THE MIDWIVES' WAR

CHRISSIE WALSH

Boldwood

First published in Great Britain in 2023 by Boldwood Books Ltd.

Copyright © Chrissie Walsh, 2023

Cover Design by Colin Thomas

Cover Photography: Colin Thomas

A CIP catalogue record for this book is available from the British Library.

Paperback ISBN 978-1-78513-481-4

Large Print ISBN 978-1-78513-477-7

Hardback ISBN 978-1-78513-476-0

Ebook ISBN 978-1-78513-474-6

Kindle ISBN 978-1-78513-475-3

Audio CD ISBN 978-1-78513-482-1

MP3 CD ISBN 978-1-78513-479-1

Digital audio download ISBN 978-1-78513-473-9

Boldwood Books Ltd
23 Bowerdean Street
London SW6 3TN
www.boldwoodbooks.com

In loving memory of my father Edward Manion who served in the RAF IN WW2
And for my wonderful family in the hope that they always find a patch of blue sky.

1

SUMMER 1969: KILMALLOW, COUNTY CORK, IRELAND

Grace Brady opened her eyes, her dream dissolving into a different world. Gone were the windswept airfield, the greasy smell of engine fuel and the low, droning of a Spitfire circling the sky then landing with a rattling thud on the tarmac. Gone was the lithe, young man leaping from the aircraft and running towards her, his flying jacket hanging open and his blond hair flopping over his forehead as he ripped off his helmet.

Slowly, her bedroom came into focus, early morning light filtering through the white linen curtains and onto the flowered wallpaper. Lying perfectly still she drew several deep breaths and waited for her heart to stop its pounding. Then, still feeling slightly disorientated she pushed aside the bedclothes, swung her legs over the edge of the bed and planted her feet firmly on the floor. She didn't have time for dreams.

In the kitchen, the shadows of the night behind her, she began the ritual of the day. When that was done, and the loaded plates keeping warm in the Aga, she washed her hands and stepped outside, exchanging the tantalising smells of fried bacon, sausages and scrambled eggs for the heady scents of lavender, thyme and the old-world roses she had cultivated in a plot close by the kitchen door. She loved her garden, and having been reared on the wild Atlantic coast of Clare where rough, tough heathers and sea spurge clung to the rocky shores in the prevailing winds, it never failed to amaze her how even the most delicate, exotic plants flourished in this quiet corner of West Cork.

Today was promising to be warm and dry, banks of high, white clouds like giant cotton wool balls shifting slowly across the horizon. Grace gazed up at them bemusedly, for though she could not recall what her dream had been she felt troubled by it, and having spent the last half hour over a hot stove she stood for a moment with her head tilted and her arms outstretched palms upward letting the gentle breeze cool her cheeks and bare arms. Then, stepping over the old golden Labrador that sprawled dozily on the doorstep she walked down the flagged path alongside the garden. The dog slowly eased itself upright and followed, sniffing at her mistress's heels.

Behind her, the long, low white farmhouse with its bright red window frames and half-leaf door sat serenely in the early morning light, a canopy of purple flowering clematis clinging to its gutters and snaking up over the grey slate roof. The garden path led to the stack yard, the barns and outbuildings, and beyond them the fields where black and white cows munched the sweet grass, ignoring the frisky, inquisitive goats that spent their time exploring the hedges. Less than a mile away was the sea, and as Grace reached the end of the path with its neat border of calendula, their fiery petals aglow, she smelt the faintest tang of salty air wafting on the gentle breeze.

With the dog padding behind, she crossed the stack yard towards the barn, the satisfying sound of gravel crunching under the soles of her stout black shoes. The dog nuzzled her hand, its wet tongue making her aware of its presence and she stopped where she was to fondle its thick, golden coat. Then, commanding the dog to 'stay, Jess' she sang out, 'Michael. Lorchan. Breakfast's ready.'

Lorchan was the first to appear, his fleshy, weather-beaten face breaking into a wide smile. He had a prodigious appetite. A big, beefy man in his late sixties, her husband had forearms like hams and hands as big as shovels. He lumbered up to Grace. 'I'm ready for it,' he said, patting her in much the same way as he patted his collie dog, Setanta. Dwarfing her with his huge frame, he smiled down at her, the breeze lifting the tufts of his salt and pepper hair that had once been a deep shade of auburn.

'It's in the Aga, ready for lifting,' she replied in the same way as she did most mornings, flicking back her hair and grinning pertly. Lorchan grinned back.

Her own tresses were a tangle of glossy, black curls and her flawless skin and slender figure had Lorchan thinking nobody would ever guess she'd never see forty-five again. He ruffled her hair affectionately. 'I'll away on in, make a start,' he rumbled. 'The young fella's right behind me.' He headed for the kitchen his step surprisingly brisk for a man of his bulk.

Grace smiled fondly at his departing back. There was much to love about kind, generous Lorchan – but she had never been 'in love' with him. They had first met more than twenty years ago, and at that time she had no room in her heart for any other man. She had given it away some seven years before she married the gentle giant, and she had never reclaimed it. Lorchan knew this, for she had never lied to him, and theirs was a marriage built on mutual respect and trust. They were happy.

Grace averted her gaze to the barn, peering across the distance into its gloomy shadows as she waited for her son, Michael. He had been four years old when Grace had married Lorchan in a hastily arranged ceremony at a registry office in Doncaster. They had known one another for less than three weeks.

Two days after the wedding they had crossed the Irish Sea to go and live with Lorchan in County Cork. It had been a dreadful crossing, strong winds buffeting the ferry from Swansea to Cork, the passenger lounge thick with the smell of vomit, and Grace's nausea made worse by her fearful apprehension of what lay before her. Could she find it in her heart to be a proper wife to Lorchan? Would his friends and neighbours accept her? Or might they think that she, more than twenty years his junior, was nothing other than a gold digger taking advantage of a lonely middle-aged confirmed bachelor who had been living a solitary life until she came along. And what would they make of the child?

She need not have worried. Lorchan had enough love for all of them, and more besides. From the start, he had cherished his newly acquired family with such gentle love and kindness that they had very easily learned to return it. Grace had buried the misery she had suffered in the years following Michael's birth in the deepest corner of her mind, and in no time at all Clonahooley Farm in the pretty little village of Kilmallow had proved to be a haven of peace and security.

By the time he was five and ready to start school Michael had, like all young children, retained few memories of his early years. For him, life was all about mammy and daddy and the everyday happenings on the farm. However, almost everyone in the little, gossipy village knew that he wasn't Lorchan Brady's natural son. Grace, afraid that he would hear it in the playground, had taken him to one side and gently told him the truth: *your real daddy was another man I once knew. He didn't know he was your daddy because he went out of my life before you were born.* Then, struggling to make what she had said seem unimportant, she had forced her eyes to sparkle and smiled brightly as she added *so I had to find a new daddy for you.* With the innocence of the child he then was Michael had accepted the facts. He had looked at her with his father's clear, blue eyes and frowned. *Like Jess's pups,* he had said thoughtfully. *Their da's Hogan's lurcher but she lives with Setanta an' us.* Grace had managed a wobbly smile and replied, *Yes, something like that.*

At that time, Michael had required no further confirmation, but in later years, when he was old enough to be curious, he had asked Grace about his real father. On learning that he had been a Spitfire pilot in the war Michael had for a while fantasised about him, imagining him to be a hero. But as he matured he reasoned that whoever his birth father was, he was of no consequence and he rarely, if ever, thought about him. As far as he was concerned he was Lorchan Brady's son. Michael considered himself blessed.

Now, out he came, and as he turned to close the barn doors behind him a ray of sunlight flashed on his cheekbones turning his recently acquired stubble to pure gold. He strolled across the yard to where his mother stood.

Grace's breath caught in her throat. Her mind flipped back to another time and place, last night's dream returning to haunt her. Yet again she saw the bleak airfield, heard the fading whine of propellers and smelled the petrol fumes as a tall, young man sauntered across the airfield's tarmac, his stride long and self-assured. As he pulled off his helmet and goggles, his thick, fair hair flopped over his brow above clear blue eyes and an aquiline nose. When he saw her, his smile quirked the corners of his full mouth and when he reached her, he pulled her into his arms and kissed her.

'Daydreaming again, Mum,' Michael said, flinging his arm lightly around her shoulders. Grace jumped as though she had been stung. The vision disintegrated. She laughed to hide her embarrassment. What would he think if she were to tell him? They began walking across the stack yard, Grace's thoughts in tatters and her feet feeling as though they didn't belong to her even though the crunching sound of gravel under them let her know exactly where she was.

She liked the feel of Michael's arm across her shoulders and missed its warm weight when he removed it to tell her about the calf he had delivered earlier that morning. Gesticulating comically with both hands, his blue eyes sparkling, he gave her a blow-by-blow report. He was in his final year at University College Dublin studying to be a vet and putting his skills into practice on his summer vacation. Still clinging to her memories, Grace was only half-listening, and when they arrived at the path leading up to the house she paused. 'You go on ahead. I'll come in a minute,' she said, reluctant to sit with them for the moment in case her eyes betrayed her. Michael loped up to the kitchen door, Grace's heart aching as she watched him go.

Then, fixing her eyes on the riot of purples, reds, yellows and greens in the garden plot but not seeing them, she let her ghosts invade her mind. Once again, as in so many times in the past, she saw the face of her first true love. The scent of his cologne and the faint whiff of his tobacco tickled her nose. His lips were curved in that lovely crooked smile and his sharp, blue eyes beckoning her to run to him. She felt as though she was floating. Then, like a dash of icy water thrown in her face, she recalled all that had happened afterwards. She shook her head impatiently, screwing her eyes tight shut. When she opened them her imaginings seemed as insubstantial as cobwebs.

What am I thinking? she chastised herself. *After all these years, and at my age, I should know better.* But she knew in her heart that it wouldn't be the last time she'd harbour such thoughts, for the older Michael got the more he reminded her of his father. Now, at twenty-five years of age, he looked like him, walked like him, laughed like him and was blessed with the same forceful personality. Having him at home was a daily reminder of all that she had lost.

Had Michael been aware of his mother's feelings or known just how much he resembled his father he would have been surprised and somewhat shocked. He knew next to nothing about him, hadn't wanted to know, and was ignorant of the fact that his mother had given him the latter part of his father's surname to keep the memory alive. She never talked about him, and Michael never asked.

Grace wiped her cheeks with the palms of her hands and fingered tendrils of hair back behind her ears. Then, she gazed up at the white, puffy clouds moving slowly across the heavens. In amongst them was a patch of clear blue sky. She smiled at it then turned and went indoors.

2

SUMMER 1969: LOWER MELTON, YORKSHIRE,
ENGLAND

Sara Carmichael flicked the right-hand indicator of her daffodil yellow Beetle and then slowed to a halt. As she waited for a gap in the stream of oncoming traffic her fingers impatiently drummed the steering wheel, irritation coupled with a hefty dose of guilt. It was five days since she'd last visited her father.

Behind her, the driver of a silver Ford Capri blared his horn. Irritation turning to rage she leaped out into the road, and after marching a few paces to the rear, she banged on the Capri driver's window. Startled, he lowered it.

'Why don't I sit here and blow your horn while you drive my car?' she snapped, her blue eyes flashing dangerously. 'Or didn't it occur to you that I'd get out of your way if I could?' She ran back to her car leaving the Capri driver with his mouth hanging open.

At the first gap in the traffic she swung the Beetle across the road and in between the gateposts of Manor Court. A few jerky manoeuvres squeezed the Beetle into a space marked:

RESIDENT'S VISITOR'S ONLY

Lousy punctuation, she thought, not for the first time, as she gathered her bags from the passenger seat. Out of the car, she hurried to the main door of the complex of the nursing home, the cloying smell of antiseptic, air freshener and sickness meeting her in the foyer. It caught in the back of her throat cruelly reminding her that although Manor Court outwardly resembled a five-star hotel it was actually home to the dying. Her dad called it the last chance saloon.

She walked down a brightly lit corridor with doors on either side, the spiky heels of her knee-high boots sinking into the thick pile of the maroon and gold carpet. In between each door, side tables displayed vases of flowers, pot plants and photographs, and from behind the closed doors she could hear the sound of music and laughter from televisions or radios, their volume turned up too high.

A turn to the right along a shorter corridor brought her to her father's suite.

She still hadn't come to terms with the idea of her father choosing to live in Manor Court rather than the fine Victorian house that had been their family home up until three months ago. Now, it was rented out to an American academic who was currently attached to the university in Sheffield. Sara had been furious when she learned that her father had made these arrangements. That he hadn't discussed it with her still hurt even though he had told her she, and his concern for her, was the reason behind his decision.

Outside his suite she swallowed her distaste for this opulent death house, as she thought of it, and pasting a smile on her face she tapped the door then opened it. As she stepped inside the light, airy room that smelt of her father's aftershave and a smell that was his alone, her irritation dissipated and her lips curved in a genuine smile. She loved him dearly, and he had enough to contend with without her behaving like a sulky teenager because he had gone against her wishes.

Richard Carmichael was sitting in a chair facing the window that looked out onto a patch of grass and a scrappy border of marigolds. Spots of yellow the only bright colour in the otherwise bland garden. Sara thought of the verdant lawns and the multitude of flowering plants and shrubs her mother had lovingly planted and tended in their garden at home. He should have been sitting looking at them she thought dismally.

The top of Richard's head was just visible above the chair back, his blond hair thinning at the crown. She smiled sadly, recalling the days when it had been thick and glossy. 'Hi, Dad, I'm back,' she called out, making an effort to stem the tremor in her voice.

He peered round the side of the chair, blinking sleep from his eyes and grimacing with discomfort as he strained to see her. Then his face lit up, and he swung the chair round with alacrity as she hurried over to him. 'Well, did you have a good trip? What was the weather like in Spain? A damned sight better than it has been here I imagine.'

Sara dropped her bags, and placing the palms of her hands on each of his leathery cheeks, she kissed him on his forehead. He put his arms round her waist, holding her close in a twig-like embrace, the knobs of his wrists and elbows pressing through her thin, white shirt. Tears sprang to her eyes. He was wasting away and there was nothing she could do to prevent it.

'Hot and sticky,' she said as he released her. 'The models were peevish and the guy whose swimwear they were promoting was so far up his own backside that he was in danger of disappearing.'

Her father laughed; a strong rumble from deep in his chest. It was one of the few things about him that hadn't changed.

'I'm sure you soon chivvied them into order,' Richard said,

knowing that his daughter had inherited his temperament for getting things done.

Sara chuckled. 'Let's say we got the shots we wanted. Lots of oiled, bare brown flesh with not a blob of cellulite in sight and sunglasses as big as wing mirrors hiding dilated pupils and the bags under their eyes. Tristan was in a filthy mood and took his temper out on me as usual, but apart from that it was grand.'

She detested having to assist at fashion shoots but they were bread-and-butter money. She far preferred photographing land-scapes and ordinary people going about their everyday business, but at twenty-three years old and fresh out of Goldsmiths she was still learning and had to go where the agency sent her.

'You've caught the sun,' her father said admiringly as she pulled up a chair and sat opposite him, her fashionably short yellow leather skirt showing off her slender legs. 'It's kissed your hair. It reminds me of your mother.'

Sara ran her fingers through her streaky blonde bob then patted her thick fringe, flattered to be likened to her late mother, an elegant woman to the end. Helen Carmichael had died suddenly almost two years ago, shortly before Richard had been diagnosed with bowel cancer. The death of a vibrant, seemingly healthy woman had shocked them to the core and it had taken some time for them to adjust to life without her.

After Helen's death, Sara had shared her free time between London and Higher Melton, dashing home whenever possible from her bedsit in Chelsea to keep her father company and make sure he was managing his illness. Then, just as they were learning to cope with their loss, they had been hit by the bombshell. Richard's cancer was terminal. The surgery hadn't cured him, and he wasn't a suitable candidate for chemotherapy. Sara was devastated when she learned that his life expectancy was limited: two years his consultant had said. Immediately, she offered to give up her job and move back home but Richard robustly refused to hear of it. Mrs Briggs, the part-time housekeeper Helen had employed, popped in on a daily basis and the district nurses called with him regularly. He continued to oversee the small firm of architects that he owned, and went to his club and visited friends, and as one year ran into two, Sara began to believe that the doctors had made a mistake: the cancerous cells weren't metastasising after all. She clung to this belief like a limpet clings to a rock on the shore even though her eyes told her that her father was wasting away, his tall, muscular frame shrinking and his handsome features drawn and weary.

Then, three months ago on her last weekend at their family home, he had told her he was moving to Manor Court. It had all been arranged and now there was nothing she could do but accept his decision. Carrying on with her work and leading the life she had led before his illness seemed to please him most and she had resigned herself to doing just that, albeit that she came to see him at every given opportunity. It was her dearest wish to make what time he had left as happy as she possibly could.

Now, sitting across from him, Sara noticed that the colour of his eyes had lost their intensity, the striking blueness that had capti-vated many women in whose company he happened to be now paled to an opalescent grey. It tugged at her heart to witness his gradual decline and she wanted to cry out to the heavens to put a stop to it. Instead, she told him a few more interesting or funny inci-dents from her time in Spain. Richard enjoyed the vicarious plea-sure of his daughter's experiences. She deliberately avoided asking him about his condition and how he was feeling. She knew he didn't want to talk about that.

A tap on the door interrupted their chatter. They turned to find Mona hovering in the doorway. The nursing orderly was a big, blousy woman with a mop of peroxide blonde hair and a florid complexion. She gave them both a wide smile, all teeth, as she came further into the room.

'Hello, Dickie, and how are we today?' she carolled pushing her trolley over to the side of his chair.

Sara saw the glint in her father's eye and waited for the sharp riposte. Richard sat up straighter in his chair and fixed his eyes on Mona.

'I'm Richard and I'm feeling quite well, Mona, thank you for asking,' he replied, his tone as sharp as vinegar. 'As for Dickie, he's not here so I can't speak for him.'

Sara hid a smile, thrilled to see that her father still had enough spirit to rebuff Mona's prattle and just as annoyed as he was at Mona's condescending use of the word 'we' – it certainly wasn't royal – and the abbreviating of his name. Richard glanced Sara's way and winked wickedly. Sara grinned back.

'Now then, open up like a good boy,' Mona trilled, holding out a tiny pot of tablets in one hand and a glass of water in the other. Richard downed the tablets and placed the pot and the glass on the trolley, then raising his gaze to meet Mona's, he gave her a simpering smile laden with cynicism. Sara suppressed the urge to laugh out loud.

'Celia will be along with your tea in about half an hour. It's salmon en croute,' Mona said enthusiastically, grabbing her trolley and clattering out into the corridor then bawling out, 'and chips.'

'God spare me from that woman,' Richard groaned as the door closed behind her, 'And the salmon en croute. It'll be cooked within an inch of its life.'

'You don't have to stay here, Dad,' Sara said heatedly. 'We can find somewhere else to live. I'll look after you and...' She lightened her tone. 'I promise not to call you Dickie.'

Richard heard the plea in her voice and raised his hand, silencing her in a weary, half-amused manner. 'No, Sara, we've been over all that. I flatly refuse to burden you with my problem so let's not go into that again.' Sara gave a resigned shrug. It was pointless to argue.

'I know you mean well,' Richard continued, 'but I'm in the right place for now, and anyway—' he gave a lopsided grin '—Monty needs the business. He's invested everything he has in this place.'

Philip Montgomery was a friend from the days Richard had been in the Royal Air Force. They had belonged to the same squadron, flying Spitfires: they had fought a war together and survived. Sara suspected that Philip had been very instrumental in persuading her father to move into Manor Court.

They carried on talking about this and that, both of them avoiding the reason why they were in Manor Court, until the rattle of crockery and tuneless singing signalled the arrival of Celia and the tea trolley. Sara glanced at her watch. Quarter to five. Why did they have to serve the evening meal so ridiculously early? They had always had it at seven when they were at home.

Celia gossiped about the weather as she laid the table, offloading a dish of wilted salad and a pot of tea along with the salmon en croute and chips. The smell of fish was overpowering. His room would stink for the rest of the evening, Sara thought miserably, and pictured the spacious, airy dining room they had had at home.

Richard got to his feet, flexed his wasted muscles and walked over to the table, Sara painfully aware his forced sprightly gait was for her benefit. She loved him all the more for it and swallowed the tears clogging her throat. She took a magazine from out of her bag. 'Eat up and enjoy, and I'll catch up with the latest news in the nefarious world of fashion,' she said in a jolly voice, keen to spare him the indignity of trying to choke down his food and hold a conversation at the same time. She kept her back to him and began flipping through the pages.

Richard picked reluctantly at the salmon. He pulled a face. 'The chef who dreamed up the idea of caging fish in cast-iron pastry should be boiled alive in one of his own stew pots,' he growled, pushing the plate aside. Sara glanced up from her magazine, disappointed to see how little he had eaten.

He got up from the table. 'Be a dear and make a strong pot of coffee to wash the taste away.' He went and sat in his chair by the window. They'd had a good laugh about the coffee maker in the little kitchen recess on Sara's first visit. 'Courtesy of Ex-Wing Commander Montgomery,' Richard had told her when she'd commented on it. 'And I quote—' he'd waved the forefingers on both hands '—"just one of the extra, little luxuries that Manor Court provides for its clients still compos enough to use one if you think you're up to it". I told him, "Decent of you to acknowledge I've still got my faculties, Monty. It's my small intestine I've had removed, not my bloody brain."'

Sara smiled as she made the coffee, reminded that her dad hadn't lost his sense of wry humour. When it was ready, she resumed her seat next to his.

'Well, how's your love life?' He sipped the strong, black brew then pursed his lips appreciatively. 'What's the bold Julian up to these days?'

'Sulking,' Sara replied and grinned. 'He was furious when I accepted the job in Spain. He's jealous of Tristan. He thinks I'm having some mad, passionate affair every time I go off on a trip, even when it's only for one night in somewhere as unglamorous as Brighton or Skegness.'

'He seems like a bit of a control freak. I'd ditch him if I were you.'

'I most likely will,' Sara said, thoughtfully. 'He was fun at first. I thought he was my type what with both of us liking the same things, going to art galleries, the theatre and taking walks in the countryside. Turns out he was just pretending. Now, all he wants to do is keep me a prisoner in his place or mine. He doesn't like my friends and I don't like his. Not that we see them any more.' She gave a careless shrug. 'I've come to the conclusion that he's not the love of my life.'

'Good for you,' Richard chortled. 'He sounds positively horrendous.'

Sara smiled a sad little smile. 'He does, doesn't he?' She laughed softly. 'I'm clearly not a very good judge of character, unlike you. You chose Mum.' Her features softened as fond memories rose to the surface of her mind.

'It wasn't a matter of choosing, it was more a case of having to,' Richard said.

Sara's thoughts still clouded with dreams of finding a perfect mate, she ignored the remark. 'I'd like to fall head over heels in love with someone who'll make me as happy as you and Mum were. Yours was a wonderful marriage, wasn't it?'

Richard didn't reply immediately. He was gazing pensively into the space above Sara's head, a glimmer of a smile curving his lips. She presumed he was remembering his love for Helen and was surprised and disappointed when he did answer.

'Hmmm.' He jutted his lips and nodded. 'I suppose you might say that. Your mother and I rubbed along very nicely,' he said, his tone matter of fact and his gaze fixed on the neat square of garden to avoid meeting her eyes.

'You make it sound like a marriage of convenience.' Sara's tone was sharper than she intended.

Richard's smile was almost apologetic. 'In a way, I suppose it was. You might say we rescued each other from the stormy seas that we were floundering in at that time. She needed me and I needed her, and when extenuating circumstances intervened, we decided to make a go of it.'

He fiddled with the frayed cuff of his sweater, his bony wrist and hand protruding from the baggy sleeve like an ancient carving of a reptilian form.

'But where was the romance?' Sara asked accusingly. 'I've always imagined that you fell head over heels in love. I thought Mum was the love of your life.'

'She was... eventually.'

Richard shifted uncomfortably in his ergonomic chair. It was clearly failing to provide the ease that the manufacturer had promised and that her father was now looking for. He twisted his wasted frame so that he was looking directly at his daughter. 'We grew on one another,' he said, the corners of his mouth twitching into a fond, little smile.

'Grew on one another! Now, you're making it sound as though you were a couple of parasites, fungus, or lichens at best.'

He heard the hint of disgust and gave a raspy chuckle, his Adam's apple bobbing inside his shirt collar that only a few months before had fitted snugly and was now sitting proud of his scrawny neck.

'It was nothing like that,' he protested.

'Then what was it like?' Sara urged. 'Here you are, likening all those years of marriage to Mum as though it was a business trans-action when, as I've already said, I thought yours was a true love match.'

'I wouldn't say that,' he said softly. 'The two people who conceived you and brought you up grew to love one another – and dearly loved you. But before that time we were people you wouldn't recognise. We both had had a life that was very different to the one you shared with us.'

He closed his eyes and folded his hands across his chest, shrivel-ling inside his baggy cardigan and shirt, his thoughts drifting to a time and place in which Sara had no part.

Sara's heart lurched. He was wasting away before her eyes. She was losing him ounce by ounce, and soon all the happy times they shared, their heated discussions – or lively debates as he liked to call them – would just be memories. Who would she have then to confide in, to pour out her innermost feelings and be listened to without judgement?

'What life?' she asked, her voice barely above a whisper. 'Tell me,' she urged, her words drowned out by a sharp rap on the door and the rattle of a trolley's wheels as Raj barged into the room.

Richard's eyes flew open and he adjusted his position so that he was sitting up as perky as a turkey cock. Sara knew that this was for the benefit of the resident male nurse. Her father was always loath to let Raj think he wasn't in good form; couldn't stand the fuss.

'Good evening, Mr Carmichael.' The sleek, young Indian nurse addressed Richard deferentially then smiled at Sara. 'I see your daughter is visiting. That is nice.'

'Yes, it is,' Richard replied tetchily, annoyed by the intrusion.

Raj pretended not to notice. 'I just need to check your sodium levels.' He lifted a pressure strap from the trolley. 'Sleeve up, please.'

Richard fumbled with his cardigan sleeves, exposing his arm above the elbow. Raj applied the strap and then deftly took the blood sample, his long, brown fingers gentle and efficient. 'What about your stoma bag, sir? Do you want help changing it?'

Richard shook his head irritably. 'My fingers might be clumsy —' he wiggled his hands '—but they're mine and they're the only ones I want fiddling with the private parts of my body.' He softened the curt reply with a smile and muttered, 'Thank you for asking.'

Raj returned the smile and left. When he'd gone, Sara looked expectantly at her father, wanting him to continue with his story. But seeing how weary and diminished he looked she changed her mind. She'd leave it until tomorrow. She stood to stoop over him, kissed his cheek and ruffled his hair.

'See you tomorrow, Dad. Same time, same place, eh? I love you.'

* * *

After Sara had left, Richard sat staring out at the darkening garden and listening to the faint rumble of passing traffic. Bands of light from nearby windows and distant street lamps broke the shadows, the sickly yellow glow matching his mood. He thought about what he had been going to tell her, and what her reaction might have been, had Raj not interrupted. Did she need to know? He wasn't sure, and he cringed inwardly when he thought about how it might affect her. She might find it hard to forgive him for destroying her romantic illusions.

He was still lost in thought when Raj returned to give him his shower and help him into his pyjamas. Alone once more, he took a small wooden box from his bedside cabinet then climbed into bed. Resting the box on his lap, he lifted the lid. Inside were his cap badge and buttons from his RAF uniform, his war medals, a small tin containing a lock of Sara's baby hair, and an enamelled brooch. On top of these were a few old photographs from his days in the squadron: photographs of Spitfires, airfields, drinking sessions in the mess, and the smiling faces of friends who had made the ultimate sacrifice. There he was, arms slung about the shoulders of his fellow pilots, grinning for all he was worth. He'd been tall and muscular then, his leather flying jacket adding to his bulk, and his thick, fair hair flopping into sharp blue eyes that sparkled with the thrill of a dangerous and exciting life.

The corner of his mouth twitched miserably as he gazed at the laughing faces of Bill Rigsby and Peter Hepworth. Rigs and Heppy hadn't made it back. They'd been lost over the English Channel courtesy of Adolf Hitler and a swarm of Heinkels. They weren't the only friends he had lost, but those two had been like brothers. He missed them still. The old familiar feeling of guilt at having survived made him clench his teeth. *I'll be joining you soon, lads*, he said under his breath as he put the photographs to one side.

Their deaths had changed the way he felt about the war and about himself. Losing them had caused him to make the most foolish decision of his life. With fingers that trembled, he lifted the photograph that was the most precious of them all. It was creased and fraying at the edges; it had been slipped in and out of a breast pocket and kissed too often. Richard's eyes moistened as he gazed at it.

The young woman who gazed back at him through luminous, grey eyes had a tangle of black, curly hair surrounding a beautifully sculpted face. There was something wild and ethereal about her that always made him think of magical creatures that inhabited dark forests. That had been his impression of Grace Murphy on the night they had first met, and it lingered now as he lovingly traced his fingertip over the curve of her cheeks and lips. His heart ached with regret.

Holding the photograph in one hand and delving into the box with the other, his fingers clasped the enamelled brooch. Withdrawing it, he rubbed his thumb gently over the familiar contours of its embossed surface before placing it and the photograph side by side, marrying them together.

The beautifully crafted brooch was shaped like a cumulonimbus cloud, its outer edges enamelled iridescent white and in its centre a Spitfire flying in a patch of clear blue sky. Richard gazed at them for some time, his thoughts apprehensive. Then he placed them and the other photographs back in the box. Tomorrow, if Sara pursued their unfinished conversation and his nerves didn't fail him, he'd take them out again.

* * *

Driving back to the bed and breakfast accommodation she used for her overnight stays, Sara mulled over what her father had told her. Phrases such as 'we rescued one another' and 'decided to make a go of it' and the worrying 'we grew on one another' tumbled through her mind. What did they really mean? She tried to imagine what her father and mother had been like when they were young and single, but the pictures she conjured were from a time when she was perhaps six or seven. How different had they been before she was born? she wondered. And what was the 'extenuating circumstance' that had brought them together?

Showered and changed, she went to Lower Melton's only restaurant, a little Italian place on the same street as the B&B. As she pushed open the door the strong, sweet smell of rich Bolognese hit her nose and her belly rumbled. Almost delirious with hunger she found a table by the window.

Bon Italia was a family-run business, three generations of Quiodos feeding the busy evening diners, Pappa Quiodo bawling orders from the kitchen where his wife sweated over pans and pots, and two sons and a daughter scurrying between kitchen and tables. From behind the till on the counter Grandmother Quiodo sat like the mistress of all she surveyed, her eyes two limpid chocolate drops and her wrinkled cheeks old wineskin sacks.

Munching on a delicious plateful of gnocchi and watching their teamwork, Sara felt a sudden pang of regret. She had no siblings, and before long she would have no parents. Soon she would be alone in the world. The gnocchi lost its taste and the wine soured on her tongue.

One of the Quiodo sons, Enrico, a handsome, swarthy lad was approaching Sara's table, no doubt to offer her dessert, when his sister, Carmelita, caught his arm and whispered something in his ear. They giggled together, their eyes on a table in the corner. Sara followed their gaze. A stout, elderly man was sitting with a blonde half his age. He was stroking her arm, a lascivious smile on his face. Sara glanced at the brother and sister. Enrico rolled his eyes then placed his lips to Carmelita's ear. She whirled away, laughing. Sara watched them enviously. How nice it must be to have someone to share an amusing moment with, or to share the pain of watching a parent die. When Enrico arrived at her table, she paid her bill and left. She had never felt more alone.

Back in her bedroom at the B&B the feeling of loneliness persisted. It was a warm night, the air in the chintzy little room stuffy and the lingering smell of the previous occupant rather unpleasant. Lying on the narrow bed unable to sleep even though she felt dog-tired, Sara stared into the void that her father's demise would leave behind and summed up her future. She'd still have a job she loved and friends for company, but without him life wouldn't be the same.

Of course, she wasn't entirely without family to turn to but that was neither practical nor appealing. Her father's younger brother and his family lived in Canada, and her mother's sister had married and then migrated to Australia shortly after the war had ended. Sara had met her cousins when their families returned for the funerals of her mother, and then her maternal grandparents, but apart from that only the annual Christmas letter kept her in touch with their lives. However, her paternal grandmother was still very much alive and living in the house in Higher Melton that had been Richard's boyhood home.

Sadly, Sara had never got on with the imperious Cecily Carmichael. As a child she had been afraid of the brittle, snobbish woman who thought children should be seen but not heard. Sara's opinion of her hadn't altered over the years. She was no longer afraid of Cecily but her supercilious attitude and her selfishness still rankled. Her grandmother had sneered at Sara's choice of occupation saying *such a frivolous, rather tawdry way to earn a living, my dear. What sort of men do you expect to meet in those circles? Politics would have been a wiser choice.*

Cecily was a social climber of the first water. According to Sara's dad, Cecily had always courted what she considered to be the elite of society, her days filled with lunches, bridge parties and influential gatherings. She had alienated her younger son, Stephen, to such an extent that at seventeen he had left home and gone to live in Canada, thus denying his father, Garvey, and his brother, Richard, the pleasure of his company. Worst of all, Cecily looked on Richard's illness as an inconvenience, as though he was letting the side down by succumbing to ill health and he not yet fifty. Consequently, her visits to him were few and far between, and her lack of sympathy for his condition not at all motherly. Little wonder that Sara's dislike for her had intensified in the past two years.

Her father tolerated his mother with wry forbearance. 'She's always been the same,' he told Sara when, after one of Cecily's rare visits, Sara had expressed her disgust at her grandmother's callous attitude. Richard had laughed it off. 'She's squeamish when it comes to people who don't meet her high standards, and I don't quite cut the mustard these days,' he'd said practically before wistfully adding, 'in fact I don't think I ever did.'

Sleep still evading her, Sara climbed out of bed and poured a glass of water from the bottle she'd bought before setting out on her journey from London. Sitting by the window gazing out to the street below, she conjured up a picture of the hard-faced, over-dressed woman that was her grandmother. Poor Dad, she thought as she sipped the tepid water, fancy having to live with a mother like her. He must have had an unhappy childhood. That thought sent her mind down a different track. She recalled how earlier that day he had told her he had been a very different person to the one she had grown up with, and it now made her realise how little she knew about his earlier life. He sometimes told her amusing anecdotes about his days at boarding school or his time in the RAF but that was all they were; funny stories fondly remembered. And like most young people who were only interested in the immediacy of their own lives, Sara hadn't delved deeply into his youthful past. But tomorrow she would, she told herself firmly as she climbed back into bed.

3

SUMMER 1942: DONCASTER, YORKSHIRE

Grace Murphy gently placed the tiny baby into a crib in the nursery at Doncaster Royal Infirmary. Three days old and weighing less than two bags of sugar the poor little mite gazed up at her with round, blue eyes. He was a pale, sickly, little thing and her heart ached for him. He had been placed in an incubator at birth, his tiny lungs clogged with mucus but today the doctor had declared his breathing was stable and he'd been brought to the nursery. Even so, Grace still worried for him and paid him particular attention. It was imperative that he survived. Three weeks ago his mother had lost her husband. His ship had been in a convoy sailing from Iceland to Murmansk, taking tanks for the Russians, when a German U-boat had torpedoed it.

Leaving the baby to sleep, Grace wandered along the row of cribs looking with a practised eye at more than a dozen babies wrapped like mummies in tight, white sheets. Most of them were sleeping, their rosebud lips put-putting as their tiny chests rose and fell. One or two grizzled, their mouths and eyes wide open. Grace settled them before their whinges changed to full-blown screams.

The slanting rays of a watery, late afternoon sun outside the long, narrow windows signalled that she was coming to the end of her shift. Grace paused for a moment listening in the near-silence, and satisfied that her little charges were all peaceful, she tiptoed from the nursery and out into the corridor.

Clodagh Flynn came skipping towards her wearing a big grin and her green eyes sparkling. 'I was lookin' for ye,' she said, slightly out of breath. 'There's a bus goin' to the RAF camp tonight at half seven. Will we go, do ye think?'

Grace wasn't sure she felt like dancing, but it was Friday and she was off duty that weekend. She heard the eager, pleading in Clodagh's voice. 'Go on then. It's bound to be better than sitting at home listening to Patsy talking to Joey the budgie.'

Clodagh giggled and rolled her eyes.

The 'home' Grace referred to was the little terrace house she and Clodagh shared with Patsy O'Grady. The girls had first met when they were training to be nurses at the Rotunda Hospital in Dublin. Each of them far from home for the first time, Grace from County Clare, Clodagh from County Cork and Patsy from County Kerry, they had somehow gelled and stuck together through thick and thin although they had very different personalities. Grace was sensible and bookish, her thoughtful dedication a calming influence on the impulsive, dizzy Clodagh, and her patience and kindness boosted Patsy's confidence no end, for the poor girl was afraid of her own shadow. By the time each of them had celebrated their twenty-first birthdays they were fully qualified and ready to take on the world.

Britain had been at war with Germany for almost two years when Grace had announced that she was going to London. Bearing in mind that a country at war needed nurses more than ever, and in answer to 'her calling' and a yearning to widen her horizons, she had made up her mind to go where she thought she might be most needed. At that time it seemed the right thing to do. Clodagh had jumped at the idea and Patsy, reluctant to be parted from her friends, had hesitantly agreed to go with them. Sadly, London had been a crushing disappointment. St Stephen's Hospital had none of the camaraderie that they had shared in the Rotunda, and being new recruits – and Irish – they were given all the worst jobs and little respect.

Grace detested the cold, unfriendly face of the city, and Clodagh rebelled at the strict regime in the nurses' home. The frequent bombing raids didn't help matters either. Whenever they were walking to and from the hospital and the sirens sounded the alarm, Patsy had had hysterics as they rushed for the nearest air raid shelter or down into the Underground. Try though they did, none of them felt settled or truly appreciated. When Clodagh's aunt wrote to say that nurses were needed in Doncaster Royal, Clodagh couldn't wait to shake the dust of Camden from her feet, and Grace was also ready for a change of scenery. Patsy tagged along, afraid to stay on in London without her friends.

Grace considered it to be a wise move. Whilst standards in the Royal were high, they were not as intense as the impersonal regime in London, and for the first time since leaving the Rotunda she felt valued and respected. Furthermore, the people in the north of England were much friendlier. Their accents were different from Londoners, words like 'about' and 'down' sounding like 'abaht' and 'dahn', and they said 'thas' instead of 'you've'. They laughed when Grace asked them to explain, and unlike the Londoners they didn't look down their noses when they heard her Irish accent. It was fair to say that Grace liked Doncaster and its people, and she loved her job.

'Hurry up an' get finished,' Clodagh said, jigging from foot to foot.

'I'm nearly ready,' said Grace. 'I'll just go and tell Mrs Butterworth that her baby's sleeping peacefully then I'll meet you at the main door.' Clodagh's eyebrows shot up in dismay. She was inclined to think that Grace got too involved with her patients.

'Don't be long. We don't want to miss the bus,' Clodagh protested walking in the direction of the nurses' cloakroom. Grace hurried to the maternity ward.

Doreen Butterworth looked anxiously through red-rimmed eyes at Grace as she approached her bed. 'Did he settle all right?'

'Like a lamb,' Grace replied.

'I just wish they'd let me keep him here by my side so I could keep an eye on him.' Doreen was tearful. 'He's so fragile he could slip away at any minute.'

'There's always someone on duty in the nursery, Mrs Butterworth. They'll watch him for you,' Grace assured her even though she knew it wasn't strictly true. In the busy, short-staffed hospital the nursery was frequently left unattended for periods. 'What you must do is concentrate on building up your strength.' Grace looked pointedly at the barely touched plate of food on the bedside table. She smiled encouragingly into the pallid face of the frightened, weary woman whose husband had lost his life when his ship was torpedoed. 'You owe it to your son to get plenty of rest and nourishment so that you'll be well enough to take him home when he's ready.' Grace continued, 'He's going to need his mother for years to come.'

Doreen managed a wan smile. 'I know what you mean, and I will try, but I don't like boiled haddock, and the mashed potato's full of lumps.' She started to weep. 'An' I've no appetite 'cos I can't stop thinking about my Norman freezing to death in the Arctic Ocean. We don't even have a grave to visit. He'll never know he has a son an' the baby will never know his dad,' she sobbed. Grace glanced surreptitiously at the watch pinned to her apron, but she knew she wouldn't ignore Mrs Butterworth's distress.

'Sure he does. The dead know everything. At least that's what we Irish believe. He'll know and he'll be looking out for you, and his son.' Grace sounded supremely confident.

Doreen blinked back her tears. 'Do you really believe that?' She sounded awfully doubting.

''Course I do,' Grace replied fervently. 'God's good and Norman's in His care. They're all watching over you and the baby.'

Doreen had had a long and arduous labour and at that moment looked ten years older than her twenty-five years. She looked thoughtfully at Grace. 'You Irish have great faith, don't you?' She gave a sad, little smile. 'Maybe you're right. It's time I bucked meself up and started to believe that I'll manage without him. I have to, for baby's sake. He's all I've got now.'

'That's the spirit,' Grace said, relieved to hear her patient looking and sounding more positive. She plumped Doreen's pillows. 'Now, you get some rest and I'll see you on Monday. I'm off this weekend but don't you be worrying. I'm leaving you and baby in good hands.' After giving her a warm, parting smile, she hurried from the ward. In the cloakroom she pulled on her navy blue cloak with the red braid trim and then dashed down the corridor to the main door. Clodagh would be on pins.

'You've been ages,' her friend said accusingly. 'What kept you?'

Grace told her how miserable Mrs Butterworth was, and that she had wanted to give the poor woman assurance that things would be all right. 'I couldn't bear to leave her in that state,' she explained.

'Your trouble is you care too much,' Clodagh complained as they hurried across the hospital forecourt and out into Thorne Road.

'It's our job to care,' Grace replied snappily. 'She's just lost her husband, and the baby's so weak he might not pull through. It breaks my heart to think that she could lose him as well.'

'That's what you get for being a nurse,' Clodagh panted dispassionately, for by now they were almost running down Zetland Road. The girls had squealed with delight when they learned they weren't being accommodated in the nurses' home but in a house bequeathed to the hospital by a deceased doctor, and they'd had a good laugh when they were told the address: St Patrick's Road.

'We can't seem to get away from Ireland, can we?' Grace had commented as they walked to the house for the first time, noticing the street leading to it was called Plunket Road. 'We've got the blessed Oliver and St Paddy to look out for us right on our doorstep.'

'As long as they keep Oliver's head in Drogheda,' Clodagh had said giving a mock shiver as she referred to the head of the saint that was kept in a museum in the Irish town, 'I wouldn't like to meet it when I'm coming home late at night.'

'Oooh, that's a horrible thought,' Patsy had squeaked before piously adding, 'and ye shouldn't be making fun of the blessed saint.'

The house in St Patrick's Road was drably decorated and furnished with a mish-mash of old furniture, but they each had their own bedroom. Grace and Clodagh in the ones overlooking the street, and Patsy choosing the box room at the back of the house. 'It'll be cosier and easier to make it look like home,' she had said innocently.

'Hello, we're home,' Clodagh shouted as she and Grace entered the lobby. Patsy was at home today having just completed a week on night duty. Wiping her hands on a tea towel, she bustled from the kitchen like a mother hen.

'I've made a mince an' tattie pie an' I'm just about to open a tin of peas to go with it,' she said, her plain, round face glowing from the exertion of her labours.

Small and dumpy, she looked nothing like her companions. Her straight, brown hair was parted severely down the centre and fastened neatly in a little bun at the nape of her neck, and her sensible tweed skirt and prim blouse with its Peter Pan collar made her look quite matronly for all she was the youngest. Clodagh was tall and skinny, all arms and legs with a mop of vivid red hair that accentuated her narrow, green eyes and freckled face, causing her to complain that she looked like a matchstick. Grace, on the other hand, although not much taller than Patsy, was slender and shapely, her extremely pretty features and opalescent grey eyes surrounded by a tangle of glossy, black curls.

'You're an angel,' Grace said, sniffing the tantalising aroma and slipping off her cloak. 'It smells lovely, and I'm starving.'

Still wearing their uniforms, Grace and Clodagh tucked into the pie and talked about what they might wear for the dance. 'Will you come, Patsy?' Grace asked.

Patsy looked doubtful. 'I don't think so,' she said, looking over at the birdcage in the corner of the counter. 'Joey doesn't like to be left on his own an' I've hardly seen him all week what with working nights an' sleeping most of the day.' On hearing his name the budgerigar fluffed his feathers and tweeted loudly. Grace and Clodagh exchanged amused glances.

'You might meet a nice fella if you come.' Clodagh's green eyes twinkled mischievously.

'Sure, I've no time for fellas,' Patsy said dismissively. 'They're all out for one thing, an' they'll not be getting it from me.'

'Me neither,' Grace said, 'but I don't mind giving them a dance or two. I quite enjoyed meself the last time we went to Finningley.'

Clodagh sniggered. 'So did I until that big, beefy public-school-boy-type started mauling me all over. I hope he's not there tonight.'

'Keep your hand on your ha'penny is what my mammy always says,' Patsy advised, standing to clear the empty plates and put the kettle on.

'Very wise too,' Grace agreed, before Clodagh could make a skittish remark about Patsy's mother. 'I'll make the tea, Patsy. You've done more than your share already.' Whereas Clodagh never gave it a second thought, Grace sometimes felt guilty about leaving Patsy to do the motherly things around the house even though she seemed to derive great pleasure from it.

Grace made the tea, and when she handed Patsy her cup Patsy took it with one hand and with the other she lifted the budgie's cage. 'Now, you go off an' get yourselves all dolled up for the dance, an' me an' Joey will away into the parlour to sit by the fire an' listen to the Light Programme. There's usually some nice music on after the news.' Patsy toddled off.

'You'd think she was sixty-one instead of twenty-one,' Clodagh groaned as soon as she was out of earshot.

'She's happy enough,' Grace said. 'Now shift yourself and let's get ready. We're

running late.'

A short while later, the two girls appeared in the parlour to say goodnight to Patsy. 'We'll lock the door behind us so you don't have to wait up,' Grace said, looking enviously at Patsy curled up on the old couch, and half-wishing she also was staying in.

'Ye both look lovely,' Patsy said, admiring Grace's navy blue cotton frock splashed with white daisies and Clodagh's green shantung skirt and white blouse. Grace did a twirl, her full skirt showing off her shapely legs. She was carrying a white cardigan that she'd wear outside to cover the dress's little capped sleeves and heart-shaped neckline. It was too warm to bother with a coat.

'Enjoy your radio programmes, and don't be teaching Joey any bad words,' Grace said cheekily. It was a standing joke between them that Patsy was trying to teach the bird to talk.

'Get him to say Staff Nurse Morris's a bugger,' Clodagh quipped still feeling resentful at being reprimanded by her for not cleaning the sluice properly.

'Away out of that,' Patsy cried. 'This boy's not learning any bad words.'

* * *

After they had left, Patsy picked up her needles. She was knitting another dishcloth; she made them for the house, and as little gifts for the nurses she worked with. Pushing her needle into the soft, white cotton she mused how much nicer it would be if she were knitting a baby jacket: she'd love a baby of her own. But to have a baby you had to have a husband, and men terrified her. Not that one would want her, she thought, she didn't have Clodagh's long legs and Grace's slender figure. For her, going to Finningley was a complete waste of time. She'd just sit there in a miserable heap pretending not to mind that nobody asked her to dance.

'Say Kerry, Joey, Kerry, Kerry,' Patsy urged. Joey didn't respond and she dropped a stitch as a sudden yearning for the little, white farmhouse on Dingle's rocky shore flooded her mind. Mammy and Daddy would just about now be finishing off the milking, she thought, and not for the first time she asked herself why she had come to England. She knew the answer. She hadn't wanted to be parted from Grace and Clodagh. She loved their friendship, and had let them persuade her to go with them to London, but the nightly bombing raids, the sirens and the madness of running to the shelters had wrecked her nerves. She'd been glad when they moved to Doncaster, even though the first thing that met their eyes was a bombed-out street of shops and houses.

'We've jumped out of the frying pan into the fire,' she had declared, but fortunately since then the town had got off lightly. Even so, she wanted to go home, but she was afraid of travelling by herself so for now she took comfort from doing her nursing to the best of her ability, and mothering her friends. Keeping busy kept her fears at bay, and on nights like this she had to make do with a budgie and the Light Programme for company. She poked her needle into a stitch and said, 'Dingle, Joey, Dingle, Dingle, Dingle.'

* * *

The bus to RAF Finningley was packed with young women, the RAF driver the only male on board. No self-respecting local lad would dream of attending a dance at the base. The rivalry between the local males and the boys in blue was hostile, and they referred to the bus by several vulgar names, most of them beginning with the letter F in the belief that that was what its feminine cargo went to the camp to do. This, however, didn't deter the girls.

Grace and Clodagh found seats at the back, the heat from fifty or more excited

warm bodies and the clashing smells of cheap perfume, hair lacquer and cigarette smoke so overwhelming that Grace wished yet again that she'd stayed at home.

A girl with bleached blonde hair turned in her seat to shout down the bus. 'Do you think there'll be any Yanks from RAF Lindholme there tonight?'

'You keep away from them Americans, Sylvia. They on'y want to get in your knickers so I've been told,' someone yelled back.

'If it means getting a pair of nylons and some ciggies I wun't mind.' Sylvia's response made several of her companions gasp, so she added, 'Letting 'em try, that is.'

'I went to see *The Philadelphia Story* last night in the Electra, an' there wa' a fight between some Yanks an' our lads,' a girl sitting in front of Grace and Clodagh shouted. 'We all got chucked out early an' never saw t'end o' t'film.'

'That's 'cos our lads are jealous of 'em. They allus start cutting up rough when they get wi' t'Yanks,' another voice shouted above the noise of high-pitched laughter and chatter.

Proper conversation impossible, Grace sat gazing out of the window as the bus left the town behind and jounced along the country roads. When it arrived at the camp gates the girls piled out, smoothing their skirts and checking that the seams in their stockings were straight or, in the absence of stockings, that the pencil lines they had carefully drawn up the backs of their legs tanned with gravy browning hadn't smudged. One stout girl, having wasted too much time gossiping, was taking the curlers out of her hair as she alighted. Clodagh nudged Grace. 'She looked better with them in,' Clodagh said cattily as big fat sausages of curls fell round the girl's moon-shaped face.

Then, hips swinging, the long line of feminine bounty filed across the tarmac
to the hangar that was used for dancing. A cavernous building, the RAF lads had done their best to make it look more like a dance hall by hanging streamers from the ceiling and pinning bunches of balloons to the walls. At one end, on a raised stage, an eight-piece band was belting out 'Boogie-Woogie Bugle Boy'. The hangar was a sea of blue RAF uniforms under a cloud of cigarette smoke. A cheer went up as the girls sashayed inside.

Grace and Clodagh wormed their way through the throng to one of the small tables at the edge of the dance floor. Finding two empty chairs, they sat down and surveyed the scene. Within a matter of minutes the dance floor was alive with couples swinging to the deafening music, skirts flaring and feet flying as the dancers followed the incessant beat of drums, piano, clarinets and saxophones.

'I'll go to the bar and get us some lemonade,' Grace said, leaving her cardigan on the chair. When she arrived back with the drinks, Clodagh was dancing with a lanky airman, his hair as red as her own. Grace set the glasses on the table and was about to sit down but before she could do so a stout lad with very prominent front teeth grabbed her hand, pulling her into the whirling throng.

'Come on, gorgeous. Give us a dance,' he yawped giving her no opportunity to refuse. He swung her energetically from one sweaty hand to the other then grabbed her round the waist, lifting her off her feet and spinning her round like a rag doll.

'Take it easy,' she protested, slapping at his pawing hands, and willing the band to take a break. Her prayers answered, she ditched her partner without another word and strutted off the dance floor. 'I'll not be dancing with him again,' she gasped, flopping down beside Clodagh. 'He near broke me ribs.'

Clodagh laughed. 'You're lucky he didn't bite your head off with teeth like that,'

she scoffed. 'If he asks again tell him you've twisted your ankle.'

'I'll more like twist his neck,' Grace replied, then took a long swig of lemonade.

'Oh, oh, here he comes again.' Clodagh nudged Grace as the lad with teeth loomed up at their table. 'He must have taken a shine to you.'

'I've twisted me ankle,' Grace said before he had time to ask her to dance. He gave her a dopey, disappointed look and ambled off. When he saw her dancing a short while later with another airman, he growled, 'Your ankle soon got better.' But Grace didn't care. She danced with numerous partners but none of them appealed enough for her to show them more than a fleeting interest.

Clodagh partnered the lanky lad with the tufted carroty hair again and again. 'His name's Ray,' she said coming to sit back down. 'He's ground crew an' he's not bad, is he?' She looked to Grace for her approval.

'Well, you certainly make a pair. You're both long an' lanky with fire on top.'

Having pointed out their similarities Grace held back her opinion on Ray's unattractive slack mouth and sloppy grin.

'We matchsticks have to show solidarity.' Clodagh giggled and got to her feet as Ray approached their table for the umpteenth time.

The doors of the hangar swung open and four men sauntered in. They looked rather dashing in their leather flying jackets with sheepskin collars and brightly coloured narrow, silk scarves.

'Oh, here come the glamour boys,' Ray sneered. 'None of us other guys get a look-in when they arrive. They're as bad as the bloody Yanks.' He grabbed Clodagh's hand, whisking her onto the floor before he lost her to a fighter pilot.

Grace was feeling rather tired, and refusing several offers, she sat content to watch the dancers and listen to the music. By now many of the young men and women had paired up for the evening. The band had slowed the pace and was playing smoochy love songs. Couples drifted by, arms round necks, and heads leaning against shoulders. Clodagh waltzed by with her arms draped round Ray's neck and his hands cradling her bottom. When she caught Grace's eye, she raised her thumbs and winked. Grace responded with a wry grin.

The band began to play 'You'll Never Know Just How Much I Love You', one of Grace's favourite songs. She closed her eyes. Then, sensing someone sitting down in the chair next to hers, she quickly opened them and glanced sideways. The brightest blue eyes she had ever seen met hers.

'All right to sit here?' The pilot leaned forward, his elbows rested on his knees and his head cocked to one side as he smiled at her. Grace's tummy flipped.

'Yes... my friend's up dancing.' Grace pointed to Clodagh who happened to be passing by in Ray's arms. The pilot slipped off his jacket. Grace caught a whiff of expensive cologne and the musky scent of warm leather. She looked directly into his handsome face, the startling blue eyes gazing into her own, as if fascinated. His thick, fair hair flopped over a broad forehead above a Roman nose and generous mouth. His cheeks were smooth and tanned. Something that Grace had never felt before fluttered in her chest. The band struck up a different tune.

'Would you care to dance?' he asked. 'I'll be delighted if you say yes.'

Grace's legs felt like jelly as she stood.

On feet that didn't feel as though they were touching the floor, she let him lead her round the floor to the strains of 'I Only Have Eyes for You'.

'Pretty apt,' he said softly, 'seeing as how I haven't been able to take my eyes

off you from the moment I saw you.'

Grace felt her cheeks burning. Then gathering her wits she replied, 'Do you say that to all the girls?'

His steps faltered, bringing them both to a halt. 'To be perfectly honest I've never said that before in my life,' he replied candidly. 'I'm sorry if it sounded too smooth. I really meant it.'

'In that case, I believe you,' Grace said, wanting to believe it with all her heart.

They resumed dancing, Grace relaxing and enjoying the strong feel of his arms. She felt as though she belonged there.

'I'm Richard Carmichael,' he said. 'And you?'

'Grace Murphy,' she replied, 'and before you ask, I'm from County Clare in the west of Ireland and I work as a nurse at the Royal in Doncaster.'

He chuckled. 'Thanks for the potted history. I'm a Yorkshire lad born and bred and I fly Spitfires for a living.'

After that they spent what remained of the evening together, dancing or sitting talking and discovering that they were both fond of reading, films and popular music. *To think I almost didn't come tonight*, Grace thought dreamily.

Clodagh was sticking to her fellow matchstick, and shortly before the dance was about to end, she came over to Grace and Richard to say, 'Ray an' me are just going outside for a breath of air.'

'Don't go too far,' Grace said, both girls knowing that she didn't mean in feet and inches: she knew that her friend was easily carried away in the heat of the moment when she really liked something, or someone. Clodagh looked at Richard then at Grace and rolled her eyes suggestively before looping her arm through Ray's and hurrying to the door with him.

Grace and Richard danced the last waltz, neither of them wanting the night to end. As the band packed up their instruments and the hangar began to empty they stood hand in hand on the dance floor each waiting for the other to make their farewells.

'It's been a lovely evening,' he said.

'It has, hasn't it?' Grace replied.

'I'll be stationed here off and on for the next couple of months,' Richard said. 'I'd really like to see you again. What are you doing tomorrow?'

A thrill of excitement tingled Grace's spine, but for some reason she couldn't fathom, instead of saying she would love to meet him the next day she ignored his question and said, 'Maybe I'll see you at the next dance.' Even to her ears it sounded flippant and mildly disinterested. She could have bitten the end off her tongue, but it was too late to take back the words.

Richard smiled ruefully.

Grace removed her hand from his and went to fetch her cardigan. Richard followed, and when she lifted the cardigan from the chair, he took it out of her hands and in a gentlemanly fashion he held it up so that she could put it on. As she threaded her arms into the sleeves, he leaned close enough for her to feel his heart beating.

Her own somersaulted and she was about to rectify her cool dismissal of him, tell him she was free all that weekend, when the bus driver burst into the hangar.

'Bus for Doncaster leaving in two minutes,' he bawled.

'I have to go.' Grace hurried to the door and out onto the tarmac. Richard, close on her heels, placed a hand under her elbow, and when they reached the bus, he brought her to a standstill.

'May I?' he said softly, bringing his face close to hers.

Grace gave an imperceptible nod.

His lips were firm and tasted sweet, and under their touch Grace's lips blossomed, opening to return the kiss with equal sweetness. Her knees trembled and a new and wonderful sensation flowed from the tips of her toes to the top of her head. She had never been kissed so beautifully before.

The bus driver let out a roar and revved the engine. She tottered up the bus steps, Richard's 'I'm glad I met you, Grace,' ringing in her ears.

'He was a bit of all right,' Clodagh gushed as Grace squeezed into a seat beside her. Grace nodded. Her lips still tingled from his kiss and she wondered why she had refused his offer to meet her the next day.

4

'Are ye not going out?' Patsy enquired as she ran a duster over the sideboard in the parlour. 'It's not like ye to be sitting in on your weekend off. You're not sickenin' for something, are ye?'

Grace shook her head dreamily and continued gazing into space, the polishing cloth she was using to shine the brasses from the mantelpiece lying idle in her hands. 'No, I'm fine,' she replied although she did feel slightly sickened at having thrown away the opportunity to spend the day with Richard Carmichael. *Why did I brush him off?* she asked herself, rubbing listlessly at a candlestick before placing it back on the shelf.

Clodagh burst into the parlour on a cloud of Lily of the Valley. Patsy glared at her. Clodagh had telephoned the hospital first thing that morning to say she was too ill to work. Now, she was going to meet Ray, the redhead. 'He's taking me on the back of his motorbike to Sandall Park and then for something to eat,' she'd crowed as she fastened the straps on a pair of flimsy sandals.

'Ye should be ashamed letting the staff down like that,' Patsy cried, flapping her duster. 'Have ye no thought for anyone but yourself?'

'She's right, Clo,' said Grace. 'It's not fair on them.'

'Ach, will ye listen to the pair of ye,' Clodagh sneered. 'You're a couple of Saint Theresas, that's what ye are.' Paying no heed to Patsy's warning that her skirt was too tight and her footwear totally unsuitable for a pillion passenger, she danced out of the house to meet her new passion. Grace watched her go, envious. Cleaning brasses was a poor substitute for a day out with a handsome man. Not that Ray the redhead qualified for that but Richard Carmichael certainly did.

'I'll go shopping with ye, if ye like,' Patsy said flapping her duster round the sideboard's legs. 'I'm not on duty till tonight.'

Grace was touched by her friend's kind offer but she didn't feel like shopping, and anyway, she was saving her coupons for a new dress. What she wanted to do was wind back the clock so that she could say, *I'm free all weekend.*

'Well, while you're thinking about it I'll away up an' get meself ready. I want to go to Verity's for some knicker elastic and then to the Co-op for some custard creams. It's my turn for the biscuits.'

Grace couldn't help smiling. The nurses took it in turn to provide biscuits for their tea break, and she knew just who would be eating most of them. Patsy had a voracious appetite for sweet stuff and had been known to demolish a whole packet at one sitting.

'Go on then,' Grace said, 'I'll come with you and whilst you're in Verity's I'll nip into the library and change my books.'

'Have ye read them already? Sure an' you've had them less than two weeks.' Patsy's eyes were wide with amazement. 'It 'ud take me near a year to read four books.' She toddled from the parlour and up to her box room.

A few minutes later, Grace went up to her bedroom. As she dressed to go into town, she couldn't help thinking that she could have been dressing for an occasion far more exciting than an afternoon in the library.

* * *

In the town centre they went their separate ways, Patsy to Baxtergate and Grace to St George's Gate. At the library, she lingered between the stacks looking for her next good read. She looked into one book and then another but her mind wasn't really on the task. The previous evening was still paramount in her thoughts and the more she thought about it the clearer it became why she had turned Richard Carmichael down. Fear at being mistaken for seeming too easy, and a silly, niggling feeling of inferiority: nothing more, nothing less.

She had known from the way he spoke that he wasn't a common working man. His funny story about boarding school and another amusing incident when he was at university had let her know that his education was that of a boy from a wealthy family. He'd mentioned horse riding, tennis parties and a holiday in Italy, not in a boastful manner but more as though everyone lived that sort of life.

In return, Grace had told him about the wild Atlantic coast of County Clare and the massive limestone formations that were known as The Burren. 'It's amazing,' she had enthused, 'just miles and miles of enormous rocks with hundreds of different plants growing there.' He'd been fascinated and seemed not at all dismayed when she went on to talk about her humble background in the small seaside town of Lahinch and the little grocery shop that her parents ran.

Yet, in her heart of hearts she had known then, and certainly knew now, that the reason she had rebuffed him was because she didn't think he could possibly be truly interested in her: that for him last night had been nothing more than a mild flirtation, and she someone to merely pass the time with. Even so, it hadn't felt like that at the time and she didn't think she would ever forget those flashing blue eyes and that wonderful kiss.

Clutching copies of *Rebecca* and *The Grapes of Wrath* and two books of a less serious nature she hurried back to meet Patsy in the little café beside the Co-op.

Patsy was on her second iced bun when Grace arrived. The bakery did specials on Saturdays, and sugar being rationed they charged the exorbitant price of sixpence for each tiny bun. Patsy thought they were worth every penny. What else did she have to spend her money on?

'Ye seem in a better mood,' Patsy remarked after Grace had ordered a cup of tea and a custard tart. The elderly waitress wasted no time in bringing it.

'I am,' said Grace, taking a bite of the tart, and telling herself that she'd done the right thing. It was a night to remember fondly, and even if she had arranged to see Richard again she would probably have ended up with a broken heart.

* * *

On Monday morning when Grace walked into the maternity ward she went straight to Doreen Butterworth's bed. Doreen was holding her son to her breast and looking much brighter.

'He's gained nearly two ounces,' she said, in much the same way as she might have said he'd won a scholarship to Eton.

Grace peered into the tiny, wrinkled face. It wasn't as yellow as it had been on Friday, and his pale, little lips were sucking feverishly on his mother's nipple.

'That's grand,' Grace said warmly, 'and by the way he's sucking now he'll soon put the weight on. What are you going to call him?'

'Gary, an' Norman for a middle name. I think Norman's a bit old fashioned, an' I love Gary Cooper.'

'That's lovely,' Grace said, helping Doreen to change Gary over to her other breast, and hoping that his namesake turned out to be as burly and rugged as the film star.

'Did you have a nice weekend?' Doreen was awfully perky this morning and Grace was glad to see it.

'Smashing! I went dancing at the RAF camp in Finningley.' She smiled as she recalled a pair of blue eyes and a rapturous kiss.

Grace was far too busy at work to dwell on her missed opportunity to see

Richard again, but at night in bed when she closed her eyes she saw his gazing back at her, amused, interested, and as blue as the sky on a summer's day. His lopsided grin at a funny remark or the way his cheeks dimpled when he smiled found their way into her dreams, and the feel of his lips kissing hers was sometimes so real that she'd woken with a start. These feelings were extremely confusing. It wasn't the first time she'd been kissed, she'd had plenty of boyfriends, but none of them had affected her like this.

It was easy to put him out of her mind during the day as she nursed new mothers and their babies or talked screaming women through difficult labours. And that sensational moment when the baby slithered into her waiting hands left little time to think of anything other than the job in hand.

Today she was doing just that. 'Knees nice an' wide apart, Mrs Hudd,' said Grace, peering under the sheet to check the young woman's progress.

'It all Mr Churchill's fault,' panted Carrie Hudd as she spread her knees. 'When he called my Bert up... he wa' droppin' his trahsers ivverytime he came through t'door... wanting to do it day an' night afore he went away even though we'd agreed... to wait a year afore havin' a babby...' She got no further as a massive contraction ripped through her.

'I can see baby's head,' Grace said calmly. 'Hold on, don't push until I tell you.' She glanced up and gave Carrie a reassuring smile then, 'Now! Let it all out.'

'Ooh! Ooh!' Carrie pressed her chin down on her chest and pushed for all she was worth.

'There we are.' Grace gently wiped the baby's airways clear. 'Thanks to Mr Churchill you've got a lovely baby boy. Are you going to call him Winston?' she said, cleaning off blood and mucus then placing the baby in his mother's arms.

'Not bloody likely! My hubby says Winnie's a warmonger. We're calling this little one Basil after me dad.' Grace left Mrs Hudd gazing adoringly at her son, and as she walked out into the corridor the hospital klaxon blared signalling the staff that they were to expect an emergency delivery of casualties. She hurried to the nurses' station in the main ward.

'Hah, there you are Staff Murphy,' Sister Morris barked, her tone suggesting that Grace had been neglecting her duties. Staff Nurse Maudie Shaw, who was standing next to the sister, rolled her eyes at Grace. They were both used to Sister Morris's overbearing manner. 'Report immediately to Dr Broadbent,' Sister Morris told them, 'there's been an air crash, and seeing as none of our mothers are likely to give birth in the next hour or so I've told him I can spare you.'

Grace and Maudie Shaw hurried through the hospital corridors to the wooden huts at the rear of the Royal. The huts had been constructed to receive wounded servicemen, and Grace always got a buzz when she was called upon to help out in an emergency. Although she believed that bringing a new life safely into the world was most important, saving lives came a close second and she felt extremely worthy as she tended injured soldiers and airmen, ARP wardens and the poor unfortunates who had been bombed out of their homes. Doncaster wasn't one of the Germans' prime targets like London, Sheffield and other major cities but it still suffered the occasional tragedy.

'I know I shouldn't be saying this seeing as how some poor souls have crashed out of the heavens, but it's a relief to get away from Morris and her nasty tongue,' Grace panted as they hurried along.

'You can say that again,' Maudie agreed. 'She can take the enamel off a piss pot when she's in one of her moods.'

'And when isn't she in one of her moods?' Grace asked cynically as they arrived at the huts to learn that a Lancaster bomber returning from a mission to the airfield at Finningley had run out of fuel and made a crash landing, killing two of its crew and seriously injuring five others.

As Grace tended a wounded airman, his face torn to ribbons by flying shards of glass and metal and his right leg broken in two places, she was tormented by the thought that this could have been Richard. He was a flyer. As she removed slivers of glass from her patient's cheeks and chin it made her realise the danger that Richard and these brave men faced every day. Glamour boys, Clodagh's friend, Ray, had called them, but there wasn't much that was glamorous about being smashed to bits or blown out of the sky. Grace shuddered.

'Bit squeamish, are you?' The airman could barely move his lips.

'Not at all,' Grace replied with a smile. 'It just came to me what a hideously dangerous job you do to keep us safe.' The sliver of metal she dropped into a kidney dish clinked ominously. The airman groaned as she applied antiseptic to the gash the metal had left behind. With gentle strokes, Grace continued to bathe his damaged face. He was a good-looking man and her heart went out to him. She wondered what his reaction would be when next he saw his pulped face in the mirror. 'There, almost finished.' She dropped a bloodstained cotton wad into the dish. 'I've removed the debris so there's less chance of infection.'

He looked at her with anxious eyes. 'How bad is it? Will I be scarred for life?' His voice trembled and he closed his eyes to stem the tears that threatened.

'It's looking pretty raw at the moment but time's a great healer, and apart from the gash on your chin I doubt there'll be much scarring,' she said confidently then added with a mischievous grin, 'and anyway, a little bit of a scar can be quite attractive. You know, the devil-may-care look that women fall for.'

He winced as he returned her grin. 'I hope you're right. I'm due to get married next month. Let's hope that my fiancée thinks the same as you do.' He looked worryingly doubtful.

'If she loves you it won't make a jot of difference. She knows what you do is dangerous, that you risk your life every time you fly, and I imagine she's awfully proud of you. She'll look on your scars as marks of honour and bravery.'

'Do you think so?' The shadows in the airman's eyes lightened.

Grace gave him a warm smile. 'I know so.'

He gave her a quizzical look. 'Do you have someone in the force you're close to

– a flyer?' he asked as she prepared to move on to another patient.

'In a funny sort of way, yes, I suppose I do,' she said wistfully. Then giving him

an encouraging smile, she said, 'Orthopaedics will be along shortly to set your leg. Best of luck for the wedding.' She moved briskly down the ward before he could ask her anything else.

The next patient she was asked to assist with had deep lacerations to his scalp. 'Shave his head, nurse, so we can see the full extent of the damage,' the doctor curtly ordered before dashing off to attend to another patient. Grace saw the look of horror in the young airman's bruised eyes. His gaunt face crumpled.

'I'll be as gentle as I can,' she said applying the clippers to his blood-soaked, matted, black curls. 'And don't worry. It'll grow back again.'

For the rest of her shift she couldn't help thinking about the danger Richard Carmichael faced every time he climbed into the cockpit of his Spitfire. She'd hate to think that he might lose his beautiful thatch of golden hair or that his handsome face might be damaged beyond recognition. War was terribly cruel.

She wondered how it was that a man she had spent no more than two hours with could have made such a deep impression on her. She'd read about people who fell in love at first sight. Was that what had happened to her? If so, she was in for a pretty miserable few weeks or months until she put him out of her mind.

Back on the maternity wing shortly before the end of her shift, she met up with Clodagh. 'How was it?' she asked, green with envy at not being chosen to attend the emergency. She liked nothing better than being in the thick of things.

'Gruesome!' Grace stripped off her stained apron and screwed it into a ball. 'A poor fella with his face in ribbons, an' him getting married next month, and a chap who was heartbroken when I shaved off his hair.'

Clodagh pulled a face. 'I've just got to change Mrs Lewis's dressing,' she said, referring to a new mum whose baby had been delivered by caesarean section, 'then we'll walk home together.' She darted off and Grace went to clean herself up before popping in to the ward to see her usual patients.

Doreen Butterworth smiled as Grace approached her bed. 'We missed you today.'

'That's nice to know. And how's Gary?'

'Ravenous!' Doreen rubbed at her sore breasts. 'The doctor says if he keeps this up we should be able to go home the day after tomorrow.' The smile fell from her face, and Grace suspected she was thinking of the empty house and no husband and father there to welcome them.

'That's good news. You'll be fine, Mrs Butterworth. I know it won't be the same without your husband but you can love Gary for both of you. The more love you give him, the more you'll get back.'

'Is that another of your Irish beliefs?' Doreen chuckled.

Grace laughed. 'It is, and it's a good one.'

* * *

Grace and Clodagh left the hospital by the main door. Arm in arm, wearing their navy blue cloaks over their uniforms, they strolled out into a glorious summer's evening. The lowering sun gleamed softly on the roofs of the nearby houses in Thorne Road and dappled the trees in the gardens. It winked on the chrome bumpers on the doctors' cars parked in designated spaces close to the main door, and on the headlamp of a motorbike near the gate.

Richard saw Grace and Clodagh before they saw him. His face lit up; his telephone call had paid off. Ever since the dance, Grace Murphy had crept, unbidden, into his mind, breaking the self-imposed rule that he wouldn't enter into any serious relationships with any of the women he met as long as he was a flyer. He had to see her again. Then he'd remembered that an old school friend, Simon Hewitt, was now a houseman at the Royal and had rung to ask him if a nurse called Grace Murphy was on duty that day.

'I presume your enquiry is purely for medical purposes.' Simon had given a dirty laugh.

'Absolutely,' Richard responded playing along with Simon, 'I need to further examine her.' It sounded distasteful but he needed to keep Simon on his side.

A few minutes later, Simon returned to the phone. 'She is, and her shift ends at six. Have fun, you filthy rogue.'

Now, he leaned against his motorbike, his leather helmet and goggles on the seat, and his flying jacket lying open over a crisp blue shirt and the brightly coloured silk scarf around his neck.

Grace saw him first. She stopped dead in her tracks, her arm yanking Clodagh to a stop. 'That's Richard Carmichael,' she gasped at the same time as Clodagh hissed,' Isn't that the fella...?'

Richard raised his arm and waved.

The tarmac beneath Grace's feet suddenly felt like eggshells as she walked towards him. He was smiling warmly, his blue eyes flashing triumphantly.

'I thought I might find you here,' he said as the girls reached his side.

'I'll see you later,' Clodagh whispered, and with a brief 'hello again' to Richard she darted off down the road. Dazed, Grace stared after her. Then gathering her wits she turned her attention to Richard.

'Hello,' she said, 'what a nice surprise. Are you here to visit someone?' She was

amazed how mildly interested she managed to sound seeing as her heart was beating a mad tattoo inside her chest.

'Something like that,' he chuckled. 'I came to see you.'

A swarm of butterflies took flight in Grace's tummy. 'How... how did you know I'd be here at this time?' she asked, her voice wobbling.

Richard ran his forefinger up the side of his nose and winked. 'Simply by deduction, my dear Watson.'

Grace giggled. 'In that case, Sherlock, it's nice to see you again.'

'Where will we go?" Richard looked deeply into her eyes.

Grace was at a loss. She couldn't think straight, and furthermore she didn't want to go anywhere whilst she was still in uniform. But she did dearly want to spend some time with him.

'Walk me back to the house and I'll get changed out of my uniform. Then we can decide what to do,' she said practically, although her heart was beating like the clappers and an unfamiliar sweetness clogged her throat.

'My pleasure,' Richard said gallantly, 'or...' he grinned enticingly '... we could ride.' He patted the motorbike's fuel tank.

Grace frowned, then visibly brightened. Why not? She'd often ridden pillion with her brother, Liam, when he got his first bike. Of course, she'd been a lot younger then and oblivious to the dangers. Now she tossed care to the wind.

'All right,' she said, 'but don't be going too fast. It's a long time since I rode on the back of a motorbike.'

'Oh, so you know what to do?' Richard sounded pleased and surprised. He put on his helmet.

'Yes, cling on for dear life and try not to pull you off when we go round

corners,' Grace said blithely.

Richard threw back his head, laughing for all he was worth. 'Let's go then.' He swung astride the bike. 'You shout the directions in my ear.'

Grace hitched up her cloak and dress and climbed on behind. She put her arms round his waist and clasped her hands together, thrilled to be holding him. He kicked the bike into motion and they set off down Thorne Road at a leisurely speed, Grace calling out 'left here' and 'left again' as they zoomed along Zetland Road into Plunket Road and on to St Patrick's Road. 'Stop here, house with red door,' she cried breathlessly. They dismounted, laughing at their achievement.

'We made it, even though you nearly had me off at the first left turn.' Richard smiled, his face full of admiration. 'What now? Do I wait here or will you invite me in?'

Grace hesitated. Clodagh might be flitting about the house half-undressed as she often did, and Patsy might be affronted by the arrival of an unexpected male visitor.

'Look, I understand,' Richard said amenably. 'I'm content to wait outside.'

That did it. 'I wouldn't dream of leaving you on the doorstep.' Grace smiled. What a gentleman he was. 'Come in and wait. I won't be long.'

Patsy went into a flap and rushed to put the kettle on even though Grace told her it wasn't necessary. Grace showed Richard into the parlour and then dashed up to her bedroom. Discarding her uniform she put on a grey tweed skirt and a mauve jumper with a cowl neck. It brought out the colour of her grey eyes. Then she loosened the chignon she wore for work and brushed her hair letting it fall in glossy back waves around her shoulders.

Clodagh poked her head round the bedroom door. 'Did ye bring him in?'

Grace nodded. 'Fancy him coming looking for you like that.' Clodagh's eyes twinkled and her grin was suggestive. 'He must be really keen on you.'

Grace nodded again, and grabbing her grey wool jacket she raced downstairs. Patsy was loitering in the hallway looking starry eyed. 'Sure, an' he's gorgeous,' she whispered, patting Grace's arm. 'An' such a gentleman.' She followed Grace into the parlour.

Richard sat clutching an unwanted cup of tea. He raised the cup and grinned conspiratorially. 'Patsy's kindly entertained me,' he said draining the cup and setting it on the tray.

Patsy blushed and bobbed a little curtsey. 'No bother,' she simpered.

* * *

They rode out of the town, the wind whipping through Grace's hair
as they travelled the country lanes to Sprotborough: Richard's
choice. Grace didn't mind where they went as long as she was with
him. She placed her cheek against his broad back, leaning into him
with her arms tightly round his waist. She had never before felt so
exhilarated.

Sprotborough was a quaint, pretty village with its little shops
and pubs, and houses and cottages whose gardens were in full
bloom. They parked the bike outside The Three Horseshoes public
house and walked along the banks of the River Don. The evening
sun shimmered on the water, golden bands of light rippling down-
stream and reflecting the overhanging trees.

Conversation came easily, both of them eager to learn more
about one another. Grace told him about her two brothers, Liam
who worked in the shop with her father and Declan who was a
bricklayer. She learned that Richard had a younger brother who
had gone to live with relatives in Canada. Bit by bit they teased out
each other's histories.

Grace told him about the men she'd nursed that day, how brave
they were in the face of adversity, and how aware it had made her of
the dangerous task of flying.

'What's it like to fly?' she asked, her tone hinting at the wonder
of it.

As she spoke a skein of geese skimmed the water, the whirring
of wings fading as they took to the sky, the perfect V-formation dark
against a bank of clouds.

'Like that,' Richard said, his eyes following the flight of the birds
as he pointed. 'Suddenly you're up there among the clouds free as a
bird and everything below you in miniature. Master of all you
survey.' His voice echoed her wonderment.

He deliberately neglected to say that the sky was often black with German bombers, Heinkels, like swarms of black wasps up ahead or on his tail and the rattle of gunfire and the hiss of tracers spraying the heavens. And he praying, *miss me this time, you bastards.*

He pointed up to where a bank of clouds had assembled. In the centre was a small patch of bright blue. 'See that patch of blue sky,' he said. 'Whenever you see one that's where I'll be – thinking of you.' He spoke lightly, but there was an underlying depth to his words.

Grace gazed up at the clouds. The small blue aperture steadily held its own place in the firmament. Silently, she repeated Richard's words inside her head. They were the most beautiful words that anyone had ever said to her. Suddenly she felt extraordinarily happy.

She smiled into his eyes. 'In that case, from now on I'll make a point of looking out for a patch of blue sky.'

Richard nodded and returned her smile.

They retraced their steps, never running out of conversation, her hand warm

inside his and her heart singing. When they arrived back at The Three Horseshoes they went inside and found a seat by the window in the cosy warmth of the busy pub. Grace ordered the ham and Richard the beef, and though the portions were sparse, rationing being the order of the day, the vegetables were plentiful and tasty.

Dusk had fallen whilst they ate, but it was still light enough for them to take another walk. Hand in hand, they strolled up to the ancient church of St Mary and there, in the shadows of its buttresses, Richard took Grace in his arms. Her hair smelled like meadow flowers, a scent that still clung to his jacket long after he had left her home.

He brushed his lips against her, as fleeting as a butterfly when it lands on one flower and then flits to another. Grace's head swam, every inch of her tingling with pure joy.

'I have a feeling you are going to be a very precious part of my life,' Richard said, his voice thick with emotion.

'I think I'd like that very much,' Grace whispered.

They rode back the way they had come, Richard's attention on the road ahead and Grace pressed against his back, each of them aware that something special had taken place.

5

In the weeks that followed that glorious day in the summer of 1942, Grace and Richard met whenever their duties allowed. The trouble was Grace never knew when or where to expect him. Neither did she know that Richard had qualms about getting too involved with any girl, letting them into his life when he didn't know whether or not he'd live to see the next day. But there was something about Grace Murphy, and he couldn't get her out of his mind.

So, duties allowing, he'd turn up at the house in St Patrick's Road or outside the Royal, having phoned his friend, Simon, to check when she would finish her shift. Then off they'd go for yet another few enjoyable hours in each other's company. Afterwards, Grace would be happy for a day or two. During the weeks in between, she lived on tenterhooks, waiting. The war was still raging with no end in sight, and every time Richard returned from duty, Grace was able to breathe again without the constricting fear that he might not be safe. And every time that Richard landed his Spitfire back in an airfield in England he thanked God for letting him survive another mission.

Whenever they were together, Grace found herself being drawn deeper and deeper into their relationship, and it wasn't just the romantic aspect that had her feeling this way. He was good company. She liked his irreverent sense of humour, his ability to talk knowledgeably about a broad range of subjects, and the way in which he did this without a hint of superiority. She also liked the look of him, the feel of him and the smell and taste of him, and the way he made her feel more alive than she ever had before. It was unexpected, and all seemed a bit too soon. She had never been in love but if that's what it was, then she was all for it. And the most wonderful thing about it was that he seemed to feel the same way.

* * *

Grace was on duty and Richard was paying his parents a fleeting visit on the same day that Doreen Butterworth was allowed to take little Gary home. Grace had grown fond of the young widow and was delighted that her son had fought against the odds and won. There had been some complications with his breathing and Doreen had had to leave him in the hospital for several weeks, visiting him every day to feed him and praying he would pull through. He now weighed more than five pounds and his skin was no longer sickly yellow. Grace walked down the corridor with her, Doreen proudly carrying Gary in her arms then putting him in the pram she'd left at the main door.

'Best of luck,' Grace said giving Doreen a quick hug. 'Look after the little fella.'

'You can be sure of that,' Doreen replied tearfully. 'Thanks for everything.

You've been lovely. Maybe I'll see you round the town one day.' Off she went, her back courageously straight as she walked across the tarmac, going home to face bringing up her son without his father to support and comfort her. Grace felt sad as she watched her go.

At the end of her shift Grace left by the main door surprised to find Richard in the car park leaning nonchalantly against a nippy Triumph sports car.

'Hop in,' he said when Grace stared, open-mouthed at the car.

'Have you borrowed it?' She roamed her eyes admiringly over the car's sleek, green paintwork and shiny chrome bumpers.

Her question made Richard smile. 'It's mine,' he said, his tone matter of fact.

'The weather's turned and I can't have you freezing to death on the back of the bike so I thought I'd bring it out of retirement. Just let's hope I can get enough fuel to keep it on the road.'

Grace climbed in, feeling rather grand as she sank into the passenger seat, the rich smell of leather and petrol tickling her nose.

Having the car meant that they were able to go further afield in the few hours they shared. They went to the Peak District and the Dales, Richard introducing Grace to the stunning scenery in his home county. Another time they visited Wentworth Woodhouse with its magnificent Georgian mansion, every outing pure joy and Grace convinced she'd found the man of her dreams.

* * *

'Where's Brylcreem boy these days?' Clodagh said, one day when Grace hadn't heard from Richard for three weeks. They had just arrived home from work.

'He doesn't use Brylcreem,' Grace replied tartly, hanging her cloak on one of the hooks in the hallway and then slipping off her heavy, black shoes before padding in her stocking feet into the kitchen, and at the same time picturing Richard's thick blond hair flopping over his forehead.

'I was just thinking he's a bit casual in the way he comes and goes, that's all,'

Clodagh said, tossing her cloak over the newel post at the foot of the stairs and following Grace. 'It seems unfair on you that you never know where he is or what he's up to,' she continued, sitting down at the table watching Grace put the kettle on ready to make their evening meal. 'He's not like my Ray. He never leaves me without making arrangements to see me again.'

'That's because he's ground crew and knows exactly what hours he's going to work.' Grace opened a tin of oxtail soup. 'Ops are different for the flyers. They answer the call at a minute's notice, and what with the Luftwaffe targeting Sheffield these past few weeks they've been kept pretty busy.'

'Just saying,' Clodagh remarked. 'I prefer to know where I stand with a feller that's all.' She stood up. 'I'll go and give Patsy a shout. She must have slept in.'

She left the kitchen to waken Patsy who had been on night duty. She was usually up by this time and more often than not she'd have a meal ready for Grace and Clodagh when they came in from their shift.

Grace poured the soup into a pan and put it on a low gaslight to heat then began paring cheese very thinly to make sandwiches to eat with the soup. There was some truth in what Clodagh had said and it made her feel uneasy. She hadn't liked the way her friend had said 'or what he's up to'. She'd made it sound as though Richard might be stringing some other girls along at the same time as he was seeing her.

Feeling decidedly unhappy, Grace placed the slivers of cheese between the six slices of bread she'd smeared with margarine; two sandwiches each. Was Richard just a charmer who dropped in on her because he had nothing better to do at that particular moment? It didn't seem like that when she was with him. And maybe the fact that she was always ready and willing whenever he called might make her seem too easily available: just another girl to fill an empty hour or two in a lonely airman's life. Then there was the niggling problem of the differences in their backgrounds. He came from money, had had a private education, owned a car, and would one day run the family business. What did he see in her? Was she, as Clodagh had implied, just a bit of fun on the side?

The soup had stuck to the bottom of the pan by the time Patsy and Clodagh returned to the kitchen. 'Sorry, I was daydreaming,' Grace said as she scraped the last of it into her own bowl.

Clodagh sniggered. 'Dreaming of when glamour boy's going to show up again?'

'An' why not?' said Patsy, sitting down at the table still wearing her dressing gown. 'I think he's just lovely.' She spooned up her soup. 'This is grand, Grace. I don't know what I was doing sleepin' so long. It's not like me.'

'Night duty does that to you after a while. It catches up on you.'

'Aye, but I like working nights, Grace. I love the wee small hours when it's mostly quiet, or the times when ye bring a baby into the world when the stars are shining.' Wearing a quaint little smile, she munched greedily on her sandwich.

Clodagh ate in silence. She was feeling guilty at being catty to Grace, but if she was perfectly honest she was envious of Grace and her fighter pilot with his dashing good looks, and a car. Still, she thought, she had Ray and although he might be a gawky redhead like herself, he was crazy about her.

A knock at the door had them looking at one another and Grace, having no appetite for her soup and sandwich, jumped up to answer it. Richard stood there

smiling. 'I thought I might catch you. Are you free this evening?'

Grace remembered her earlier misgivings about being available. Tossing them to the wind she said, 'As a matter of fact, I am.'

They drove down into the town to a pub on Fishergate where Grace drank a lemonade and Richard a pint of stout. 'What do you say to a walk?' he suggested when their glasses were empty.

'There's a park nearby. We could go there.' Grace would have gone anywhere as long as she was with him. They strolled through the streets to Sandall Park. The trees were wearing their autumnal garb, the russet, yellow and red leaves adding to the small park's natural beauty. They were walking towards the lake finding plenty to talk about as they usually did when they saw two young airmen and their girls in the near distance. They were strolling arm in arm chatting and smooching as they wandered along a path bordered by a dense shrubbery.

Suddenly, a gang of youths broke through the bushes, quickly surrounding the courting couples. The girls screamed, and dragging their arms free, they began to run. The local lads let them go, shouting after them, 'Mucky tarts,' and to the airmen, 'They're our lasses, keep your bloody hands off,' along with a string of similar insults. The two young airmen glanced wildly from one another to their assailants. The local gang closed in.

'Bloody fools! Wearing their uniforms,' Richard growled and set off running. Grace ran after him, her heart in her mouth as she saw one of the airmen crash to the ground under two of his attackers. It was five men to two, neither airman able to defend himself or his mate.

Richard waded into the hail of flying fists and feet yelling, 'Break it up, lads!' But the local boys having the upper hand, they ignored him. Richard backhanded one of the youths with a powerful slap to his chin, and at the same time kicked out his right foot bringing another lad to his knees. The lad scrabbled to his feet and ran after his mate who was nursing his jaw. The rescued airman stood, swaying on his feet and fingering his broken nose.

Grace ran over to the airman who, flat on his back, was writhing under a swarm of kicking and stamping feet in pitmen's boots. 'Stop it! Stop it!' she screamed at the top of her lungs. 'You're going to kill him.' She lunged forward and grabbed at the hem of a jacket yanking its wearer backwards.

'No! Grace, no!' Richard yelled, and fearing for her safety, he charged to her side, kicking out at the thug. Her intervention had caught the local lads off guard and when Richard dived in amongst them, they too turned and ran.

Grace dropped to her knees running a practised eye over the inert body of the wounded airman. He struggled to sit up but Grace pushed him gently back down.

'Lie still,' she ordered, checking for any signs of broken limbs or heavy bleeding. Finding only a deep gash on the back of one hand, she gently rolled him into the recovery position. 'Breathe, love, breathe,' she said softly as she rubbed his back and kept on rubbing until the airman gulped a lung full of air. Richard hovered over her.

'He's in shock,' said Grace looking up at Richard. 'Bend down and raise his legs up on your knees.' Richard did as she asked, her calm proficiency twitching the corners of his mouth into a little smile. The airman's pal staggered over to them, blood pouring from his nose onto his uniform jacket. 'Doug,' he croaked, 'are you all right, mate?' He turned panicked eyes on Grace. 'Is he dead?'

'No, but these broken veins need staunching.' She got to her feet and lifted her skirt. The airman looked away, blushing, and Richard raised his eyebrows as she whipped off her waist slip. Biting through the cotton material with her teeth, she ripped it into two parts. 'Here.' She handed broken nose a piece saying, 'Nip the bridge of your nose tight.' Then, down on her knees again she bound Doug's hand tightly. 'Can't afford too much blood loss,' she muttered.

Once again she ran her hands over Doug's bruised and battered body. 'His uniform saved him from worse,' she said getting to her feet. 'The thick material took the brunt of the kicking. I don't think anything's broken except his front teeth.' Doug groaned and struggled to sit up. Grace stooped to assist him. She looked up at Richard. 'Help me get him to his feet,' she said briskly.

Richard placed his hands under Doug's armpits and Grace supported his legs until he was upright. 'Okay?' she asked Doug. He nodded, and between them Grace and Richard steered him to a park bench. 'Go and bring the car to the park gate,' she said without looking at Richard, and devoting all her attention on Doug.

'Orders understood, ma'am.' Richard appeared none the worse for his part in the foray as he set off running. He was back in minutes and between them they half-carried Doug to the car. He seemed to have recovered his senses. Apart from flinching at every movement he didn't appear to have suffered any major damage.

'Right, hospital first stop,' Grace said as she helped Doug into the front passenger seat.

Richard hesitated. 'Hospital or camp?' he said addressing Doug.

Grace drew a sharp breath. What was he thinking? 'Hospital,' she snapped.

'Not the best idea,' Richard said shaking his head. 'The medics on the camp can see to him. If it gets out that he was in a fight in the town in his uniform he'll be in deep shit. He won't want that on his record.' He looked at Doug.

'Camp,' Doug mumbled through his broken teeth, 'and thanks, Flight.'

'Don't thank me. Thank your lucky stars Staff Nurse Murphy was on hand to assess your injuries and treat them.' He then addressed Grace. 'What about you? Where will you be when I come back?'

'What about Larry?' Doug gestured to his pal still nursing his nose.

Before Grace had time to answer either question an army truck trundled towards them. She ran out into the road and flagged it down. After a hurried exchange Larry climbed aboard.

'There, that's him sorted,' Grace said efficiently. 'I'll walk back to the house. I'll see you when you get back.'

Richard looked at her with something verging on awe then climbed into the driving seat and sped off to Finningley.

* * *

'You are one amazing woman, Grace Murphy,' Richard said as she led him into the parlour when he returned. He continued praising how she had dealt with the two young airmen as they sat on the couch.

'I was just doing my job,' she said glowing under his words.

'Not when you were dragging that thug off by the back off his jacket, you weren't. You scared the hell out of him – and me.' Turning in his seat, he looked deeply into her eyes, his expression full of admiration – and something else.

Grace's heart fluttered. 'I wasn't going to stand by an' watch them beating that poor lad when he was down,' she said, her voice wobbling for he was still looking at her in a way that made her insides feel as though they were melting.

'You could have been hurt,' he said, his voice thick with concern. 'When you whaled in to stop that lout, I was scared of what could have happened if he'd turned on you. It confirmed just how much I care about you.' He placed his arms round her pulling her closer. Grace snuggled into him feeling warm and safe. 'You know I once told you that I thought you were going to be a special part of my life,' he whispered against her hair, 'well, now I know that you are. I love you, Grace Murphy, and I can't imagine life without you.'

After Richard had gone back to camp Grace went up to bed. As she lay wide awake his words played inside her head. He had told her he loved her, and she knew without a doubt that she loved him too.

It was late December when Grace next saw Richard. His misgiving about letting a woman into his precarious life had been forced out of him by his love for Grace, and her doubts that he was just playing her along had fizzled and burned. By now they both accepted they were an item. At her suggestion they went into the town to buy Christmas gifts, something new for a change, not second-hand. She'd been saving her ration coupons and her money, and now on the arm of the most handsome man in the county she felt like a million-dollar princess.

However, from the outset Richard seemed distracted, Grace wondering if he, like a lot of men, disliked shopping. After all, it had been her idea. His unusual long silences made her nervous and her excitement palled as she made her purchases from the meagre stock the shops had to offer: a striped scarf for Clodagh and gloves for Patsy.

Grace was looking in a shop window deliberating whether or not to go in and try on a dress like the one in the window display when Richard dropped his bombshell. 'I'm being transferred to Duxford,' he said gloomily.

'Duxford!' Grace lost all interest in the dress. 'Where's that?'

'The other end of England,' he replied dolefully, 'Cambridgeshire to be exact.'

Grace's heart sank: too far to nip and see her when he wasn't flying, not to mention being able to get petrol for such a lengthy journey. 'When do you go?'

Her voice sounded scratchy, her throat suddenly clogged with tears.

'The day after tomorrow.' He looked so miserable she put her hand to his cheek stroking it comfortingly. He gave a wan smile. 'I won't be celebrating Christmas with you this year, or seeing in the New Year,' he continued, 'but as soon as I get leave I'll be back, don't doubt that.' He pulled her into his arms, and oblivious to the shoppers passing by he kissed her. Grace clung to him, not wanting to let go.

In a desultory manner they carried on shopping, but the pleasure had gone out of the day. In Binns department store they separated, Grace to buy underwear, and he to purchase something for her. Then they went to the café, and over tea and scones they sat silently for much of the time, each lost in their own thoughts.

Would he forget about her once she wasn't near at hand? Grace wondered. Might he go to a dance in Cambridgeshire and find some other girl to spend his free time with? How would they keep in touch? The house in St Patrick's Road didn't have a telephone. She wasn't allowed phone calls at work, and neither was he. Sod the war, she thought bitterly, why did it have to come between her and all her hopes for the future. Then she thought of the poor, wounded men she had nursed, and Doreen Butterworth who had lost her husband. It made her feel petty. She was alive, Richard was alive, and if their love was as strong as it seemed to be they would survive being parted for a while.

Would she write him off now that he would be too far away to see on a regular basis? Richard pondered. Had these months been nothing but a beautiful interlude not meant to last. He was certain he loved her and she seemed to love him, but were they just caught up in the thrill of the moment influenced by a world at war where their lives could be snatched away at any minute. He didn't want to believe that but he was plagued by the thought of losing her.

They drove back to the house, and finding themselves alone, Patsy and Clodagh on duty, they sat in the parlour. Richard pulled Grace close so that she was almost sitting on his lap. Their kisses were greedy, for soon they would only be memories. When they said goodnight they both knew that sleep would evade them.

'Tomorrow's the last time I'll see you for a while,' he said as they walked out to the car. 'Where will we go? What would you like to do?'

Grace wanted to say *run away to where no one will find us, and spend the rest of my life with you.* Instead, she said 'Take me to Sprotborough again.'

* * *

They walked along the banks of the River Don, but unlike their previous visit on that glorious day in summer a cold, fretful wind ruffled the rushing water, crests of white horses racing to the distant sea. The grassy banks were devoid of flowers and the trees, stripped of their leaves, stood stark against the skyline, their blackened branches like witches' talons. Underfoot the path was crisp with a light coating of frost.

'It's still beautiful even if it's lost all its finery,' Grace said, her breath clouding in front of her as she fondly recalled the first time they had strolled this way. Richard's arm was draped across her shoulders, its weight making her feel warm and wanted.

'Everywhere is beautiful when I'm with you,' he said pulling her closer. 'When this rotten war is over we'll go to Paris and stroll along the boulevards, then to Venice where I'll hold you in my arms as we glide down a canal in a gondola. And I'll kiss you under the stars in Sorrento. What do you think to that?' He stopped walking and pulled Grace into his arms, kissing her so thoroughly that she couldn't think let alone speak. Her heart felt as though it might explode to know that he was promising to be with her for years to come.

He let her go. 'We'll fly our kites before we settle down and have kids,' he said confidently. Grace's heart somersaulted at the thought of having his children.

'I think it sounds absolutely perfect. I can't think of anything I'd like better.' She thought about telling him just how much she loved him.

'I love you, Grace Murphy,' he said softly against her hair. 'I want to spend the rest of my life with you.'

'I love you,' she replied, those three little words imbuing all she had been about to say. 'I want to grow old with you for I'll never feel this way about any other man as long as I live.'

A few hours later, having driven back to St Patrick's Road under a sky speckled with frosty stars, when they entered the parlour Patsy jumped to her feet and rushed to put the kettle on. Grace left Richard sitting by the fire and followed Patsy into the kitchen.

'He's asked me to marry him,' she whispered excitedly then paused, 'well, sort of.' He hadn't actually used those words.

'By all the saints in heaven,' Patsy gasped, clanking the kettle on the stove. 'Did ye say yes?' Her eyes were like saucers.

'More or less. I'd be a fool not to. I love him more than anything in this world.'

She lifted cups from the cupboard. 'Where's Clodagh?'

'Out with your man, the red-haired fella.' Patsy raised her eyes to the ceiling. 'She's never done seeing him.' Ray being ground crew, he and Clodagh managed to spend a lot of time together. Grace felt slightly envious as she told Patsy that Richard was going away and she didn't know when she would next see him.

'Ye take the tea in an' I'll make meself scarce,' Patsy said sympathetically.

Grace hugged her for her thoughtfulness. Patsy was a dear.

When Grace entered the parlour, Richard was standing with his back to the fireplace, a small elegantly wrapped package in his hands. Grace set down the cups and looked at him expectantly.

'Here,' he said handing her the package, 'something to remind you of me. Merry Christmas.'

Grace removed the dark green and gold paper carefully. The scarf, in muted shades of blue and green, was similar to the ones he himself wore. She unfolded it, the silk, light as a feather, slithering between her fingers as she draped it about her neck. 'It's beautiful,' she said breathlessly, overwhelmed to think that he had chosen something for her that was so much a part of himself. 'I'll treasure it for the rest of my life.

'Be back in a tick,' she said, hurrying from the room to fetch the present she had bought for him more than a week ago. She hadn't bargained on giving it to him so soon. Back in the parlour, she handed him her gift.

'I'll feel as though I'm holding your hand every time I wear them,' he said, slipping his hands into the suede gloves with crocheted string backs. After taking them off then stuffing them in his jacket pocket, he took her in his arms and kissed her. She kissed him back.

'Tea's getting cold,' she said in an attempt to calm the thudding of her heart. Richard sat in one of the armchairs and Grace in the other whilst they drank their tea. Then, putting his cup down, he patted his knee and she went on to it without hesitating. In between kisses, they talked. Richard came up with the idea that every Wednesday and Saturday, duties allowing, he would make a call to the telephone box at the end of Plunket Road at nine on each of the nights. Grace thought it was a marvellous idea.

'That way, I can hear your lovely voice,' he said kissing the tip of her nose, 'and I'll send you an address when I get one.' He gave a rueful grin. 'I've not had much practice writing love letters, but I'll expect you to write at least once a week.'

Grace laughed. 'I'll write every day and you'll never be out of my thoughts.'

'Nor you mine,' he said solemnly then kissed her so passionately that her insides felt as though they were on fire.

'I'll miss you dreadfully,' Grace whispered against his chest. His departure now imminent, and the frightening thought of never seeing him again uppermost in her mind, she voiced the fateful question: a question that thousands of women must have thought or asked during the past three years. So many loving couples had had their dreams ripped apart by this terrible war. She took a deep breath. 'What if you don't come back – anywhere – ever?'

The implication in those few words made Richard hesitate. He smiled sadly. 'That's something you'll have to deal with when the time comes. Don't fear things that might not happen.'

'It's hard not to.' Grace's voice wobbled pathetically.

'Don't try to swim against the current, Grace, swim with it. What will be will be. Short or long, life is precious and I intend to keep mine so that I can spend the rest of it with you.'

When it was time for him to leave, Grace swallowed her tears determined not to cry and make him feel more desolate than she knew he already felt. She followed him out to the pavement and as they stood by the car he chucked her under her chin and said, 'Remember, Grace, a patch of blue sky.'

It had become their watchword and, as he drove away, the Triumph's shrouded headlamps barely lighting the road ahead, Grace stood in the darkened doorway and waved until he was out of sight. Already, her body ached with a desperate longing for him and her skin yearned for his touch. Then, gazing up into the dark sky she picked out the brightest star, the one she thought was the Pole Star, and said a little prayer to it.

6

'Thank God there were no fatalities. It always seems worse if someone dies at Christmastime,' Grace commented, her breath clouding in the cold evening air as she and Clodagh trudged through the darkened street. It was Wednesday night, three days before Christmas Day, and they were both bone-weary having just spent four gruelling hours attending to a team of injured fire wardens. A gang of kids playing in the ruins of a bombed-out building had set it alight and as the wardens were dousing the flames an unexploded bomb had detonated.

'Yeah, it's awful.' Clodagh sounded thoroughly disinterested. She was dwelling on her own problems and not those of the fire wardens. 'I'm still not sure if I'm supposed to be spending Christmas in Chesterfield with Ray's family, and the bloody RAF are keeping him working right up to Christmas Eve. I need to know for certain if it's still on,' she whined.

Grace's thoughts still with the injured men, she didn't respond. The deprivations of living in a country at war seemed all the harder to bear in the winter months, what with having lost an hour of daylight when the clocks went back, and the darkness of the blackout at night adding to their misery. Now, there were five men in hospital who wouldn't be celebrating with their families.

'Are you listening to me?' Clodagh dug her elbow into Grace's side as, arms linked, they watched their steps on the thick frost on the pavement. 'I said Ray's on duty right up till Friday.'

'Think yourself lucky he's only a few miles down the road and not at the other end of the country,' Grace said, thinking of Richard. 'At least you know you'll see him then, and celebrate Christmas with him.'

'Yeah, I suppose you're right, although I'm not sure I want to go.'

'Why? I thought you were really keen on him.'

'I am, but I won't know anybody, and his parents might not like me. Then I'll be miserable all over Christmas,' Clodagh groused.

'Of course they'll like you,' Grace said heatedly. 'What's not to like? And Ray clearly thinks you're the bee's knees, otherwise he wouldn't have asked you to meet his family.'

Clodagh groaned. 'I know, but he's as daft as I am when it comes to thinking things through properly. He most likely asked me on the spur of the moment just to get his way with me.'

'I hope he didn't,' Grace cried, wondering what he'd received in return for the invitation. 'An' I hope you didn't give him what he was after. You need to be careful, Clo, you don't want...' Her words were drowned by the wail of the air raid siren, its eerie warning resounding off the gable end walls in Plunket Road.

'That's all we bloody need,' Clodagh yelled. Picking up their heels the girls

slipped and skidded towards the shelter at the bottom of the street, jostled by other frightened folks with the same intention.

Inside the shelter they huddled together, crammed in by the inhabitants of

Plunket Road and others who like themselves had been on their way to somewhere else. Grace detested the shelters and tried to avoid using them, at the same time appreciating the safety they provided when faced with imminent danger. They were dank and depressing, and made worse by the smell of sweaty bodies, beery breath and fear.

Standing bust to bust with Clodagh and her bum wedged against that of a fat, elderly man who smelled of fried onions, Grace clenched her teeth, resigned to waiting it out in the cramped space. Behind Clodagh, a young girl with a toddler in her arms stared pale-faced into nothing. An older woman, whom Grace presumed was the child's grandmother, was stroking the little girl's face and softly singing 'You are my sunshine, my only sunshine'.

'You can blame this on my missus,' a middle-aged man joked. 'She allus gets the ARP to blow t'siren when I'm on me way to t'pub. She says if Hitler dun't stop me boozing nowt will.'

A ripple of laughter was suddenly silenced as they heard the heavy rumble overhead. As the rumbling grew louder several pairs of eyes were raised to the shelter's roof whilst others gazed pensively into the faces of those standing nearest. Those who had managed to find places on the narrow beds built into the shelter's walls sat up, alert. The shelter shook as the planes roared overhead and kept on going until their engine noise faded.

A united whoosh of stale breaths was released.

'It looks like them poor buggers in Sheffield are in for it again tonight,' the

smelly onion man said. Sheffield was a prime target for the German bombs, the Luftwaffe doing its best to wipe out the steel-works there.

A second wave of bombers passed overhead. The air grew stuffier. Listless conversations were exchanged, babies cried and little children wittered and the singing granny carolled 'Run rabbit, run rabbit, run, run, run.' Some of the people joined in but Grace didn't. She was mulling over what Clodagh had said before the siren went off. Clodagh wasn't the same since she started going out with Ray. In the past she'd been ebullient and game for anything. She'd plunge into things without giving them a second thought, and could always have been relied on to be the life and soul of the party, but just lately she didn't do anything without Ray's approval. And like him, she was sarcastic and catty about people that she perceived had more than she had. At one time she wouldn't have cared less, and it saddened Grace to see the change in her.

One hour dragged into two, Grace on pins willing the siren to blow again.

At last, the all-clear sounded. 'Music to my ears,' someone shouted. The door opened and the crowd surged towards it, Grace and Clodagh carried along in the sway. Outside, they gulped mouthfuls of clean, wintry night air. Grace undid the top buttons of her coat and flipped up the little watch pinned to her uniform. It was seven minutes to nine. 'You go on, Clo. I'm going to the phone box. Richard might be trying to ring me.'

She ran back to the telephone box on the corner only to find it occupied. She glared at the back of the young woman chatting and laughing into the receiver. When she tucked it under her chin and delved in her pocket for a packet of cigarettes, Grace groaned out loud. She pictured Richard dialling the number again and again, only to find the line engaged. Before the woman had a chance to light up Grace opened her cloak so that her uniform was on full display. She tapped on the glass then opened the kiosk door.

'Sorry to interrupt, but it's an emergency.'

Clocking Grace's uniform, the woman shouted down the phone, 'Sorry, I'll have to go. There's a nurse wanting to make an emergency call.' She put the receiver down, and giving Grace an apologetic smile, she stepped out of the box. 'Sorry to keep you waiting.'

Grace took her place, her breath pent as she waited for the phone to ring. It didn't, and after forty-five minutes it still hadn't rung. The notion of Richard ringing her had sounded marvellous at the time, but it had only worked on the Wednesday after his departure. She'd waited an hour last Saturday and again on Wednesday, pretending to be deep in conversation when someone came to use the box, and peeved when a man had banged on the window telling her to *bloody well be quick, she was hogging the phone.* Cursing under her breath, she'd relinquished the phone and stood outside shivering with cold and bad temper.

Now, her heart in her boots, she trudged home. Perhaps she'd never hear from him again, she thought. Absence didn't always make the heart grow fonder. She knew that for a fact. When she'd moved from Clare to Dublin to start her nurse's training, she'd felt sad at leaving Dara Kerrigan behind. He'd begged her to stay, but for all she'd been courting him for several months once she was in Dublin she soon forgot about him, and he her. On her first visit home some weeks later, she'd learned two things: that Dara Kerrigan was engaged to Mary Kelly, and that she, Grace Murphy, didn't give a damn. Was that the way it would be with her and Richard? she wondered dismally as she let herself into the house. Would they become no more than pleasant memories in each other's minds?

* * *

On Christmas Eve, Clodagh packed her overnight bag in the hope that Ray would remember he had arranged to collect her and take her to Chesterfield. Standing amidst a clutter of rejected garments scattered over her bedroom floor, she ranted and raved about meeting his family. Grace and Patsy, on hand to assist, exchanged bemused glances.

'What are you getting so uptight about?' Grace picked up a shoe placing it alongside its partner to bring order to the chaos. 'It's not like you to get in a state over meeting new people.'

'But they're not just any people,' Clodagh wailed. 'They're his parents and I want to make a good impression.'

'Then just be your lovely wee self,' Patsy said sagely, folding a discarded jumper and putting it in a drawer.

A knock at the outside door had Clodagh whirling like a dervish as she rammed last-minute toiletries into her bag. 'That'll be him,' she cried, lifting the bag and haring downstairs, Grace and Patsy at her heels.

Ray gave Grace and Patsy a sloppy grin then letting it slip he looked at Clodagh. 'Do you still want to come?' he said grumpily. Grace thought he sounded as if he was having second thoughts about taking her with him.

'Of course I do.' Clodagh lifted her bag. Ray's mate revved the engine of the jeep they would travel in and making no attempt to open the jeep's door or help her with her bag Ray jumped into the seat next to the driver. 'Get in the back then,' he called out. Crestfallen, Clodagh climbed aboard and gave a pathetic, little wave as the jeep sped away.

'He's no gentleman,' Patsy scorned as Grace closed the house door. As they

went into the parlour Joey tweeted noisily. Patsy clapped her hands. 'Did ye hear that? The wee darlin' just said Merry Christmas.' She rushed over to his cage to congratulate him.

Grace thought it sounded nothing like it, but she held her tongue and put another piece of coal on the pathetically small fire. The shortage of coal meant that they had to ration every piece they burned, and she knew the coal cellar was almost bare. 'I do hope things turn out all right for Clodagh,' she said anxiously. 'I'm worried for her. She's changed since she started going out with Ray. She seems to have lost her confidence. She never used to care what other people thought about her, but now she's all nerves.'

'Aye, I'd noticed that,' said Patsy as she sat down opposite Grace. 'She goes out of her way to please him, even when she doesn't want to.' She screwed up her face. 'An' he's not that much of a catch. I think he's a bully. Take the other night for instance when she wanted to go to the pictures an' he wanted to go to the pub.' Patsy sniffed disparagingly. 'Guess who won?'

'She must really love him, though God knows why,' Grace said thoughtfully. 'Look at the fellers she went through when we were in Dublin. She had them dancing on strings an' didn't give a hoot what they wanted.' That reminded her of what Clodagh had said about Ray's invitation. *He'd only issued it to get his way with her.* Grace sighed. 'I do hope she doesn't do anything silly.'

Patsy giggled. 'Sure, she wouldn't be Clodagh if she didn't.'

* * *

At nine o'clock that night Grace stood inside the telephone box waiting for Richard to ring. Surely, on Christmas Eve he'd make the effort to get in touch, or was he now celebrating with someone new? She shivered at the thought. When the receiver jangled, she almost jumped out of her skin. She lifted it, her hand and voice shaking as she said, 'Hello.'

'Merry Christmas, darling.' At the sound of Richard's voice Grace's blood pulsed and her mouth went dry.

'Merry Christmas,' she croaked, swallowing unshed tears and wishing she didn't sound so pathetic.

'Not the best way to spend Christmas Eve, is it?' Richard told her that he missed her and how much he loved her. Grace responded likewise but she wasn't feeling happy.

In the background she could hear music and laughter. 'Where

are you calling from?' she asked, picturing a party of revellers drinking and dancing, and suddenly feeling jealous.

'Officers' Mess. We're having a wing-ding.'

'Don't be falling for any of the girls there.' Grace tried to sound perky but she was crippled with jealousy.

'God, no! Why would I do that when I've got the best girl in the world even though she's miles away? And anyway, there's a whole load of Americans stationed here so chaps like me don't get a look in.'

Grace breathed a sigh of relief. Thank God for the Yanks with their nylons and chocolate and long American cigarettes. Even so, without any of those lures there were still lots of girls who couldn't fail to be attracted to Richard.

'Come on, Carmichael, you're missing all the fun,' she heard a masculine voice yell. Her heart sank.

'Shove off, Rigs, I'm talking to the woman I love,' Richard replied, making Grace's heart soar again.

They exchanged more words of love, longing and affection then, the noise in the background making it almost impossible for Grace to hear what Richard was saying and a definitely female voice screeching, 'Richard, I'm dying to dance with you,' he ended the call with 'Look, I've got to go. Merry Christmas, Grace.'

She replaced the receiver not knowing whether to feel happy or sad. His words of love had filled her with joy but the fact that he was now at this very moment drinking, and maybe dancing with a pretty girl made her feel lonelier and emptier than she had felt for some time. *Some Merry Christmas this is, and all because of the rotten war*, she thought. *I hope your Christmas is as miserable as mine, Mr Hitler.* She walked back home to Patsy and Joey. At the door she paused gazing up into the starry sky. No chance of a patch of blue sky tonight.

* * *

The next morning, Christmas Day, Grace and Patsy left early for work, both girls cheerfully accepting that they were on duty all over the festive period. There was a light covering of snow on the pavements making it slippery underfoot.

'Here, hang on to me,' Patsy said, her kindness making Grace feel like crying. Arms linked, they made their way to the Royal looking forward to the day ahead. Christmas Day in hospital was usually fun, even though there were sick patients to nurse and babies to deliver.

'Isn't that just gorgeous?' Patsy gushed as they walked by the huge, beautifully decorated spruce in the hospital foyer. 'It makes our wee tree look like nothing.'

'Ours is just perfect,' said Grace praising Patsy for having the initiative to buy a little fir tree. It hadn't occurred to her. She didn't feel at all Christmassy. These days her mind was elsewhere. Where was Richard spending Christmas Day?

'Well, what have we got so far?' Grace asked as soon as they entered the

maternity ward. Christmas babies always seemed special.

'A boy two minutes after midnight and two girls before six o'clock,' Maudie Shaw announced cheerfully. 'An' now I'm off home an' leavin' 'em for you to see to. The kids will have been up from the crack of dawn opening their pressies. My old man'll be tearing his hair out if he has to mind 'em much longer.' She grinned. 'Not that he has much. He started going bald not long after he married me.'

'And we all know why.' Grace laughed along with the plump, jolly staff nurse. Maudie was one of the few married nurses in the Royal that had been brought back into work to make up the shortfall caused by so many of their colleagues going off to hospital field stations on the front line. She waddled off, her duty done, and

Grace and Patsy went to the nursery to view the new arrivals. They read the cards on the end of the cribs that identified the babies to their mothers. Some simply said 'Baby' and the mother's surname.

'Ah, would ye look at that now.' Patsy pointed out a card with 'Noel Sykes' written on it. 'Sure an' isn't that just lovely giving the wee feller a Christmas name?'

'It's a damned sight better than Horace,' said Grace pointing to another card where the baby had already been named. Giggling, the girls checked that all the babies were comfortable then went on their way.

The maternity ward was suitably festive with streamers and balloons, and all the mothers in the beds were in good health and good spirits. At quarter to ten Grace and Patsy delivered another boy. At eleven they sang carols to the accompaniment of the Salvation Army Band, and at one o'clock they ate overcooked chicken and piles of sprouts. 'I'll be farting all afternoon,' Patsy said as they made their way back to the ward.

'I'll remember to keep downwind of you then,' Grace chuckled as she went to assist Mrs Darwin who was having trouble feeding her new daughter.

In the afternoon the radio was turned up to full volume so that the patients could listen to the World Service deliver Christmas messages from servicemen and women in far-off places. Then it was time for the King's Speech. A drum roll and the solemn strains of the national anthem stilled the chatter of the women in the ward as they listened to the halting words of their monarch, King George VI.

'Eeh, that poor man! It's giving me a pain listening to him,' Mrs Hawkes exclaimed, bored already, as the king spoke of loyalty to the nation and strength to fight on and win the war.

'He can't help his stammer,' Mrs Lawson cried. 'I think he's very brave.'

The women began to argue amongst themselves. The king praised the men and women in the forces, Grace's heart lurching when he said, 'and those who fly our aircraft'. Was Richard listening? If so, did he feel honoured?

'Thank God that's it,' Mrs Hawkes commented as the king blessed his people. 'I know he means well but I'd rather listen to a nice bit of music.'

She got her wish, but when the song 'What'll I do when you are far away and skies are blue' came on, Grace rushed into the sluice to hide her tears.

* * *

In Chesterfield, Clodagh was also listening to the King's Speech in the Barnes's crowded living room. She wasn't enjoying herself. They'd arrived late the night before, the little house already packed with relatives and friends celebrating Christmas Eve. Music was blaring, drink flowing and the noise deafening.

Above the din, Ray had introduced her to his mother. She'd looked from Ray to

Clodagh and back to Ray. Clodagh had instantly known that she wasn't expected. She'd given Ray a dirty look, but he'd ignored it and sloped off to get a drink.

Vera Barnes had taken a swig of her gin and tonic then breathing its fumes into Clodagh's face she'd asked, 'Where are you staying, luv? Are you visiting with somebody down here?' The fat, blowsy woman hadn't seemed too interested. Clodagh had felt the urge to run. But where would she go?

'Ray invited me to stay with you.' The palms of her hands moistened and she'd mentally kicked herself for agreeing to come.

'Oh, he did, did he, the cheeky bugger? Well, I don't know

where you're going to sleep. They're all home for Christmas.' Vera had tottered away.

'Why didn't you let your mother know I was coming?' she'd spat when Ray came back and flung his arm round her shoulder. She'd shrugged him off.

'I thought I had,' he'd said uncaringly, and before she could vent her feelings he'd wandered across the room to catch up with some old mates who were calling his name. Clodagh had spent the rest of the evening seething and making pointless conversation with drunken people. The only person who had made any sense or taken any notice of her was the man who had driven them down in the jeep. It turned out he was Ray's cousin, Geoff. He was pleasant enough but he wasn't Ray. She had shared a bed with one of Ray's sisters. Pauline had drunk too much and snored so loudly that when Clodagh woke from a restless night's sleep she wasn't in the mood to celebrate Christmas Day.

She had somehow thought they would go to church in the morning, but when she went down into the shambles of a kitchen no one else was up. She found some bread and a jar of jam and made a sandwich and a cup of tea. She couldn't believe how neglectful of her Ray had been. She'd hardly spoken to him all night. She stemmed her tears, cursing herself for falling in love with him. For she did love him, even though he was a bit demanding, always wanting his own way and always wanting more than she was prepared to give him. She was in two minds to get her bag and go back to Doncaster, but common sense had told her there would be no buses on Christmas Day.

Now, here she was in the shabby sitting room with its outdated wallpaper, squashed on the settee with Ray listening to a boring speech. Every few minutes Ray's dad jumped to his feet and saluted drunkenly. His mother sat nursing a tumbler of gin and tonic, her eyes glazing over. Clodagh was beginning to think they were all slightly mad: they weren't at all like her own family. Strong drink had never passed her mother's lips. By the time they had eaten a tepid, dried-up Christmas dinner and had far too much to drink, Clodagh was in the depths of despair.

Towards evening, the house began to fill up again, people of all ages roistering in with bottles of beer and mince pies. Clodagh looked at the crowd of people laughing and drinking, their happy faces flushed as they bantered in the way friends do. But she knew nobody except Ray, and he seemed to have forgotten about her. She stood there with a sick feeling in her chest, suppressing the impulse to go find him.

'I thought the Irish were the big drinkers, but this lot...' Clodagh said to Geoff who happened to be standing at her elbow and looking as out of place as she felt.

'Aye this lot 'ud give 'em a run for their money,' he muttered as Vera swayed past, glass in hand. Clodagh left Geoff to go and find Ray. He was in the kitchen, his arms round a very pretty blonde girl wearing too much make-up. He was laughing at something she'd said, his face too close to hers for Clodagh's liking.

Pauline sidled up to Clodagh. 'That's Jean, our Ray's sweetheart. They're

getting married when the war's over.' Her eyes gleamed maliciously. A spurt of anger flared in Clodagh's chest and before she could stop to think she marched across the kitchen and slapped Ray's face. He reeled back, shocked to the core.

'What the bloody hell...?'

'In case you forgot, it's me you're supposed to be celebrating with. Not some slapper you hung about with before you met me.' Clodagh's cheeks blazed.

'Aw, don't be like that. Jean's an old...' Ray blustered, looking slightly guilty.

'An old tart you were knocking off before you tried it on with me,' Clodagh cut in sneeringly. By now, all eyes were on her and Ray.

'Here, who are you calling a tart?' the blonde screamed, grabbing at Clodagh's hair and pulling her off balance. Clodagh lashed out in defence.

'We were only having a bit of fun,' Ray bawled. 'Don't go spoiling it for everybody.' He tried to pull Clodagh away but she was having none of it. She grabbed at Jean's hair, spitting and scratching until Geoff stepped in and broke it up. Clodagh ran from the kitchen into the hallway and sat on the stairs. Ray didn't follow her. She heard his mother slurring something about *mad Irish* and *you should have hit her back!*

Christmas was ruined and Clodagh wanted it to be all over and done with so that she could escape back to Grace and Patsy and the little house in St Patrick's Road. She pressed her lips together, determined not to cry as she wondered what to do next. Geoff came and plumped down beside her. She looked into his sympathetic face as if to say *what now*? He was an ugly lad, his lips too thick and his cheeks pocked with acne, but his brown eyes were warm and kind.

'It it's any help, I'll give you a lift back to Doncaster,' he said.

Clodagh gave him the same sort of look a drowning man gives a lifeboat when it suddenly appears out of nowhere. She knew he was making the offer out of pure kindness. He was supposed to be staying until the Boxing Day to take her and Ray back then.

'Really?' she gasped. 'Do you mean it?' Then not wanting to prey on his thoughtfulness. 'I don't want to drag you away.'

'You're not,' he said firmly. 'I'd forgotten how bloody awful me Auntie Vera an' that lot are. I only came 'cos I'd nowhere else to go.'

Clodagh could have cried for him as well as herself. 'I'll get my bag.' She stood ready to mount the stairs. 'We don't have to tell anybody we're leaving, do we?'

'I don't think they'd be that interested,' he said dolefully.

* * *

It was well after midnight when Geoff pulled the jeep to a halt outside Clodagh's door. They'd covered the miles from Chesterfield to Doncaster mainly in friendly silence, or chatting about their work and films they had seen. Neither of them had mentioned Ray. 'I'll see you around,' Geoff said as Clodagh climbed down to the pavement and he prepared to drive on to Finningley.

She leaned back into the vehicle and gave him a warm smile. 'Thanks, Geoff, you're a lifesaver.' She meant every word. 'I'll look out for you if I ever go to a dance in Finningley again.' She sounded as though it would be highly unlikely but she felt she owed it to him.

'I don't go to the dances. I've no time for such stuff.' His tone was matter of fact. 'You take care now, and don't let that bloody cousin of mine pester you. He doesn't deserve you.' He revved the engine, anxious to be on his way. Clodagh thanked him again and slammed the jeep's door. Then she fished in her bag for her door key.

Up in her bedroom, Patsy opened her eyes then froze, listening. Someone was opening the front door. She'd know the sound of that creaky hinge anywhere. She lay for a moment, panic seeping through her veins. Were she and Grace about to be murdered in their beds? Or were they being robbed? She'd better warn Grace.

Slipping out of bed, she put on her candlewick dressing gown. No murderer or thief was going to catch her in her nightie. Whoever it was down below, they weren't being quiet about it. She padded on the landing to Grace's room and crept in. 'We're being broken into,' she hissed shaking Grace's shoulder. Grace woke with a start. Her eyes flew open. Patsy was peering down at her.

'Patsy! What's wrong?' Grace sat up at once.

Patsy placed her fingers to her lips. Grace nodded. 'What is it?' she whispered.

'Downstairs. There's somebody there.'

Then Grace heard the sound of the water running in the sink. She climbed out of bed. Together they crept stealthily along the landing and down the stairs. At the bottom they paused, looking at one another anxiously.

'A weapon, 'Grace hissed, lifting her umbrella with the pointed end out of the hallstand. Patsy darted into the parlour and came back wielding a brass candlestick. The hiss of the kettle and the clink of crockery came from behind the closed kitchen door.

'The cheeky blighter's makin' himself tea,' whispered Patsy.

Grace took a deep breath. 'We'll charge in and catch him off guard. Ready?'

Grace threw open the door and they barged in, Patsy's plump backside wedging them between the jambs. Eyes boggling, they stared at Clodagh sitting at the table drinking tea and weeping. Grace and Patsy shrieked in unison. 'What are you doing here?'

'I live here,' sobbed Clodagh raising her tear-stained face.

* * *

'I can't believe I got into a fight over him,' Clodagh exclaimed for the umpteenth time as the girls nursed cups of cocoa round the kitchen table. 'I've never fought over any feller. It's usually them fighting over me.' Her misery had turned to anger but it didn't last long. 'But I really love him and I thought he loved me,' she wailed, beginning to weep again.

Grace and Patsy offered all the comfort at their disposal, Patsy declaring, 'He's one dirty, heartless beast, so he is,' and Grace saying, 'He doesn't deserve you, Clo, you can do better than the likes of him,' but it hadn't been enough to ease her heartache. She went off to bed still weeping. Her weary friends followed her.

* * *

'What are we going to do about Clodagh?' Patsy asked, as she and Grace walked to the Royal the next morning. They had left her sleeping, feeling envious as they'd looked in on her for both of them were decidedly underslept.

'There's not much we can do other than be there for her,' Grace said flatly.

'We can't make Ray into a decent feller, and she can't stop loving him just like that. It's not like turning off a tap,' she continued, aware that Patsy had no idea what it was like to be in love: unless you counted Joey the budgie.

7

SPRING 1943: DONCASTER, YORKSHIRE

The weeks went by, winter's snow and freezing fog giving way to an uncertain spring. In Doncaster, the persistent drone of aircraft coming and going to and from Finningley and Lindholme day and night, and the undulating wail of the air raid siren was a constant reminder that the country was still at war, but of late, the town had been lucky. In previous years there had been a spate of attacks, the town centre demolished, and more recently a lone German bomber on his way back from bombing Sheffield had unloaded the last of his deadly cargo over the railway line at Balby. The town's inhabitants had grown used to rationing and the blackout, and wailing sirens and Anderson shelters. They also suffered the ever-present worry for loved ones working on the home front or scattered to places in the world they had never before heard of or thought about, but the country was at war and they had learned to accept it. Further afield the Germans had surrendered at Stalingrad and the Americans had taken Guadalcanal and were holding back the Japanese, but still the war raged on.

Grace, Clodagh and Patsy continued to deliver babies and nurse their mothers and at the same time each of the girls dealt with their personal problems in different ways. Whenever they weren't working Patsy hid her yearning to go home to Dingle by tidying the house and mothering her friends. Clodagh salved her heartache by dating one hospital porter after another, and Grace found comfort in writing cheerful, newsy letters to her parents in Lahinch letting them know she was safe and well, and long, loving letters to Richard in Cambridgeshire.

Grace missed Richard so much that she often felt she had lost part of herself.

She lived for the Wednesday and Saturday night telephone calls which, sadly, were very hit and miss. In fact, a lot more miss than hit. When she did hear his voice her knees trembled, and there was so much she wanted to tell him that her words came out garbled and too filled with emotion. On the occasions he did manage to call they reminisced rather than recount her daily routine or his, for Richard's work didn't bear talking about. He was careful to spare her the horrors he endured. The calls always ended with declarations of love, and Grace would walk home on a cloud and sleep peacefully, her dreams sweet.

Sometimes she received hastily scribbled letters telling her of amusing incidents on the base and other trivia, but the words she liked best were those that told her how much he loved and missed her. His letters were never more than a page or two whereas hers were so long she felt embarrassed as she wadded them in the envelope, but writing them made her feel closer to him.

She took to plane spotting, her eyes fixed on the skies every time she heard

the distant roar of an aircraft. Soon she was able to recognise a Lancaster from a Wellington, a Tiger Moth from a Spitfire. When she saw a 'Spitty' as Richard called them, she fantasised that it might be him coming back to Finningley.

Clodagh had spent weeks after Christmas moping, and red-eyed for much of the time, but as daylight lengthened and the weather became warmer, she appeared to bounce back to her former bubbly self. When Clodagh announced that she no longer loved Ray, Patsy was delighted. 'Sure an' what did ye want with a dirty spalpeen like that?' Only Grace suspected that Clodagh was acting.

On a lovely evening in June Grace walked home alone, her thoughts dismal. It had been a miserable day on the ward. That morning she had delivered a stillborn baby, and another one had died within an hour. It wasn't her first experience of such calamities, and it certainly wouldn't be her last – she was wise enough to know that – but whenever things didn't go as planned she was inclined to feel she had failed both the mothers and the babies.

Clodagh and Patsy were on night duty and Grace was looking forward to the meal she knew they would have ready for her. She also knew that they would understand her reason for feeling sad and comfort her with kind words. She had done the same for them in the past.

As she walked down Plunket Road she saw the dusky pink mopheads of a hydrangea bush peeping over a garden fence. They made her think about how the seasons lapped and reeled each with their own signs of what was to come. Spring was about new life, new beginnings and summer was everything in full bloom. Sadly, she didn't feel as though her life was blooming, in fact sometimes she felt as though it was withering. It seemed like a lifetime since she had seen Richard's handsome face and felt his touch, his hand in hers, his lips tasting hers and the feel of his strong, warm body against her own. She needed him to make her blossom and bloom.

The smell of something tasty tickled her nose as she entered the house, but she forgot that her tummy was empty when she saw the letter on the hall table. She snatched it up and held it to her heart before opening the envelope and withdrawing the flimsy blue page.

She read what was written on it, her cries of pure joy bouncing off the walls of the narrow hallway.

'What is it?' Clodagh yelled dashing from the kitchen. 'What does he say?'

She'd recognised Richard's loopy scrawl on the envelope and felt jealous. She swore she was over Ray and had been dating the same hospital porter for the past two weeks, but she still hadn't really recovered from losing the man she thought was hers. 'It's not bad news, is it?' she asked, half-hoping that it might be, and then feeling ashamed.

Grace flung her arms wide dancing Clodagh into the kitchen. 'Quite the opposite,' she chortled. 'He's been granted eight days' leave. He's arriving on Friday.' She let Clodagh go, tears of happiness streaming down her cheeks as she plumped down into a chair at the table.

'There, there, darlin',' Patsy comforted, putting a plate of pale, pink Spam and a dish of champ in front of Grace then placing her arms round her. 'Sure, an' didn't I say all along it 'ud not be long before he was back.'

'It's been six long months,' Grace sobbed wiping her cheeks with her fingers, 'and I'll not know what to do with meself from now until Friday.' She gave a wobbly laugh. 'He'll be here for eight whole days,' she gasped in wonderment. 'It's like a dream come true.'

'Aye, an' you'll be on duty for most of 'em.' Clodagh took a rather spiteful

pleasure out of putting a damper on Grace's euphoria.

Grace's smile fell from her face. She looked frantically from Patsy to Clodagh.

'What can I do? I've got to get leave.'

* * *

The next morning, Thursday, Grace approached Sister Morris, her insides fluttering with apprehension and her fingers crossed behind her back. Her uniform immaculate – she'd pressed it that morning – and her shoes glistening, Grace held herself tall and straight as she requested leave. 'I know it's short notice, Sister Morris, but my fiancé has been granted eight days and I'd like to spend some of them with him.' She thought that the little white lie about Richard being her fiancé might add weight to her request.

Sister Morris pursed her lips. 'It is indeed very short notice, Staff Nurse Murphy but...' her severe face softened, 'let me look at the rota. Staff Nurse Shaw is due to go on leave for a few days. She might agree to swap with you.'

Sister Morris stalked off, her back ramrod straight as she marched into her office. Grace's heart thudded painfully. Please God be kind, she prayed as she took a bedpan from under the pale, young girl who had been admitted late two nights before. The girl averted her head so that she didn't have to meet Grace's eyes. She had spent much of yesterday sulking and refusing to answer Sister Morris's questions. Grace felt pity for her. Just sixteen, unmarried and pregnant, she had a hard road ahead of her.

Sister Morris came back waving the rota. 'It's as I thought. Staff Nurse Shaw has booked five days starting from Monday. You may go and ask her if she's willing to exchange them. She's in the nursery.' She gave Grace a tight, little smile. 'Of course, Matron will have the last word.'

Grace left the bedpan in the sluice and hurried into the nursery. Maudie Shaw was bottle-feeding a new arrival whose mother had no milk and a nasty chest infection. She looked up, smiling when she saw Grace.

'Poor little mite has an appetite like a baby bird,' she said, gently nuzzling the teat on the bottle against the baby's tight shut mouth.

In a different mood, Grace would have shown concern for the

baby, but right now she couldn't think of anything other than begging Maudie to swap her leave.

Her heart in her mouth, she broached the question.

'Aye, I will,' Maudie agreed instantly. 'I booked them days ages ago when Archie thought he'd be coming home on leave, but now he's not coming till next month. He's been promoted,' she added proudly. Archie, Maudie's husband did something in the Signals, and Grace blessed him for not being able to get away.

'Oh, thanks, Maudie! You don't know what this means to me,' Grace gushed.

Maudie grinned. 'I think I do. I was young once, you know.' She gave a fat, wheezy chuckle. 'You have them days an' enjoy 'em, love. An' when my Archie comes you can stand in for me.'

'Oh, I will, Maudie, I will!' Grace felt faint with relief. Now all she had to do was square it with Matron. She didn't relish the thought of asking the stern-faced, big- bosomed woman who prowled the wards with an eagle eye always on the lookout for something that didn't meet her high standards. She went back to the ward, her fingers crossed.

'What did she say?' Clodagh hissed, coming up behind her. She found herself hoping Maudie had refused. She knew it was mean of her to think like that but she just couldn't help it. She missed Ray dreadfully.

'She said yes!' Grace's eyes were dancing.

'Good old Maudie,' Clodagh said unenthusiastically.

'I'd best get on,' Grace said. 'I don't want to put a foot wrong today.'

'Staff Murphy!' Sister Morris's bark made Grace cringe. Summoning an expression of obedience and willingness, she turned to find her sour-faced superior marching towards her. Without a trace of the tolerance she had shown earlier the sister snapped, 'Don't stand gossiping, nurse, you've already wasted time attending to your own needs. Go and see to that impudent little madam in the end bed. She's sorely trying my patience.'

Grace scurried off thinking, *What patience is that, Sister Morris?*

'You haven't touched your breakfast, Ruth,' she said to the young girl when she saw the untouched food on the tray. 'You've got to eat for you *and* the baby.'

'Don't want it!' Ruth Slater turned her head away. Grace presumed she meant the lumpy porridge and singed toast. She flinched hard when Ruth cried, 'I don't care if it dies 'cos I wish I wa' dead.'

'Oh, Ruth, you mustn't think like that. It's not the end of the world,' Grace said gently. 'I know it must seem difficult at the moment but once your baby's born you'll fall in love with it, because you won't be able to help yourself.'

'Will I?' Ruth sneered. She looked Grace up and down, her cold, pale eyes and the lines etching her mouth making her look much older than her years. 'What do you know about it?' she scoffed. 'Did you have a kid when you were my age and wa' left to bring it up on yer own?'

'No, I didn't but...'

'Well, keep your bloody mouth shut, an' don't keep telling me what to do,' bawled Ruth tossing over in bed with her back to Grace.

'That attitude will neither help you nor your baby, Ruth,' Grace said sternly.

'It's time for you to grow up and face reality.' She often used such tactics with patients who refused to help themselves, believing that sometimes you had to be cruel to be kind. She lifted the tray and left the girl to sulk.

'She needs her arse slapped,' Mrs Ackroyd said when Grace arrived at her bedside. 'Talking to a nurse like that. It's not on.'

Grace sighed. 'She's frightened and feeling very much on her own, I suppose. Maybe you could try talking to her. You've had five so you know what it's about.'

'Aye, an' my five were all born in wedlock,' Mrs Ackroyd said piously.

'We all make mistakes,' Grace said wearily. She went to the nursery to start bringing the babies in to their mothers for feeding. Twice she gave the wrong baby to the wrong mother, and red in the face, she had to apologise. Her mind wasn't on her job. She muddled through the rest of the morning thinking of little else other than would her leave be granted.

Shortly after lunch a probationer came onto the ward looking for Grace. 'Matron wants you in her office, now.' She smirked.

Grace tidied her uniform as she hurried down the corridor to Matron's office. Outside the door, she adjusted her cap and glanced down at her shoes to check they were still shining. She knocked the door with a hand that was visibly shaking. So much rested on the next few minutes.

'Enter.' Matron's gravelly tones sounded ominous in Grace's ears. She went in and stood to attention several feet from Matron's desk. Elsie Parr looked her up and down in much the same way as Ruth had earlier that morning. Grace's heart sank. The back of her neck itched but she dared not scratch it.

'Staff Nurse Murphy,' Matron said, not unpleasantly. 'Sister Morris has brought it to my attention that you've requested a period of leave and would like to take

it as soon as possible. Might I ask why?' Her gimlet eyes behind wire-framed spectacles drilled into Grace's face.

Grace flushed. There was no use pretending there had been a death in the family or something like that, and it hadn't crossed her mind that she could have used that excuse until after she'd spoken to Sister Morris. She would have to tell the truth. She drew a deep breath.

'My fiancé is a fighter pilot and he's stationed in Cambridgeshire. I haven't seen him for months and now he's coming on leave. He arrives tomorrow.' She was amazed by how calm and succinct she sounded.

Elsie Parr cocked her head on one side, interested. 'What does he fly?'

Grace, taken completely by surprise stuttered, 'A... a Sp... Spitfire.' She felt utterly foolish.

Matron smiled. 'So does my dear nephew. What would we do without our boys in blue, Staff Nurse Murphy?' Grace had no answer to that.

Matron folded her large, capable hands under her chin and gave Grace a steely look. 'I've considered your request, Staff Nurse, and in view of your impeccable timekeeping, your efficiency and dedication to duty I've decided to grant you leave albeit that Staff Nurse Shaw is in agreement.' She sat back in her chair.

'She is, Matron,' Grace assured, trying to calm the rapid beat of her heart that had quickened with every one of Matron's words of praise. She pulled herself up straight in an attempt to look just as Elsie Parr had described her. 'Thank you, Matron, I really am grateful.' She bobbed a brief curtsey.

Elsie smiled beatifically. 'Dismissed, Staff Nurse Murphy.'

Grace floated down the corridor in search of Clodagh. She was in the sluice. 'I can have five days from Monday.' Grace almost screamed, 'isn't that just perfectly marvellous. Matron was ever so nice about it. Her nephew flies Spitfires.'

'Does he now?' Clodagh intoned her jealousy flaring as she wiped a bedpan dry. 'So ye told the old battleaxe about glamour boy an' his Spitfire an' touched her heart, did ye? Ye'll be best friends next.'

'You don't sound very pleased for me, Clo.' Grace sounded disappointed.

'Oh, take no notice of me.' Clodagh clanked the bedpan on top of another and decided to tell the truth. 'To be honest I'm green with envy.' She blinked back threatening tears. 'You've got Richard, and I've got nobody.'

'Aw, Clo, I'm so sorry. Here's me flaunting my happiness and being thoroughly selfish,' Grace said hugging Clodagh comfortingly. 'You're still missing Ray, aren't you?' She felt Clodagh's head nodding against her shoulder.

'Yeah,' sniffed Clodagh. 'I thought I'd get over him but I can't. I honestly thought he was my match... er... stick,' she giggled, trying to make light of her misery. 'Every time I think back to when I slapped him and started a fight with that girl, I can't believe I did it. I ruined everything.'

'I think it was Ray that ruined everything, Clo.' She patted Clodagh's back. 'Don't be so hard on yourself. Somebody else will come along, I'm sure.' She let her go. 'I'd best get back on the ward, keep on Sister's good side.'

'What side's that?' Clodagh asked dolefully. 'Her big, fat backside.'

* * *

Grace had washed her hair and shaved her legs and was now languishing in a bath of hot, soapy water fragrant with the bath salts Patsy had bought her for Christmas. She was annoyed at having had no success in encouraging Ruth Slater to eat, or getting her to talk to the other mums on the ward, but now she pushed aside those thoughts in anticipation of seeing Richard again. In his letter he'd said he would call at the house around five and if he didn't find her there he would meet her outside the hospital. Having to work tomorrow was a bind. She didn't want him seeing her again for the first time in months, her wearing her uniform and looking frazzled after a day on the ward. She wanted to look like she had on the night they first met.

She climbed out of the bath, and as she vigorously towelled her body she reminded herself to take her make-up bag to work. She didn't wear make-up at work, but tomorrow she'd find time before the end of her shift to slap some on. She'd also wear the scarf he had given her at Christmas. It being so precious she only wore it on Sundays when she went to mass, but tomorrow was special. Silently cursing at not having tomorrow off she put on her dressing gown and went downstairs to join Clodagh in the parlour. Patsy was on night duty so there was only the two of them in the house.

Grace knelt in front of the fire to dry her hair. 'I'm a bag of nerves,' she said running her fingers through her wet hair. 'I feel like I'm about to explode.'

'I'm going to the dance in Finningley tomorrow night,' Clodagh announced, deliberately ignoring Grace's reference to meeting Richard again. Grace looked up, surprised. Clodagh had avoided the RAF dances since the debacle with Ray.

'Won't you feel a bit uncomfortable if Ray's there?'

Clodagh tossed her long, red hair. 'Why should I? I wasn't to blame, an' I'll not let a toerag like Ray Barnes stop me enjoying meself. I'm not becoming a nun just because of him.'

Grace frowned. Only yesterday she had been saying she missed him, and now she was acting as though she couldn't care less. But then, Clodagh was a mass of contradictions, and tonight she sounded so sure of herself that Grace hadn't the

time or patience to worry about her. 'I'm going to have an early night,' she said. 'I've a big day to look forward to tomorrow.' She had no sooner spoken than the sirens wailed their mournful note. 'Oh, no! That's all we need.' She jumped up dashing from the room to gather up the blankets and the basket they kept tea and biscuits in.

'Bloody Hitler an' his rotten Luftwaffe,' Clodagh yelled, grabbing the milk bottle and their gas masks that were on the kitchen table. After turning out the lights and locking the door they blundered the length of the back garden to the Anderson shelter they shared with their immediate neighbours.

Mr and Mrs Johnson, the elderly couple from next door were already inside, huddled together on a camp bed holding hands. Grace thought how sweet they looked, so loving after all the years they had been married. She wondered if she and Richard would be like that in fifty years' time.

The girls had just dumped their baggage on their camp beds when Lucy Moorhouse hurtled in, her baby daughter, Norma, screaming in her arms and her three-year-old son hanging on to the hem of her coat. 'Bloody hell! Listen to that,' she exclaimed as the strange whining noise overhead followed her into the shelter. The five adult occupants pricked their ears. The whining suddenly stopped. Then, a distant thud followed by a mighty explosion had them looking at one another as they wondered which poor souls had copped that one.

The Anderson's walls shook and a shower of dust escaped from its roof. Mr Johnson began to cough, his wife patting his back to loosen the phlegm. In the lull they heard the rattle of the ack-ack guns from the nearest battery. 'They're too damned close tonight,' Clodagh grumbled, flopping down on a camp bed and covering her head with her hands. The adults sat in silence waiting for further explosions. Norma continued screaming, Grace unsure which was worst, the sound of the bombers or the terrified cries of the child.

The roar of the bombers' engines faded and it was quiet again. 'Must be Sheffield in for it again tonight,' Mr Johnson croaked.

'Thank goodness for that,' his wife said then quickly corrected herself. 'Not that I wish anybody there any harm.'

Another wave of aircraft passed overhead, and Grace reluctantly prepared to stay put for the night. 'Tonight of all nights,' she moaned. 'I'll be a complete wreck in the morning.'

'That's if we live to see it.' Clodagh shuddered as more rumbling and roaring shook the shelter. 'An' if that child screams much more I'm getting out of here an' taking me chances with Hitler's madmen,' she whispered.

Grace lit the small primus stove they kept in the shelter and made tea for the grown-ups and cocoa for the children. She handed round the biscuits. Mrs Johnson produced slabs of fruitcake. 'Left over from Christmas,' she said as she doled it out. 'My sister's husband does the black market. He got me two bags of raisins and sultanas.'

Norma stopped crying and fell asleep, a ring of cocoa round her mouth. The others munched the delicious cake then lay down on their camp beds ready to make a night of it. Grace prayed that Richard's journey north wouldn't be delayed by the destruction the German bombers might have caused elsewhere.

At five in the morning the all-clear woke them. Bleary-eyed and groggy they made their way back into their homes.

An hour later, as Grace and Clodagh wearily trudged to the Royal, they met another neighbour. Bill Walmsley, an ARP warden, grinned when he saw the

shadows under their eyes. 'Rough night, lasses?'

'Something like that.' Grace forced a smile. 'What about you? Where was that awful explosion around midnight?'

'The Decoy at Tickhill,' he said referring to the false airstrip that had been constructed to deflect German pilots from the real airbase at RAF Finningley. 'They see the lights, you see, an' the murdering buggers think they've found their target but there's nowt there but scrubland.' He laughed. 'We're not as daft as Jerry thinks we are.'

'Thank goodness it wasn't Finningley. If anything happened to

R—' Clodagh clapped her hand to her mouth then continued '—to any of those lads there it would be terrible.'

Grace knew that Clodagh had been about to say Ray's name and knew that her protestations of not caring about him were nothing but thin air, but she let it pass as they hurried on their way down Zetland Road without speaking: Clodagh because she knew she'd nearly given the game away, and Grace too concerned with getting this day over and done with in time for Richard's arrival.

8

Breakfasts over, the women on the ward who had already given birth were feeding their babies and Grace going about her duties when Sister Morris barked, 'Staff Murphy! Screen *Miss* Slater's bed. I'm to examine her to see how advanced her pregnancy is.' Her expression one of utter distaste, she marched off and Grace went to Ruth's bed to pull round the screens.

Ruth was sitting up in bed, a scowl on her face as Grace approached.

'How are you this morning, Ruth?'

'What do you care?' Ruth stared straight ahead.

'I care because it's my job and I'm worried about you.' Grace unfolded the screens then put her hand to her mouth to hide a yawn.

Grace had felt sorry for Ruth from the moment the ARP warden had brought her to the maternity unit. 'I found her lyin' in a shop doorway when I wa' coming' off night duty,' he'd said. 'Seems she'd been there all night. When I saw what condition she wa' in, you know, I thought I'd better get her straight round to you.'

Ruth had been brutally unhelpful when Sister Morris had

asked her when her baby was due, shouting, 'Bugger off an' leave me alone,' and clamming up when questioned. Now, she eyed Grace warily asking, 'What are you doing?'

'Sister Morris wants to examine you.'

'She's not!' Ruth drew up her knees. 'I'm not letting her touch me.'

'Don't be silly. We need to know how far on you are so that we can look after you properly.' Ruth slid down in the bed as Sister Morris parted the screens and stepped inside like an avenging angel.

'Now, Miss Slater,' she snapped rubbing her palms together then leaning over Ruth's supine body, 'I'm going to ascertain how soon you're likely to give birth.' She pulled back the sheet and snatched at the hem of Ruth's hospital nightgown.

Wham! Ruth's leg shot out, her foot catching Sister Morris under the chin and sending her steel-rimmed glasses flying. Sister Morris screamed. Grace lunged to restrain Ruth who was now kicking and screaming for all she was worth. 'Calm down, Ruth,' she cried gripping the girl's shoulders and trying to push her flat on the bed. Morris would more than likely blame her for this debacle just when she needed to keep on her good side. But Ruth fought back, rearing up and swiping Grace's cap from her head along with a handful of hair.

Blinded by fury and the loss of her spectacles, Sister Morris lashed out, the flat of her hand connecting with Ruth's face in a resounding slap. The stinging blow stunned Ruth into silence, the only sounds behind the screen being Grace's shocked gasp and the sister's laboured breathing. Then Ruth began to wail.

Grace picked her cap and Sister Morris's spectacles up off the floor. The sister was shaking with rage, her face livid. When Grace handed over her spectacles, she clawed them from Grace's hand and stamped off without another word.

'That was a very foolish thing to do, Ruth, you could have harmed your baby,' Grace panted putting her cap on and struggling to slow her thudding heart.

'Don't care,' wailed Ruth. 'That bitch hit me.' She dragged the sheet over her head. Grace pulled back the screens and walked slowly up the ward to Sister Morris's office dreading the tongue-lashing she was sure she would get and ignoring the nursing mothers' cries of 'Eeh, what wa' all that about?' and 'Is that lass all right, nurse?'

Sister Morris was slumped at her desk struggling to regain her composure. 'We can't afford to keep her here if she has another week or so to go,' she growled without a hint of compassion, her bent spectacles askew on her nose and two bright spots burning her cheeks. ''You're good with patients, Murphy, see if you can get her talking.'

Grace hid her surprise at being let off so lightly. She was, however, aware that the sister had broken every rule in the book by slapping a patient in anger. The least said about it the better.

'I'll try, Sister.' Grace backed out of the office and went back to Ruth's bed as much to help Ruth as to obey Sister Morris. Ruth was sitting up staring sullenly into space.

'Were you sleeping in the shop doorway because you had nowhere else to go?' Grace began softly. Ruth shot her a quick look. Grace gathered she'd touched a nerve so she pressed on. 'I'd hate to think you had nowhere to go and no one to care for you.' Ruth slid down in the bed. Grace persevered. 'There are people who can help,' she said. 'You don't have to go through this difficult time on your own.'

'I've been on me own for years,' Ruth muttered.

'Why's that?' Now that Ruth was responding, even though it was reluctantly, Grace felt she was having some success.

'I'm an orphan, aren't I?' Ruth sneered, looking directly at Grace for the first time since she'd arrived by her bed. 'Nobody ever wanted me.' Tears welled in her pale, grey eyes. She brushed them away roughly with the back of her hand.

'Am I right in thinking that there was someone that you once thought did want you – very much? Someone you thought loved you.'

The girl blinked her wet eyes, surprised by Grace's perspicacity. 'Yeah,' she croaked. 'How do yer think I got like this?' She patted her swollen belly.

'Tell me about him,' Grace said kindly. 'Did you love him?' They seemed to have arrived at a plateau of understanding so she pulled a chair to the bedside. 'The man I love is coming home on leave tonight. I haven't seen him for ages and I'm worried that things might not be the same when we meet again.' Admitting that to this lost, lonely girl took Grace by surprise but she pressed on. 'Is that what happened to you when he found out you were having his baby?'

Ruth nodded, tears threatening again. 'I thought he loved me, but when I told him about the baby, he got his mam to chuck me out. I wa' working in their pub. I lost me job an' me home all at one go,' she said bitterly. 'I've been on t'streets since then.' She hung her muttering, 'I on'y let him do it once.'

'Sometimes that's all it takes,' Grace said sympathetically. 'How long ago was that?'

'Harvest Fair,' Ruth mumbled. 'He told me he'd stop loving me if I didn't let him,' she said tearfully. Then hardening her voice she added, 'He told me nowt could happen if it wa' t'first time an' you did it standin' up.' She began sniffing and hiccupping. 'An' look at me now.' She turned wild eyes on Grace.

'Don't cry, Ruth.' Grace patted the girl's skinny arm. 'There are people we can contact to help both you and your baby. I'll tell Sister Morris to get in touch with them.' She stood. 'I'm glad you told me,

Ruth. Now we can make plans.' She smiled, and for the first time since her arrival on the ward, Ruth smiled back.

'You're kind, you are,' she said.

'I try to be,' Grace said then grinned. 'Now I'd better get on and do some work. Sister will have my guts for garters, sitting here talking to you all this time.'

Ruth actually laughed. 'She's a right cow, isn't she?'

Grace was dying to agree. Instead, she went back and reported, 'She's more or less full term, Sister. She conceived last September.'

Sister Morris pulled a face and sniffed, 'It looks as though we'll have to keep her then, but she'd better mend her ways if she knows what's good for her.'

Grace wanted to say: *For God's sake, woman, have a bit of compassion*, but she held her tongue and continued with her duties. The hours dragged, each one seeming longer than the one before. Five minutes before her shift ended, Grace nipped to the sluice and washed her hands and face then carefully applied her make-up. She couldn't do anything about her hair. If she walked back on the ward with it flowing round her shoulders Sister Morris would no doubt have a blue fit, so she tidied the disarray Ruth's clawing fingers had caused then teased little tendrils onto her cheeks and forehead to lessen the severity of her chignon.

'You look pretty, Nurse Murphy,' commented Mrs Hawkes when Grace went back on the ward. 'You should wear a bit of lippy more often.'

Sister Morris gave Grace a sharp look but passed no remark. Grace hurriedly completed her final chores then bidding the mums goodnight, she went in search of Clodagh. The last she'd seen of her was in the nursery.

'She's gone,' Nurse Walker said, 'nipped off early. She's going dancing.'

Grace frowned. It wasn't like Clodagh not to wait for her.

Pushing aside her sensitivity, she walked briskly down the corridor. She wanted to run but that was strictly forbidden. Stepping out into the evening sunlight her eyes swept the hospital forecourt searching for Richard. The flame of longing and desire that had carried her down the corridor flickered and died. He wasn't there.

She lifted her feet and ran, her breathing shallow as she quickened her pace down Thorne Road. He must be waiting for her at the house. On the corner of Zetland Road she met Patsy on her way to do the night shift. Before she could ask, Patsy said, 'I see your man hasn't arrived yet.' Grace's face crumpled.

'An' I'll tell ye somethin' else,' Patsy continued sagely, 'that Clodagh one is up to somethin'. She's as giddy as a wee schoolgirl tonight.' She flipped her fob watch up from her breast. 'God, is that the time. I'd best run.'

Grace stood on the corner to catch her breath and ease the stitch in her side. Her heart felt like a lead weight. There was no longer any need to hurry.

Or was there? He might this very minute be only a street away. Sure that her face must be bright red with exertion, and not wanting him to catch her looking like that, she patted her cheeks to cool them then pulled out her chignon, stuffing the pins in her pocket and ruffling her fingers through her hair. A glorious mass of shiny, black curls sprang to life. She glanced back the way she had come but there was no sign of his car. Her heart plummeted again.

Never mind, she told herself as she arrived home. Now she'd have time to change out of her uniform and into the new summer dress she had bought in Verity's. She'd been saving her clothing coupons for months. She glanced into the parlour then the kitchen expecting to see Clodagh there, and still wondering why she hadn't waited to walk home with her. She poured herself a glass of water, her hands unsteady as she tried to stem the dreadful thoughts tumbling through her mind. Perhaps his leave had been cancelled at the last minute. It happened. Or maybe he'd crashed the car. She almost choked at the thought of it. She trailed upstairs, the anticipation of putting on her new dress and making herself look her best well and truly quashed. Clodagh was in her own bedroom, singing 'We'll Meet Again', at the top of her voice.

'Somebody's happy,' Grace said, poking her head round the edge of the open door. Clodagh was vigorously brushing her long, red hair. She waved the brush in acknowledgement and called back, 'Me, I'm always happy.'

She stood up from the dressing table, looking lovely in a green and white checked cotton frock. Her eyes were sparkling. Then suddenly looking rather cynical she said,' I gather he hasn't turned up yet.'

Grace thought she detected a hint of maliciousness in her tone. She was about to ask her why she hadn't waited for her at the end of the shift then decided she couldn't be bothered. 'Have a good time tonight,' she said. 'Enjoy the dance.'

In her own bedroom, she stripped off her uniform then went to the bathroom. She'd have a quick bath to freshen up. But when she turned on the taps there was no hot water; Clodagh had used it up. She'd have to make do with a quick rub down with a damp flannel: 'a prostitute's wash' her mother called it. Back in her bedroom she reapplied her make-up and put on the blue-grey linen dress that brought out the colour of her eyes, its nipped in waist and gently flowing skirt making her appear taller, and the fitted, short-sleeved buttoned bodice showing off her pert bosom. Grace thought she looked rather elegant but it did little to cheer her. After listlessly going back downstairs and into the parlour, she sat hopelessly staring into space, her fingers in her lap worrying one another.

Richard still hadn't arrived when Clodagh left on a cloud of Lily of the Valley to catch the bus to Finningley. 'Looks like you've been let down,' was her parting shot. Grace nodded miserably, at the same time hurt by Clodagh's catty manner. Grace was hungry, but Richard might want to go out for a meal *if* he came at all, so she ignored the rumbling in her tummy and picked up a book.

She must have dozed off, last night's stay in the shelter and the fraught day at work catching up on her. Someone was hammering the door. She leaped to her feet and, hastily rubbing her hand over her mouth in case she'd dribbled in her sleep, she rushed to open the door.

It was their coal-mining neighbour. 'Here you are, love,' he said winking as he humped a bag of coal he'd smuggled out of the pit into the hallway. 'It fell off t'back of a lorry. It'll keep you going for a bit.'

Choking back disappointment, Grace thanked him and he went off whistling, leaving her feeling guilty at seeming ungrateful. It was good of him to risk his job to keep them warm, and it was ridiculous to think that coal in Doncaster was rationed; there were a dozen pits close by. She dragged the sack through to the kitchen careful not to get coal dust on her dress. She washed her hands trying to hold back tears. It wouldn't do to have red eyes if Richard did turn up. She put the kettle on. A cup of tea was in order. The leaves she was spooning into the teapot scattered as the knock on the door had her racing to answer it.

Her heart stumbled when she saw him. He was wearing his RAF blues, his jacket hanging open. His striking blue eyes were just as she remembered them, and his smile was so warm and tender that Grace felt as though she was melting. She flung herself against him and he wrapped his arms about her, kissing her on the forehead as he gently pushed her backwards into the hallway. He kicked the door closed with his heel, and his lips found hers, the kiss so deep with yearning and desire it spoke more than words ever could. She felt the beat of his heart through his blue cotton shirt, beating in tandem with her own. Grace wanted to stay in his arms forever, but conscious that he had driven hundreds of miles she reluctantly pulled away and offered him tea.

'Are you hungry? Do you want to go out for something to eat?' she asked as she refilled the kettle that had almost boiled dry.

'Where are Patsy and Clodagh?' Richard glanced round as if expecting them to bounce in at any moment.

'Patsy's on night duty, and Clodagh's gone to the dance at Finningley.'

Richard's lips twitched into a little smile. 'Then we have the house to ourselves,' he said speculatively, his eyes twinkling.

'We do,' Grace replied, surprised at how calm she sounded although her tummy was doing somersaults at the thought of it.

'Then we'll eat here. Anything will do.'

Grace made Spam and lettuce sandwiches and as they washed them down with cups of tea Richard told her about his journey. A crater in the road north of Coventry had necessitated a lengthy detour through the countryside. He'd had to crawl for miles behind a massive troop convoy that moved at snail pace. The food might have been tasteless and the tea weak but to Grace it tasted like nectar. Richard ate ravenously, and as he talked Grace listened to the cadence of his deep baritone voice and watched the movement of his lips and every tiny facial nuance, her own rapt expression leading one to think he was relating some fabulous legend rather than a tedious road trip.

When they retired to the parlour, Grace piled precious pieces of coal on the fire to celebrate. Richard sat on the little sofa and beckoned her to sit beside him. When he leaned over and kissed her, Grace relaxed against the cushions so that he was almost lying on top of her. In this way, they explored the sense of taste and touch. She inhaled the scent of him; soap, cologne and something she couldn't quite define that was his and his alone. Her head swam.

Richard ran his fingers up her arm, light as a butterfly's wings against her bare skin. He rested them below the short sleeve of her dress, his thumb reaching out and gently stroking the top of her bosom. When Grace made no objection he cupped his hand and caressed her breast, his fingers sending delicious little shocks like electricity through the fine linen.

She brought her hand up to his, guiding his fingers to the buttons down the front of the bodice. Somehow it seemed the right thing to do. Here in this room it was just them and the way they felt about one another. 'Go on,' she said, so softly that she wasn't sure he had heard her.

He hesitated, his eyes searching hers, then he lowered his mouth to hers, kissing her as his fingers loosened the buttons. Grace's blood tingled as he slid his hand around her back and snapped open her brassiere then returned it to gently knead her soft, warm flesh. Her nipples sprang to attention, and pushing her bra aside Richard kissed them. She felt his manhood hard and throbbing against her thigh and slowly she lowered her hand to stroke it.

His breathing quickened. Grace felt an intensity of desire like never before telling her she would go wherever he led, give herself to him completely even though she had made a solemn vow not to lose her virginity outside of marriage. Then, he lowered his hand, catching hold of hers and stilling it.

'I want you desperately,' he panted, 'but I'm not going to make love to you. It wouldn't be fair.' He groaned loudly. 'We'll just have to make do with...'

Grace bolted upright, her cheeks burning. Had she been too wanton? She hastily adjusted her clothing, her fingers fumbling with the buttons on her dress as she gave an embarrassed sob. He saw the humiliation on her face and placed his hands on her burning cheeks, gazing deeply into her eyes.

'If you had any idea... If you only knew how much I want you...'

His voice was low, his words coming out in jerks. 'I love you too much to compromise you. I can't make love to you now when I never know if I'll live to see tomorrow.' He was almost crying.

'Oh, my love, my precious love. My wonderful man.' Grace choked on her words as she pulled his bowed head to her breast. Gently, she stroked his hair, her humiliation forgotten. He wanted her as much as she so obviously wanted him but out of respect for her he was denying himself the pleasure.

'We did get rather carried away, didn't we?' she said, in an attempt to lighten the moment and to let him know she understood. Richard groaned again, and raising his face he mustered a rueful smile. She saw the love and yearning in his blue eyes, and her respect for him knew no bounds. She loved him all the more.

They held each other, content just to feel close. After a while Richard said, 'Seeing as how you have to work tomorrow, I'll go and see my parents but I'll be back in time to meet you from work. We'll go for something to eat and then to the cinema. How does that sound?'

'Perfect.' Grace kissed his cheek. He was about to return the kiss when the outside door rattled. Grace and Richard moved apart, and in the next minute Clodagh burst into the parlour. Her hair was mussed and her lips looked as though they had been stung.

'Oh, oh,' she yawped. 'Nearly caught you at it.' She was quite tipsy.

'Hello, Clodagh,' Richard said. 'Did you enjoy the dance?'

'Yeah! It was fa-a-abulous,' she drawled, flopping into an armchair and spreading her long legs wide as she kicked off her shoes. 'What about you?'

'We've had a fa-a-abulous time too,' Grace said mockingly. Richard chuckled.

'I'd best be on my way.' He got to his feet. Grace stood also.

'Goodnight, Clodagh, good to see you again,' he said as he walked to the door.

'You too, glamour boy.'

Grace raised her eyes to the ceiling and followed Richard into the hallway.

'See you tomorrow,' he said taking her in his arms and kissing her tenderly.

'I'll be waiting,' she whispered wishing he didn't have to go to the cold, empty room he'd reserved in the Danum Hotel. Richard was thinking exactly the same thing. Suppressing the urge to change his mind, he kissed her again.

Grace stood at the door until the Triumph's taillights disappeared, hugging herself with sheer joy. He was here and she'd see him again tomorrow and every day after that for a whole week. At that moment life seemed perfect.

She closed and locked the door then popped her head round the parlour door. 'I'm going to bed, Clo. Goodnight.'

'Hey, come back,' Clodagh slurred. 'I want to hear about what you an' the Brylcreem boy got up to.'

Grace pretended she hadn't heard and climbed the stairs. The wonderful moments she and Richard had shared were theirs and theirs alone. She'd most surely have sweet dreams tonight.

9

'Darling, what a lovely surprise!' His mother's brittle voice met Richard as he entered The Grange, the house that had been his home before the war. His mother was dressed for going out, her smart tweed costume and elegantly coiffed hair making her look hard and unapproachable.

Cecily Carmichael adjusted her green felt cloche in the mirror then came and dropped a brief kiss on his cheek. She smelled of something expensive. Richard returned the kiss just as briefly: mother and son were sparing with their signs of affection. 'You caught me just as I'm on my way to one of my committees,' Cecily said. 'There's a ghastly problem with a bunch of itinerants who've parked their caravans on the village green. We have to get rid of them.' She patted Richard's arm. 'Must dash, dear.' She moved past him to the door. 'Catch you later, darling.'

Richard stood in the familiar entrance hall with its high, elaborately corniced ceiling and its antique furnishings. 'Nice to see you too, Mother,' he muttered and went in search of his father.

He found him exactly where he knew he would be: in his study that looked out onto a paved terrace. 'Hello, my boy,' his father said looking up from his desk and greeting his son as though he had last seen him six hours before rather than the six months that had elapsed since Richard's last visit.

'Hello, Dad,' Richard said, noticing that his father's hair seemed to be much greyer than it had been and his face creased with lines that hadn't been there when last he saw him. He sat down in a chair by the French windows where fragrant curtains of purple wisteria hung from the pergola framing the rolling lawns beyond. 'How's it going? Is the business surviving?' He was referring to the architectural firm his father owned.

Garvey Carmichael ran his fingers through his hair. 'More or less – there's not much call for new buildings when Hitler's mob are busy smashing hell out of the ones we already have,' he replied cynically. Garvey had made a small fortune during the thirties when a government initiative had ordered the clearance of slum dwellings and then replaced them with new council houses. Now, the war had put an end to that. He shuffled the plans lying on his desk and sat back. 'What about you? Still giving the Hun a run for his money?'

Richard grinned. 'I'm doing my best.' The grin slipped from his face. 'But it gets harder with every passing year. Barnes Wallis's bouncing bomb has wreaked havoc on German industry but as for us lads up in the air, we never manage to rid the skies of Heinkels and Messerschmitts.' He rubbed his hand over his face as if to wipe away an unpleasant memory.

'It's not all bad though,' he continued, his smile returning. 'I met the loveliest girl when I was stationed in Finningley. I'm thinking of inviting her to meet you seeing as I'll be here for the next eight days.' He told him about Grace.

His father smiled fondly. 'Good for you, son. We all need something, or someone, to brighten our days at times like this.' He turned and gazed out into the garden his eyes wistful. Richard wondered how much his mother did to brighten his father's days. Her constant social climbing and endless committee meetings left little time for her to consider anybody's needs but her own.

Once again, Garvey shuffled the plans on his desk anxious to get back to them. 'Is there anything I can do for you?' Richard found himself feeling rather sorry for his father.

'Not really,' Garvey replied wearily. 'Enjoy your leave, lad. I'm sure you're in need of some relaxation after what you've been through.'

Richard left him to it and went in search of something to eat. Mrs Trotter was in the kitchen chopping vegetables. Her face lit up when she saw him.

'Eeh! Richard, lovely to see you safe an' sound.' She tossed the paring knife aside and waddled over to hug him. Richard hugged her back. She smelled of onions and green sap, but Richard relished the feel of her plump, warm cheek against his. Maggie Trotter had been the daily help at The Grange for as long as he could remember.

'Are you still knocking hell out of them bloody German bombers, love?' She gave a throaty chuckle.

'With the greatest pleasure,' Richard quipped. 'And I've told Adolf that if he doesn't surrender then I'll send you over to deal with him. That shook him, I can tell you.'

Maggie threw back her head, roaring with laughter. 'I'd give the bugger the rounds of the kitchen if ever I got chance,' she chortled. 'Now, what do you want to eat? Your mother's gone off to give the gypsies short shrift but she should be back for lunch at one.' Maggie sniffed her disapproval. 'I thought she might have cancelled her meeting seeing as you've turned up.'

'What, and miss the opportunity to run some poor tinkers off the village green? You must be joking. Mother rarely gets her priorities wrong.' He was grinning, but Maggie knew that he had always felt as though he came a poor second to any of Cecily Carmichael's interests. Hadn't she, Maggie, made up for it when he was a small boy, mothering him and his younger brother, Stephen, like she mothered her own sons?

'Well, it's lovely to have you back, so sit down and get your jaws round a nice piece of Lord Woolton pie to tide you over till lunch.' She gave a sarcastic grimace. 'Bloody Lord Woolton! I'll bet he doesn't eat his pies. He most likely has a nice bit of steak an' kidney. Still, the vegetables are ours. When my Arthur dug up that side lawn, he wa' definitely digging for Britain. We've never been short, an' half the village gets a share an' all.' She lifted a jug from the meat safe and poured gravy into a pan. 'I'll just warm this up to go with it.'

Richard sat back in a chair at the table, smiling at her chatter and glad to be in her company. 'I've met a lovely girl,' he said. 'I'm thinking of bringing her down here next week.'

'At long last,' Maggie crowed. 'Tell me all about her.'

* * *

'Go on then, tell me what you and Richard the glamour boy got up to last night,' Clodagh said as she and Grace sat down to eat their lunch in the Royal's canteen. They had both overslept that morning and running to work, late, had left no time for conversation. She began to scoop up the watery stew, her eyes flashing as she waited for the details.

Grace broke off a chunk of dry bread irritably. 'Will you stop referring to him as a glamour boy,' she snapped, dipping the bread into her dish. 'And as for what we got up to is my business and his, an' all I'll say is, it was marvellous.' Her eyes took on a dreamy look as she popped the bread into her mouth.

'Did ye do it?' Clodagh chirped, slopping a blob of stew on the table.

'Do what?' Grace carried on chewing.

'You know...' Clodagh licked her lips lasciviously.

Grace laughed. 'If we did, I wouldn't tell you. You'd have it all round the hospital by teatime.'

'Then you did.' Clodagh smirked, and leaning across the table she gushed, 'Me an' Ray are back on.'

Grace almost dropped her spoon. 'After what he did to you,' she cried. 'Are you having me on, Clo?'

Clodagh shook her head dismissively. 'All that's in the past. He was ever so sorry about it. He blamed it on the excitement of being at home and having too much to drink – an' I believe him,' she said forcefully when she saw the disbelief on Grace's face. 'He's crazy about me, an' I'm crazy about him so there's no need for you to look down your nose.'

'I'm not,' Grace said firmly. 'I just don't want him to hurt you again. You were dreadfully miserable last time, and I don't like to see you unhappy.'

'Well, now I'm not.' Clodagh's smile was smug. 'So now it's not just you with a fabulous love life. I've got one too.'

* * *

Cecily Carmichael arrived home shortly before one o'clock in a dreadful temper.

'Those ghastly itinerants wouldn't listen to reason,' she grumbled, peeling off her gloves and tossing them into a chair in the drawing room. 'We told them quite clearly that our village doesn't welcome their sort, that their caravans are a blot on the landscape.'

'I'll bet that went down well.' Richard looked up from the book he was reading. 'What harm can they do? They have to rest somewhere and they never stay long in one place.'

'That's because no one wants them to,' Cecily snorted, coming to stand in front of the fireplace like Boadicea guarding the gates to Icene. 'As for your tolerance, you don't have to live here and put up with trash like that.'

'No, Mother, I have to live in a Nissen hut with a dozen or so other chaps. Sometimes, on good days, I manage four or five hours' sleep, and if I'm lucky I might grab a bath. But that doesn't happen too often. The same goes for meals. I eat when I can in a canteen that's a far cry from a Michelin star restaurant. I don't have to put up with anything as distasteful as gypsies on my doorstep.'

'But that's because there's a war on, darling, otherwise you'd be here at home,' Cecily twittered without a hint of compassion or understanding.

'Yes, Mother, I am aware of that.' He stood up, a conciliatory smile twitching his lips. 'Look, before we have lunch there's something I'd like to ask you.'

Cecily glanced at her watch impatiently.

'I'm off for eight days and I'd like to invite someone to spend them here with me, if that's okay with you.' He gazed out of the window to avoid meeting her eyes, preparing himself for the onslaught of questions he was sure would follow.

'Oh, darling, is it anyone we know? Do tell me it's that delightful girl we met at your passing-out parade. Your commanding officer's daughter,' Cecily gushed.

'No, she's a nurse I met whilst I was based at Finningley. She's...'

'A nurse!' Cecily screwed up her nose. 'Do you mean the hospital sort, or a children's nanny?' She clearly didn't approve of either.

'The hospital sort,' Richard replied through gritted teeth. 'A very worthwhile occupation under present circumstances, you must admit. She works at the Royal in Doncaster. She's Irish and she's...'

'Irish! My goodness, Richard! It gets worse. What on earth were you thinking?' Cecily flapped her hand in front of her face as though she was feeling faint.

'I'm thinking she's the most wonderful girl I've ever met and that I intend to spend the rest of my life with her,' Richard snapped, his patience at an end. 'And when I bring her here you will do me the courtesy of making her welcome for one day she's going to be your daughter-in-law. With or without your approval.' He jumped up angrily.

'But, darling, I'm only thinking what's best for you. I had hoped you'd make a go of it with Sir Humphrey Warrington's Patricia but you let that relationship fizzle out, and then there was that lovely girl related to the Scottish laird. What was her name?'

'For God's sake, Mother. Listen to yourself, ' Richard roared. 'I had no interest in either of them or any of the others you tried to foist on me.' He softened his tone and gave her a pleading look. 'I love Grace, and it's only right that she meets my family if she's to become one of us.' He gave a lopsided grin. 'You'll like her too when you meet her. No one could fail to.'

He stalked from the room, certain that his father would make Grace welcome and sincerely hoping that his mother's high standards of propriety would at least prevent her from being obnoxious to the woman he loved.

'I've just been talking to Mum about bringing Grace down for a few days,' Richard said. 'She didn't seem too keen. She was a bit disappointed that she's not a titled heiress or an Air Commodore's daughter. You'll make her feel welcome won't you, Dad?'

'Most certainly, my boy,' Garvey said heartily. 'And don't worry too much about your mother. She'll be so busy playing the perfect hostess she won't have time to be rude.' He chuckled throatily. 'Or better still, she'll be up to her armpits running itinerants out of the village.' He gave Richard a fond smile. 'You bring your girl down, lad. I can't wait to meet her.'

* * *

Grace and Clodagh hurried off the ward at the end of their shift. Sister Morris had been in a vile mood for most of the day and they were both glad to shake the dust of the hospital off their heels.

'I wouldn't be surprised if Ruth Slater goes into labour tonight,' Grace said as they walked to the main door. 'She's been having twinges all day.'

'The snotty little cow deserves more than twinges,' Clodagh sneered. 'She was downright ignorant to me when I told her to take a bath.'

'She's terrified, poor thing,' Grace defended. 'The only way she feels in control is to put on that rough exterior. She's not used to people being nice to her.'

'I wasn't,' Clodagh sneered. 'I told her what an ungrateful little sod she was.'

'Oh, Clodagh,' groaned Grace. 'Tell me you didn't.' She gave her friend a concerned glance as they stepped outside. 'I don't know what's got into you just lately. One minute you're as happy as a sand boy and the next you're as bitter as lemons. Is it something to do with Ray?'

'You'd like it to be, wouldn't you?' Clodagh snapped and on the same breath, 'Oh look who's here. If it isn't the glamour boy himself.'

Richard was waiting by his car. Grace too irked to take Clodagh to task ran to meet him. He pecked her cheek. 'I've missed you,' he said opening the car door. 'Hey, Clodagh! Squeeze in beside Grace,' he called out as she drew nearer. 'I'll give you a lift seeing how we're going to the same place.'

Clodagh accepted rather ungraciously. Squashed in the passenger seat with Grace she simmered at the unfairness of it. Ray didn't have a car.

'How was your trip to Higher Melton?' Grace asked as Richard drove out of the car park. 'I'm sure your parents were pleased to see you.'

'For the most part, yes,' he replied thinking of his father and Maggie Trotter. He fell silent as he negotiated the corner into Zetland Road, and whilst Grace was puzzled by his comment, she left him to concentrate on driving.

A short while later, after Grace had changed out of her uniform, they drove into the town centre to the Danum Hotel. Richard had booked a table in the restaurant. There they ate a sparse, limp ham salad, neither of them noticing the poor quality of the fare they were so wrapped up in each other. Then they went to the Electra to see *In Which We Serve*, the only film on offer though neither of them particularly wanted to watch a war film.

'Thank God I'm not in the navy,' Richard said as they came out into the twilight. 'Clinging onto a raft with nothing but sea all around you and watching your ship sink isn't my cup of tea.' Grace said she thought it was a safer option than falling out of an aeroplane and clinging to a cloud. Richard laughed at that.

They walked through the town centre past the shells of buildings that had been bombed earlier in the war. Outside a house with its front blown off Grace looked up at what had once been a bedroom, its wallpaper flapping loosely on one of its walls behind the remains of a bed that teetered on splintered floor joists. 'Isn't that sad?' She pointed upwards. 'Not long ago that was somebody's home. I only hope they got out alive.' When they passed the grand villas in Regent's Square, Richard commented on the large bay windows, saying they were houses full of character. Grace loved the way he always found topics of interest to talk about rather than dwelling on the awfulness of the war.

They came to a little park and strolled hand in hand under the trees. In a dark, quiet corner sheltered by dense shrubs they stopped to share kisses and fond embraces almost, but not quite, as passionate as the ones they'd shared the previous night. Then they sauntered back to the car. Richard was tempted to take her up to his hotel room, but common sense kicked in. Last night's struggle to restrain his desire still fuelling his thoughts, he knew where that might lead.

For her part, Grace had wondered if he would suggest they go up to his room. When he didn't, she understood; he was saving them both, for she knew that she wouldn't be able to resist if he chose to make love to her. She felt a flicker of disappointment as she climbed back into the car, but she knew that his reason for holding back was probably for the best. They drove back to St Patrick's Road both of them silent for once, and each of them imagining what could have taken place in a bedroom in the Danum Hotel.

* * *

The next morning when Grace arrived on the ward Sister Morris barked, 'Staff Nurse Murphy, that Slater girl has been in labour for most of the night and she's asking for you.' The sister strongly objected to her nurses forming bonds with one patient in preference to the others and her disapproval was plain on her hatchet face. 'Go and see if you can't calm the silly girl down. She's putting herself and the baby in danger.' Sister Morris swept off as though she was personally holding back the Armada. Grace hurried to the labour ward.

Ruth was as white as a sheet, her eyes tight shut, and she howled like a banshee as another contraction shot through her. Grace rushed to her side and gripped her hand. 'I'm here, Ruth,' she said reaching out with her other hand to stroke the girl's fevered brow.

Ruth's eyes fluttered open. 'I can't do this, Nurse Murphy,' she gasped. 'It hurts, an' I want it to go away.' Another contraction almost lifted her off the bed.

Staff Shaw left the new mother whose son she had just delivered in the care of a probationer and hurried over to Grace's side. 'That one was just like shelling peas,' she said, smoothing her hands over her apron, and then lowering her voice she whispered, 'but this one's not coming easy. It's not breech. The head's down but her pelvis is as tight as a duck's arse. I said we should get Doctor Simpson but you know how Morris is about that. She thinks she delivers better than Father Christmas so she said to hold off.'

Grace told Ruth to raise her knees then lifted the sheet and peered into the girl's nether regions. 'Try not to push, Ruth, just take deep, slow breaths.' Grace was afraid that the amniotic sac might tear and cause infection.

'I'm trying,' Ruth gasped, her face screwed into an ugly grimace, 'but I can't stop when the pain comes.'

'You stay with her, Maudie. I'm going to tell Morris to send for Doc Simpson.' She gave Ruth an encouraging smile. 'You're doing just fine. Keep up the breathing and try not to push.'

'Squeeze my hand instead, love.' Staff Shaw shoved her plump, capable hand into Ruth's. 'Squeeze as hard as you like. I'll not complain.'

Grace barged into Sister Morris's office without knocking. 'We need to get Doctor Simpson for Ruth Slater. I think she's so small she'll not deliver naturally. I think it will have to be a caesarean.'

Sister Morris's eyebrows almost disappeared into her hairline.

'Are you trying to tell me how to do my job, Murphy? That silly girl's just making a fuss. This is my ward, and we don't need a doctor.'

'You might not,' Grace argued, her cheeks blazing, 'but Ruth Slater does – and immediately – otherwise you risk losing both her and the baby. Not to mention your reputation in the eyes of the nurses and mothers on the ward.'

That seemed to hit home. Sister Morris got to her feet. 'Move along, Staff Murphy,' she snapped, 'don't stand in my way.'

* * *

'That was touch and go. That baby sure was in distress.' The voice with a strong Dublin accent came from behind Grace as she stood in the queue in the Royal's canteen. Recognising it she turned to face Sean Maguire, the young doctor who had whipped Ruth Slater away and performed the emergency caesarean that had saved Ruth's and her baby daughter's lives.

'I'm glad you came when you did and saw the need for it,' Grace said, smiling warmly and pleased to have been proved right. She accepted a plate of sausage and mash from the girl behind the counter. It had been a stressful morning and Grace was starving.

'Do you mind if I join you?' Sean asked as they moved out of the queue to the tables. 'The sausages might taste better in company.'

'Not at all,' Grace chuckled as she led the way to a table by the window. They sat opposite each other, Grace noting his soft brown eyes that shone with intelligence in his lean face, a face almost too thin that made her think he most likely didn't eat often enough. She reckoned he was somewhere in his thirties, and if she'd been asked to describe him she would have used the words ascetic, rather like a monk.

'So, what brought you to Doncaster from...' He paused quizzically.

'Clare,' she replied cutting in to the gristly sausage. 'Lahinch to be precise. And am I right in guessing you're a Dubliner?'

'Away outta dat! However did yez guess?' Sean grinned, deliberately thickening his accent. 'Oi'll have yez know oi've been lurrnin' to spake the King's Engerlish ever since oi' got off the boat.'

Grace laughed. It felt good, and as she chewed on a piece of unpalatable sausage she thought about the trauma of the morning and the frightful row she had had with Sister Morris after Ruth had been taken away for surgery. It was perhaps as well that she'd be off duty for the next five days. It would give time for things to cool down.

'So why Doncaster?' Sean repeated, his kind, dark eyes gleaming with interest.

Grace swallowed a tasteless mouthful of mash. 'It was London at first – you know – wanting to be where you thought you'd be most needed, but that didn't work out. When we heard about jobs in the Royal, we moved up here.' She went on to tell him about Clodagh and Patsy. Sean was easy to talk to. 'What about you?' she said.

'I'm for London shortly,' he said pushing his plate aside. 'This is just a stopgap. I applied to one of the big teaching hospitals there but they won't have a vacancy until later in the year so they offered me this.' He sat back in his chair and smiled. 'It's not a bad place, and Mister Simpson's a good old stick. He lets me try me hand so I'm honing me skills rightly.' Mr Simpson was the Royal's chief gynaecologist due to retire at the end of the year.

Grace nodded understandingly. 'Sister Morris should try taking a page out of his book,' she said morosely.

'Jeez, yes!' Sean exclaimed. 'That woman's a stickler of the first water.'

On their way back to the ward, Grace to continue with her duties and Sean to check on Ruth, they talked about Ireland and their home places. It buoyed Grace up no end. The intervening hours until she left to meet Richard wouldn't seem half so long.

Ruth was still drowsy but none the worse after her emergency surgery. She complained of feeling sore, but when Dr Maguire sat down and gently told her that he had made the smallest incision possible and that it would heal in no time she seemed mesmerised by his softly spoken words and stopped whining.

'Your wee girl's in an incubator and we'll keep her there for a day or two to clear her lungs,' he said, 'but she's a beauty like her mum, I can tell ye that.'

Ruth blushed scarlet and gave a little smile.

'He's lovely,' she said after he had gone. 'Do you fancy him, Nurse Murphy?'

Grace grinned and shook her head. The only man she fancied would be waiting outside the hospital when her shift finished, and she couldn't wait to see him.

10

Clodagh and Patsy were on night duty so Grace and Richard had the house to themselves again. They had stopped on the way back to buy fish and chips and were sitting at the kitchen table to eat them. As she chewed, Grace imagined that this was what it would be like when they were married and had a house of their own. *But I'll learn to cook delicious meals for him coming home each day,* she told herself, her thoughts veering to the creamy, homemade butter they had in Clare as she helped herself to another slice of bread smeared thinly with margarine. 'One day I'll take you to meet my parents,' she said. 'You'll love Lahinch with its beaches and cosy little pubs where the fiddlers play great Irish music.'

'I'd like that,' Richard said rather distractedly then carried on eating. Grace gave him an anxious look. He'd seemed preoccupied from the moment he'd picked her up at the hospital. Was it because they had the house to themselves again? Was he worrying about having to restrain his feelings for her and be the perfect gentleman that he was? she wondered. She'd have to make sure she didn't put him in that awkward position again.

'Talking about meeting parents,' he said, setting his knife and fork neatly on his empty plate. 'What do you say to us spending a few days at my home so that you can meet my parents?'

He had pondered long and hard over whether or not he should issue the invitation. Could he rely on his mother to be civil and welcoming? He hated the idea of placing Grace in an embarrassing situation, but he dearly wanted his father to meet her. Let both his parents see what a wonderful girl she was and what a marvellous choice he had made in his future wife.

'Oh, Richard, I'd love to meet them.' A thrill of excitement and apprehension shot up Grace's spine. This was serious stuff. He wanted her to meet his mother and father. When he'd talked of them marrying, he must have meant it. Not that she had really doubted him, but one never knew. Words were cheap, and the war allowing them to meet only sporadically sometimes meant it was easy to say things that, in the heat of the moment, had no substance.

Her eyes sparkling and her smile wide, she leaned across the table to him. He didn't return the smile, and feeling disappointed she wondered if taking her to meet his parents was the cause of his distractedness. Suddenly she was beset with misgivings.

'That's if you really want to,' she said, her voice wobbling. 'You don't have to if there's something else you'd rather do.' Feeling utterly deflated she got up and cleared away the plates.

'But I do,' Richard insisted. 'I want nothing more than for them to meet you and for them to get to know you. You're going to be my wife, for Christ's sake.'

Shocked by his distress, Grace dropped the plates into the sink with a splash. 'Then why are you so prickly?' She looked directly into his eyes. His gazed back at her, bleak and troubled.

'It's my mother,' he said quietly. 'She can be rather abrasive.' He glanced round the kitchen, searching for words. 'She has fixed ideas about her place in society. She...' He gave a grim chuckle. 'She's an arrant snob, for want of a better description.' He sounded so boyish that Grace wanted to laugh. Instead, she carried on washing the dishes.

She'd have had to be some sort of a fool to not realise that his background was very different to her own, she thought. Surely he'd realised that from the tales they'd exchanged about their youth. But attitudes towards the social classes had changed: two world wars had seen to that.

'So, what you're saying is that I might not meet your mother's expectations, that the daughter of a small-town Irish grocer isn't a suitable prospect for a future daughter-in-law.' She couldn't help following that with a giggle.

'Something like that,' Richard muttered. 'But don't let that bother you. It doesn't bother me,' he went on, sounding more cheerful. 'As far as I'm concerned you are perfect. No one else's opinion counts.' He stood, and walking over to her, he brushed his lips against hers then increased the pressure, as if to seal his words.

'I'm glad to hear that,' said Grace, resting her head on his shoulder and nuzzling his neck. But curious to learn more she led him back to the table and sat down on his knee saying, 'Now that you've prepared me for what to expect, tell me about her.'

Richard screwed up his eyes and pursed his mouth. 'She a bridge-playing lady who lunches with those she thinks are the cream of society. She's involved in committees that consume so much of her time there's none left over to spend on the people who should really count.' Grace saw the wistful look in his eyes and the downward curve of his mouth as he spoke and her heart went out to him. He continued to joke about Cecily, a socialite with a passion for acquiring people with titles or positions of importance into her social circle, concluding with, 'She's so busy climbing the social ladder it's a wonder she hasn't fallen off and broken her neck.'

But Grace saw beyond his cynical humour, seeing the neglected little boy he must have been, packed off to boarding school at the tender age of eight and most likely ignored when he was at home, his mother too busy feathering her own ambition. Right then she almost hated the woman she would be meeting within the next day or so. However, not wanting to dwell on the gloomy aspects she determined to comfort the man she loved.

'She can't be all that bad,' she said reassuringly, 'otherwise she wouldn't have reared a man as kind and thoughtful and wonderful as you.' She dropped a kiss on the end of his nose then gave him a loving smile. Richard thought of Maggie Trotter and returned Grace's smile with a lopsided, rueful grin.

'On the bright side, you'll love my dad,' he said, his expression softening. 'He's a splendid chap, and he doesn't have a snobbish bone in his body. So, what do you say to us going to Higher Melton tomorrow?' He didn't add that if they got the visit over and done with early in the week it would leave a few days for them to salvage what might be the biggest mistake of his life.

'If that's what you want, then I'm more than willing.' Grace climbed off his knee. 'Let's go into the parlour and you can tell me what I need to bring with me to wear.' She giggled. 'It's important that I make a good impression.'

Grace had woken early filled with nervous anticipation and childish excitement at the prospect of meeting Richard's parents, and more so for the five days she would spend with him on what she now thought of as their holidays. She'd had a bath and then packed her small suitcase with enough clothing for a few days, carefully deliberating over which garments were most suitable for countryside excursions and what to wear in the evenings. Now, she was scrambling two precious eggs, courtesy of Mr and Mrs Johnson's chickens. The elderly couple often gave the girls eggs, or vegetables from their garden patch.

The front door opened. Clodagh and Patsy trudged into the kitchen weary from doing night duty. Grace gave them a big smile. 'There you go, girls,' she chirped putting two plates on the table each with a dollop of egg topped with a sliver of fried streaky bacon. She knew they would be hungry. As for herself, she was too excited to eat more than a round of toast and drink a cup of tea that tasted more like dishwater it was so weak. She wondered if Cecily Carmichael's tea would be as weak. She thought not.

'Thanks, Grace, this is grand.' Patsy took off her cloak and sat down to tuck in.

'Just what the doctor ordered,' said Clodagh, following suit, 'especially when the doctor's as dishy as Doc Maguire. If my heart didn't belong to somebody else, I think I could quite fancy him.'

'He is lovely, isn't he?' Patsy agreed, her mouth full of scrambled egg.

'He was brilliant with Ruth Slater,' said Grace. 'How are she and the baby doing?' Hearing that they were both doing well Grace smiled then drained her cup. 'I won't be here for the next few days. Richard's taking me to meet his parents.'

'Aw, Grace, that's just lovely,' Patsy mumbled through a mouthful of egg.

Clodagh gave Grace a cynical smile. 'So, you're going to inspect the family pile and they are going to inspect you,' she quipped.

Grace frowned. 'Nobody's inspecting anything or anybody,' she replied curtly although she didn't quite believe that. 'I'm just going to meet them, that's all. And what do you mean by "the family pile"?'

'The mansion in Higher Melton,' Clodagh said flippantly. 'Ray says they live in this massive house and that they have pots of money. Very posh,' she drawled, a sneer twisting her lips.

'And Ray would know, would he?' Grace got to her feet, the colour going out of the morning. 'I'll go and finish getting ready,' she said feeling hurt. Clodagh could be a right bitch just lately.

* * *

It was a glorious summer morning, the sun shining and hardly a breath of wind. They drove out of town into the countryside, Richard concentrating on the road, and Grace enjoying the gentle breeze ruffling her hair. She turned sideways in her seat to look at him, admiring his tanned, capable hands on the steering wheel, and the firm set of his jaw. A ray of sunlight flashed on the windscreen turning the fine stubble on his cheeks to purest gold. Her heart flipped. She wanted to rub her own cheek against his, kiss the crinkles at the corners of his eyes and feel his lips on hers. Suppressing the urge, she silently and sternly admonished herself. *Calm down you lovesick fool, or you'll both end up in the ditch with the car on top of you.*

'You seem quiet,' he said. 'Not having second thoughts?'

'About what?' She frowned uneasily, fiddling with the tails of the scarf that he had bought her for Christmas, and which she only wore on special occasions such as this.

'Meeting the parents.'

The question was quite unexpected. Her face registered surprise. 'No, of course not,' she protested. 'Why do you ask that?'

'Because of what I said last night about my mother.'

'Oh, that,' she said flatly, wondering if it was him who was having second thoughts. 'I'm looking forward to meeting her,' Grace said eagerly, desperately wanting him to believe her, 'and I'm enjoying the journey,' she added, just as desperate to change the subject. 'The countryside's wonderful at this time of year. It's nice to get out of the smoky town with its sad bombed-out buildings, and it's even nicer to get away from the hospital and Sister Morris for a few days.'

Richard seemed to relax. Grace told him about Sean Maguire and how he had most likely saved the lives of Ruth Slater and her daughter. She didn't say that she had been the prime mover in making it happen. He talked about Mussolini, saying that in his opinion his days were numbered, and then he told her about the book he was currently reading: Steinbeck's *The Moon is Down*. This prompted Grace to tell him the plot of *A Tree Grows in Brooklyn*. Swapping the stories of whatever they happened to be reading was a favourite occupation.

Half an hour into the journey they caught up with a long line of army trucks. Richard didn't attempt to overtake. He seemed quite content to crawl behind them at snail pace. Grace didn't mind either for as they drew nearer to their destination she felt the tension building in the back of her neck and unwanted thoughts cluttering her mind.

Richard steered the car off the main road and into a long, winding byway covered with a canopy of trees. Sunlight lanced the leafy branches dappling the road ahead and Grace and Richard's faces. She turned her gaze on him, his face one minute in shadow and then gilded by a flash of light, the flickering changes making her feel as though she was playing a role in a film where light and then shadow were a portent of a dramatic event. She even imagined she could hear thrumming music inside her head.

Richard drove the car down an incline in the road into a pretty village of small cottages interspersed with larger, grand houses. 'This is Higher Melton,' he said as they drove past a pub, a row of shops and a church with a square tower. On a large circle of grass rutted with deep wheel tracks two men were picking up rubbish. Richard glanced their way, a sardonic smile twitching the corners of his mouth. His mother had obviously got rid of the travellers.

He slowed down and swung the car in between a pair of large gateposts topped with what Grace thought looked like pineapples. Very impressive, she mused as the car continued up a long driveway lined with rhododendrons, their leaves green and glossy against the fading pink and purple flowers. Grace remarked on how splendid they must have looked in full bloom.

'Yes, it is rather colourful,' Richard replied in an off-hand manner. He steered round a bend and the house came into view. Grace drew a sharp breath. She had expected something grand, but nothing as large or as opulent as this.

'My, it's beautiful, isn't it?' she breathed, gazing at the mellow stone façade, three long windows either side of a stout, oak door and six windows above. Virginia creeper clustered round the door and clung to the walls above and beneath the windows, its green leaves contrasting with the yellow stone.

'It's at its best in autumn when the leaves turn red and gold.' Richard didn't seem at all impressed by the house. But then why would he? Grace thought. He'd lived here all his life and was used to it.

He brought the car to a halt on the gravel sweep and climbed out. As he opened Grace's door for her to alight he said, 'Welcome to The Grange.' Deep down he desperately hoped that she would be. After lifting out their suitcases, Richard headed for the door, and with Grace at his heels they went inside.

Grace's first thoughts were what would her mother make of the entrance hall. It was larger than their sitting room in Lahinch and furnished so elegantly she was afraid to touch anything. She glanced up at the chandeliers, crystals winking in the sunlight that shone through the glass panes around the door. She felt completely overwhelmed.

Richard dropped the suitcases and reached for her. Before she could stop him he wrapped his arms round her and kissed her. She pulled back, glancing about her to check they were not being observed, but they were alone. Then she realised that his kiss was as much to bolster his own confidence, as it was hers. She was beginning to wish they hadn't come.

'Come on,' he said, 'let's go and find some signs of life. He took her hand, and leading her to a door at the far end of the hall, they emerged into a short passage and then into a large, airy kitchen. An appetising smell filled Grace's nose. A plump, middle-aged woman turned away from the stove as she heard them enter, her ruddy face cracking into a warm smile when she saw them. Surely this wasn't Cecily Carmichael, Grace puzzled.

'Eeh! Richard!' The woman waddled forward to give him a hug. 'So you've arrived then and brought your lovely girl with you.' She turned to Grace and looked her up and down. 'And she is lovely, I'll say that for her.'

'Grace Murphy, allow me to introduce you to Maggie Trotter. When God made her He broke the mould.' Richard chuckled.

'Aye, he did but it was on'y for health an' safety reasons,' Maggie said wryly, but she had blushed at the compliment. Grace liked her immediately.

'Pleased to meet you, Mrs Trotter.' Grace meant every word of it.

'Sit you down, the kettle's boiled,' said Maggie. 'I'm sure you won't say no to a cup of tea.' She waddled about the kitchen setting cups and a milk jug and sugar bowl on a tray. Richard pulled a chair from the large, deal table for Grace and then sat beside her. Suddenly, Grace began to feel much better about things.

'Where are Mum and Dad?' Richard didn't seem at all surprised that neither of his parents was at home to welcome them. Grace had expected they would be.

'Your dad had to pop into the office. Something to do with the plans for the rebuilding of somewhere in Sheffield,' Maggie said, putting the teapot on the table. 'Eeh! They haven't half had it bad in

Sheffield. The poor beggars have been bombed to buggery. Fancy having to sleep every night in one of them shelters.' She filled three cups and then trotted over to a cupboard, coming back with a plate of freshly baked scones and a pot of jam. 'Your favourites, love, though there's no cream to go with 'em,' she said to Richard and to Grace she said, 'Help yourself, love, I baked them specially.'

Maggie sat down and helped herself to milk and two hefty spoonfuls of sugar. Fleetingly, Grace wondered if rationing didn't apply to Higher Melton and The Grange. The tea was strong and the scones delicious.

'And where's Mother?' Richard blobbed jam on half of his scone. Maggie sniffed. 'Organising the flower rota in the church. Seems she had a bit of a fall out with Lily Brooke an' May Smith an' they've withdrawn their labours.'

Grace detected a wicked gleam in Maggie's eye. 'She'll be back afore long. We're having lunch at one.' She got to her feet. 'An' I'd best get on 'cos there's eight of you sitting down to it.'

Richard's heart sank. His mother had done exactly what he had hoped she wouldn't do. He had wanted her and his father to meet Grace when it was just the four of them. Grimacing, and dreading the answer he asked, 'Who's coming?'

'Bishop Clotworthy, an' that chap in charge of the Council, Henry Miles,' Maggie replied dryly. 'Then there's Miss Bradbury from the library and Sir Sydney Spencer's lass. She's just back from finishing school in Switzerland, so I heard. I don't know what they've finished her off like 'cos they didn't have much to start with.' She pulled a face as she looked at Grace, woman to woman. 'She's one o' them pasty little creatures that's been spoiled to death all her life. A right hoity-toity madam so Hetty Collier tells me. She's their cleaner,' she added for good reference.

Grace giggled and Richard snorted. 'My God! What a crew,' he said before looking at Grace apologetically. 'The bishop's a bore.

Henry Miles is a smarmy get, and as for Miss Bradbury, she's so insipid she fades into the wallpaper.' He reached for Grace's hand and squeezed it. 'Sorry to burden you with this.'

'That all right,' she said, telling the lie through clenched teeth, 'I'll take everybody as I find them and I hope they do the same with me.' She gave him a brave smile.

'You do right to, love. It's the best way,' said Maggie scooping flour into a bowl.

Grace gave her a grateful smile.

'Richard tells me you're a nurse,' Maggie continued, cracking an egg into the flour then adding milk and water. 'I think nurses an' doctors are the salt of the earth,' she said stoutly, 'an' where we'd be without 'em at times like this I just don't know. You must be kept very busy, love, what with folk getting caught up in the mess that Luftwaffe keeps causing.'

'I see a bit of that, but I'm a midwife for most of the time. Delivering babies and caring for their mothers is more in my line.'

'Ooh, that's lovely,' Maggie exclaimed. 'Bringing new lives into the world when that bugger Hitler's trying to kill us all off.' She began beating the batter as though it was the Fuhrer's head.

Richard looked at Grace, nodding towards the door as if to say let's go. She nodded back. He got to his feet and Grace did likewise. 'Which bedroom's been made ready for Grace?'

'The one overlooking the kitchen garden.' Maggie's face and tone suggested it didn't meet with her approval. 'Your mother's idea, not mine.'

Richard frowned. It clearly didn't meet with his either thought Grace as she saw the frown and the annoyed shrug of his shoulders. 'Come on, I'll show you the way and you can freshen up before lunch,' he said. At the door he called back, 'Thanks for the tea and scones, Maggie.' The way he said it made Grace aware that he was also thanking her for the warm welcome.

She followed him up the sweeping staircase, Richard carrying their suitcases.

Outside a room that Grace took to be at the front of the house he propped his own suitcase. 'This is mine,' he said. 'Yours is down here.' They walked along the landing, and eventually came to the room that was to be Grace's. 'In here.' He threw open the door. 'I hope you'll be comfortable.'

Grace had been wondering from the looks on his and Maggie's faces if she had

been relegated to the box room. She needn't have worried. The room was large and airy and beautifully furnished. 'This is lovely,' she said walking over to the window and looking at the kitchen garden surrounded by a rosy, red-brick wall.

Neat rows of vegetables and fruit-bearing shrubs filled the beds below.

'Somebody's a keen gardener,' she remarked.

'Maggie's husband, Arthur, takes care of all that,' Richard informed placing her suitcase on a lacquered ottoman at the foot of the large double bed. 'There's a bathroom next door. Take your time. There's no hurry.'

He stood, looking rather at a loss, and Grace went and put her arms round him. 'Stop being so anxious,' she said, kissing his jaw. 'Everything's going to be just fine.' He responded by dropping little butterfly kisses from her brow to her lips, and when he reached them he kissed her so thoroughly he took her breath away. 'Back for you in half an hour,' he said winking wickedly.

11

Grace had told Richard that everything would be just fine, and to her amazement it was. In fact, at times it was hilarious. After very briefly introducing Grace to his mother who had arrived with the bishop in tow, the other guests started to arrive and a melee of confused people bumped elbows in the entrance hall.

Grace thought she was handling a bunch of twigs as Cecily put her long, bony hand into hers and with a saccharine smile said, 'So pleased to meet you, my dear. Now, have you met Bishop Clotworthy?'

The bishop had bumbled forward and grasped Grace's hand in his meaty paw. 'Delighted, Miss Murphy,' he mumbled. Then followed a dizzying round of hand shaking: Miss Bradbury's cold and clammy, Henry Miles' lingering for too long, and Verity Spencer's limply unwilling. Grace noted that Verity's long, pointed nails had been recently manicured and painted a very dark shade of red. As her hand made contact with Verity's silky-smooth palm, she was conscious that her own had spent too much time scrubbing bedpans soaked in disinfectant, and that her clipped nails were far from glamorous.

Just as they were filing into the dining room, Richard's father arrived.

'Late as usual, Garvey,' his wife said coldly. Garvey Carmichael seemed not in the least perturbed.

He made a beeline for Grace. 'You must be Grace,' he said warmly, clasping her hand and shaking it vigorously. 'It's lovely to meet you. Do enjoy your stay.'

'Garvey, you're holding up proceedings.' Cecily caught Grace by the elbow. 'Miss Murphy, you sit here,' she said almost dragging Grace to a chair in between two others at one side of the beautifully arranged dining table. Grace sat with Henry Miles on her right and Bishop Clotworthy on her left. Henry pressed his thigh against Grace's as he made himself comfortable. Grace pulled her knees together. Richard was seated between Miss Bradbury and Verity Spencer. Garvey and Cecily took their places at the head and foot of the table respectively.

Cecily beamed round the table, clearly delighted with her arrangements. Richard smiled across at Grace and raised his eyebrows. Grace wanted to giggle. Maggie Trotter, and a young woman who Grace later found out was Maggie's daughter, began serving salad greens in Marie Rose sauce for starters.

Cecily began complaining about the itinerants on the village green. 'I soon let them know they weren't welcome, and after a deal of provocation they saw reason and moved on,' she said imperiously.

'Good for you,' Bishop Clotworthy boomed. 'A lazy bunch of ne'er-do-wells the lot of them. The men should be fighting for king and country not traipsing the roads making a nuisance of themselves.'

'How right you are, Bishop,' Miss Bradbury simpered, turning pink as she dropped a blob of Marie Rose sauce on her blouse.

'Personally, I say live and let live,' Richard commented. 'They have their way of life, we have ours.'

'Really, Richard!' his mother exclaimed. 'You surely don't believe they serve any useful purpose in the community.'

'Where would people get their clothes pegs from or have their knives and scissors sharpened and their pots and pans mended?' he replied, his blue eyes flashing provocatively. Grace hid a smile.

'Don't be facetious, darling.' Cecily turned her full beam on Verity. 'You must tell Richard about your time in Switzerland, my dear. He'll be frightfully interested. He often flies over the continent.' Richard looked at her askance.

Verity fluttered her eyelashes at him. She said something in French then tapped her long, red nails to her bright red lips. '*Excusez moi*,' she said coquettishly in a very bad accent. 'I keep forgetting which country I'm in.' Richard concentrated on chasing a piece of tomato round his plate and tried not to groan out loud as she began to talk about Switzerland.

As the conversation flowed, Maggie served roast beef and Yorkshire pudding for mains, and then apple pie for dessert. You'd never know there was a war on or a ration coupon in sight, Grace thought as she tucked in and listened to Henry Miles' tedious account of his stamp collection at the same time trying to fend off his roaming hand and pressing thigh. No matter how far over she sat on her own chair his knee kept brushing against hers, and twice his hand had somehow managed to come into contact with the top of her leg.

'Miss Murphy, is that an Irish accent I detect?' Bishop Clotworthy's question couldn't have come at a better time. With relief, Grace turned her attention on him at the same time batting Henry's wandering hand away.

'It is, Bishop. I'm from Clare in the west of Ireland.' Her grey eyes lit up as she spoke, and Richard admired their opalescent beauty from across the table.

'Are you acquainted with Bishop Cleary? He ministers in Clare,' the bishop continued. 'I once met him on a retreat several years ago.' He leaned forward waiting for her answer.

Grace almost choked on her coffee. She swallowed noisily. 'Not personally,' she replied, 'although I have heard of him.' The bishop looked disappointed but that didn't prevent him from rambling on about his visit to Ireland.

Then Cecily fired her barbed arrow. 'I'm so pathetically muddle-headed that I've never quite understood whose side the Irish are for in this war,' she said rather girlishly. 'Is it us, or are they in league with the Germans?' She glanced round the table, her smile inscrutable and her eyes narrowing as they came to rest on Grace. Grace flinched and looked across the table at Richard then at his father. Whatever had a nice man like Garvey Carmichael seen in such a bitch?

'No war talk,' Garvey growled.

'Not at the dinner table,' Richard snapped. He pushed back his chair and darting round the table he levered Grace out of hers. He squeezed her arm gently, but his blue eyes were dark with fury. 'Thank you for a nice lunch, Mother. Now, if you'll excuse us, we have somewhere else to be.' Nodding courteously to the rest of the diners he led Grace to the door, pausing as they passed by his father's chair to pat his shoulder and say, 'We'll see you later, old man.'

They walked out into the garden, Grace shaking with laughter as she clung to Richard's arm. 'My goodness,' she gasped, collapsing against him, 'what an ordeal. I almost choked when Bishop Clotworthy asked me if I knew old Cleary. I wanted to say wrong side, Bishop. He's Episcopalian. I'm Catholic. And what with Henry Miles's straying hand, I was nearly sitting on the bishop's lap at one point.'

She felt the tension leave Richard's body, and heard the rumble in his chest as he began to laugh along with her. Relief flooded her veins. She didn't want his mother's remarks to become an issue. And if she was perfectly honest, far from finding the last hour intimidating, Grace had found it truly bizarre. Even Cecily's spiteful comment about the Irish had seemed ridiculous. Of course, Grace was well aware that it had been a deliberate ploy on Cecily's part to let her know that she disapproved of her. But she didn't care. She'd decided she didn't want the approval of such an obnoxious woman.

Richard pulled Grace to a halt and held her close. 'You really are a most remarkable woman, Grace Murphy. There was I, beating myself up for subjecting you to such a shambles, and all the while you were having a good laugh.'

'Your dad didn't have much to say.'

'He never does at times like that. He hates the sort of people Mother loves.'

'Poor Miss Bradbury couldn't say a word after spilling sauce on her blouse. I felt sorry for her.'

'And that silly little girl next to me never knew when to shut up.'

'You weren't seduced by the fluttering eyelashes and the French accent then,' Grace said mischievously.

'Excusez moi!' Richard mocked Verity's dreadful pronunciation. 'How could I be? I'm in love with you.'

* * *

Garvey Carmichael welcomed them fulsomely when they dropped into his study a short while later. 'I see you're none the worse for having had a preview of what hell must be like,' he said, inviting them to sit by the window and offering them a drink. Grace settled for sweet sherry, and Richard a brandy.

'Get that into you, son.' Garvey handed Richard his glass. 'Fortify yourself against the pleasures of life at The Grange.'

'I don't know how you've managed to stick it for all these years.' Richard said. 'I certainly couldn't.'

Garvey chuckled. 'I don't often have to. Your mother and I are like ships that pass in the night. She has her meetings and I have my office, and when we are both in residence I hide in here.' He attempted to sound awfully upbeat, but Grace thought she heard the same wistfulness that she had heard in Richard's voice when he'd told her about his mother.

'As long as you're happy, Dad.' Richard thought his father looked a bit peaky. There was a greyish tinge to the skin on his cheeks and the whites of his eyes were faintly yellowed. He was about to ask him about his health then thought he would leave it until they were alone. He didn't want to embarrass him in front of Grace in case he had something unpleasant to divulge.

'So, Miss Murphy, or can I call you Grace, whereabouts in Clare are you from?' Grace told him, and to Richard's surprise his father said, 'Ah, Lahinch. A lovely place as I recall. That wild rocky shore and miles of beach, and the best pints of Guinness I've ever tasted. We spent many a happy hour in the little pubs drinking creamy stout and listening to stirring Irish ballads.'

'I thought you only went to Dublin that time you were in Ireland,' Richard said, his amazement showing.

Garvey shook his head. 'We were in Dublin for a few days, then the chap I was with suggested we go and visit his relatives in Clare, so off we went.' He turned to Grace. 'This was a long time ago when I was young and single,' he explained. 'I'd just qualified as an architect and we were exploring different cities to compare the building and layouts to see what made them tick.'

Grace asked had he visited the Burren, and from then on the conversation flowed back and forth in a most enjoyable manner.

That was the first of several pleasurable hours they spent in Richard's father's company during the next four days. Of his mother they saw very little; she was rarely at home. 'Can't drop everything, darling, just because you're here,' she had said one morning before going off to play bridge and have lunch with her cronies.

The rest of the time, Grace and Richard toured the countryside or simply sat in the garden, the weather being gloriously hot and sunny.

One day they paid a visit to his father's offices in Pontefract. There they met John Morgan, Garvey's lifelong friend and manager. Grace was fascinated by the detailed plans and drawings of houses and public buildings. When they came away and were on their way to Brodsworth Hall, a stately home that Richard thought Grace would like to see, she asked him if he would be an architect once the war was over.

'Most likely,' he said. 'It's what I trained for, and the business is there.'

Grace liked that idea, and as they walked around the huge Victorian pile that was Brodsworth Hall, she was fascinated by Richard's depth of knowledge as he pointed out various aspects of its architecture.

'Of course, I prefer the modernists such as Le Corbusier and Lloyd Wright. Their buildings are the sort of thing I'd like to design,' he said casually.

Grace had no idea who Le Corbusier and Lloyd Wright were. However, she liked it that Richard thought she did. She determined to look them up the next time she visited the library.

* * *

On what was to be the last afternoon of their stay at The Grange, Cecily was at home. Going in search of Grace and Richard, she found them on the terrace outside Garvey's study window. 'Darlings,' she cried, 'so here you are.' She gave them an unctuous smile, her vivid red lips in her long, bony face garish against her pale skin. Grace thought she looked scary.

'Now then, my dears,' Cecily continued addressing herself to Richard. 'I'm going to do something terribly naughty and steal Grace away from you for a while. We've hardly had chance to get to know one another.'

'And whose fault's that?' Richard muttered. Grace suppressed a giggle.

'What was that, darling?' Cecily cocked her head quizzically. Richard didn't bother to reply. He looked at Grace, his eyes questioning.

Grace got to her feet. 'That would be very nice,' she said, her stomach suddenly churning as she prepared to go with Cecily.

'Don't let it take up too much time,' Richard said resignedly. 'We're heading back to Doncaster shortly.' Again, he gave Grace a meaningful look, but the smile she gave him was confident at the same time letting him know she understood his concern. 'I'll go in and interrupt Dad then until you come back.' He opened the French doors and stepped inside the study where Garvey was bent over his desk.

Cecily led Grace to the drawing room. They sat in the claret velvet armchairs either side of the huge marble fireplace. Cecily elegantly crossed one leg over the other then smoothed the skirt of her finely tailored mauve silk dress. Everything about Cecily Carmichael spoke of money from her kitten-heeled, purple suede shoes to her pearl jewellery. She's no beauty but she certainly knows how to dress, Grace thought, fingering the sleeve of the blouse that had used up the last of her clothing coupons. Cat-like, Cecily watched her, her expression bordering on a sneer as she leaned back into the chair, very much in command.

'This is a lovely room,' Grace commented, for want of anything better to say.

'Isn't it?' Cecily's long, bony fingers toyed with the pearls at her throat. 'This is Garvey's family home, you know, he inherited shortly after we were married. His father made a fortune in engineering. The Carmichaels are a highly respected family in Yorkshire, as are my own.' She gave a simpering smile. 'We've even got a sir or two in the family – knighted by the king,' she added as though she thought Grace might not understand.

Grace smiled her response. What on earth could she say to all that? *The*

Murphys of Lahinch have a grocer and a cobbler in the family. Not to mention the one who came to a grizzly end in Kilmainham jail during the nineteen-sixteen uprising. She waited silently to see where this tête-à-tête was leading. She already had her suspicions.

Cecily leaned forward in her chair, her gimlet eyes probing Grace's own grey eyes that looked calmly back at her, although Grace's heartbeat had quickened and her hands felt clammy. *By the pricking of my thumbs, something wicked this way comes*, she thought, and steeled herself.

'Now, about this... er... relationship you appear to have formed with my son.' Cecily paused, plainly waiting to see the impact she had made.

'What about it?' Grace was amazed how calm she sounded.

'You do realise it can't possibly have a future.'

'And why is that? Do you think that Richard might lose his life in this terrible war, that he'll pay the ultimate price?' Grace said curtly, although it pained her to even think such a thing let alone say it out loud.

Cecily waved her hand dismissively, Grace thinking that her painted nails looked like bloodstained talons fresh from the kill.

'No, of course not, you silly girl! I'm merely stating that a person of your...' for a moment she floundered, 'background... hmm, nationality... social standing... call it what you may, is hardly a suitable match for my son.'

Grace gazed back sceptically. Cecily might have had to search for her words but when she found them she'd certainly made herself clear.

'So, what you are saying, Mrs Carmichael, is that the daughter of a small-town Irish grocer isn't good enough for your son. Surely, that's for him to decide.' Grace let the words hang in the air for a second before adding, 'And I'm fairly certain that he already has.' She had difficulty suppressing a smirk.

Cecily's eyebrows shot up and her mouth became an ugly, twisted cavern. 'But it's preposterous. Irish! Your father a grocer! And you a nurse! Really, Miss Murphy, it's quite unacceptable. And you—'

'And you are afraid of what to tell your friends when they ask about me,' Grace cut in, her hackles rising and her eyes flashing dangerously. 'It would be a different story if I was the Earl of Clare's daughter, wouldn't it?' she sneered. 'But let me tell you, Mrs Carmichael, my father is just as good as you, and as for me being a nurse, I can't think of a more worthy occupation.' She got to her feet, her cheeks blazing but inside she felt icily calm. 'I've no intention of sitting here to let you belittle me and try to persuade me to stop loving your son. I'll never do that.' She marched to the door. 'I don't think we have anything further to say, do you? Thank you for your hospitality, and thank you for giving birth to such a wonderful man. Clearly, he takes after his father.'

Cecily sat gasping like a fish out of water, her red lips opening and closing like those of a speechless clown. She wasn't used to being put in her place. Suddenly, she recovered her wits and leaped to her feet. 'Come back!' she bawled. 'I haven't finished with you yet.'

'No, but I've finished with you,' Grace said more to herself than Cecily as she left the room, closing the door carefully behind her.

* * *

'What did Mother have to say?' Richard wanted to know as soon as Grace returned to the terrace. He had seen her through the study window and he had instantly leaped to his feet and come outside, closing the French doors behind him. His voice was light but Grace sensed that under his casual unconcern he was anxious to hear all about it. She briefly contemplated sparing his feeling, but still fired up with disgust she changed her mind.

'I'd rather not say,' she said heatedly, 'but let's just say it wasn't flattering.' She tossed her head, her fingers sweeping back her long, black hair, and her lips curving at the corners in a triumphant, little smile. 'Mind you, I gave as good as I got.' She looked through the window at Garvey's bent head thinking what a lovely, kind man he was, and not wishing to trouble him she said, 'Let's walk.'

They went into the orchard, and when Richard pressed her, Grace gave him a verbatim account. 'I think I shocked her from the soles of her expensive kitten-heeled shoes to the top of her elegant coiffure,' she concluded sarcastically.

Richard gave a grim chuckle as he took Grace in his arms. 'Go pack your bag. I'll be back shortly.' He gave her a swift kiss. Then as though the hounds of hell were after him he ran round the corner of the house out of sight.

'How dare you?' he bawled, bursting into the drawing room where Cecily was still attempting to regain her composure. 'You arrogant, overbearing bitch!' He strode across the room to where she sat and towered over her, his handsome face mottled with rage and the glint in his eye almost murderous.

Cecily cowered back in the chair, her face paling. 'But... but, darling... I was only telling her...' she spluttered, blinking her eyes rapidly.

'I know exactly what you told her,' he growled.

'I was doing it for your own good, darling,' Cecily whined.

'My own good?' Richard gave a harsh laugh. 'Whenever did you do anything for me? You were always too busy currying favour with the local gentry to even notice me,' he sneered. 'Maggie Trotter brought me up, and Stephen. Hers was the only motherly love we ever knew. You didn't have any to spare because you've only ever loved yourself. Well, I don't need your love or your approval for what I do, Mother. We're finished as far as I'm concerned.' He stepped back, wiping his hands together as if to rid them of something nasty.

Cecily's face was ashen. Twice in one day she had been spoken to in a manner that shocked her to the core, and it left her reeling. Frantically, she sought to regain control. 'Your father will have...'

Richard shook his head sadly. 'My father is in complete agreement with me,' he said, his voice low. 'You have made his life a misery but I won't allow you to interfere in mine. Goodbye, Mother.'

By now, tears of self-pity were coursing Cecily's cheeks. 'But darling, we can...' Richard turned on his heel and headed for the door, his mother's pathetically whining pleas ringing in his ears.

Richard went straight back to the study. 'We're leaving shortly, old man,' he said fondly. 'Thanks for making Grace so welcome. I really appreciate it.

'The pleasure was all mine, son. She's a lovely girl. Take great care of her, and yourself of course,' he said, his voice thick with emotion.

giggling, an' her dropping hints about a *big day* an' wondering what the weather's like in Scotland.'

Grace was well and truly puzzled. 'What "big day" and why Scotland? Do you think he's taking her on holiday?' She put the tea and corned beef sandwiches on a tray. Whatever Clodagh was up to wasn't Grace's prime concern. Soon she would have to say goodbye to Richard and she wanted to make the most of their last hours together.

'As I said,' Patsy continued, 'there's something funny going on. You button her about it when she comes in.' She threw her cape round her shoulders. 'Now, I'll have to dash or I'll be late. It's lovely to have you back.' She hurried off to do her night duty.

Grace forgot all about Clodagh and her mysterious goings-on as she sat on the sofa in Richard's arms. In between talking they kissed and cuddled, sealing the taste and touch of their love for one another until they would meet again.

When Clodagh bounced into the parlour with Ray behind her the four of them exchanged greetings. Then, as Clodagh and Ray clattered upstairs to her bedroom, Richard said, 'I suppose I should go. I'm leaving first thing tomorrow.' He sounded like a man who had the weight of the world on his shoulders. He placed his arms around her. Grace felt the tension in his body, and saw the nervous flick of his long, fair lashes and the uneasy smile on his beautiful mouth as he prepared to say goodbye.

He gazed into her pure, grey eyes, almost silver, and up close a sprinkling of freckles on her nose. The sweet sight of them almost broke his heart and he kissed them lightly before finding her lips. Grace clung to him, returning his kiss with a passion so strong it made her feel quite dizzy.

'I don't know when I'll next see you,' he said miserably as they walked to the front door. 'I'll telephone on Wednesday, and write when I can.' Grace's suitcase still sat by the door; a reminder of the wonderful days they had just shared.

Grace held back the tears that were forming behind her eyes and gathering in her throat. 'I love you,' she said raggedly.

'And I love you,' he said his voice cracking under the strain. 'Never forget that.'

12

When Grace went on duty the next morning, she felt on top of the world. Granted, it had been hard to let Richard go, but the memory of the wonderful days they had just shared kept on playing in her mind, making the most arduous tasks bearable. She was pleased to hear that in her absence Ruth Slater had bonded with her baby daughter, and had been discharged into the care of a home for unmarried mothers and babies.

'They're very good at St Vincent's. Ruth an' her baby will be well cared for,' Staff Shaw said as they sat waiting for Mrs Jenkins to go into the last stages of labour. A fifth- time mother, Mrs Jenkins wasn't making any fuss. Grace recalled Ruth's wailing and her protestations that she didn't want the baby. Ah, well, she thought, it had a happy outcome. She wondered if she would ever see Ruth again. She'd grown quite fond of the lost, frightened girl, and wondered what she herself would do if she was faced with the same predicament.

Mrs Jenkins let out a groan as a contraction almost lifted her off the bed. 'I think this is it, girls,' she said, wincing as another one swiftly followed it.

Grace sprang into action, glad to be doing something positive. It made the day go quicker and kept up her spirits for better things to come. There was no way she was going to allow herself to sink into the doldrums just because she and Richard had been parted yet again. She'd keep on watching for that patch of blue sky.

* * *

Patsy was doing the night shift and Grace was alone in the parlour listening to the wireless and trying to ignore the rhythmic thud of wood against plaster. Clodagh and Ray were upstairs in her bedroom. Richard had been gone for more than a week now, and Grace had never felt so bereft. Spending those five glorious days with him had spoiled her, leaving her wanting more.

The knocking ceased, and she breathed a sigh of relief for she had realised not only was it annoying, it had the capacity to make her feel jealous. She wondered what it was like to make love in the real sense of the word rather than the petting she and Richard indulged in. A hot flush crawled over her skin and her blood pulsed as she imagined herself naked, her skin against his and his hands caressing parts of her body that had yet to come alive under a man's touch.

She closed her eyes, picturing his head on the pillow next to hers, his hair touching her face as she breathed in his fresh, clean smell. Her mind's eye saw the golden hairs that she knew covered his chest, and in her dreamlike state she traced the tapering line down her lean torso to his manhood. She felt a hot sensation spreading through her, emanating from her groin and as she moved to her own rhythm she felt a pleasure so intense it made her moan out loud. The sound reached her ears and her eyes flew open. She glanced round wildly to make sure she wasn't being observed, almost jumping out of her skin when she heard the cultured, baritone voice. She sat bolt upright, her hands flying to hide her burning cheeks then sliding slowly into her lap when she realised that the voice came from the wireless.

Drawing in a few deep, calming breaths she heard the announcer say that almost sixty thousand Jews in the Warsaw ghetto had been killed or captured in the recent uprising, that many of the resistance army of Polish Jews had been burned alive by Hitler's troops and the survivors transported to Nazi-run extermination camps in Majdanek and Treblinka.

Grace shuddered violently. She had read newspaper reports about Hitler's death camps and her heart bled for those who were incarcerated in them. Yet the rich, baritone voice, speaking in the received English pronunciation common to all BBC announcers, had shown not one jot of compassion as he delivered his horrendous report. Grace pondered on how he managed to sound so cool and calm. She knew she couldn't talk about death in such a dispassionate way.

The thud of feet on the stairs broke into her thoughts, and the next moment the parlour door opened and Ray Barnes loped into the room. He gave Grace a sloppy grin. 'I hear the glamour boy's back in Duxford,' he said smugly. 'An' here you are "Left all alonio, all on your ownio",' he sang tunelessly, 'except that Dickie boy doesn't have an ice cream cart. He has a Spitfire.'

Grace heard the envy in his voice. 'If you must sing, Ray, at least do it in tune.' What on earth does Clodagh see in him she asked herself? Just then Clodagh popped her flushed face round the door. She gave Grace a self-deprecating smile.

'All right,' said Ray, 'I'm going. I just wanted to say goodnight to Grace.' He loped to the door humming the tune to 'Oh! Oh! Antonio' then calling back over his shoulder, 'Be seeing you, Grace.'

'Not if I see you first, you won't,' she muttered.

In her opinion, Ray Barnes was thoroughly obnoxious and he

was a terrible influence on Clodagh. Grace sighed deeply. It was sad because at one time they had been such good friends. Now, there was a superior smugness about Clodagh that Grace didn't like, and although they often worked together Clodagh rarely gossiped with her as she used to, neither did they sit chatting in the house at night or go to the cinema. She, who at one time would have told everything, her green eyes flashing and her hands gesticulating – a Sarah Bernhardt if ever there was one – was reticent and secretive. Her entire world revolved around Ray. Patsy had never done complaining about Clodagh and what she called *that carry on*, raising her eyes to the ceiling to make sure Grace knew what she meant.

The front door slammed, and Clodagh sauntered into the parlour. She flopped down in the chair facing Grace. Grace couldn't help giving her a sad, bemused look. Clodagh's eyes narrowed and she sat up straight drawing her knees together, her manner confrontational.

'What are you looking like that for?'

'Like what?' Grace asked innocently. She didn't want an argument so she picked up her book and opened it.

'All holier-than-thou, as though butter wouldn't melt,' Clodagh scoffed. Before Grace could respond Clodagh said,' You don't have to look down your nose at me. I'm not doing anything I shouldn't. Me an' Ray are getting married in a couple of weeks so...'

'Married!' Grace dropped her book and stared at Clodagh, amazed.

'Yeah. Ray's applied for a special licence.' Clodagh's casual reply didn't quite

hide her underlying anxiety, and the way in which she began chewing on a lock of her long, red hair only added to it. 'I wasn't going to say anything until it came through,' she continued, 'but I might as well put you right seeing as how you're looking at me like you'd look at a backstreet Dublin doxy.'

'Oh, Clo, I wasn't,' Grace protested, her friend's tone having gone from casual to accusingly bitter. 'It's just... it's just a bit of a shock, that's all.' She sought Clodagh's eyes with her own. 'I really do care about you, Clo, and I don't want you rushing into something that might mean you getting hurt again.'

'I'm not likely to.' Clodagh sounded supremely confident. 'Ray's been promoted. We're moving to Scotland after the wedding.' Then her face crumpled into a beseeching smile. 'Come on, Grace. Be happy for me. Please.'

Something in the way she made her final plea told Grace that Clodagh was also doubting the wisdom of a hasty marriage; that she was doing her best to make it sound like the joyous occasion it should be. And not wishing to spoil her friend's happiness she jumped to her feet then pulling Clodagh to hers she hugged her. 'If it's what you want then I am happy for you.'

'It is,' Clodagh said fiercely as much to reassure herself as to reassure Grace. They hugged again and then sat down.

'Two weeks doesn't leave much time to plan a wedding,' said Grace, keen to let Clodagh know she was interested. 'Where are you getting married? You're not going home to Cork, are you?' She looked puzzled.

'No!' Clodagh seemed amazed that Grace should even think that. 'We're doing it here, in the Register Office, you know, that big building down Watergate.'

'Why not St Peter's?' This was the Roman Catholic Church they attended if and when they went to mass.

'No can do,' Clodagh said flippantly. 'Ray's a Protestant.'

'Oh, I hadn't thought of that,' said Grace. 'Will your parents be coming over?'

'No chance.' Clodagh rolled her eyes. 'I rang home to ask if they wanted to come but Mammy says it's sinful. She says it's not a proper marriage if it's done in a Register Office and that I won't be married at all in her eyes or the eyes of God.' She sounded as though she didn't care, but her eyes told a different story.

'She's what?' Patsy exclaimed, the following morning when Grace imparted Clodagh's plans. 'By all the saints and the Blessed Virgin.' Patsy flicked her fingers from her forehead to her breastbone then from shoulder to shoulder. 'That'll be no marriage at all. 'Twill be like signing for your ration coupons, not a priest or holy blessing in sight.'

By the morning of Clodagh's wedding on the third of August, Grace had had one short letter from Richard and managed to speak to him twice over the telephone, the crackling line making both calls deeply dissatisfying. As they filed into the Register Office, she thought how pleasant it would have been if he were here to attend the ceremony. She also felt slightly envious. Whilst she wouldn't want to marry a twerp like Ray Barnes, she did wish that this were her own wedding day. But she wouldn't want to exchange her vows with Richard in a bleak room panelled with dark wood and smelling of dust and sweaty bodies, and just one paltry vase of past-their-best chrysanthemums.

Clodagh looked beautiful in a cream linen two-piece, the jacket's peplum waist and its narrow skirt accentuated her tall, slender figure. A neat pillbox hat sat at a saucy angle on top of her mane of red wavy hair, and her slingback, peep-toed red shoes finished off her outfit. Grace and Patsy had given her their clothing coupons and a pair of pillowcases as wedding presents.

Grace wore the green and white checked cotton dress with the buttons that Richard had undone on the night they had almost made love, and Patsy her uniform as she had been granted an hour off duty to attend the ceremony. As a grim-faced, elderly woman conducted the proceedings in a rather offhand manner, Grace fingered the buttons on her dress and wondered what Richard was doing at that moment. In less than ten minutes it was all over, Clodagh Flynn now Mrs Ray Barnes, and Patsy grumbling that she needn't have bothered asking for time off for such a poor show. 'It's not the same without a priest an' a nuptial mass,' she moaned.

Ray was wearing his best RAF blues, and apart from his sloppy grin and stubbly, carroty hair he looked quite presentable. As he marched Clodagh down the aisle between the rows of chairs his parents and friends jostled them, cheering and shouting lewd remarks. 'Ye'd think that they were at a hooley,' Patsy complained. 'They're a rough lot of hallions, if ever there was.'

Outside, they stood on the Register Office steps in the sunshine to have their photographs taken. 'Say cheese,' screeched Ray's mother, haphazardly clicking the button on her Box Brownie camera as she tottered on heels too high, and her gaudy silk frock showing every lump and bump of her roly-poly figure. She was three sheets to the wind, Patsy remarking that she bet she had a bottle of gin in her capacious, pink handbag.

Two ground crew friends of Ray's linked Grace's arms and almost forcibly trailed her along with the other guests down to the Crown and Anchor in Fishergate. Grace wished that like Patsy she could make the excuse of having to return to work. However, the lads turned out to be good company and she found herself caught up in the mood.

In the pub, Clodagh came and threw her arms round Grace.

'Isn't it terrific?' She flashed her wedding ring. 'I'm Mrs Clodagh Barnes,' she giggled tipsily. Then the smile slipped from her face and her voice wobbled as she said, 'Thanks for coming.' She blinked back sudden tears.

'I wouldn't have missed it for the world,' Grace said sincerely feeling Clodagh's pain for she and Patsy had been her only guests, and she knew that her friend was sorely missing her family on what was a momentous occasion in her life. She smiled brightly, and with forced jollity she said, 'Congratulations, Mrs Barnes. I wish you all the happiness in the world.'

One of Ray's friends came and shoved drinks into their hands, and as they sipped cheap, sparkling wine they watched the melee of guests who were rapidly getting plastered. Ray was ogling a girl with large breasts, one hand placed familiarly on her shoulder and a pint glass in the other. Clodagh looked anxiously over at them. 'He'll be sozzled by the time we catch the train to Scotland. I think she's his cousin.' She sounded uncertain. Grace felt sorry for her and angry with Ray.

'Do you think you'll like living in Scotland, Clo? I imagine it'll be more like Ireland.' Grace desperately wanted to divert Clodagh's attention away from her feckless husband of less than an hour. He's just married the loveliest girl in the room, she thought, the spark of anger in her chest bursting into flame, and there he is slobbering over that little tart.

She was never to find out what Clodagh imagined her new home would be like for just then Ray's mother staggered over and dragged Clodagh away. 'Come an' say hello to our Arthur and Phyllis, love,' she slurred. 'You're one of us now.'

* * *

'It was absolutely awful. You were well out of it,' Grace told Patsy later that day as she described the drunken wedding reception and the dreadful scene at the train station, Clodagh in tears as Ray's mates bundled the legless bridegroom into the carriage. 'She looked so miserable, lost and afraid, that I wanted to go and grab her and bring her back here.'

'It's too late now. An' would she have let ye? No! She would not. She's made her bed an' now she has to lie on it,' Patsy replied philosophically.

13

Richard sat back in the cockpit, his Spitfire rising higher and higher until it was above the cumulus clouds. This was the best bit. Riding the clouds, free as a bird, his squadron pals Rigs and Heppy on his left and right. He gave them a signal then, adrenalin flowing through every vein, he looped the loop showing off and having a bit of fun before he got down to the serious stuff. That's what he liked about his Spitty. Once he was up in the air he could make it do whatever he wanted, and that feeling of freedom was pure ecstasy. He came out of the roll and zoomed back into position. He knew the fun couldn't last for long.

They'd been scrambled only minutes earlier. He'd been lying on his back on the grass with his pals around him on a warm September evening thinking of Grace when the order came. It took less than twenty seconds for him to run across the tarmac, put on his flying suit and climb aboard the aircraft, its engine already running courtesy of the ground crew. Then he was up and away, saying a brief prayer as he always did that God would be kind and give him another day. Now, flying high over England's south coast and trying hard not to feel afraid, he felt the tension in his muscles tighten and his breathing quicken.

Suddenly the sky was black with Heinkels and Messerschmitts. Like a swarm of locusts they were coming towards him at great speed. Bastard Krauts, he thought, trust them to spoil a lovely evening. Sweat broke out on his forehead, misting up his oxygen mask for a second or so before it cleared. Then, with icy calm he opened up the throttle and zoomed in for the kill. The trick was to see Jerry before he saw you, hit him hard and take him out. Richard always tried to aim for the machine rather than the man. After all, the poor blighter was only doing his job, just as he, Richard, was. But he had to let him have it. Up here there was no time for second thoughts. There were no second chances.

He fired. Yak-a-yak-a-yak! A Heinkel caught it full blast, one of its wings in tatters as it spiralled down to the English Channel in a trail of black smoke. Again and again, his actions as familiar as breathing. Richard dodged and dived, the rattle of gunfire and the hiss of tracers drumming in his ears. The surviving German bombers slewed off, heading for home to fight another day. Richard's radio receiver crackled, and as the dogfight fizzled out with a few departing shots he obeyed the command to turn for home. He had survived another day.

He circled the airfield bringing his Spitty into a smooth landing, pleased to see Rigs and Heppy doing the same. Ripping off his oxygen mask and unclipping his harness, he leaped to the tarmac, the smell of cordite still in his nose. Then he looked round warily for those who hadn't yet returned. This was always a tense moment. Rejoicing with those who had made it back and sorrowing for those he would never see again.

As he was making his way across the tarmac a clerk came running towards him. He'd clearly been watching out for him. He was waving a slip of paper in his hand. 'Telegram for you, Flight

Lieutenant,' he panted. 'It came an hour ago.' Richard's stride faltered. He nodded his thanks and tore open the envelope. Then he started running, blinded by his tears.

* * *

The house in St Patrick's Road seemed empty without Clodagh. Grace and Patsy took no comfort from the fact that it stayed much tidier. They missed picking up her scattered clothing from the parlour and kitchen, or finding hairpins next to the sugar bowl and stockings draped over the towel rail in the bathroom. She had been gone for almost a month and they hadn't had any word from her, and as she hadn't been given her new address on the camp in Scotland at the time of her departure, they couldn't write to her. For now, she played no part in their lives other than in fond memories.

It was September, and Grace felt as though she was playing a waiting game. Each letter and the odd telephone call brought Richard closer for an hour here and there but they were small consolation. His absence created an aching void that hollowed out the core of her very being and there were nights when she could think of little else except when she would see him again. The five days they had spent in Higher Melton more than two months ago took on a dreamlike quality as though she had only imagined them and she was afraid that one day they would fade from her memory, leaving her with nothing.

Even the news that Mussolini had surrendered and that Italy was now joining the allied forces couldn't bring a smile to her face. Nor did the news that the bombing of Hamburg had crippled the German economy and its industry, although everyone else talked about it being a real turning point in the war. Britain was on the way to victory. When Grace listened to the talk in the hospital canteen, all she could think about were the thousands of innocent women and children who had been killed, or at best made home-less. She had never felt so depressed in all her life.

And today wasn't helping. She was down in a hut behind the hospital cleaning the wounds of miners who had been injured in a roof fall in a nearby pit. The unfortunate miners had been temporarily trapped underground and were now suffering from broken bones and lacerations.

'Hello, Seth, this is a bad do,' Grace said to the miner who occa-sionally slipped the girls a bag of coal that he always said had fallen off the back of a lorry. She sliced the leg of his filthy trousers from turn-up to waistband with a sharp pair of scissors shuddering as she added. 'You must have been terrified when the roof came crashing down all round you.'

'I'm more bothered abaht me bloody trahsers that you've just cut to ribbons,' he joked, his teeth shining white in his blackened face. He winced as Grace swabbed the deep gash on his thigh with antiseptic.

'You were lucky to get off so lightly,' she said, glancing at the man in the next bed whose leg was completely shattered. 'You'll need several stitches but there's no major damage.'

'It should never have bloody happened,' Seth grumbled. 'It's them bloody Bevin Boys that caused it. The useless buggers don't know what they're doing.'

Grace nodded sympathetically. Doncaster being a mining area, she had heard the objections from various quarters about the men who had been conscripted by Ernest Bevin, the Minister for Labour, to take the place of miners who were serving in the forces. She'd also heard the story of how these conscripts were selected.

'We might be shorthanded dahn t'pit but we need them as knows summat abaht diggin' coal, not bloody schoolteachers an' fellers what worked in banks,' Seth continued, as Grace covered his wound with a loose dressing.

'Yes, I've heard about them.' She grimaced. 'Apparently, one of Ernest Bevin's clerks places bits of numbered paper into Bevin's Homburg hat, and if the numbers withdrawn match the last number of a man's National Insurance number he's sent to work in the pit.' She giggled. 'Now I know what it means when they say your number's up.'

'Aye, they bloody do,' said Seth, 'an' I can't help feeling sorry for t'poor buggers but I don't want them puttin' my life at risk.' He screwed up his face thoughtfully. 'Do you know, I were only thinkin' t'other day when I read summat in t'paper that the worst bloody jobs are them that are either as deep down or as high up as you can go. Take us in t'pit for instance an' them poor buggers in submarines at t'bottom o' t'sea, you can't get much bloody lower than that. An' then there's them lads what fly t'fighter planes up higher than t'stars. That takes some bloody courage. I'd rather be dahn below any day.'

Grace's breath caught in her throat. Dealing with the injured men hadn't left room for thinking about Richard, and now Seth's words opened up her own wound, the one that pierced her heart.

'My young man's a fighter pilot – Spitfires.' A flush of pride lit her cheeks.

'Is that right?' Seth's voice was full of admiration. 'Well, good luck to him. I hope he comes home safe to you.'

'So do I,' Grace said, choking back unprofessional tears and thanking God that Sister Morris was nowhere in sight.

* * *

At the same time as Grace attended the injured miners, Richard was driving frantically up the A1 from Duxford to Higher Melton. He didn't arrive at The Grange until the early hours of the morning.

The house was silent. It was too early for Maggie Trotter to have arrived, and his mother must still be sleeping. He glanced into the drawing room, and then the dining room and library. Not finding what he was looking for, he frowned, the furrows in his brow receding when he realised why. Of course, he thought cynically, his mother wouldn't want to clutter the reception rooms in her house with anything inappropriate. He went down to his father's study.

The coffin lay on a wheeled bier in front of the desk, its lid leaned against the end of it. Richard steeled himself before slowly walking towards it. The study smelled cloyingly sweet, and he presumed the smell came from the large, white lilies in vases on the side tables. They reeked of death.

He gazed down into his father's face, smooth and waxen, and peaceful. Garvey's eyes were closed, but Richard imagined he could still see the sharp, bright blue so like his own. It took his breath away. His heart felt heavy inside his chest with the weight of so many unspoken words. When had he last told his father he loved him? He couldn't remember. Tears welled in his eyes and he let them fall unheeded.

Garvey's hands were clasped neatly on his chest. Richard placed his own hand over them. They felt cold and hard. He recalled how, as a boy, he had watched those deft hands make model aeroplanes for him or show him how to hold a pencil and draw. They had swung him up into the air for fun, had picked him up and brushed him down when he fell and held him tight whenever he was in need of comfort. It shocked him to think that he'd never again feel their warmth, or hear Garvey's deep, gentle voice telling him a story or explaining the intricacies of an architectural design. They wouldn't go fishing again or tinker with a motorbike or a car in the garage. An icy hand clutched Richard's heart as he realised that he was already missing those wonderful times spent with his father. His cheeks wet with silent tears, he leaned into the coffin and brushed his father's forehead with his lips. 'Goodbye, Dad,' he whispered. 'You were the best in the world. If I can be half the man you were I'll be satisfied.'

When he came upright, he gazed into his father's peaceful face, and unwilling to leave him alone, he went and sat in Garvey's chair behind the desk. He closed his eyes letting the memories of their time together wash over him. When next he opened his eyes, he realised that he had slept, he didn't know for how long but hearing movement from up above, yawning and stretching, he slowly got to his feet.

He walked from the room, a cold anger searing through his veins, and hearing movement from up above, he bounded up the stairs. Without knocking, he threw open his mother's bedroom door. Cecily, in her dressing gown, was standing in front of a cheval mirror holding a black dress against her skinny body, her head moving from side to side as she deliberated the dress's suitability. She turned quickly, a look of outrage on her face. When she saw Richard, she gaped.

'Darling, you quite startled me,' she whined clutching the dress to her body.

'Why did you wait until the day before the funeral to let me know?' he yelled, his face incandescent with rage. 'Why didn't you call me sooner? I could have been here to say goodbye.'

She lowered the dress, letting it trail on the floor. 'Oh, darling, do calm down. There was nothing you could have done. His heart gave out and that was it.' She sounded as though she was describing a clock that had suddenly stopped ticking.

'But why not call me immediately? Not five days later.'

Cecily gave him an imploring look. 'Darling, there was so much to do. The funeral to arrange, our friends and his business acquaintances to notify, I simply didn't have the time.' She held up the black dress. 'What do you think to this, darling? Yes or no?' She walked over to her wardrobe as she spoke.

Richard stared askance, his cheeks blazing. 'I'm his bloody son, for God's sake! How is it that when you were letting every other Tom, Dick and Harry know, I came at the end of the line? And have you let Stephen know?'

Cecily took another dress out of the wardrobe. 'You know that Stephen and I don't speak,' she said sourly.

'And we all know why that is,' Richard snarled. 'You only got pregnant with me to keep Dad on your side. But Stephen! You hated him from birth. He interfered with your bloody lifestyle, just like I did. No wonder he left home.' He clenched his fists in case he was tempted to put his hands round her throat and wring her neck. 'And as for the dress, who the bloody hell cares?'

'I appreciate that you're upset, dear. So am I,' his mother sighed, 'but his funeral will be attended by some very important people and one has to keep up appearances.' She pulled another black garment out of the wardrobe and held it up speculatively.

Richard felt sick. Before Cecily could ask his opinion, he fled from the room and clattered downstairs. The smell of frying bacon reached his nose and he headed for the kitchen. There he found solace in the arms of Maggie Trotter and a bacon sandwich. 'He was a lovely man was Garvey Carmichael,' she said fondly, her tears tripping her, 'a true gentleman, an' you're just like him.' She placed two juicy rashers between two slices of bread, a teardrop or two sizzling in the hot fat as she put the pan to one side. 'Now, you think on, love,' she said as Richard munched. 'Get this day over an' done with then live on your beautiful memories. You'll have plenty of 'em.'

* * *

The urgent knock at the door startled Grace. Who could it be at this time of night? It was after eleven. She put down her book and then turned off the wireless. Perhaps something was wrong at the John-sons', she thought, as she went into the hallway and cautiously opened the front door.

She almost screamed her delight when she saw Richard standing there, but when she saw how haggard he looked, his eyes bleak and unsmiling she hastily swallowed her joy. He fell into her arms, burying his face into her shoulder.

'What is it? What's happened?' Grace's voice was high with alarm.

Richard raised his head. 'I've just buried my father,' he gulped.

'Oh, my God! My poor, poor darling,' Grace gasped, and taking his hand she led him into the parlour. Richard slumped on the sofa, and she sat beside him, cradling his head against her chest. She could hear the rapid thud of his heart, and her own quickened. 'When did he die? And how?'

'Five days ago. A heart attack,' he mumbled into her blouse. Then forcibly regaining his composure he sat up and told her how he'd received the telegram the night before and had driven to Higher Melton in the early hours of the morning. Grace swallowed her disgust when she heard that Cecily had let five days elapse before she had notified him.

'And your mother?' Grace's voice was icy. 'How is she coping?'

Richard snorted. 'Still worrying as to whether the outfit she wore for the funeral was suitable, and did we put on a good enough show to impress Sir Sydney Spencer,' he said bitterly, his lip curling at the memory. 'Weren't the flowers absolutely lovely, darling?' he said, mimicking Cecily's syrupy voice. He dropped his head into his hands, his shoulders heaving.

Yet again, Grace's intense dislike for his mother flared, and she did her best to comfort him, stroking his cheek with the back of her fingers then running them through his thick, fair hair, each gesture a symbol of her love. She felt his heartbeat steady as they sat entwined, content just to be holding one another. They stayed like this for some time.

'Is Patsy on night duty?' Richard asked after a while. Grace told him she was.

He started to kiss her, slow, lazy kisses strung out along her chin and then her throat. His hand was stroking her arm, bare below the sleeve of her blouse, and she felt her blood tingling. Gently he pushed against her so that she was lying flat on the sofa then he covered her body with his own.

Grace closed her eyes, quivering under the intimacy as he continued to caress her arm then her breast through the thinness of her silk blouse. Her nipples tingled and the sensation miraculously reached deep down inside her body. His hand strayed down to her thigh and then under her skirt. Earlier, she had taken off her stockings to wash them, and his probing fingers moved higher and higher up her bare leg. It felt so nice she didn't stop him.

Her heart was beating so fast now that it took her a moment to realise that his had also accelerated. His kisses were hot and passionate but his fingers were cool and calm as he slipped them inside her knickers gently sliding them into her most secret parts. She gasped, shaken by the thrill that shuddered through her body. She arched her back, moving with him and wanting more.

He groaned and withdrew his hand, and Grace felt a sudden chill course through her veins. She wondered had she done something wrong. She looked into his eyes. They reflected hers, wild with desire.

'Look,' he said gruffly, 'if we're going to do this let's do it like grown-ups.' He got to his feet pulling her with him, and leading her out of the parlour he began to climb the stairs. 'Which is yours?' he said when he saw the four doors on the landing. Grace opened her bedroom door and they went inside.

He stripped off his shirt and then his vest, Grace's eyes greedy as she took in his muscular shoulders and the fine, golden hairs on his chest that tapered down towards the belt on his trousers. He unbuckled it, and letting his trousers fall to his ankles he shucked them off.

Grace watched, then barely able to breathe she hurriedly pulled her blouse over her head, slipped off her skirt then removed her petticoat. He took her in his arms, kissing her in places that had never before been kissed, not hurrying but lingering just long enough for her to feel the thrill of his lips. She felt the heat emanating from his body and warming her own as he held her close. Then he scooped her up and carried her to the bed.

After that, Grace couldn't really have described what happened, but as he removed her underwear and then his own, the feel of his skin against hers was so intense that she moaned with pleasure. 'I want it to mean as much to you as it does to me,' he said softly against her hair.

Grace didn't reply. She just let her senses take pleasure from his caresses and his warm, wet mouth gently sucking at her nipples then moving up to kiss her lips. He propped himself up on his elbow, tracing the curve of her body with dreamy eyes. 'You are so beautiful,' he whispered, and she suddenly felt shy and vulnerable. He seemed to sense this and said, 'I won't hurt you. I promise.'

She felt the hairs on his legs tickle her own as he gently parted them with his knee. Then she could feel him filling her with his manhood, feel his muscles tense and pulsing and she arched her back, moving rhythmically with him until her insides exploded with something so exquisitely overwhelming, she saw stars. Richard groaned, and shuddering convulsively he collapsed on top of her. He lay like that for a moment then rolled off her. 'Are you all right, Grace?'

Grace wasn't sure whether or not she was. Her heart was

hammering and her insides felt like jelly, and although she felt deliriously happy, she wanted to cry.

'I feel wonderful,' she managed to say through unshed tears. Richard moved slightly away from her, settling his limbs tenderly around hers in a close embrace. Within minutes his breathing became slow and measured and she realised he had fallen asleep.

Grace lay with her eyes wide open, and in the dim light of the bedside lamp she could see the fine line of his jaw, his powerful shoulders and the steady rise and fall of his chest. She knew that this wasn't the first time he had made love. She'd be a fool to think that; he was a twenty-five year-old healthy man with a lust for life. But it didn't matter. She didn't care. She wondered if he had sensed that it was the first time for her. She had an inkling that he had.

Her eyes travelled the long, strong shape of him and she loved him more than ever. Better still, she had never felt so loved. Something light and winged fluttered in her stomach. The last half hour had been unimaginable: like waking up to warm, bright, sunshine after living for years in shadow. With those thoughts in mind she fell into a deep untroubled sleep.

She was the first to waken. She looked at his sleeping body and felt a thrill of anticipation. Last night, this man had touched her in ways and places that made her blush yet she knew that she wanted him to do it all over again.

Richard wakened and looked at her uncertainly. When he saw that she had no regrets he made love to her again, at first slow and languorous then gradually taking her up the spiralling path to where she lost all control and clung to him as though she would never let go.

'I have to get up,' she said reluctantly. 'I'm on duty at eight.'

Richard groaned. 'And I have to go back to Duxford. I only got a forty-eight-hour pass.' He rolled out of bed and began pulling on his clothes. Grace did the same. It seemed as though it was something they had being doing for years so easy did they feel in each other's company.

Over a quick breakfast they talked about everything and anything, and after sharing a parting kiss outside the Royal she forced a cheerful grin in an attempt to lessen their pain. 'Patch of blue sky, Flight Lieutenant,' she said softly.

'Orders understood. Over and out,' he replied touching two fingers to his temple then climbing into the car. He started it up, revving the engine, and Grace was left in a cloud of petrol fumes wondering when she would see him again.

* * *

Richard struggled with his conscience all the way to Duxford. He knew that he had stolen Grace's virginity, and whilst it had been the most pleasurable and wonderful experience, he felt shrouded with guilt. He'd let his feelings run away with him. The terrible loss of his father, and his mother's selfish callousness had distorted his thinking. He'd desperately been seeking comfort and Grace had given it so willingly it made him feel callow. He had promised himself he wouldn't make love to her until they were married, a promise he'd found hard to keep, and now he'd broken it. He couldn't in all honesty say he regretted what had happened but he did feel anxious as to what the consequences might be.

They hadn't taken any precautions.

Arriving back at Duxford, he was walking to his quarters when Leggy Burke shouted to him from the doorway of the workshop. 'Carmichael, your order's ready and waiting.' Richard grinned and walked towards him. Long, lean Leggy had been training to be a jeweller before he joined the RAF, and he had the most wonderful knack of turning bits of semi-precious metals, wire and solder into the most exquisite necklaces, brooches and rings. Weeks ago, Richard had placed an order for a brooch.

The workshop smelled of grease and hot metal, and under its bright strip lights Richard examined the brooch he had designed and Leggy had crafted. It was in the shape of a white, enamelled cumulonimbus cloud, and at its centre a small patch of vivid blue from which a tiny Spitfire was emerging.

'Wow!' Richard exclaimed. 'You really pulled the stops out with this one, Leggy. It's terrific.' He pulled the narrow silk scarf he was wearing from his neck and wrapped the brooch in it. When he entered his quarters he strode over to his bed and placed the bundle in his bedside locker. He'd give it to Grace when they met next, whenever that would be.

14

The weeks dragged by. Autumn's glory fading, soggy, brown leaves clogged the pavements as the trees shed the last of their burnished colours. Grace trudged through them on her way to the Royal, sometimes with Patsy for company and more often than not on her own. Patsy purposely volunteered for night duty preferring the quiet solemnity of the wee small hours to the bustle of the day.

Whenever Grace bumped into Sean Maguire in the canteen they always shared a table. She enjoyed his ready Dublin wit and they had many a good laugh, often at the expense of the Irish.

'My mammy thinks I'm living in a heathen country,' Sean said in one of their lunch breaks as they ate a tasteless concoction of Spam and chips. 'She worries that I'll lose me faith by spending too much time in the dens of iniquity that she thinks dirty, ould Enger-land is full of.' He chuckled, and Grace laughed too. Irish mothers were known for clinging to their sons.

'It's my da who frets about me,' Grace said. 'He's never done warning me about fast English men out to take advantage of me.' She said it without thinking then flushed as she recalled the last wonderful night she had spent with Richard.

Sean seemed not to notice. 'If Mammy only knew what my life's really like she'd have no cause for worry,' he continued. 'I work most of it, an' the only excitement I get is from going to the pictures.' He paused, smiling. 'Talking of which, I'm off duty tonight, an' *Yankee Doodle Dandy* is on at the Electra. Do ye fancy joining me?'

Grace thought for a moment. It would make a change from sitting moping and listening to the wireless. 'I'd like that,' she said. 'What time shall we meet?'

'Seven,' Sean said, his face lighting up. 'I'll meet you outside.'

* * *

Grace had bought a bag of peppermint humbugs and Sean some lemon sherbets, and in the dark, smoky cinema they sat chewing and laughing at James Cagney's vaudevillian capers. They howled when he said the famous line *'You dirty rat, you killed my brother.'* Then, as Grace reached for a sherbet, her hand collided with Sean's. His fingers somehow entwined with hers and she pulled them away quickly. He glanced at her, a quizzical smile on his face.

Not wanting him to think she saw him as anything but a friend she whispered, 'I'm already spoken for, Sean. Sorry.' Her cheeks burned as she spoke.

Sean laughed softly. 'So am I, Grace,' he hissed back. 'In fact, I'm leaving the Royal next week to join her. She's a doctor at the Royal Free in London.'

Grace felt foolish. She'd read too much into his clasping her hand. He was just having a bit of fun, as was his way. Her cheeks burned even brighter. Humiliated, she watched the rest of the film through blurred eyes.

After the film, as they were walking through the town Grace felt the need to make reparation for her foolish mistake. 'So, tell me about your lovely doctor,' she gabbled. 'Is she an Irish girl?'

Sean sensed her embarrassment and pretended not to notice. 'She is,' he said enthusiastically. 'Sure an' aren't they the best?' Grace chuckled. 'We met at medical school in Dubs,' he continued, 'an' we're getting married next spring. What about your feller?'

'Richard's a fighter pilot based in Duxford,' Grace replied dismally. 'Like you and your lady doctor, we don't get to be with one another as often as we'd like but...' she lightened her tone, 'after next week that won't be a problem for you.'

Sean heard the yearning in her voice when she mentioned Richard, and this time he deliberately took hold of her hand and squeezed it comfortingly. 'This rotten war won't last forever, Grace. Before ye know it, he'll be back home an' then ye'll have the rest of your lives together.'

Grace stood in the telephone box waiting for her nine o'clock call, thankful that the lashing rain was keeping everyone else indoors. Nobody would venture out on a night like this to chat over the phone if they had any sense. She was still wearing her uniform and she pulled her cloak tighter, shivering as she willed the handset to make its tinny shrill. It remained silent, a Bakelite black monster refusing to respond to her prayers.

She opened her cloak and flipped the watch pinned to her apron. Its little face gleamed back malevolently: twenty five past nine. She pushed open the door and put one foot outside, a cold gust of rain spattering her face. Then she leaped back in, the door slamming against her shoe as she grabbed for the telephone and killed its chirruping ring. Suddenly, she felt warmer.

'Hello,' she cried breathlessly, rubbing her bruised foot against the back of her leg. 'Hello! Richard?'

'Grace?' The line crackled, then Richard's voice came again. 'Grace, is that you?'

'Yes, love yes, it's me,' she cried, her heart leaping at the sound of his voice.

'Grace... Grace... I...' He sounded strange, distracted.

She opened her mouth to speak. A sound like sobbing travelled down the line.

'Rigs didn't make it back today.'

'What? Oh, my God! No! Please say I didn't hear you right.'

The line hummed, Richard's silence sending icy cold shivers from her head to her toes. She gripped the handset tighter. 'Richard? Richard? Is he...?' The word stuck in her throat. She couldn't bring herself to say *'dead'*.

Another long silence then, 'Shot down over Kent. We'd just... we were on our way back from the op...' Grace could tell that Richard was crying now. 'A stray bastard Kraut took him out and I...' He sounded as though he was choking.

'Oh, my poor love,' Grace groaned, feeling utterly impotent. Silently, she cursed the distance between them. How could you truly comfort someone over a telephone line? Words meant nothing. Even so, she groped for something to say.

'I'm so sorry. I know how close you were.'

Richard gave what sounded like a harsh laugh. 'I killed the bloody Kraut,' he shouted. 'Blasted him out of the fucking sky in bits.' He paused and gulped. 'But not quick enough to save poor Rigs.' Grace listened to his muffled sobs and was about to say something when he cried, 'My God! If only I'd been quicker. Next time, I won't hesitate. I'll kill them all and let them kill me. It's what I deserve. He shouldn't have died. It should have been me.'

Grace almost screamed. Her first inclination was to beg and

plead with him not to think like that, but the cold hand of reason caught her in time. Hysterics would serve no purpose. She breathed deeply. You're a nurse, she told herself firmly. You deal with traumas day in and day out. Be professional, Grace.

'Richard, you mustn't blame yourself. Rigs wouldn't expect you to. He knew he was taking his chances, just like you all do.' She sounded soothing and quite calm but her stomach was churning and her thoughts tumbling crazily.

But she had to make him understand it wasn't his fault.

'It's this rotten war,' she continued. 'It does terrible things, things that seem unacceptable but we have to learn to live with them and hope for better things to come.' She paused, aware that she was rambling, and maybe not making sense, then added, 'Don't give up, darling. There has to be hope.'

Grace thought she could sense Richard's anger burning through the holes in the earpiece. 'Yeah, next time I go up I hope I kill every fucking Fritz that ever took to the skies,' he snarled sarcastically. He fell silent, and all she could hear was his ragged breathing. Then, 'I'm sorry, Grace. I shouldn't be talking to you like that. Please forgive me.' He sounded so desperately lost and lonely her heart bled for him. She wanted to hold him so badly that her arms ached.

'It's all right, love. I understand,' she said softly. 'I don't like to think of you killing anybody but I know it's what you have to do.' By now, tears were trickling down her cheeks, and she had never before felt so helpless and hopeless. Even so, she kept on talking, garbled words of sympathy and encouragement sliding from her tongue in a desperate attempt to comfort him. When she ran out of words there was only the buzzing on the line.

'Richard, are you still there?' she shrieked.

An eerie silence. Then.

'I... I... love you, Grace,' he mumbled. Another long pause, and all she could hear was heavy breathing. Then, a stream of disjointed words, sobs and groans, as incoherently he told her what their last night together had meant to him.

'I love you too, darling, more than words can say,' she cried. 'That night was the most wonderful night of my life and we'll have...'

An ominous clunk stabbed her eardrum.

'Richard? Richard? Are you still there?' But the line was dead.

Shocked beyond belief, she stood in the kiosk trembling from head to toe and feeling as though her heart had been ripped from her body. Then leaning with her forehead pressed against the cold glass panes she asked God why He was doing this to her, and to Richard. She stayed like this for several minutes then ducked out into the lashing rain.

On her way back to the house she pondered on the awful grief Richard was suffering: first his father, now his best pal, Rigs. How much more would he have to bear before this ghastly war was over? He'd been pushed to the limits. Fearing he might do something reckless, she quickened her pace. She'd write to him straight away, instil in him the belief that his life was precious, something to be nurtured, and not ruled by bitterness and revenge. She'd show him that her love for him was strong enough to get them through this awful patch, and that he had everything to live for.

Seated at the kitchen table she covered page after page, writing down all that was in her heart, and when the letter was ready for sending she pulled her cloak round her shoulders and ran to the post box. The letter made a little plopping noise as it landed on top of the others in the box, and silly as it seemed when she heard it she was filled with the sense that everything was going to be all right. That the words she had written would help to heal Richard's troubled soul.

Each day after that awful night she hurried home from work

praying there would be a letter in reply waiting for her. She wrote to him again, and again.

Days became weeks, and still she waited, neither sleeping nor eating enough. At home Patsy fussed over her, and at work Maudie remarked on how distracted she seemed and how pale she looked then offered comfort when Grace explained why she was so miserable.

As for Grace, she felt as though she was a shadow of the girl she had once been.

In Duxford, Richard was slumped over the bar in the officers' mess calling for another whisky. He'd lost count of how many he had already downed, but in the certainty that he wouldn't be on ops for the next two days, he didn't care. The young fellow behind the bar gave Richard a dubious look then set the drink in front of him. Almost three weeks had passed since Rigs had been killed.

Richard sipped, oblivious to the noise around him as his pals laughed and chattered, making the most of being off duty. At one time he would have been in the thick of it, his charismatic personality drawing a crowd round him, but since Rigs's death, just as he avoided them, they also avoided him. His surly nature and cruel jibes, and his sudden bursts of fury a stark reminder that life was tough enough. They still acknowledged that he was one of the best Spitfire pilots in the squadron, that he took the most amazing risks, and they were proud to fly along with him: he had the killer instinct. But his off-duty behaviour didn't make him pleasant company.

He raised his fingers to attract the bartender's attention then banged his empty glass on the counter when the lad ignored him. 'Hey, are you blind or what? Give me another,' he slurred. Reluctantly, the lad filled Richard's glass. He downed it in one gulp, slid from the stool and staggered to the door. As his pals watched him go, they exchanged rueful glances.

Richard stumbled to his quarters, his thoughts muddled. Inside, he made his way unsteadily to his bed, sank down on it and pulled open the drawer of his bedside locker. Grace's most recent letters stared up at him. He hadn't replied to any of them. There was nothing worth writing. Not even her long letter telling him he had everything to live for and that their love was strong enough to carry them through this nightmare had touched him. Neither had he telephoned her. He had nothing to say. He pushed the letters aside and scrabbled in the drawer for a pen and notepad. He was going to write to Grace for the very last time. Tell her he was being transferred to Malta and say goodbye forever.

He found his writing pad under the silk scarf with the brooch wrapped in it. Uncapping his pen and propping the pad on his knee he began to write, his scrawling strokes like demented spiders as he filled the page. He addressed an envelope and stuffed the page inside, and keen to send the letter on its way and be rid of it he tottered out of the hut, reeling as the fresh air met him. One of the ground crew happened to be passing by and caught him before he hit the ground.

'Okay, Flight, I've got you,' he said placing his arms firmly under Richard's armpits. 'Let's get you back inside and to bed.'

Richard shook him off angrily. ''M all right,' he growled. 'Don't need bloody help.' He shoved the letter into the man's hand. 'Posht thish for me.' He spun on his heel and bumbled back into his quarters, slamming the door behind him.

The ground crew man shook his head in despair. Flying Spitfires killed men in more ways than one he thought as he dropped the letter into the Post Sergeant's office on his way back to his billet.

Richard lay on his bed, his eyes closed. He felt lighter, cleansed, relieved of responsibility. He'd done the right thing. Grace didn't deserve him. She deserved someone far better. It would be unfair to keep her tied to the likes of him. The thought brought a sob leaping from his throat. What was it she had said? *I don't like to think of you killing anyone.* Yes, that was it. But that's what he did. Yesterday he'd killed at least one man.

The memory of it filled his fevered brain. He saw it clear and vivid in his mind's eye. Fritz couldn't have been much older than eighteen. Richard had been so close to him he'd seen the terror in his blue eyes, and the shock of white blond hair sticking up childishly from his forehead as he'd ripped off his oxygen mask in some vain effort to save himself before his Heinkel exploded, hurling him battered and broken into the sea below.

Richard had laughed then, but not now. He hated what he had to do, and his self-hatred was eating away at him. He didn't trust himself any more. He no longer felt human. He was a killing machine. He couldn't subject someone as beautiful and sweet-natured as Grace to a life shared with the sort of man he had become. She'd understand when she read the letter: that he'd saved her from him. He smiled fondly thinking how much he loved her, and as sleep claimed him he knew that he would never forget her.

15

SUMMER 1969: LOWER MELTON

'So, Dad, tell me about the young man you were before I was born. The one you said I wouldn't recognise.' Sara handed him a cup of coffee and sat down beside him.

They had been out for a drive and a bite to eat, a tour of the local countryside and a Sunday pub lunch. Now they were back in Manor Court Sara thought this was the right time and the right place to bring up the subject that had kept her awake for most of the previous night.

Richard gave a slow smile. 'I should have known you wouldn't let it drop,' he said dryly. 'It gave me a restless night too.'

'Why? Were your younger days so murky that I'll be shocked out of my socks? Are there skeletons in cupboards or bodies in the garden?'

Richard grinned and shook his head. 'No skeletons, no bodies, I promise you

that. Just a whole heap of fond memories and bitter regrets,' he said softly.

'Go on then, dish the dirt. I'm all ears.' Sara's cheeky response was delivered with a grin even though she didn't like the sound of bitter regrets.

Richard hesitated, unsure where to begin. He flicked his hair back from his forehead, a gesture Sara knew well, and his blue eyes crinkled at the corners.

'You know I was a flyer during the war, that I flew Spitfires on ops against Hitler's Luftwaffe,' he said. Sara nodded, her eyes sparkling with interest.

'Well, after I'd done my training in Canada, they sent me to Lincolnshire. I flew my first missions from there. Scary as hell they were.' Richard grimaced. 'Then, when the brass thought I was proficient enough to pass on my knowledge they sent me to Finningley.' He paused, a sad little smile playing round his lips.

'At that time I thought I was top dog. Flyers like me were called the glamour boys, the risk-takers fighting for king and country. The girls loved us. Even the guys who were as ugly as sin got the girls just because they were flyers.'

'You must have been doubly lucky, with your good looks,' Sara cut in.

Richard chuckled. 'We'd swagger into the bars and the dances, an arrogant bunch of bastards wearing our flying jackets and boots, our silk scarves draped round our necks letting the girls know what we were, and forgetting that only hours before we had been shit-scared of not making it back from the op.' His face crumpled at the memory.

'Don't talk about it if it hurts.' Sara placed her hand on his arm.

Richard patted her hand. 'No, I need to talk about it. Get it out of my system. It's been bothering me just lately thinking about the things I did and the things I should have done.'

'Oh, Dad! That sounds so sad, and if it helps to talk about it then I'm more than willing to listen. Mum used to say I should never bury what was troubling me. She said it would only fester.' Sara's smile was nostalgic.

'Your mother was a very wise woman,' Richard agreed. 'I'll take her advice.'

He settled himself more comfortably in his chair, and clasping Sara's hand he rested it on his knee. Then he cleared his throat nervously.

'Well, as I was saying, they transferred me to Finningley. I was reluctant to go. I thought I was missing out on where the big action was.' He gave a little shrug. 'Less than a week later, I'm thanking my lucky stars. You see, I met this girl...' His eyes misted over and his lips curved in a fond smile.

'Mum,' Sara intervened, her smile as fond as his.

'No, not Mum.' Her father raised his hand impatiently as if to say *don't stop me now.* 'She was called Grace. She was a nurse at the Royal in Doncaster. Irish,' he mused, 'met her at a dance in the summer of forty-two and fell in love, head over heels, hook, line and sinker.' He raised his eyes to the ceiling remembering how it had felt. Sara swallowed her disappointment at the girl not being her mum and silently waited for him to continue.

'I'd more or less promised myself not to get romantically involved, life being what it was in those days. We never knew if we'd see tomorrow, so it was better that way. But meeting Grace changed all that. I couldn't help myself.'

'Wow! It sounds as though you really loved her,' Sara said on her breath, but still feeling sad that it wasn't her mum he was talking about.

'Get me that small wooden box from my bedside cabinet,' Richard said.

Sara did as he asked. She'd seen the box before but not its contents. Now she was curious about what it held and her fingers tingled as she lifted it out of the cupboard and handed it to her father. He opened it up.

'This is me and my pals.' He handed Sara a photograph of him with his arms slung round Rigs and Heppy's shoulders. 'You can see what sort of chaps we were,' he said wryly. 'Those guys were like brothers to me.' He swallowed noisily. 'Neither of them lived to tell the tale.'

'Oh, Dad, I am sorry.' A stab of pain pierced Sara's heart.

He took out another photograph. 'That's me again with Rigs and Heppy, and there's good old Monty on the end.' Sara looked at a young Philip Montgomery. He bore no resemblance to the beefy owner of Manor Court that she now knew.

'He hasn't aged well,' she commented, 'unlike you. You've hardly changed at all.' Sara wished she could bite back the words as her father looked at her askance then went back to leafing through the photographs.

'This is Grace,' he said softly. He handed her a photograph, its fraying edges showing signs of much handling. A girl with a lovely face and luminous grey eyes looked back at her, her fine-boned features surrounded by a cloud of long dark curls. Sara's breath caught in her throat.

'She's beautiful,' she whispered, not wanting to disturb the dreamlike expression that she now saw on her father's face.

'Yes, she is, isn't she?'

'What happened to her? Where is she now?' Sara asked breathily.

Richard shook his head. In a low, wistful voice he said, 'I've no idea.'

'You mean she just disappeared out of your life, just like that?' Sara waved her hand, thoroughly bemused.

'Not quite like that.' Richard's face crumpled. He closed his eyes and drew a deep breath in a valiant attempt to gather his composure. 'Look, it's getting late and you've got to get back to London. Can we leave it for another time?'

'Of course we can, Dad,' Sara said fervently, and seeing how tired and drawn he looked she stood up. Richard struggled to his feet and she hugged him close, loath to leave him. 'See you next week.' She dropped a kiss on his sunken cheek.

'I'll look forward to it. Drive carefully, darling.'

Driving down the A1, Sara mused on where her mum fitted in to her dad's story.

16

AUTUMN 1943: DONCASTER, YORKSHIRE

The flap on the letterbox rattled and a letter fell on the mat behind the door just as Patsy reached the bottom of the stairs. She picked it up and seeing that it was from her mother her spirits soared. A letter from home always made her feel closer to the ones she yearned to be with so she eagerly tore open the envelope and began to read.

Grace also had heard the rattle of the letterbox and her heart lurched. Had Richard replied to her letter? Resisting the urge to tempt fate by rushing to find out she continued smearing margarine on slices of toast as Patsy's cry split the air. 'Oh, no! No!' Patsy wailed, her cries so distraught that Grace dropped the butter knife. She sprinted into the hallway, her friend's distress banishing all thoughts of the letter she so desperately awaited.

'What is it, Patsy?' What's the matter?'

'It's Daddy. Mammy says he's fallen through the barn roof,' she squawked.

'He's in the hospital in Tralee. They say he's critical.' Patsy began to sob. She shoved the letter into Grace's hand. 'Here, read it for yourself.'

Grace scanned Mrs O'Grady's neat, round writing. It certainly did seem as though Patsy's father was seriously injured.

'Dears a boys, what am I to do? Jesus, Mary an' Joseph, so help me!' Patsy's voice rose to screaming pitch. 'I have to go home, Grace, I have to go home,' she yelled, her plump, little body turning aimless circles in the narrow space.

Grace threw her arms round Patsy and brought her to a standstill. 'I'm so sorry, Patsy, so sorry,' she said, rocking her like a child. 'Now, if you're going to go home we need to get you organised.' She thought it was better for Patsy to be doing something positive rather than working herself up into a state of hysteria. Gently, she led her into the kitchen. 'Sit down and have your breakfast and we'll talk over what you have to do.'

'Oh, Grace, how am I going to get there? Suppose he dies before I get back. I should never have left Dingle,' Patsy moaned in between sipping her tea and popping bits of toast into her mouth. 'I knew all along it was a mistake to come here.' She thumped her fist into the palm of her hand.

'Eat up, Patsy,' Grace said firmly. 'You'll need something inside you if you're to make the journey. When you're done, we'll go upstairs and get your things together. If you leave now and get the train to Holyhead you can catch the night boat to Dublin. You'll be home by tomorrow afternoon.'

Grace's calm delivery of a sensible plan galvanised Patsy into sensible action. She finished her breakfast then up in her bedroom she pulled a large suitcase from under her bed, and then a smaller one.

'Will you need both?' An anxious thought crossed Grace's mind as Patsy began pulling open drawers and haphazardly tipping the contents into the cases.

Grace lifted a pair of shoes from under the bed, her chest tightening as she asked the question to which she thought she already knew the answer. 'You're not coming back, are you?'

'Indeed, I'm not,' Patsy said fervently, her plump, tear-stained face red with exertion as she stripped dresses from the hangers in the wardrobe. 'I never should have come in the first place. An' if Daddy needs nursin' then I'll be the one to do it.'

Grace dumped the shoes into the small suitcase. Already she was feeling lonely. First Clodagh, then Richard, and now Patsy leaving her here alone. Suddenly, it felt as though her life was unravelling.

* * *

They made a strange sight as they trudged to the train station, Grace lugging the two suitcases and Patsy carrying her handbag in one hand and Joey's cage in the other. The budgerigar was tweeting furiously and battering his little wings against the bars. *I can't leave him behind*, Patsy had wailed when Grace had protested that taking him wasn't feasible. Every now and then Patsy lifted the cage to eye level saying, 'Hush now, Joey, ye're goin' on a wee trip to meet your granny an' granda,' and the little bird ceased his flapping until they set off again.

At the ticket office Grace took charge, jotting down the details the clerk gave her whilst Patsy stood pathetically by like a lost child being sent on a journey to the moon. Joey drooped miserably in the bottom of his cage.

'Here's your ticket.' Grace handed it over then gripped Patsy's arm in the hope of getting her full attention. 'Listen carefully. You have to change trains at Chester and go from platform four to platform seven. I've written it down for you.' She pushed the paper into Patsy's open handbag. Patsy, dazed and tearful, nodded, the panic in her eyes making Grace wonder if she would make it as far as Holyhead, never mind from Dublin to Dingle. As they made their way to the platform, Grace glanced down at Joey. He was lying quite still in a ruffled heap. She drew a sharp breath.

'Patsy,' she said, her heart in her mouth, 'Patsy, I think Joey's...'

Patsy, fraught at having to change trains, had forgotten her little charge. A glance brought her to a sudden halt. She let out a scream, and sinking to her knees she opened the cage and gave Joey a cautious prod. He didn't stir. Her piercing wails reverberated off the station's glass roof as she scooped him up. 'Breathe, Joey. Breathe,' she pleaded stroking his tattered feathers.

'He's dead, darlin'.' Grace pulled Patsy to her feet. 'It was all too much for him.' She took the bird from Patsy's hand and placed him back in his cage. Then she held Patsy and let her sob her heart out.

The train for Chester chuffed into Doncaster station. Grace heaved the bigger suitcase into a carriage, and then the smaller one. She smiled at the only occupant of the carriage, an elderly woman: at least Patsy would have company as far as Chester. Then, back on the platform she flung her arms round Patsy and felt the trembling in her plump, little body.

'Ye'll give Joey a decent burial, won't ye?' Patsy sobbed. Grace told her she'd bury him under the apple tree in the back garden.

'He'll like that.' Patsy sniffed giving Joey one last forlorn look.

'Write and let me know how your daddy is. Tell him get well from me,' Grace said, sincerely hoping he would be alive to receive the message. A porter ran along the platform slamming doors. 'You'd best get on,' she said, bundling Patsy into the carriage and urgently asking the elderly woman, 'Are you by any chance going to Holyhead?'

'That I am,' the woman said in a thick Dublin accent.

Grace breathed a sigh of relief and nodded at Patsy, huddled in her seat and weeping copiously. 'Would you ever keep an eye on her? She's had bad news an' is nervous about travelling on her own.'

The woman smiled and said she would. The guard blew his whistle, Grace leaping for the platform just in time to avoid being carried on to Chester.

'God go with you, Patsy,' she yelled as the train pulled away. Patsy gave a limp wave in return. Feeling rather foolish carrying a cage with a dead budgie in it Grace trudged back to St Patrick's Road. As she unlocked the house door the fact that she was now the only occupant hit her with a gut-wrenching emptiness. She stepped inside and dumped the cage on the floor. Turning to close the door she saw that the postman had made his second delivery of the day.

* * *

Grace sat in the parlour in the dark, the tear-stained pages on her knee. She didn't need to turn on the light to read them by; she already knew them off by heart. Even so, she still couldn't make head or tail of Richard's letter. It was a mass of contradictions. He had started it by saying that he was being transferred to Malta: that much was clear. Then he'd written:

I do not want you to wait for me. I have nothing decent to offer you. It's far better if we make a clean break of it before I ruin your life. Mine is already in tatters. I am doing this out of love for you, Grace, because I love you more than life itself.

He'd then written several lines telling how and why he loved her, the handwriting straggling and smudged over the page to such an extent that she'd had difficulty making out some of the words. When she did, she had blushed. His account of their last night together was so poignantly beautiful that she felt as though her heart was being torn from her body.

Finally, he had scrawled:

I will not write to you again, and though it breaks my heart to say this, it is for the best. Don't put your happiness in my hands. Find someone who deserves you. I am not that man. I wish you all the love in the world. I will never forget you. Goodbye, my darling Grace.

'Why are you doing this if you love me?' she asked the empty room. She scooped the letter in both hands screwing the pages into a ball and tossing it across the room. After a while, having cried until she was empty, and feeling remorseful, she went and picked it up. It was a horrible thing to do. The letter had been in Richard's strong hands; it had felt his touch and was smudged with his tears. She smoothed the wrinkled paper and read the letter once more.

Something flared inside her. He hadn't meant to write those awful words. He'd written in the heat of the moment, the loss of his father and Rigs's death, and the dreadful stress of his flying missions must have driven him to it. Strangely, this thought pleased her. Yes, that was it, she convinced herself. She jumped up and fetched her own pad and paper. She'd write and tell him she understood the grief he was suffering, that he was the most decent man she had ever known and that she wanted no other but him. Come what may.

17

The fog was thick and the air dank and chill as Grace walked to the Royal. It was the first week in November and she knew for certain she was pregnant. She had been sick again that morning before she left the house, a house that was empty and devoid of happiness. At first when she missed her period, she put it down to being stressed by the events of the past few weeks, but now she had missed a second one and the nausea was as good a sign as any. Not only that, her tea tasted funny and twice when bacon had been served to the mothers on the ward she'd had to rush for the lavatory.

In her handbag were the letters she had written to Richard in the past month, each one bearing the cruel words *Return to Sender*. There had been no more telephone calls although she had waited in the telephone box on Wednesdays and Saturdays. In her last letter to him she hadn't told him she thought she might be pregnant. She had wanted to be certain and hopefully tell him face to face.

Now she knew that was just a pipe dream.

Her deep sense of loss stunned her, leaving her confused and frightened. Her hands would start to shake at the most inconvenient times and her breath catch in her throat. It was astounding to think about it and she tried not to, yet it was never far from her mind, and as one miserable day followed another she faced up to the truth. He didn't want her any more.

Sometimes her sadness turned to burning anger and she raged at his defection. But no matter how bitter her thoughts of Richard sometimes were she never for a moment felt that way about the little life growing inside her. She wanted his baby, wanted it for her so that she could give it all the love she would have lavished on him, had he wanted it.

'You're looking peaky this morning.' Staff Shaw gave Grace a concerned look as she walked into the nursery. Just for an instant, Grace was tempted to tell her why. She was closer to Maudie Shaw than any of the other nurses, but she dreaded being the focus of gossip behind her back. Instead, she made the excuse of coming down with a cold then lifted a bonny, two-day-old baby boy from his crib ready to take him to his mother for feeding.

'Don't breathe any of your germs on him,' Maudie remarked sceptically.

Grace mumbled a reply and walked out of the nursery and into the ward. She laid the baby in his mother's arms and helped her latch him on to a nipple. He sucked ravenously, the soft slurp-slurp causing Grace to feel a tingling in her own breasts. On the ward she watched the mothers nursing their sons or daughters and thought *in seven months' time that'll be me.*

Then where would she be and who would be taking care of her? she wondered. It wouldn't be here in the Royal, she was sure of that. Sister Morris would have a field day. The surly bitch would no doubt laugh her leg off as uppity Staff Nurse Murphy gave birth to a child out of wedlock. As she went about her duties she began to think crazy thoughts. She could pretend that she and Richard had married. Then she remembered that the hospital would demand a marriage certificate so that her wages could be paid under her new name.

Abandoning that idea, she suddenly had another. It was imperative to let Richard know he had fathered a child: her child. The baby was as much his as it was hers. He had a right to know. Then, when he knew that and she knowing what a decent, good, kind man he was it would make it impossible for him to ignore her letters. She'd write to his commanding officer, tell him that a matter of extreme urgency demanded that she contact Richard. She wouldn't divulge the reason why.

Feeling more in control with her dilemma, she carried on with her duties.

* * *

The weeks dragged by, each one more miserable than its predecessor. Grace came to the conclusion that there was nothing worse than waiting. On the ward it wasn't too much of a problem, being kept busy and trying to work as efficiently as she had always done left little time to dwell on her predicament. But as the days went by without any news of Richard, she knew that she would have to face up to making plans for her and the baby.

This morning, lying in bed after another restless night, she had felt a tiny pulse of movement inside her like a bubble bursting. She had placed her hands on her stomach and gently stroked the little bump that was growing week on week. Then, a rush of tenderness had infused her body, but now as she filled a bath with warm, soapy water for a patient she was aware of her thickening waistline. How long would it take for one of her colleagues to notice the small bulge under her apron?

'You seem tired,' Mrs Collins remarked as Grace helped her into the bath. Grace shrugged and smiled. The worry was wearing her out. Even the simplest tasks left her feeling exhausted. She stifled a yawn and muttered, 'I didn't sleep well last night.'

In fact, she couldn't remember the last time she had. Even when she did fall asleep she'd suddenly wake a short while later sweating profusely and feeling panicked. Each evening walking home from work she prayed for a letter on the mat. Yesterday there had been two, and her heart had jumped in her throat, hope soaring only to be crushed when she saw that one was from her mother and the other from Patsy. Her father had been released from hospital, his broken bones healing nicely, Patsy wrote, but he still required a great deal of care and she was staying at home to nurse him. Grace was pleased that Mr O'Grady had survived his fall and that he was getting better, but she felt deeply saddened to think that she'd most likely never again see Patsy's chubby, smiling face or hear her old-fashioned remarks. There had still been no word from Clodagh.

Now, on a cold, miserable day in the week before Christmas, as if things couldn't get much worse, Grace had delivered a stillborn baby. A stillbirth on the ward was always a terribly sad occurrence for the bereaved parents and the staff. Grace had struggled to hold back her tears.

Walking home that evening through a thick fog her spirits were so low that she felt as though she was treading on them. She was shivering uncontrollably, not because the evening air was damp and chill but because the stress of living every day with uncertainty was making her ill. She unlocked the house door and stepped inside, almost treading on a stiff blue envelope with an RAF crest on it. She stared at it for a moment then picked it up and tore it open, hope surging through every vein.

She hadn't truly expected the commanding officer to reply but he had, or at least someone had replied for him. It was signed p.p. for the commanding officer. Grace knew by its brevity that the reply was not what she had hoped for. Her shoulders slumped and her eyes filled with tears as she read.

Dear Miss Murphy,

With regard to your enquiry: Wing Commander Richard Carmichael is no longer based at RAF Duxford. It is contrary to RAF policy to provide you with further information as to his whereabouts.

Grace felt as though her world had fallen apart.

So, he'd been promoted to Wing Commander was her first thought, her second was how dare they refuse to give her his address in Malta, if indeed he was there. A burning rage seared through her and she screamed insults up at the ceiling. 'Damn the bloody war! To hell with the RAF! Sod the bloody glamour boys!' Then she sank down on the bottom step of the stairs, great wracking sobs tearing at her throat as she denounced the man who had promised one thing and then delivered another.

She had no idea how long she sat there, but when she got to her feet her legs buckled and her chest felt bruised as though she had been kicked. Strangely, however, her mind was clearer and she felt calmer than at any other time during the past few weeks. Richard was no longer part of her life. She had to accept that and go on alone.

Filled with a steely determination she went into the kitchen, and after taking off her cloak she began to make something to eat. She had to keep up her strength. 'It's just me and you now,' she said patting the bump under her apron, 'just you and me. And we'll manage just fine, whatever it takes.'

She stood at the sink by the window to peel potatoes gazing out at a mass of rolling grey clouds. There wasn't a patch of blue to be seen.

* * *

'Ah, Staff Murphy, busy as usual, I see?' Sister Morris's sarcasm didn't escape Grace as she pinned a sprig of holly to the ward door. A porter had delivered a bunch earlier that morning. It being Christmas week, Grace and the other nurses in the maternity unit were making the ward look festive for the benefit of the women who would miss being at home with their families.

'Yuletide festivity, Sister,' Grace replied tersely, her apron taut across her stomach as she stretched to adjust the holly.

Sister Morris gave a vinegary smile. Then she cocked her head to one side, her eyes narrowing as she said, 'And you, Staff Murphy? How are you?'

Grace was so taken aback she clutched the sprig of holly crying 'Ouch!' as it pricked her fingers. 'I'm perfectly well, Sister. Thank you for asking.' She stooped to hide her reddened cheeks and lifted the bunch of holly at her feet. 'Will I put some on the windowsills?' she asked calmly even though her insides were churning. Had Sister Morris spotted what Grace was doing her best to hide?

Christmas came and went, and when Grace wasn't working she stayed alone in the house. She had refused several invitations from the other maternity nurses to celebrate the season with them in their homes, making excuses for having prior engagements. The truth was she didn't want to celebrate with anyone other than Richard, and he was gone. She felt gutted. Sitting in the parlour on Christmas Eve, the silent house oppressive, she had asked herself how long would it take for her to forget him? She knew the answer. Forever. Her baby was a constant reminder.

18

It was well into February when Sister Morris called Grace into her office, her hatchet face grimmer than usual. She looked Grace up and down over her steel-rimmed spectacles. A stab of fear pierced Grace's chest. She straightened her spine and looked directly at her tormentor preparing herself for what she was sure was about to happen.

Sister Morris made a steeple of her fingers and rested her chin on them, her mouth turned down at the corners. 'Staff Murphy, is there something you would like to tell me?'

Grace had no desire to tell her anything, but knowing it was inevitable and that sooner rather than later she would have to come clean she took a deep breath. 'I'm pregnant, Sister Morris. Five months to be exact. I suppose I should have informed you sooner than this but it's important I keep my job for as long as possible.' Her eyes moistened and she found herself looking at Sister Morris's formidable face through a haze of tears. 'I need the money,' she said brokenly.

'Am I to understand that the father isn't prepared to marry or support you?'

Sister Morris's lip curled distastefully.

Grace's insides curdled. 'He's no longer with us,' she said, her voice barely above a whisper. Sister Morris's stern expression softened slightly, and Grace assumed she thought that Richard was dead. The thought made her shiver.

'Then you have a predicament.' There was a hint of compassion in Sister Morris's tone, but she quickly dispensed with it. 'You are aware that you will have to resign from your position, and that your accommodation will no longer be available to you.'

Grace nodded. She was so aware of those facts that she had barely slept for weeks. Hearing them now in cold, hard terms turned her blood to ice. 'Yes, Sister Morris, I understand. When would you like me to leave?'

The sister glanced at the roll-top calendar on her desk and pursed her lips.

'I'll allow you to work until the end of the month. That should give you time to find alternative accommodation.' She paused to muster a wintry smile. 'I must say I'm rather disappointed in you, Staff Murphy. You have the makings of a good nurse.' She gave what sounded to Grace like a sigh of regret then with a wave of her hand she said, 'Dismissed.'

Dismissed indeed, in more ways than one, thought Grace as she made her way back to the ward. She looked at the women in the beds, some of them feeding their babies, and her heart felt as though it had been sliced through the middle. She'd miss the thrill of delivering a baby and sharing the delight of its mother, or comforting those in distress and calming their fears. The next baby she would deliver would be her own. She trembled at the thought.

There was little point in hiding her condition any longer, and when she took her tea break with Staff Shaw she told her, 'I'm leaving at the end of the month.'

To Grace's surprise, Maudie Shaw didn't look at all shocked. She put down her cup and reached across the table to squeeze Grace's hand. 'I suspected as much. I noticed how you kept having to dash off to the lavvy or the sluice in the morning to be sick.' She chuckled wryly. 'I haven't been a midwife all these years not to notice the symptoms.'

Grace gave a rueful smile. She thought she'd hidden her condition rather well. 'I should have known nothing would get past you, Maudie.'

'Is he going to marry you?'

Grace flushed. 'I don't know where he is. I haven't heard from him in months. He doesn't even know I'm pregnant.' Each grim statement tore a piece out of her heart. She slumped on the edge of the table with her elbows, her chin resting on her clenched fists.

'Where will you go? Will you go back to Ireland?'

Grace shuddered at the thought. 'Ireland doesn't exactly welcome unmarried mothers, my dad would lose half his customers once they heard he was sheltering a pregnant daughter who didn't have a husband,' she said, trying to make a joke of it. 'To be honest I haven't thought that far ahead.' She sat up straighter and thrust back her shoulders. 'But come what may, I want this baby more than anything else in the world, and I'll make damned sure it has the best upbringing I can give it.'

Maudie patted the back of Grace's hand. 'That's the spirit, love. An' if there's anything I can do to help, you only have to ask. I'll miss you when you go 'cos you're great to work with. You're a bloody good nurse.'

There it was, another compliment in the space of a morning. Grace had never doubted her own nursing abilities but it was cheering to hear someone else praise them. She wondered when she'd next be able to use them after the end of the month. It was less than two weeks away, but for now she would go back to the ward and prove what a good nurse she was.

'Thanks, Maudie, you're a pal,' she said sincerely. 'I'll miss you too, and everything that's here. Even Sister Bloody Morris.' The two women laughed as they returned their cups to the trolley and went back on the ward, but it was laughter tinged with sadness.

* * *

Grace listened to the burring of the telephone, and as her call was connected she dropped coins into the slot, her fingers fumbling nervously. 'Hello, is that The Grange in Higher Melton? I'd like to speak to Mrs Cecily Carmichael.'

'Madam is not in residence today,' a voice she didn't recognise replied.

'Then can I speak to Mrs Maggie Trotter?'

'Mrs Trotter is no longer in madam's employ.'

Grace's shoulders slumped. Cecily had obviously made some changes since Garvey's death. 'Will you please tell Mrs Carmichael that Grace Murphy called and that I will call again tomorrow evening?' She heard the edge of annoyance and desperation in her voice and put down the receiver before her frustration made her lose control. It had taken no small amount of courage and a great deal of pride-swallowing for her to contact Cecily, but Grace thought she might know how she could get in touch with Richard. She had to let him know about the baby even if he didn't want her any more. Expect me tomorrow evening, she silently told the kiosk and headed home.

* * *

'Grace Murphy,' she announced when the same stranger's voice answered her call the following evening. The palm of her hand holding the receiver was moist.

'Madam will accept your call.'

After a few seconds of silence Cecily's plummy tones floated down the line. 'Miss Murphy, how may I help you?'

Grace took a deep breath. 'I seem to have lost contact with Richard,' she said evenly. 'I wondered if you might help me get in touch with him again.'

There was a long pause. 'I'm afraid I can't do that. Richard and I haven't spoken since Garvey's funeral.' Cecily gave what sounded like a raspy chuckle. 'It's fair to say we didn't part on the best of terms – the silly sensitive boy – and I have no idea where he is.'

'That's disappointing, Mrs Carmichael, because I have something extremely important to tell him.' Before she could prevent herself from saying what she had never intended to say Grace said, 'I'm pregnant.'

Now there was no mistaking the raspy chuckle. 'Oh, my dear, that's the oldest trick in the book,' Cecily cackled. 'I don't know what you hope to gain by...'

Grace slammed the receiver back into its cradle. She should have known better than to expect any support from Cecily Carmichael.

* * *

Two days before she had to quit the house, Grace was using her two days off duty to search for new accommodation. She had searched the newspaper adverts without success and now she was on her way to another estate agency, the one she'd just left having told her that with so many dwellings having been destroyed by the bombings the demand for rented accommodation far exceeded supply.

She was walking down Fishergate when she saw a frail, young girl coming towards her. She looked familiar. Grace realised that it was Ruth Slater.

'Ruth,' she cried as the girl slouched nearer. Ruth raised her gaze, the bleak eyes in an ashen face clocking Grace. 'Nurse Murphy,' she muttered.

'How are you, Ruth, and how's your daughter?'

'Dunno.' Ruth glanced down the street as though she wanted to escape.

'What do you mean, you don't know?' Grace's concern sharpened her tone.

'They took 'er off me, di'n't they? Gev 'er to somebody better off,' Ruth growled.

'St Vincent's did that to you?' Grace sounded disbelieving.

'Yeah. They kept her an' chucked me out,' Ruth said sourly. 'You an' that Sister Morris told me they'd look after us proper but you were bloody lying.' She looked Grace up and down, her eyes settling on Grace's bump. 'Did you get married?'

Grace gave a rueful smile. 'No, I've ended up a bit like you. A baby on the way with a father who doesn't want to know,' she said.

Ruth's jaw dropped. 'Aye, well, if you're thinking of going to St Bloody Vincent's to help you out, don't bother 'cos they'll on'y take it off you,' she snarled, and pushing past Grace she ran up the street. Grace stared after her.

Saddened by the sorry outcome of Ruth's experience at St Vincent's, Grace walked on telling her bump that there was no way she'd be going there for help. She'd manage on her own. Nothing and nobody would part her from her baby.

The next estate agent offered Grace a room in Balby. 'It's a bit shabby and the elderly couple who are renting it out are not awfully fussy about cleaning, if you know what I mean,' the woman said confidentially having noted Grace's tidy appearance, 'but it might be worth a look.'

Grace was on her way to the bus stop to go and view it when who should she meet but Doreen Butterworth. 'Well, if it isn't Nurse Murphy,' Doreen exclaimed smiling broadly. 'We've often thought about you, haven't we, Gary?' She leaned into the pram and chucked her chubby, little son under his chin.

'Mrs Butterworth, it's lovely to see you. And Gary,' Grace gasped. What a coincidence to run into two ex-patients on the same day. She reached out and patted Gary's cheek. He gurgled, his smile displaying four small, white teeth.

Doreen nodded her head acknowledging Grace's rotund belly. 'When's it due?' She looked immensely pleased for Grace.

'June.'

'An' is your hubby away fighting or is he one of the lucky ones here at home?'

Doreen's face crumpled as she spoke, and Grace knew she was remembering her own husband who had been lost at sea on the Arctic convoys.

'I'm not married,' Grace replied flatly. There was no point in hiding the truth. 'The father and I split up some time ago. He doesn't even know I'm pregnant.' She realised she was saying too much but it felt good to share the pain.

'Ooh, I am sorry.' Sympathy and embarrassment made Doreen's cheeks pink. She placed a comforting hand on Grace's sleeve. 'It's hard, isn't it?' she said.

'Worse than that, I have to find somewhere to live but I'm not having much luck.' Feeling lighter as she shared her problems Grace abandoned the idea of a shabby room in Balby. 'Do you have time for a cup of tea? My treat.'

They went to a café down the street, and over tea and biscuits Doreen talked about Gary and how well she was coping. 'Although it is lonely without Norman,' she said, dipping a biscuit into her tea, silently lost in memories of her husband.

Suddenly her face brightened. 'Look, if you're wanting a place to stay why not come an' live with me till you get properly sorted? We'd be company for one another, an' it'll help with the rent. I'll not be greedy. I had thought of renting out a room an' it's better to let it to somebody I know. Perhaps you'd give me a hand wi' Gary when I'm at work.'

Grace was completely taken aback by the offer. 'Are you sure?' she asked. When Doreen said she was Grace sipped her tea, mulling over Doreen's offer. It did appeal to her, and she had nowhere else to go. They chatted about the arrangements over a second cup of tea.

Two days later Grace moved into Doreen's two up and two down council house in Wheatley. For the first time in her pregnancy Grace felt free to think about her baby without having to worry about having a roof over their heads. However, her savings wouldn't last indefinitely and she needed to think about earning money. She needed to find a job, and quick. She said as much to Doreen.

'Maybe you can get set on at my place. They're allus looking for lasses to fill t'shells,' Doreen said. She worked part-time at Compton Parkinson's ammunition factory leaving Gary with a neighbour when she did her shifts.

Grace jumped at the idea. 'We could work split shifts, that way I could mind Gary when you're working. It'll save you having to pay your neighbour,' she said pleased to think that she'd be helping Doreen out and earning money for herself.

The next morning, Grace presented herself at the munitions' factory.

'Are you sure you're fit to work? Ramming shells is heavy work,' the foreman asked, his eyes fleetingly resting on Grace's swollen belly.

'I'm perfectly fit,' Grace assured him. 'I'm a nurse by profession and that involves a lot of heavy lifting and shifting, believe me.'

The foreman scratched his head thoughtfully. 'A nurse, you say? Qualified?'

'I was a staff nurse in the Royal in Doncaster up to a few days ago,' Grace informed him. 'Sadly, they don't employ pregnant nurses.'

'They might not,' the foreman said, 'but we could do with one here. We have a vacancy an' Government orders are that we have to have one on site in case of accidents. Would you be interested in that job?'

Grace could have kissed him. She had been rather anxious as to how she would cope further into her pregnancy, Doreen having told her that filling shells was backbreaking work. She left the office on winged feet.

'He says if I work during the day he'll give you a regular evening shift,' she told Doreen when she arrived back. Doreen was delighted. She could now spend all day with her son and leave him in good hands each evening when she went to work. They celebrated with a cup of tea.

* * *

Grace considered herself more than lucky to be earning again. She thoroughly enjoyed her work, and as her pregnancy advanced she half-regretted agreeing to someone taking her place when she would have to give it up. But she dearly wanted to spend the first crucial months of her baby's life caring for it. The thought of handing it over to someone else didn't bear thinking about. Now on her last day in the factory, she was busy as usual.

'There we are, Florence, that should do it,' said Grace as she finished applying a dressing to the nasty burn on Florence's forearm. She had accidently splashed liquid TNT, trinitrotoluene, on her wrist, one of the many dangers the women faced when making explosives. 'Keep the dressing on and my replacement will look at it tomorrow. Next time take more care when you're pouring acid.'

Florence nodded her thanks. Like most of the women who filled the shells the ends of her hair were bleached blonde and her small, pinched face was tinged yellow, just two of the many side effects of working with TNT. No wonder they call them the canary girls, Grace thought, turning to her next patient with a brisk, 'Next please.'

Ken Haines, the foreman, looked on as Grace attended to a gash in the palm of one of the few male machine operatives. Ken admired the nurse he'd employed on the spur of the moment. Grace had been an asset from the start. Not only did she tend to injuries caused by using dangerous machinery or the handling of lethal materials, she had introduced a number of safety measures in the factory to lessen these daily occurrences. She also ensured that the workers got their daily ration of milk and a bun to line their stomachs at the beginning of each shift to prevent the damage caused by the fumes TNT gave off.

'Hold still now,' Grace told the injured man as she inserted the needle into his palm. 'By the time I've finished you'll be as good as a Burton's fifty-shilling suit. Hand-stitched.' The operative grinned. 'Don't apply too much pressure on it for the next couple of days,' she said then turned to Ken. 'Maybe Keith can have light duties for the rest of the week.' Ken agreed, and Keith went back to work, happy.

'I'm going to miss having you about the place, Grace.' Ken smiled ruefully.

'And I'm going to miss you, and this job. I've loved working here and I can't thank you enough for setting me on.' She gave him a warm smile. 'But this baby won't wait much longer.'

Grace began tidying up bandages, scissors, salves and dressings. She didn't want her successor to think she hadn't run a tight ship.

When that was done she said, 'I'm just going to take a walk round for one last time.'

'Aye, right you are,' said Ken looking miserable.

On her way into the factory, Grace pondered on how fortunate she had been to land such a pleasant job. There had been the occasional fraught moments when she had had to deal with major accidents such as an explosion in the grenade shed that had injured four men, and several machine wounds or burns that had required hospitalisation. Then, she had given life-saving medical care until the ambulances arrived, but other than that her daily duties were far less strenuous and she had easily managed right up to today.

The biting, metallic stink of TNT made Grace wrinkle her nose as she walked into the 'cleanway' as the danger areas were called. The women were singing as they tamped shells. It made her smile. She had grown close to these hard-working wives, mothers and daughters who had answered the country's call. Lots of yellowish faces greeted her cheerily.

'That's another one for my Bert to fire up the arse of a bloody German,' Molly Bickerstaff chirped, placing a detonator into the top of a shell case. Grace tensed. One tamp too many and Molly was in danger of blowing them to kingdom come.

'I came to say goodbye,' Grace called out. 'It's my last day.' Over cries of how much they would miss her, somebody started to sing 'We'll Meet Again'. Tears sprang to Grace's eyes as all the women joined in.

She was on her way back to the nursing station when Ronnie Fletcher came swaggering towards her. 'Came to see where the real work takes place, did you?' His words dripped with sarcasm.

Grace ignored his remark. She didn't particularly care for Ronnie. However, Doreen did. Of late, she frequently spent her free time with him. He took her to the cinema or the pub, leaving Grace to babysit Gary. Grace didn't object to that, but whenever Ronnie visited the house she did find his arrogant manner and the way in which he dominated Doreen extremely annoying. Furthermore, he was short-tempered with Gary, often reducing the little boy to tears. Up until Doreen had taken up with Ronnie their household had been a very female one, but now he barged in whenever he liked expecting to be fed, and for Doreen to dance to his tune. Grace was very fond of kind-hearted Doreen and didn't like where all this was leading.

Now, as she made to move past him and go back to the nursing station, he blocked her way. 'You're leaving today, aren't you?' He smirked. Grace nodded. 'And when are you moving out of Doreen's?' he asked, a threatening sneer adding impact to his words.

Startled, Grace retorted, 'None of your business!' and pushing him aside she hurried on. The pleasure had gone out of the day, and a cold hand clutched at her insides. Had Doreen told him she wanted rid of her? Was he intending to move in? Whichever it was, it made her feel anxious.

On her way home, Grace reflected on the matter. She didn't want to be forced to seek either new accommodation, or work, again. She wondered how long her savings would tide her over before it became inevitable. She wanted to spend as much time as she could with her baby, in pleasant surroundings without having to worry about the struggle to make a living.

Whenever she dwelt on the future she felt afraid and sad and angry. She thought how different it could have been if only Richard had stood by her. She didn't crave for wealth or the lifestyle that had been his, but she did feel aggrieved to think that her child, and his, might face years of living in impoverished circumstances. She wanted only the best for her baby.

19

Three days later, on the fifth of June, Grace knew from the moment she wakened that her baby would be born that day. The sun was streaming through the thin curtains, and already the heat in the small bedroom felt oppressive. Pushing aside the bedcovers then lifting her nightdress she lay back against the pillows with her eyes closed and her hands on the mound of her bare belly. Under her fingers she could feel the gently undulating movements of her son or daughter. She thought of Richard's strong, warm hands, his gentle touch on the night he had caressed and kissed the same skin that she was now stroking. Slow tears trickled from her eyes and into her hair as she imagined how wonderful it would be if he were here with her to share this exquisite moment.

She must have dozed, for suddenly she felt an urgent shifting in her womb.

Her eyes flew open and her hands darted to her belly, her right one coming into contact with a small protrusion. She looked down and saw the perfect shape of a tiny fist bulging under her skin. She gazed in awe, her heart bursting with love. It wasn't the first time she'd seen such a thing, but then that little fist had been inside some other woman's womb. This was her body, her baby.

She cupped her hand over the fist, felt it press against her palm and then subside as quickly as it had appeared. She had never before felt so alive, so exhilarated. Then her thoughts turned to the practicalities. She must get up and get ready.

She swung her legs over the edge of the bed but as she came upright a sharp pain rocketed through her spine. It was so violent that she almost lost her balance. Gasping and swaying, she sat back down. The pain came again then ebbed, and then came again. Grace knew she was definitely in the first stages of labour. Keep calm, she told herself, don't do anything that might harm the baby. 'Hold on,' she told it. 'Don't be too eager. I've managed to carry on living without your daddy but I couldn't bear it if I lost you.'

Cautiously, she made her way out of the bedroom and along the landing to Doreen's room. She tapped on the door then opened it. 'Doreen, sorry to disturb you but the...' Another contraction almost shot her into the room. She clung to the doorknob and took a deep breath. 'Doreen...' she gasped.

Doreen sat bolt upright, her pink curlers bobbing furiously and a look of sheer panic wiping the last vestiges of sleep clean off her face. 'Is it...? Are you...?' She scrambled out of bed. In his cot, Gary moaned but he didn't waken. Doreen flapped towards Grace, little nervous squeals accompanying every step.

'I've started,' Grace panted, 'will you give me a hand to deliver the baby?'

She turned to go back to her own bedroom. By now, she was sweating profusely.

'But I won't know what to do,' cried Doreen following Grace into her room then jigging from foot to foot and glancing round wildly.

'I'll tell you,' Grace said as she lowered herself back onto the bed. 'I'm a midwife, remember, I've delivered hundreds of babies. I'm sure I can deliver my own and...' she clenched her teeth as a contraction shot through her, 'this baby's in a hurry so we'd better get a move on.'

* * *

The sun was high in the sky, the bedroom bathed in its gleaming light as Grace lay with her son against her breast. She looked deliriously happy, her cheeks flushed and her eyes sparkling. Doreen sat with Gary on her knee by the bedside, her face wreathed in triumphant smiles.

'I told you there was nothing to it,' Grace chuckled. It had been an easy birth, and Doreen had followed Grace's instructions to the letter. However, when it came to cutting the cord she had lost her nerve, and Grace had cut it.

'To think that I brought a baby into the world with me own hands.' Doreen looked at her upturned palms in amazement. 'I feel ever so proud.' Gary's expression puzzled he touched the tiny, bare toes peeping out from under the white sheet. The toes wiggled and Gary laughed.

'What will you call him?' Doreen put a restraining hand on Gary's.

'Michael,' Grace replied softly, as Gary grabbed for the baby's toes again.

20

'Look, Doreen,' said Grace, her expression concerned, 'I know I've asked you this before but now I'm asking you again. Have I done something to upset you?'

They were sitting on the back step with a cup of tea taking advantage of the warm September evening. Gary was playing with a wooden truck at their feet on the flagstones and Michael, now three months old, was sleeping peacefully in his pram. He was an easy baby and Grace, delighting in his presence, had pushed aside her anxieties at maybe having to move out.

However, in the past few days, Grace had been painfully aware that Doreen was nervous around her, unable to meet her eye or chat in the friendly way they usually did. She reiterated her question, adding, 'You must tell me if I have.'

Doreen looked flustered. 'No, no... not at all,' she denied, her cheeks blazing as she ducked her head and began chattering to her son.

Grace sighed then stretched out her bare legs to catch the last of the sun. She might have looked relaxed but she was anything but.

The uneasy silence hanging like an ominous cloud between her and Doreen assured her that Doreen wasn't telling the truth.

Doreen set her cup down on the step then pulled Gary up to her knee holding him like a shield as she said, 'Ronnie's coming round later.'

This came as no surprise to Grace. He was rarely off the doorstep. 'Is he taking you out?' She spoke casually but something in the way Doreen had made the announcement had her worried.

Doreen flicked Grace an anxious glance. 'No, we're staying in. We've something to discuss.' Her voice wobbled as she spoke.

'Sounds serious.' Grace had an uncomfortable feeling that it was her they would be discussing. Michael woke with a lusty cry. Grace jumped up, relieved to escape the tense atmosphere. 'This wee feller's hungry. I'll go in and feed him.'

Up in her bedroom, sitting by the window, she unbuttoned her blouse and put Michael to her breast. His rosebud mouth latched on and as he sucked, his bright, blue eyes, so like his father's, gazed up at Grace. They only increased her sadness.

She heard Ronnie arrive, his loud, bullying voice penetrating the ceiling below.

'Get out from under me bloody feet,' she heard him bawl. Seconds later she heard Gary's frightened wails. She put Michael into his crib, stroking his forehead and smoothing his fine, fair, wispy hair. In time it would thicken and be exactly like Richard's. A stab of pain shot through her chest. Try as she did to keep Richard from her thoughts there was always something to remind her. She stooped over the crib and kissed her son's rosy cheek then went downstairs.

Ronnie gave her a dirty look as she entered the kitchen. Doreen was dishing up a plate of shepherd's pie, her hands unsteady and her features tense. Grace felt sorry for her. Gary was crouched in the corner, his little face covered in tears and snot. Grace went and picked him up. He gave a grateful little smile, his bottom lip wobbling as he tried to hold back more tears. Doreen shot her a grateful glance then put the pie on the table in front of Ronnie. Without a word of thanks he began shovelling food into his mouth.

Doreen leaned against the sink, looking anxious. Grace played with Gary, the only sound in the kitchen their chatter and Ronnie sloshing pie. The atmosphere was tense and Grace looked for an excuse to escape it. 'Will I put Gary to bed?' she asked. Doreen nodded, her eyes fixed on Ronnie.

'Come on, Gary, let's get you into your pyjamas,' Grace said turning to go upstairs.

'Hold on a minute.' Ronnie pushed his empty plate away. 'Doreen has summat to tell you.'

Grace gazed directly at Doreen, her grey eyes calmly meeting Doreen's brown eyes. They were brimming with tears. Grace put Gary down at her feet. 'Sit a minute, love, while I talk to your mam,' she said ruffling his hair. Doreen gave a nervous cough then looked at Ronnie. He lit a cigarette and stared up through the smoke at the ceiling.

'Grace.' Doreen hesitated then drew a deep breath. 'You'll have to find somewhere else to live. I need the room for Gary,' she spluttered, the words tumbling out of her mouth as though she wanted rid of them.

'Aye, she does,' Ronnie growled. 'I'm not having him sleeping in with us once we're wed. He's enough bloody nuisance during t'day without him spoiling stuff at night, if you know what I mean.' He gave a dirty laugh.

Doreen gulped back a sob. 'I'm sorry.'

Grace gave Ronnie a despising glance then addressed Doreen.

'I'm sorry too, but I understand. I'll move out as soon as I can.' She forced a smile. 'I didn't know you were getting married. Congratulations. When's the big day?' She was hoping it would be months away, giving her time to move out in a dignified manner to somewhere suitable and affordable.

Doreen looked anxiously at Ronnie. 'We haven't actually set a date, have we? But Ronnie wants to move in straight away, don't you?'

'No point in hanging around,' he scoffed. 'We're as good as married already.'

Grace's eyes searched Doreen's face. Couldn't she see what a despicable character Ronnie was? Doreen hung her head, unable to meet Grace's gaze. Her cheeks were crimson with shame and her shoulders heaved as she tried to suppress her tears.

Grace didn't know whom she felt most sorry for: Doreen or herself.

'Don't upset yourself, Doreen. You've been more than good to me and I'll always be in your debt. I'll start looking for somewhere straight away. Please don't feel bad about it.'

'Why the bloody hell should she?' Ronnie sneered.

Grace didn't dare answer in case she made matters worse. She marched out of the kitchen and up to her room.

'We're moving on, Michael,' she whispered to her sleeping son. 'I don't know to where but wherever it is we'll make the best of it.' Michael's lips pouted and he blew a tiny bubble. Grace smiled. Life was a bit like a bubble. One minute it was perfectly formed and luminous, reflecting the most beautiful colours. Then splat! It burst leaving behind it a tiny teardrop that would soon disappear without trace. Richard Carmichael had been a bubble.

* * *

Once again, Grace scoured the rooms-to-let columns in the newspaper and visited the estate agents without success. Anything available was either too expensive or if it was within Grace's budget it stipulated that children and dogs were not welcome. Some land-lords even went as far as to include blacks and Irish. As one week ran into two, she had never before felt so helpless. The atmosphere in the house was strained, Doreen constantly tearful and apologetic, and Ronnie champing at the bit to move in.

* * *

In late October Grace went to a view a room in a house in Raby Road.

'I don't usually take women lodgers, and certainly not them with children,'

Clarice Thorpe announced in answer to Grace's enquiry, 'but seein' as how you're a nurse I'll let you have it.' She heaved up her pendulous bosom with her elbow then pulled her grubby candlewick dressing gown tighter around her rolls of fat, a sour smell wafting in the confined space of the lobby. She's clearly not a friend of soap and water, Grace had thought, a wave of despair washing over her as she followed her up the stairs to a room at the back of the house. It was small and shabby, the wallpaper faded and the lino cracked and grimy. Her heart heavy, Grace said she would take it. She had run out of options.

* * *

'Don't cry, Doreen. I'm not going to the ends of the earth. I'm sure we'll see you again,' she said later that day as, with Michael in her arms, she prepared to leave.

'But I feel so awful,' Doreen sobbed, holding onto Gary and her wet, brown eyes shifting from Grace to Michael. 'Give Auntie Doreen a bye-bye kiss.' She gulped. 'He's another little lad who'll never know his dad.' She sniffed.

Doreen looked so pitiful that Grace had the distinct impression she regretted succumbing to Ronnie's bullying tactics and already doubted that he'd be a good stepfather. But Doreen had said more than once, 'I need a man about the place. I'm lonely without one.'

Grace knew exactly how she felt. She too would love to have a man to share her life with, but latching onto just anybody to fill the void was not the answer. Her friend deserved better than Ronnie. Making careful note not to make the same mistake, Grace put Michael into his pram and set off to their new home.

Regrettably, having no means of transportation, she'd had to leave his crib behind. Money was tight and she couldn't afford the luxury of hiring a van so she had packed their belongings into a suitcase and a large bag and with them propped on the front of the pram she made an unwieldy journey across the town. Then, after a minor confrontation with Clarice about leaving the pram in the alcove under the stairs, she lugged their belongings up to the room.

'This is your new bed, Michael,' she said laying him on one of the two single beds then padding pillows on either side to prevent him from rolling. Exhausted, Grace sank down beside him and kissed his cheek. His bright, blue eyes roamed his new home then settled on his mother's face. He smiled. Grace returned the smile then let her gaze take in the rickety wardrobe and the chest of drawers, its top scarred with cigarette burns. Through the small window she could see the back of the Royal Infirmary where she had once worked. Lying with her cheek pressed to Michael's she felt as though her heart might break.

A short while later, Michael sleeping, Grace went in search of Clarice.

'Are you suggesting I don't keep a clean house,' Clarice snarled, outraged when Grace asked for a bucket, a scrubbing brush and soap to wash the grimy lino then enquired on what day was the bed linen changed. 'Don't come all hoity-toity with me, madam. I've run a respectable house since before you were born,' she huffed opening a cupboard in the kitchen. 'Cleaning stuff's kept here. Make sure you put it back when you've finished and,' she delivered her parting shot, 'mind you keep that brat quiet. I don't want him disturbing my other lodgers.' Clarice scuttled back to the downstairs rooms she occupied.

The other lodgers were four rough, working men whom Grace met fleetingly in the evenings in the squalid kitchen as she made a hurried meal to take up to her room. Three of them were older men, worn and grizzly, and the fourth a hairy, unwashed fellow of a similar age to Grace. The older men tended to ignore her as though they had lost all interest in life, but Alfie leered at her unnervingly or made suggestive remarks about her being a woman on her own whenever their paths crossed. Grace dreaded using the kitchen at night when he was there.

It was a strange way of living. Of Clarice she saw little and had no desire to do so, Clarice having more than once complained 'That bairn kept me awake last night with all that yawping.' Grace knew it was a downright lie. Michael rarely cried during the night. However, she couldn't say the same for herself.

During the day, Grace walked Michael in the park or, if the weather was inclement, she kept to the room reading and puzzling over how to better her situation. Her savings wouldn't last forever, and at night she wept at the futility of providing Michael with a decent future.

And if living in such impoverished circumstances wasn't bad enough, she had another problem to contend with. More than once, in the hours of the night, she thought she had heard someone turn the knob on her bedroom door. She had a fair idea who it was and always kept the door bolted whenever she was in the room. Angered at being subjected to such night fears and hating the aimlessness of the days she struggled on, unable to find a solution.

Finding a job to eke out her rapidly dwindling savings would be counterproductive for to do so meant leaving Michael in someone else's care, and paying them for the pleasure.

Things came to a head a month or so later; the weather too foul to spend time outdoors and too wet for Alfie to work on the building site where he was employed.

Grace was in the kitchen heating a pan of soup when Alfie loped in clad in just his trousers and vest. He came up behind her at the stove, close enough for her to smell his sweaty armpits and his beery breath. He pushed himself against her. She froze.

'This is nice,' he slobbered, 'just you an' me, an' all the time in the world.'

'I've no time to waste, Alfie. I need to take this soup up whilst it's still hot.' Trying to sound light-hearted Grace attempted to sidestep him, but Alfie wasn't for letting her go. A cold fear clutched at her insides as, hemmed in between the stove and the sink, she sought to escape. Before she could fully gather her wits one big beefy hand grabbed her arm and the other yanked her skirt up to her thighs. 'Come on. Stop playing the stuck-up bitch. Give us a bit of that there.'

This can't be happening, Grace thought, her heart hammering. She had to do something – and quick. 'I'll give you something all right,' she screamed. Reaching out with her free arm and grabbing the pan of hot soup she upended it, the scalding liquid pouring over his bare shoulders. Then it was Alfie's turn to scream. He sprang away from her, yelling for all he was worth.

'Hey up! What the hell's going on in here.' Clarice appeared in the doorway.

'She... she... bloody well...' The pain stripped him of words.

'Did you do that?' Clarice eyed Alfie's soup-stained back then the pan Grace was still holding.

'With good reason,' Grace snapped defiantly.

Clarice's lip curled. 'I knew it was a mistake letting you in. Pack your bags. I want you and that brat of yours out. Now! This minute, or else I'm sending for the police.' She swabbed a dirty dishcloth in the sink and applied it to Alfie's blistered back. 'There, lad, that'll take the sting out,' she soothed, and to Grace, 'Be off with you. Out! Now!'

'Don't worry. I'm going.'

Grace marched out of the kitchen then hared upstairs reappearing a short while later with a hastily packed suitcase and bulging bag. Clarice stood in the hallway, arms folded across her chest and a belligerent look on her face. Ignoring her, Grace ran back upstairs and came back down with Michael in her arms. She put him in his pram, and heaving the suitcase and bag on top turned to Clarice. 'Don't dare ask me for this week's rent. Otherwise, it'll be me calling the police.'

Her head high Grace pushed the loaded pram up Raby Road. She had no idea where she was going, and within minutes she was regretting her hasty departure. She needed time to clear her head and think, so she headed for the park. Seated on a bench with her hands resting on the pram's handle she rocked it gently but her thoughts tumbled and crashed as she considered her next move. By now the light had faded from the day and a chilly dampness seeped into her bones. She needed to find shelter for the night.

She set off walking towards the town centre, the pram heavy and unwieldy. Michael was sleeping but soon she'd need hot water to make his feed. There was nothing for it. She would have to take a room in a cheap hotel for the night. Her head and heart aching, she plodded on. She was passing the railway station when Michael woke up, roaring with hunger. Without thinking twice, she wheeled the pram under the arch, bought a platform ticket and made her way to the tearoom.

Inside the stuffy little tearoom she ordered tea and a sandwich then asked the elderly woman for a jug of hot water. 'I need to make him a bottle,' Grace said, the desperation in her request touching the woman's heart for by now Michael's cries were splitting the air.

''Course you do, love. Go an' sit down an' I'll bring it over.'

Grace sat at a table in the corner as far away as possible from the other two customers. Lifting Michael out of the pram she soothed him with kisses and soft words. The woman planted a jug on the table. 'He's a good pair of lungs on him,' she said, smiling. 'Give him here while you mix the bottle.'

Grace delved in the bag, producing a tin of dried milk and made Michael's feed. The woman handed him back laughing as his lips grasped the bottle's teat. He sucked ravenously. Lolled back in his mother's arms, his eyes closed, she fumbled in the bag for a box of rusks. Softening one in a saucer with a drop of her tea she spooned it into his ready mouth.

The woman glanced from Michael to the large clock on the wall behind the counter. 'If you're wanting to catch the last train to Sheffield it'll be in in five minutes,' she said, her tone suggesting Grace had better get a move on.

Grace turned to look at the clock. It showed twenty minutes to ten. She put a dozing Michael in the pram. Then, taking another feeding bottle from her bag, she filled it and the one Michael had just emptied with the remains of the hot water. That should see him through the night. 'I'm meeting his daddy off the train,' she lied, gathering her belongings ready to move on.

'That's nice,' the woman said. 'Is he coming on leave?'

Grace nodded and got to her feet. 'He's stationed at Finningley,' she replied wishing it were true as she wheeled the pram to the door.

'I'm locking up at ten,' the woman called out to the two remaining customers. She followed Grace to the door. 'Enjoy your time with your hubby, love. He must be right proud of that lovely little lad.' She gave Michael a fond smile.

The train chuffed into the station, clouds of steam billowing up to the glass roof. Grace moved down the platform out of sight of the tearoom. As the train halted the doors flew open disgorging several young airmen in blue uniforms. Grace's heart lurched, the sight of them making the lie she had just told all the more poignant. If only Richard was one of them. With the sound of their laughter and chatter ringing in her ears she wheeled the pram into the waiting room. It was empty. Seated by a radiator that gave off a faint heat she rested her head on the pram's cover and let her tears fall. Michael slept.

Grace woke to the cries of her son and the dulled words of the night guard. 'There are no more trains tonight,' he said almost apologetically.

Grace lifted her head. Blinking through bleary eyes she was startled to see where she was. She sat bolt upright, embarrassed as she looked into the young man's face. 'I'm not waiting for one,' she heard herself say reaching into the pram to soothe her son.

The lad looked bemused. His job was to patrol the station and move on the beggars and drunks who often took refuge in the waiting room at night. But this girl was neither. He peered into the pram smiling when he saw Michael's red, angry face. 'He must be hungry,' he said turning to look searchingly at Grace.

'Have you nowhere to go?'

Grace struggled to gather her wits. 'What time is it?'

'Going on for two o'clock.'

Shocked, Grace repeated his words. How had she slept all that time?'

'I saw you earlier when I wa' doin' me rounds. I thought you'd be gone when I got back.' He looked both anxious and concerned.

'Truth is, I don't have anywhere to go,' she said dismally giving a wan smile.

The lad weighed her words. 'Well, I don't suppose you're doin' any harm. There's another guard on duty but he patrols down t'other end so he'll not bother you.' He shuffled off, Grace noting that he dragged his left foot as he walked. She lifted Michael into her lap then fed and changed him. Her throat was parched and she contemplated drinking some of the milk from the second bottle, but she resisted knowing that come morning Michael's need would be greater than her own.

A short while later the lad returned carrying two mugs of tea and a packet of biscuits. 'I thought you might be thirsty,' he said shyly. Grace could have kissed him. His name was Bobby and he'd been injured in Belgium on his eighteenth birthday. 'I'll never walk again properly, an' I on'y got this job 'cos me dad's friendly wi' the station master,' he told Grace. They chatted for a while about the war before Bobby went off on his rounds again.

Grace returned Michael to his pram then went and picked up a copy of the *Telegraph and Argus* left behind by an earlier traveller. Reading would help keep her awake. Bobby came again and they talked some more. After he left, Grace slept again until Bobby woke her with a gentle shake and another mug of tea. 'It's turned six an' I'm off home. I hope things get better for you,' he said sincerely.

'Thanks, Bobby. You're a hero,' Grace replied just as sincerely. 'You made last night so much easier to bear. I'll not forget you. Best of luck.'

After he had gone, Grace fed and changed Michael then tidied her hair ready to face the day. Bobby's kindness had given her fresh hope. Two early morning travellers came into the waiting room and Grace picked up the newspaper again. She'd read most of it and was skimming the adverts again when one jumped out at her. She must have missed it the night before.

Wanted, woman to share house. Cat or dog acceptable. Apply
Miss Pamela Armitage.

There was an address in Barnsley and a telephone number.
Suddenly, Grace was filled with the urge to shake the dust of
Doncaster off her heels. Richard wasn't coming back for her. A
flame of anger spurted in her chest. She was sick of the insignifi-
cance that dominated her life. She didn't have to stay here. She
could go wherever she pleased.

* * *

The next two hours seemed interminable. Thankfully, Michael was
fascinated by the arrival and departure of trains on the busy platform, and at the more respectable hour of nine o'clock Grace
rushed to the telephone box.

'Yeah, it's still available, come an' have a look if you want.' The
woman who answered the phone sounded quite young and easy-
going even though there was a wheezy breathlessness in her voice
that Grace associated with someone who had a bronchial problem
or smoked too much. Grace asked for details. The rent was surprisingly cheap, and in return she would have her own bedroom, and
share the bathroom and kitchen. Her spirits rising she said, 'I don't
have either a cat or a dog, but I do have a baby. He's five months
old.' She held her breath and wondered why was it that some of the
worst moments in her life took place in telephone boxes.

'Aw, that's lovely. I love kiddies. I don't have any meself. I've got a
poodle.' Grace tried not to laugh. She asked for directions then
made enquiries at the ticket office for the next train to Barnsley.
Was it foolish to move to a town she knew nothing about? she asked
herself. You knew nothing about Doncaster, an inner voice replied
and yet, coming here changed your whole life, most of it for the

better. You met the man of your dreams. You loved and were loved in return.

Grace waited on the platform, musing that some people waited a lifetime and never experienced the wonderful love she had known, a love she would never forget. She gazed down at the proof of it in the bright, blue eyes that were watching her. Leaning over the pram handle she smiled into Michael's face.

'Coming here changed my life, Michael,' she whispered. 'Now it's time to change it again. We'll go and create some new memories, and let's hope they are just as beautiful as the ones we made here.' Michael blinked and gave her a gummy smile.

When the train to Barnsley arrived, a guard put Michael's pram and the suitcase in the luggage compartment, then helped Grace into an empty carriage. As the train chugged out of the station she gazed through the window. In amongst the banks of cumulus clouds was a patch of blue sky. She winked at it.

* * *

Grace immediately liked the look of Barnsley. There was a busy open market with lots of stalls selling a wide variety of goods from fresh vegetables to crockery, clothes and books. And the people seemed friendly as she asked directions to Old Mill Lane. However, with the suitcase and bag balanced on the front of the pram she couldn't help feeling that it looked rather presumptuous to arrive with all her possessions. Perhaps Miss Armitage wouldn't like the look of her or maybe the accommodation would be unsuitable. It couldn't be worse than Clarice Thorpe's, Grace assured herself as she pushed the pram to the end of a terrace of Victorian houses their front doors opening directly onto the street.

'Oh, so you found it then,' Pamela Armitage said breathlessly in answer to Grace's knock. Grace smiled and introduced herself. At first glance, their age was about all they had in common. Whereas Grace was slender and petite, Pamela was squat and rotund. But her broad smile above chins on chins was welcoming.

'Come in, come in,' she wheezed pressing her bulk back against the wall to allow Grace to ease the pram into the narrow hallway. A dusty collection of cheap, chalk ornamental dogs cluttered a table against one wall.

'Oooh, let's be havin' a look at him,' Pamela gushed leaning into the pram. 'Oh, he's ever so bonny.' She wiggled her chubby fingers at Michael. He gurgled delightfully and Pamela laughed. 'The room's upstairs,' she said pointing to the flight of stairs immediately in front of them. Grace lifted Michael and began to climb, Pamela crowding the space behind them. 'I had other enquiries but I didn't get a feel for 'em, not like I did wi' you, so I told 'em I'd already let it,' Pamela panted mysteriously. Grace wondered what she meant.

The bedroom was large and the furniture good quality. A double bed with brass and iron ends faced a window that looked out into a tidy, enclosed garden. Grace imagined putting Michael out there in his pram on fine days, and if one ignored the dust and the clutter of ornaments on every flat surface the room wasn't bad at all. 'It's very nice,' she said.

Pamela clapped her fat, little hands then led her along the landing to what had clearly been a box room but was now fitted out with a lavatory, a washbasin and bath. 'We had this put in when me mam took poorly an' couldn't get down to the outside lav,' she said, with more than a hint of pride. Grace was pleased to see that whilst it was sparklingly clean it too was overloaded with ornaments.

They went back down the stairs Pamela holding onto the banister rails and plodding step on step and Grace's eyes resting on the wobbling mass of Pamela's backside. She was wearing a bright pink, rather girlish dress that did nothing to hide the rolls of fat wreathing her body from head to foot.

The kitchen was messy, but it had all the usual appliances along with a plethora of vases, pot dogs and other knick-knacks on the windowsills, shelves and mantelpiece. 'You surely have a lot of ornaments,' she said.

'They were me mam's. She bought summat every time she went to the market. I keep meanin' to have a clear out but I never get round to it,' Pamela wheezed. Grace was beginning to think that there was nothing wrong with the house that a bit of order couldn't put right. It was affordable and near the town centre. She might even be able to find some part-time work there. She was about to say she would take the room when a furious yapping erupted from the room next door.

'That's Percy,' chuckled Pamela. 'He's just letting me know I'm neglecting him.' They went into the room at the front of the house and a tiny, white poodle leaped into Pamela's arms and settled on her enormous bosom, his paws round her neck. 'This is my baby,' she crowed, 'and he just loves his mummy, don't you?' She kissed Percy's nose and he licked her cheeks. 'He's a miniature, you know, so he'll not grow any bigger and he's ever so good with kiddies. Say hello to Michael, Percy.' She held the little dog up for Michael to pat. His eyes grew big as he stroked the dog's curly hide. At that moment Grace's heart swelled and as she looked into Pamela's twinkling blue eyes and her flushed, chubby cheeks she knew she had found the right place.

'If you'll have me, I'll take the room,' she said.

'I knew you would,' crowed Pamela. 'I had that feeling about you.' She put Percy down. 'I'll make us a cup of tea. I'm sure you could do with one.' She waddled back into the kitchen and set the kettle to boil.

Grace was beginning to warm to this friendly, open young woman. There was something childlike and innocent about her that she found appealing, and as they chatted over a cup of tea and several biscuits in Pamela's case, she learned that Pamela had recently lost her mother and was uncomfortable living alone. A neighbour had suggested she find someone to share the house with her. She also told Grace to call her Pam.

'Nobody calls me Pamela. Everybody round here calls me Fat Pam. They allus have done.' She didn't seem to consider it an insult.

'Right. Pam it is,' said Grace.

21

After the insularity and squalor of Raby Road, life in in Old Mill Lane was a revelation. As Grace brought order to chaos, confining most of the ornaments to the cupboard on the landing, Pam played with Michael or entertained her many callers. The door knocked frequently.

'If anybody comes just show 'em into t'parlour,' Pam had told her. 'I allus see 'em in there.' The callers were women of all ages, some staying for a matter of minutes and others for an hour.

One evening at the end of her first week in Old Mill Lane as she and Pam sat in the kitchen over a cup of tea Grace remarked, 'You surely have a lot of friends, Pam.'

Pam grimaced, her fat cheeks turning crimson.

'I wouldn't call 'em friends exactly,' she said then hastened to add, 'although some of 'em are. They're more like what you'd call clients.' She giggled.

'Clients?' Grace echoed, wondering what sort of service Pam provided.

'Yeah,' Pam replied, looking embarrassed. 'I didn't say owt about it 'cos some people think it's spooky, an' there's them that say it's the devil's work but...' she shuffled uncomfortably on her chair, 'I'm what they call a medium, a clairvoyant. I see an' hear stuff that other people can't. I didn't want you to be put off 'cos I liked you the minute I saw you an' I wanted you to take the room.'

Grace felt slightly shocked. She'd always thought of clairvoyants as women who wore strange clothes and sat in darkened rooms or tents at fairs. Pam was a bubbly, bouncy girl who wore girlish gingham frocks and pinned bows in her blonde curly hair. 'What do you do?' Grace said, intrigued.

'I talk to the dead, an' do the cards an' the tea leaves. I'll do yours if you like,' she said as casually as if she was offering to make Grace a cup of tea.

'But how do you do it?' Grace was fascinated.

Pam's fat shoulders bounced in a careless shrug. 'I don't know. It's summat I've allus been able to do from when I wa' little. It started wi' me granny talking to me, an' she wa' dead afore I wa' born,' Pam said offhandedly. 'An' I've allus been able to tell when summat's gonna happen. Like that time when I wa' about seven an' I told Mrs Roberts to take her little girl into t'house 'cos if she didn't summat bad 'ud happen.' Pam screwed up her face and in a wobbly voice she added, 'She wa' run over by t'coal lorry an' killed.'

'Oh, my goodness! How awful,' Grace gasped. 'And you knew that was going to happen?' She looked at Pam. astounded.

'Not exactly,' Pam said, 'I didn't know it 'ud be t'coalman. I just get feelin's or messages in me head. If I concentrate on somebody, they sometimes talk to me. It helps people to know what's happened to 'em. It's a comfort when their loved ones reach out to 'em through me.' She looked at Grace nervously. 'I haven't put you off, have I?'

'Not at all,' said Grace thinking that her landlady was rather amazing.

* * *

Three months on, and Grace had grown used to entertaining Pam's callers, and her own circle of acquaintances had widened considerably. Grace blessed the day she had come to live in Old Mill Lane. Pam's heart was as big as her roly-poly body. She never groused or grumbled, and her sweet spontaneous affection for Michael made Grace feel blessed.

Grace had brought order to the house from top to bottom as much for her own and Michael's benefit as for Pam's. Pam had just let her get on with it, not at all offended when Grace threw out piles of unnecessary clutter. Pam just giggled, and carried on playing with Percy the poodle and Michael. The growing boy adored Pam and Percy as much as they did him.

Grace had no qualms about leaving Michael in Pam's care and got a part-time job in Barnsley's Beckett Hospital. They were in need of qualified nurses who could step in whenever the hospital received an influx of wounded soldiers, or miners. She rarely delivered babies these days.

Unlike the city of Sheffield with its huge steel industry that the Germans regularly targeted, Barnsley escaped any serious bombing. Still, there were nights when the sirens blared, and Grace had to chivvy Pam into the Anderson shelter they shared with their neighbours.

'I hate it in here, an' me sixth sense tells me they're not coming for us,' Pam complained seeking solace in the biscuit tin.

'We have to do it just in case they mistake their target,' Grace warned every time there was a raid as, huddled with Michael in one of the narrow cots and occasionally thinking of Richard on a flying mission, they waited for the all-clear.

In the week running up to Christmas, Pam was busier than usual. Grace also had plenty to occupy her. She'd been called in to cover several evening shifts, the money she earned replenishing her sadly depleted savings, and making it possible to buy little extras for Christmas.

The day before, Grace had worked what she hoped would be her last shift that week. She glanced at the clock. Three o'clock. There was a knock at the door and Grace knew who the caller would be. Some women had appointments at the same time every week. 'Is Fat Pam ready for me?' the woman whom Grace now knew as Lily Pickersgill asked when Grace answered the door.

'Not quite,' Grace replied with a smile, 'but she shouldn't be long.' She nodded her head in the direction of the kitchen. 'Have a cuppa while you wait.'

'Right you are.' Lily followed Grace into the kitchen and sat at the table. She looked round admiringly at the neat, orderly room that smelled clean and fresh. 'By, but you haven't half made some changes,' she said fulsomely. 'It used to be a right mess. But Pam never was tidy an' neither was her mam.'

Grace hid a smile as she put the kettle on. Lily passed similar remarks at every visit. 'Milk no sugar, Lily?' She got out two cups. Michael was propped up on cushions on the hearth rug with Percy at his side. They were playing tug-o-war with a soft, fluffy rabbit, Michael's chubby hands holding the rabbit's ears and Percy's little, sharp teeth clamped round its feet.

Lily nodded at Michael. 'He's dribbling. Is he teething?'

'Yes, he's already got his two front teeth and the bottom ones are just coming through,' Grace said proudly. 'He'll be six months old on Friday.'

'What date's his birthday?'

'Fifth of June.'

Lily flicked her fingers, silently calculating. 'Hmm, that's not bad. Them's good numbers. He could be lucky.'

By now, Grace was used to the strange superstitions Pam's

clients held. 'How come?' she asked, not really believing a word of it.

'His numbers add up to twenty-nine an' if you add them together it makes eleven. Then add them again an' it makes two. Two for joy.'

Before Grace had time to get her head round Lily's explanation, Pam appeared in the hallway, and the woman who had been with her in the parlour scurried out of the front door. Pam waddled into the kitchen. 'Sorry to keep you waiting, Lily, but you know how it is. Some spirits don't want to be contacted.' She gave Grace a grateful smile. 'Thanks for looking after Lily,' she wheezed, and to Lily she said, 'Come on through.'

Grace still hadn't drummed up the courage to let Pam tell her fortune. In truth, she thought it was a lot of nonsense, but suddenly she felt the urge to know what the future might hold. So, later that evening, Michael in bed and she and Pam sitting in the parlour sipping sweet sherry a client had given Pam for a Christmas box, when Pam said, 'Do you fancy a reading?' Grace thought she must have read her mind. 'Go on then,' she said, chuckling and putting aside the cardigan she was knitting for Michael.

Pam picked up the pack of large, beautifully decorated cards from the table and shuffled them. She looked closely at Grace through her small, blue eyes. 'Now before I do the reading I'll tell you what's happened to you in the past. That way you'll know what I see in the cards is true.' She shuffled them again and cut the pack.

Grace gave a cynical smile. She didn't wear it for long.

'You've known great sorrow,' Pam intoned. 'Had your heart broken.'

'Who hasn't?' Grace commented as Pam had closed her eyes and slowly rocked back and forth in her chair, one hand wringing the other.

'I see a man... with wings... he flies high in the sky... he doesn't like what he's doing,' Pam wheezed, her face screwed up as though she was in pain.

A cold shiver trickled down Grace's spine. She wanted to cry 'stop' but the word stuck in her throat. She hadn't mentioned any of this to Pam. She had just told her that Michael's father was no longer part of their lives, and left it at that.

'He's not alone... the sky's black with wings... lots of noise... flashes of fire... it sounds like guns. I think he's laughing... but he could be crying. His eyes are bright blue... like Michael's... but his eyes are sad, very sad,' Pam continued breathily. Then she paused, her head tilted as though she was listening carefully. 'His heart is heavy with the mistakes he's made. He's sorry, very sorry,' she whispered. Her plump body sagged and she sat perfectly still for a long moment as if in a trance. The silence in the room hung like shrouds.

Grace sat rigidly on the edge of her chair, her heart thudding and the palms of her hands moistening. 'Where is he now?' she asked brokenly.

Pam eased her bulk nearer the table and turned a card. 'I don't know,' she said flatly, then after a long, silent pause in which she turned one card then another, 'but the cards are telling me that you're going to meet another man who will make you very happy. You'll travel across the sea and have a good life.' She sat back looking deflated, as though she had used up all her strength.

Grace didn't know what to believe. Her tears were falling thick and fast. Without another word passing between them, Grace stumbled to her feet and went up to her room. Lying on the bed with her son wrapped in her arms she went over all that Pam had told her.

Was Richard sorry? Not as sorry as I am, she told herself as tears dripped from her cheeks into Michael's hair. A tear wet his forehead and he blinked. Grace brushed it away with her fingertip. He gazed up at her, his blue eyes watchful.

Later that night, Grace did something she hadn't done for some time. She dreamed about Richard. The dream was, like most dreams, erratic and confusing. One moment they were walking along a riverbank where geese were flying in a perfect V formation, the next they were in the house in St Patrick's Road, Richard's naked body covering her own as they made love. She felt the heat of skin against skin and savoured the passionate kisses. Then suddenly she was standing on a bleak airfield, a bitter wind chilling her bones as she gazed up into a solid grey sky with not a patch of blue in sight. She woke with a start, her heart racing and her head swimming. The dream was so vivid Grace was shocked to find she was lying in her warm bed in the house in Old Mill Lane.

* * *

On Christmas Day morning, the kitchen was redolent with the smell of roasting rabbit and the sweet scent of mince tart. The rabbit was payment for a reading from one of Pam's clients and the mince from a jar that Pam had found in the bottom drawer of her late mother's dressing table. 'She was always putting stuff by for a special occasion,' she'd cried the day before, waddling into the kitchen her face wreathed in smiles. 'Once she put some apples in the drawer an' forgot about them. By the time she remembered them they'd gone to mush.' Her laughter sounded like dried peas rattling in a tin.

Neighbours dropped in bringing Pam small gifts in appreciation for her services, Grace offering them a tot of sweet sherry and peeling vegetables as she listened to their tales of how Pam had brought them comfort in their times of grief, giving them hope for better things to come.

'Eeh! Do you remember when I came to her just after the army sent me a telegram telling me our Billy wa' missing in action believed dead, an' she told me he was safe in a church in Italy,' Lily said in an awed voice. Then turning to the other neighbours who had all heard it before but were happy to hear it again, she cried, 'An she wa' right. Six weeks later he wrote and said some monks had found him and hidden him till he got back to his unit.'

Pam sat munching on mince pies, a smile on her face.

'Aye, she put my mind at rest when she told me that me mam wa' looking after

our Connie after she got run over by the bus to Darton,' another woman said with tears in her eyes. She caught Grace's eye and added, 'My little lass had just started walking when the angels took her to heaven. You'll have to watch him.' She nodded at Michael in his pram sucking on a crust of bread. 'Once they're on their feet you need eyes in the back of your head.'

Grace promised she'd be careful. She'd grown fond of these outspoken, hard- working, friendly women who believed in omens and signs, and took comfort from the words their dead relatives conveyed to Pam. Most of them were bringing up families on their own whilst their husbands were fighting a war. Many of them worked in munitions, or drove trains, buses and delivery vans. Some worked on the railways, each doing their bit to keep the country functioning in the absence of their men and Grace considered it a privilege to live amongst them.

'Well, that's us,' said Lily getting to her feet and the others following suit. 'I'm off to put the custard on me trifle, an' take me brisket out of the oven.' The other women commented likewise on their Christmas preparations and with shouts of 'Merry Christmas' they went to their own homes.

'I can't remember when I last had such a lovely Christmas,' Grace commented after they had eaten their own dinner.

'Me neither,' said Pam demolishing the last of the Christmas pudding. 'It's lovely when you can share it with friends.' She reached out a plump hand patting Grace's affectionately. 'I'm glad you came to live here.'

'So am I,' said Grace.

Later in the afternoon, Pam's brother and his wife paid a visit. Sydney Armitage was on leave from whatever it was he did in the army. He wasn't on the fighting front. Small, thin and arrogant, he wasn't remotely like his jolly sister. His wife, Sheila, was thin-lipped and peevish. They'd married before the war began but they still had no children for Pam to lavish her affections on.

'You're fatter than ever, Pam,' Sheila said by way of greeting her sister-in-law.

'Good of you to notice, Sheila,' Pam chortled. 'An' a Merry Christmas to you.'

'Have you owt left to eat?' Sydney grunted, roaming the kitchen like a predatory weasel.

Grace made him a sandwich. He looked her up and down as she handed it to him, a gleam in his eye. Grace decided she didn't much like him or his wife. She left them chatting to Pam and went up to her room to put Michael down for a nap. She sat and read until he dozed off.

When she stepped out onto the landing to go to the bathroom, she found Sydney lolling in the doorway. She suspected he'd been there a while. He leered as he pulled a sprig of mistletoe from his tunic's breast pocket. He must have pulled it from out of the bunch of holly and mistletoe hanging in the hallway.

'No use letting it go to waste,' he said lunging towards her. Before Grace could protest, he planted a wet, sticky kiss on her lips. She pushed him away, forcing a laugh but utterly repelled by his sour breath and his outrageous behaviour. Not wanting to cause a scene or bring it to Pam and Sheila's attention she pretended it was just a bit of fun and skipped downstairs. When Pam took Sheila into the parlour for a quick reading, leaving Grace to make a sit-down Christmas Day tea, she found herself playing a game of cat and mouse as Sydney stalked her with his sprig of mistletoe. Thank God he doesn't come here often, she thought, as she and Pam saw them off later that evening.

22

'Ball! Red ball!' Michael demanded, toddling over to Grace at the sink and pulling on the hem of her skirt. He'd been walking independently for a few weeks now and was revelling in his new-found freedom. 'Out, Percy want out,' he lisped, demonstrating yet another of his recent achievements.

Grace dried her hands, her heart swelling. Every day Michael presented her with something new: a word, spooning up his porridge, building a tower of bricks, or tottering after the ball on the grass. In her eyes he was a little miracle, and there were times when she ached for his father to be there to share those wondrous moments. As it was, Auntie Pam celebrated with her as much as if he had been her own. It was a warm, sunny day in September and, as Grace, Michael and Percy the poodle played with the red ball on the grass in the little enclosed back garden behind the house in Old Mill Lane, Grace reflected on what had happened that summer.

In April Hitler had committed suicide in his bunker with Eva Braun by his side, and a week later the Germans had, at long last, admitted defeat and surrendered. The inhabitants of Old Mill Lane, along with the rest of the country, had celebrated in grand style with one street party then another, all the neighbours singing and dancing and sharing whatever food they found in their cupboards. Grace had helped set up the tables down the middle of the road, and baked iced buns and made huge pots of tea. She'd joined in the merriment but all the time in the back of her mind was the thought that Richard's war was also over. She'd wondered if he would come looking for her, then feeling foolish she'd reminded herself that he had no idea where to find her. Now, on the second of September, Japan had finally surrendered and the world was at peace.

'Catch, Michael,' she cried, tossing the ball to him and chuckling with delight as he toddled after it, Percy at his heels. She felt a great surge of happiness, thankful for all she had, but deep down inside there was always that underlying need for something more. She tried not to think about it. But it didn't go away.

One afternoon towards the end of September she was coming back from the shops with the rations, a pitiful amount of butter wrapped in greaseproof paper, three slices of bacon, two eggs and a small bag of sugar barely covering the bottom of her basket. Would rationing ever come to an end, she wondered?

Outside Lily Pickersgill's house a tall, young man in an army greatcoat had just set down his kitbag and was lifting his hand ready to knock the door.

Grace slowed her pace, curious and wanting to share Lily's delight when she answered the door. This must be the son who had been rescued by the monks in Italy. The door opened, and Lily's scream pierced the street. 'Billy! Billy! Oh, my God!' she squealed as the young man swept her up in his arms and swung her clear of the doorway. Laughing and crying, mother and son hugged and jigged on the pavement.

Lily caught sight of Grace. 'Grace! This is our Billy. Home at last.' Lily wiped her cheeks on her apron, and Grace thought: *My goodness! She looks ten years younger than she did yesterday.* She tried to imagine what it would be like if she was parted from her own son for four long years. It didn't bear thinking about.

Billy's grin was wide, but his lean, tanned face still bore the marks of the hardships of fighting for his country. The shadows under his brown eyes and the lines etched around his full mouth had been hard earned. 'So, you're Grace,' he said looking her up and down. 'Mam's mentioned you in her letters.' Grace showed her surprise, and Billy laughed. 'She's kept me well informed of what's gone on in Old Mill Lane while I've been away,' he said, and winked.

'I'll bet she has,' Grace chuckled. 'I suppose you know all our secrets.'

'Not all,' he said, 'but I wouldn't mind getting to know a few more. Maybe you'll go out with me one night so I can hear the rest,' he added roguishly.

Grace was taken aback by the suddenness of his request on such a short acquaintance. Lily giggled. 'Don't mind our Billy,' she said fondly. 'He never was one for letting t'grass grow under his feet.' She linked her arm through his. 'Now, I'm going to get my lad inside an' feed him up. He looks as though he needs it.'

Grace thought that the tall, muscular fellow still smiling at her looked perfectly fit and healthy. 'Welcome home, Billy,' she said and went on her way. As she stepped into her own hallway it occurred to her that if Billy Pickersgill was home from the war, then Richard might also be back. She paused by the hall table and gazed at the telephone. Before she could change her mind, she rang The Grange.

The same voice that had answered her call almost two years ago came down the line. 'Mrs Cecily Carmichael's residence,' it purred. 'May I ask who is calling?'

'Grace Murphy. Is Mr Richard Carmichael at home?'

'Mr Carmichael does not reside here.'

Grace put the telephone on its cradle and stared at the wall.

* * *

'What do you fancy then? *This Happy Breed* is on at the Ritz an' *Champagne Charlie*'s on at the Globe.' Billy Pickersgill took Grace's hand as they walked down Old Mill Lane. There was a sharp nip in the air, and the last of the autumn leaves lay blackened and crushed on the pavement. A cloud of black crows suddenly took flight from the bare branches of a copse of sycamores, cawing harshly as they darkened the sky. Grace was reminded of her second visit to Sprotborough, although this time there was no river, and no Richard. Suddenly, Billy's hand felt foreign.

'I think we'll give *This Happy Breed* a miss,' Grace said. 'It's about the war and we've had enough of that to last a lifetime.'

'You can say that again,' Billy replied heartily, the smoke from his cigarette wafting into Grace's face and making her eyes water.

'Then we'll go and see *Champagne Charlie*. I've heard there's some good songs in it. That's if you like musicals.'

'They're all right,' Billy said unenthusiastically, 'but it's lady's choice.' Grace heard the reluctance in his voice. She knew he was trying to please her. The trouble was he couldn't, not completely, because he wasn't Richard.

This was one of several evenings Grace had accepted Billy's invitation to go to the cinema or out for a walk, or to the Miners' Welfare Club for a drink. The latter being Billy's favourite idea of a night out. He was easy-going, full of fun, and Grace enjoyed his company, and the change of scene. However, try as he might he didn't arouse a romantic spark in her. They'd shared a few goodnight kisses but Grace had been quick to explain she wasn't ready for a full-blown love affair. Billy had reluctantly accepted that and, in between the nights he spent in the Miners' Welfare, he still persisted on seeing her fairly regularly.

Pam thought it was beautifully romantic and encouraged Grace to meet him whenever he asked. Pam had never had a boyfriend, and she lived vicariously through Grace's friendship with Billy. 'If you married him he could move in here and he'd still be near his mam,' she speculated breathily.

'I've no intentions of marrying anyone at the moment,' Grace laughingly protested. 'He's a lovely man – but he drinks a bit too much for my liking – and I don't feel that way about him. I sometimes wish I did.'

'Is it because of that chap that's Michael's dad?' Pam sounded concerned and sad. 'Him what flies the planes?' Grace had since told her about Richard and how he had suddenly gone out of her life.

'I suppose it is,' Grace replied wistfully. 'Maybe I'm meant to be one of those women who only have one great love in their life. You know, the sort you read about. No man I've ever met compares with Richard, and I loved him so much I've none left to give. I'm resigned to being a single woman for the rest of me days.' She grinned. 'I reckon I'll just have to be content with loving Michael.' She glanced out of the window. It was snowing again, another Christmas fast approaching, and it being Michael's first proper Christmas now that he understood the meaning of it Grace and Pam wanted to celebrate in grand style.

One afternoon Pam plodded into the parlour with a box of decorations and a little battered imitation Christmas tree. 'Me mam had these from when I wa' little. They were in t'bottom of her wardrobe,' Pam panted. 'We haven't had 'em up for years, not since me dad died, but we've got to put 'em up for Michael.'

Grace stood on a stool to pin streamers from the corners of the ceiling, criss-crossing them in the centre and hanging a paper lantern where they met. 'Come on, Michael, let's me an' you trim the tree,' Pam wheezed in a complete tizzy, her excitement far surpassing that of Michael's.

Two pairs of pudgy hands got to work, and in no time at all the little tree was so laden with baubles and tinsel that its spindly branches sagged under the weight. 'Isn't that just beautiful?' Pam gasped, heaving herself back on to her feet with the help of the armchair then clapping her hands. Michael clapped his, his blue eyes wide as he gazed entranced by the gaudy, sparkling mish-mash he'd helped to create. Grace fell in love with her son and Pam all over again.

The next day, Pam, who never travelled far from her own doorstep, insisted on going with Grace and Michael to the open market. There, she travelled from stall to stall buying little gifts to put under the tree, most of them for Michael. Grace bought him a wind-up train set. As they made their way back to the bus stop, Pam kept stopping to catch her breath. Puffing and panting, her face was pale under the two bright red spots that burned her cheeks.

'Are you all right, Pam?' Grace's voice was high with anxiety.

''Course I am!' Pam shrugged off the hand Grace had placed under her arm.

'I've just overdone it.' She attempted a giggle that ended in a rattling cough. 'I'm not used to all this walking.'

* * *

Come Christmas Day, Pam appeared to have recovered from the toll the shopping trip had taken, and was her usual jolly self. She squealed with unconcealed delight as Michael tore the wrapping papers from his gifts, and ate a hearty Christmas dinner so Grace ceased worrying.

The only downside during the lovely, festive day was Sydney

and Sheila's annual teatime visit. Once again they inflicted their miserable, carping presence on the house. Later that evening Sheila wanted yet another reading in her pursuit of getting pregnant and she and Pam went into the parlour. Sydney leered at Grace when they found themselves alone, and having no mistletoe as an excuse for a kiss – Grace had deliberately neglected to buy any – he just pushed himself up against her and made do with groping her breast. She slapped his hand.

'Don't be like that,' he hissed wetly in her ear. 'You'll be seeing a lot more of me now that the army don't need me.' He made it sound like a threat. Grace recoiled at the feel of his hot, sour breath on her neck, and roughly pushing him aside she ran upstairs and locked herself in the bathroom. She didn't mention anything about what had gone on between them because the next day Pam took ill.

'I feel awful,' she moaned as she sat hugging the fire in the kitchen, her chest wheezing like an old barrel organ and an unhealthy flush on her cheeks. 'One minute I'm red hot an' the next I'm freezing cold.'

'I'll make you a poultice,' said Grace going to the cupboard for a tin of Kaolin. 'It'll ease your breathing, but you need to be lying down so off you go upstairs and I'll bring it up when it's ready.'

Grace placed the tin in a pan of boiling water to soften the clay and when it was reduced to a paste, she smeared it on two squares of flannel that she'd placed on a warmed tray. Then, with Michael, she went upstairs to Pam's bedroom. 'Shoo, Percy! Shoo!' she cried setting the tray down and waving her hands at the poodle sitting on Pam's chest. 'That'll not help your breathing, Pam, push him off.'

'But he's keeping me company, aren't you, Percy?' Pam wheezed then giggled as his little tongue lapped her chins. 'He's licking me better.' Grace snorted her opinion. Reluctantly, Pam shoved the little dog off the bed and he gambolled over to Michael who dropped to his knees rolling on the carpet with Percy.

Grace applied a poultice to Pam's chest above her mountainous bosom and the other on her back. 'Ouch!' Pam yelped. 'They're bloody red hot.'

'They're meant to be,' Grace said sternly. 'Now, lie still and rest. I'll bring you a cup of tea and a biscuit in a couple of minutes.'

'Three biscuits, please.' Pam's eyes glinted mischievously. She'd grown used to Grace rationing the amount of sweet stuff she ate.

* * *

Nineteen forty-six announced itself with a vengeance, thick snow falling for several days. During that time Grace concocted every treatment at her disposal to ease Pam's congested chest. During the day she held her head whilst Pam breathed in the steam from a bowl filled with hot water and a few drops of camphorated oil, and at night she slapped on the Kaolin poultices. Grace insisted that she spent most of the day in bed, Pam grumbling and Grace turning away disgruntled clients looking for a reading to find out what the New Year had in store for them.

'Pooh! They stink bloody awful,' Pam gasped one night as Grace covered her back and chest with the clay-smeared flannel, 'I feel like a blooming sandwich. Talking of which. Can I have a jam sandwich for me supper?'

Grace laughed at her incorrigible landlady. 'What will it take for you to lose your appetite? You can have a spoonful of this instead.' She lifted the bottle of foul-tasting linctus she'd bought on the chemist's advice.

'You're downright cruel, you are,' said Pam, but she was smiling. Then suddenly serious she added, 'But you're awful good to me.'

'Likewise,' Grace replied. 'I bless the day I came to live here with you.'

* * *

By mid-January, Pam seemed well enough to start seeing her customers again, but she tired very quickly and Grace insisted on her seeing the doctor. He was new to the surgery, very young and extremely brisk. He gave Pam a cursory examination. 'You need to lose weight,' he said, his hand hovering over the bell he used to call in the next patient. Grace wasn't satisfied.

'Maybe a more thorough investigation might...' She got no further. The doctor pinged his bell and an elderly man on sticks clattered into the surgery. 'Good day, Miss Armitage,' the doctor said dismissively and Pam waddled out of the room, a mutinous look on her face. Grace had no alternative but to follow her.

'See, I told you it would be a waste of time,' Pam said crossly. 'I don't need him to tell me I'm fat. I've allus been fat.'

Once word got round that Pam was well again, the superstitious, the desperate and the downright nosy came in droves having missed their weekly fix of news from the other side. No amount of persuasion on Grace's part would convince Pam to turn them away. Late one afternoon she plodded out of the parlour looking absolutely drained. 'I feel lousy,' she moaned. 'Me head's aching an' I've got this pain in me chest.'

'What did I tell you?' Grace's anger made her speak in a way she had never before done to Pam. 'I told you it wasn't wise to take on so much but you wouldn't listen. From now on, I'm turning them away no matter how much they beg to see you.'

Shocked by Grace's harsh words, Pam's eyes filled with tears. She looked like a little girl who'd been caught with her hand in the sweetie jar. Grace immediately felt contrite. 'I'm sorry, Pam. I'm saying it for your own good. Now, go and lie down on the couch in the parlour and get some rest. And don't answer the door to anyone.' Pam wheezed and smiled, saying she'd be right as rain in a few days; she'd had attacks like this before. But Grace was worried.

Pam settled on the couch with Percy tucked in beside her. Grace fetched a blanket and when she went back Pam was sleeping. Back in the kitchen Grace looked out at the deep, pristine blanket of snow covering the back garden.

She'd been so busy attending to Pam that Michael had been stuck indoors for days. He was missing out on the pleasure of it.

'Let's make a snowman,' she said, wrapping him up warmly in dungarees and a thick, tweed coat she'd bought on the open market. It was second-hand but hardly worn. He looked a proper little man in it.

'Pam come,' he yelled as Grace popped a woolly hat over his thick, fair hair. The hat had earflaps and she was suddenly reminded of the helmet Richard had worn when he was riding his motorbike. Her breath caught in her throat, and the aching pang in her chest left her thinking that she would live the rest of her life with painful memories of Richard Carmichael.

But today we'll make new memories, she thought, bundling Michael out into the garden then beginning to roll a ball of snow. 'Like this, Michael, make a big ball for his head,' she sang out. Michael began to form a snowball. Watching him, Grace thought how fortunate she was to be able to share days like this with her son, for at his age almost everything was new and wonderful.

'Pam come. Get Pam,' Michael yelled again as he threw soft snow up into the air. It fluttered down round him, and he stuck out his tongue to catch the flakes.

'Pam can't play today,' Grace said, her face clouding with concern. 'She's got to rest and keep warm.' Michael threw a handful of snow at Grace and she threw one back. Then she made a pile of snowballs and to his delight she encouraged him to pelt her with them. Laughing and shouting and covered in snow they stayed out for almost an hour before they went back indoors. Michael's snowman was now wearing a bright red scarf with a carrot for a nose. 'I mind him,' Michael said, so Grace left him in the open doorway. Pulling off her coat she hurried into the parlour.

Pam lay under the blanket, her face pale and sweaty. Grace placed her cold hand on Pam's forehead and felt the heat pulsing from her moist skin. Pam stirred drowsily, her breath rasping in her chest, and the mucus filling her airways made a sickening gurgle that increased Grace's anxiety. Chastising herself for leaving her unattended for so long Grace softly urged, 'Pam, love! Pam! Listen to me. I'm going to ring the hospital for an ambulance. You need to go to Beckett's straight away.'

Pam mumbled something unintelligible. Grace ran to the telephone. This wasn't just a chest infection. Grace cursed her own ineptitude as she dialled the hospital. *For God's sake I'm a nurse. I should have recognised the signs.*

The ambulance arrived, the ambulance men struggling as they carried Pam down the narrow hallway, Grace crying, 'Don't bump her head against the walls.'

'She's a rare weight,' one of them huffed. 'She's heavier than that old sideboard of me mother's that I moved last week when she wa' cleaning.'

It angered Grace to hear her dear friend being compared to a bulky old piece of furniture. Michael began to wail. Grace lifted him and followed the ambulance men out into the street. The ambulance had attracted the neighbours' attention and they stood on their doorsteps watching as the men loaded Pam inside.

'Is she in a bad way?' Lily Pickersgill shouted to Grace.

'Bad enough,' Grace called back, tears stinging her eyes. She climbed in beside Pam curtly saying, 'I'm going with her,' when one of the ambulance men gave her a funny look. Only when they arrived at Beckett's did Grace realise that she wasn't wearing her coat. She thanked God that Michael was still wearing his outdoor clothes. She was freezing.

They sat in the corridor, Michael fascinated and uncomplaining as he watched white-coated doctors and nurses in uniforms like his mam sometimes wore going up and down the corridor on soft-soled shoes, and in and out of doors that they always closed firmly behind them. An hour passed without anyone letting Grace know how Pam was faring.

'Hello, Grace, what are you doing here?' A nurse whom Grace had worked with on some of the shifts she'd covered stopped when she saw her. She glanced at Michael. 'It's obviously not for him,' she said, smiling at his rosy cheeks. 'He looks to be in tip-top condition.'

'It's Pamela Armitage, my landlady,' Grace said. 'I think she's got pneumonia.' She shook her head, annoyed with herself for not spotting it sooner.

'That'll be Fat Pam you're talking about, the one that tells the fortunes,' the nurse said knowingly.

Grace nodded. 'Can you find out what's happening? I'm awfully worried about her but I can't stay here too long – not with Michael.'

'I'll see if there's any news.' The nurse walked briskly down the corridor.

She came back ten minutes later, frowning. 'It's not looking good,' she said, in that pragmatic way nurses talk to one another about their patients. 'Her lungs are full of fluid, and Dr Griffiths is concerned about her heart. All that weight you know.'

Grace nodded again. She thought of all the biscuits and cream buns Pam devoured albeit Grace had tried to persuade her to avoid them. I should have been firmer, she thought, but it was hard to get tough with Pam. She was such a lovable, innocent girl that even when people said the most insulting things about her size, she just agreed with them and laughed it off.

Eventually, a weary-looking young doctor came to speak to

Grace. 'Don't blame yourself,' he said when Grace told him about the Kaolin poultices and the steaming bowls of camphorated oil. 'You did your best, but it's not her chest that's the problem. It's her heart. It can't cope with both the infection *and* the toll her weight puts on it. I'm surprised she hasn't had a heart attack before now.'

Grace froze. Poor Pam. She loved life and lived it to the full in her own sweet way, quite content as long as she could eat what she liked, give hope and comfort with her readings, and have plenty of friends to keep her company. She never grumbled at not being able to get about as easily as other people, she didn't moan that life was unfair, she just filled every day by being happy and making those around her happy too.

'We'll keep her here, see how she does,' the doctor said, his mind already on other matters. Grace thanked him and, carrying a very sleepy Michael in her arms, she left the hospital and took a taxi back home. The dreadful occasion seemed to merit such an expense, that and it had started snowing again and Grace had no coat.

She'd no sooner alighted from the cab than several doors in the street opened. 'How is she?' Lily shouted sounding very concerned. She had clearly been keeping an eye out, as had half the street so it appeared. Grace told them what the doctor had said as they gathered round.

Lily pursed her lips. 'Her dad went t'same way. He wa' only forty-one. Alfie Armitage wa' allus a big fat lad, wa'n't he?' She glanced at her neighbours for confirmation. They nodded in agreement, their faces solemn. Everybody loved Pam.

Grace went into the house which felt strangely empty. She heated up some stew left over from the day before, and after feeding Michael and getting him ready for bed she ate a little of it herself but the food stuck in her throat. The house wasn't the same without Pam.

Sitting alone in the parlour, Michael upstairs sleeping, she felt totally bereft. Billy Pickersgill had finally got the message that his romance with Grace was going nowhere, and shortly after getting a job as a coalminer at Redbrook pit he'd taken up with the sister of one of his workmates. Grace missed his company but she was happy for him and they remained friends. Now she desperately felt the need for someone to hold her and comfort her, someone who would stand by her and ease the pain of what, she was fairly certain would be dark days ahead.

23

The huge crowd of neighbours, friends and clients trudged from the cemetery leaving behind the newly dug plot, its fresh, black soil a raw symbol of their grief. The recent snows had turned to blackened slush, the pavements hazardous as the mourners made their way through the rain to the Miners' Welfare Club to celebrate Fat Pam's life.

Grace lingered by the grave, Michael at her side, and oblivious to the drizzling rain she shared one last moment with her dear friend. Pam's big, kind heart had failed and she had died peacefully with Grace at her side, Grace's slender hand clasped inside Pam's fat, pudgy fingers that had gradually loosened their grip as she slipped away. She had witnessed many deaths in her job but none had affected her quite as much as Pam's.

The days following Pam's death had been a nightmare. In the immediate days before Pam's passing Grace had informed Sydney that his sister was gravely ill. He hadn't made an effort to visit Pam in hospital, but once Grace notified him of her death, he'd barged into the house in Old Mill Lane and taken over.

'How much money did she leave?' was his first question. 'Did she leave enough to bury her?' was the second. Grace, shocked and disgusted by his lack of compassion, told him she didn't know. Pam's financial affairs were none of her business. 'Well, I'm not spending any of my hard-earned cash on a big send off,' Sydney had continued, 'so give me her death certificate an' I'll go an' see if she has owt in t'bank.'

Grace hadn't bothered to hide her derision. 'She never went to the bank. I think she kept her money in her bedroom,' she'd snapped.

Sydney had barged upstairs returning with a biscuit tin. 'There's enough to bury her twice over,' he'd smirked tucking the tin under his arm and leaving.

Now, as Grace walked to the cemetery gates, she saw Sydney and Sheila waiting for her. She didn't feel in the least like having anything to do with them but it was unavoidable.

'I'll be wanting a word wi' you after we've been to t'Miners' Welfare,' Sydney said bluntly. 'There's things to discuss.'

The Club was packed with mourners glad to be out of the rain as they helped themselves to the repast Grace had made earlier. Sydney had refused to pay for a proper funeral breakfast so Grace had made large quantities of vegetable soup and bought crusty loaves that she'd sliced into small chunks and then taken to the Club that morning.

'Eeh! She'll be sorely missed,' and 'She wa' a beautiful soul wa' Fat Pam,' were the phrases on every tongue as Grace moved amongst them in the Club's lounge. She agreed and commiserated, all the while longing to escape back to the house yet not wanting to go there to be confronted by Sydney. At one point she found herself standing next to him and Sheila. He gave Grace a greasy smile.

'You stay here, love, an' see to things,' he said to Sheila. 'Grace an' me have a few things to discuss down at the house.' Sheila nodded obediently.

Sydney took Grace by the elbow. She shook him off. 'Can't it wait?' she said, dreading the thought of being alone with him.

'No, it bloody can't,' he muttered. 'I hold all the cards now, an' it'll pay you to keep on the right side of me.'

Her heart in her boots, Grace went and asked Lily if she'd mind looking after Michael for a while. Feeling slightly sick, Grace followed Sydney down the street. He muttered impatiently as she fished for the door key in her handbag. Locking the door was something she'd taken to doing since Pam's death to prevent Sydney from barging in on her. Prior to that, like most of their neighbours, they'd left the door unlocked. In fact, it would be fair to say that some householders in Old Mill Lane would have had difficulty finding their keys it was that long since they'd used them. They trusted their neighbours. But Grace didn't trust Sydney.

She marched down the hall into the kitchen, her back straight as a ramrod. Keeping her coat on, she went and stood with her back to the sink, her arms folded across her chest. 'Well,' she said, her gaze challenging.

He came and stood in front of her, near enough for her to smell his sweaty armpits. He gave a simpering, smile. 'Now, Grace, love, let's me an' you get down to business,' he said, his voice as thick as treacle. 'You do understand that now Pam's dead the house belongs to me, don't you?'

Grace gave a curt nod. Sydney moved a step closer.

'Well, I've been doing a bit of thinking.' He dragged out the words suggestively. 'If you want to carry on living here an' paying the same rent as you gave our Pam then you're going to have to be a lot nicer to me.' The leer on his weasel-like face made Grace's stomach churn.

'Whatever do you mean?' Her insides turned to water as she digested the full import of what he was suggesting.

'Oh, Grace, stop playing hard to get,' he sneered. 'You know I've fancied you from the start, an' you must be lonely for a bit of...' He winked lasciviously. 'So, like I say, you'll be doin' yourself a favour if me an' you can be good friends.'

Grace shuddered. She had no intention of being Sydney's 'good friend' but she had to think of Michael. She couldn't suddenly uproot him without somewhere to go. She needed time to find somewhere else for them to live. Her heart was hammering against her ribs but her mind was crystal clear. She cast her eyes down to the floor and gave a shy, little smile.

'This is all a bit sudden, Sydney. I didn't know you had feelings for me. I'll need time to get my head round it.' She raised her gaze to meet his and fluttered her eyelashes pathetically. 'It's been a long time since I...' She hoped the blush she was trying to muster to her cheeks looked suitably convincing.

Sydney's smirk was triumphant. 'Oh, I've got more than just feelings for you, Grace,' he drawled seductively pressing himself up against her. Grace flinched as the edge of the sink bit into her back. 'Now, how's about me an' you seal our bargain with a little kiss to be going on wi'?'

His breath was foul with stale beer, and Grace struggled to prevent herself from gagging as his thin, wet lips smothered hers. The kiss seemed to last an eternity, and when he let her go, he grinned lasciviously. 'There, that wasn't too bad was it?' He fondled her breast. 'Now, think on, I'll not wait too long. You know what you've got to do.'

Rigid with humiliation but bent on playing the game, Grace managed a feeble smile, but the urge to vomit and wash her mouth clean was so strong that she simply nodded her head in reply.

'Right, I'd best be off. Sheila dun't like to be kept waiting.' He walked into the hallway, and as he reached the front door he removed the key from where Grace had placed it on the inside of the lock. 'I'll take this with me so I can let meself in whenever I feel like it. You can go in an' out the back. I'll be round tomorrow.'

Grace had no fight left in her. 'I'm working in the hospital tomorrow and Friday,' she mumbled.

After he'd gone she raced upstairs and in the bathroom she scrubbed her face until it stung. Then, on leaden feet and her mind working overtime, she went back to the Miners' Welfare to collect Michael.

'I've two shifts at the hospital to cover,' she told Lily, 'tomorrow and Friday. Will you look after Michael for me?'

''Course I will, love. He's not a bit of bother,' Lily replied. 'He can play with our Marlene's kids. I'm minding her two youngest for her.'

That night, before she went to bed, Grace propped a chair firmly under the knob on the front door. Key or no key, she wasn't letting Sydney Armstrong creep in on her whenever he liked. Lying in bed unable to sleep, she was tempted to pack their belongings and flee. But she couldn't do that to Michael. Above all, she had to make the move seem as natural as possible. She didn't want her son's early years marred by being dragged from pillar to post as his mother fled from one place to another in order to avoid the consequences of her life. She wanted him to have stability, a home, to grow up with friends around him and never have the worry of wondering where he would lay his head at night.

She climbed out of bed, and pushing back the damp tendrils of hair sticking to her brow, she crossed to the window and gazed out into the empty street. The stars glinted brightly in the purple night sky and as her eyes roamed the constellations she thought of what she must do. First, she'd have to find alternative accommodation. That could take days if not weeks, she mused sadly, the prospect of finding somewhere to live as far distant as Orion's Belt. And worst of all, she'd have to keep Sydney at arm's length until she and Michael could make their escape. The Pole Star winked back at her as if agreeing with her plans. Taking it as a good omen and feeling thoroughly exhausted she went back to bed and fell into a deep sleep.

Morning came too soon. The house felt strange without Pam's presence, and Michael constantly asking 'Where's Auntie Pam?' didn't help matters.

'Gone to live with the angels, darling,' Grace told him as she set a dish of porridge in front of him. She'd tried to explain as gently as she could why Pam wasn't coming back but something so unthinkable was beyond Michael's comprehension.

'Don't want it,' he said rebelliously, sticking out his bottom lip and banging his spoon on the table. Grace's spirits sank. Was this a portent of things to come? Michael was already unsettled by Pam's death. How on earth would he cope when they had to leave the only home he'd ever really known? She watched as he slid off his chair and trotted into the parlour in search of Pam.

He found Percy lolled morosely on the blanket on the couch that Grace had wrapped Pam in on the day she had gone into hospital. Michael climbed up beside the dog and laid his cheek against Percy's curly fur. Leaving the untouched breakfast, Grace went into the parlour, her heart lurching when she saw her unhappy little boy and an equally unhappy poodle.

She knelt down by the couch, stroking thick, fair hair with one hand and knotted, white curls with the other. She wanted to cry but that wouldn't help, so swallowing her tears she lifted Percy and helped Michael to his feet. 'Come on, you two. Mam's got to go to work. Lily's going to mind you today.'

Michael clung to her skirt, his bright, blue eyes filling with tears. Grace saw Richard's eyes. That's how they'd looked on the night he had come to her after his father's funeral: the night Michael had been conceived. She put Percy down and gathered her son in her arms.

'Barry and Joan are at their Granny Lily's,' she whispered against Michael's hair in a desperate attempt to lighten the situation. 'You can play with them.' Instantly, Michael perked up and wriggled from her arms. Isn't it marvellous the way little children can so easily forget their grief? she thought, as she followed Michael into the hall. And it's perhaps as well they can, she told herself as she helped him into his coat.

'He wouldn't eat his breakfast,' Grace told Lily as she dropped Michael off at her door, 'and I'm afraid you've got Percy as well.'

'The more the merrier,' Lily chortled as her daughter Marlene's children came rushing to the door. Barry scooped up Percy and Joan took Michael's hand. He went inside without a backward glance. At least, someone's happy, Grace thought as she hurried down Old Mill Lane to catch the bus to Beckett's hospital.

* * *

'You're in with the geriatrics today, Staff Murphy,' the Charge Nurse told her briskly. 'Report to Sister Venables on ward fourteen.'

When Grace arrived at the ward, Sister Venables introduced her to the nurse on duty. 'This is Nurse Dunne. Unfortunately, there's just the two of you. The rest of my nurses are off with the flu so you'll be kept busy.' She marched off.

Grace smiled at Nurse Dunne and said, 'Grace Murphy.'

'I'm Irene,' Nurse Dunne said with a grin, 'but don't be calling me that in front of Venables. She can be a right cow.'

'I know what you mean. I've come across her sort before.'

They went into the sluice and began preparing the bowls of washing water. 'Have you nursed geriatrics before?' Irene asked.

'Once or twice,' Grace admitted. 'I'm trained in midwifery but here I step in wherever I'm needed. I quite like nursing the elderly. It's not as rewarding as maternity but it's similar in some ways.

Spoon-feeding, washing and toileting patients at the end of their lives isn't all that different from bottle-feeding babies and caring for their mothers.'

Irene laughed. 'I can see I'm going to like working with you.' They loaded the bowls of warm water onto trolleys and wheeled them into the ward.

'Watch out for Miss Cotterill in the end bed,' Irene said, as they began their rounds. 'She can be a right cranky bitch. A bit too quick with her hands, is that one. She gave me a right clout yesterday.'

Grace glanced down the ward. Most of the patients were still huddled under the covers, but in the end bed a rather imperious-looking woman was sitting up reading, her glasses perched on the end of her sharp nose and her iron-grey hair immaculately rolled. An exotic silk shawl draped her shoulders. 'She looks like the Queen of Sheba,' Grace giggled.

'She bloody acts like her,' Irene snorted.

'What's she in for?'

'Broken femur. It should have been her neck.'

Grace moved from bed to bed, waking the occupants then washing wrinkled faces and shrivelled hands, brushing hair and putting in false teeth. Eventually, she arrived at the end bed. 'Miss Prudence Cotterill' she read on the card fastened to the bed head.

'Good morning, Miss Cotterill, I'm Staff Nurse Murphy, how are you this morning?' Grace smiled warmly into eyes as hard as brushed steel. A withering look met this pleasantry and was accompanied by a disdainful sniff.

'How am I? You might well ask,' Prudence scorned. 'Not that you are all that interested, I'm sure. But seeing as how you've taken the trouble, I'll tell you. I'm hungry, bored witless, and tired of being treated like an imbecile.' Her cultured articulation was like gravel washing over stones.

'I'm sorry to hear that,' Grace replied calmly. 'Now, will you wash yourself or would you like me to do it for you?'

'Thank goodness for that!' Prudence barked. 'At last, someone who has the wit to realise that I'm not completely incapable. The other fools seem to think that because I've broken my damned leg that I've lost the use of the rest of my body, not to mention my faculties.' She snatched the dampened flannel Grace held out and began rubbing her face vigorously. Grace proffered a towel then rinsed the cloth and handed it back. Prudence wiped her gnarled, swollen knuckles. 'Arthritis,' she snapped tossing the cloth back to Grace.

'Breakfast will be served shortly,' Grace said, 'and in the meantime is there anything else I can do to make you comfortable?'

Prudence laughed harshly. 'My goodness, I do believe you really care.'

'I do,' said Grace. 'It's my job to care. Now, if there's nothing more I'll press on.' She wheeled her trolley away.

Prudence Cotterill watched her go, a glint of admiration in her eye.

'How did you get on with Shrewdence Prudence?' Irene was washing the bowls in the sluice and Grace drying them as they waited for the arrival of the breakfast trolleys. 'Did she start carping about wanting to go home?'

'No, but she told me she was bored witless. Looking at her I'd say she was pretty active before she broke her leg, and her mind's as sharp as a razor.'

'So is her tongue,' Irene sneered. 'I wouldn't want to be the one looking after her when she goes home. Her nephew'll have a job finding somebody who'll put up with her.' She washed the last of the bowls and handed it to Grace. 'He's put a notice up on the board in the foyer asking for a live-in nurse. He asked me if I knew of anybody who might be interested. He says it's not just until she gets back on her feet, it's a long-term companion he's looking for. If he gets one to stay more than a week he'll be lucky.'

'Where does she live?' Grace was intrigued.

'Cawthorne.'

The rattle of the trolleys alerting them, they hurried out to begin serving breakfasts.

'Are you not going to force-feed me spoonful by spoonful, nurse?' Prudence hooted when Grace set a dish of porridge on the table over the bed.

'I don't think that's necessary, do you?' Grace replied briskly and moved on.

Before she left the hospital that evening, she made a telephone call. Nigel Cotterill agreed to meet her after work the next day.

* * *

Grace had just put Michael to bed, and back downstairs in the kitchen she made a cup of tea and sat cogitating on the scant information Prudence Cotterill's nephew had imparted during the brief telephone conversation. He had sounded anxious and rather desperate, and Grace was now questioning the wisdom of applying for the post. But, she told herself, as she sipped her tea, it offered accommodation and a more than generous salary. Beggars couldn't be choosers.

Weary after her first day on the geriatrics ward and aware that she had another shift the next day, she decided to have an early night and sleep on her problems. She had just put on her night-dress when she heard the rattle at the front door.

She froze. Oh, my God, she'd forgotten to wedge the chair under the doorknob.

She glanced at Michael sleeping soundly in the cot beside her bed. She couldn't risk Sydney coming into the bedroom. At the foot of the stairs, she almost collided with him as he loped out of the parlour and into the hallway.

'I wa' looking for you, an' it looks like you were expecting me,' he said lasciviously, eyeing her state of undress.

Grace crossed her arms protectively over her chest, silently cursing her decision to have an early night. Although her nightdress was made from thick winceyette and covered her from neck to toe, she felt naked.

'What are you doing here?' she hissed. 'Creeping into my house uninvited.'

'I think you're forgetting yourself, love,' he leered, 'this is my house an' I'll come an' go as I please.' Catching her by the elbow he pulled her into the parlour. Grace wrenched her arm free.

'Keep your voice down! My little boy's sleeping.'

Sydney smirked. 'We'll not be disturbed then.'

Grace's mind in turmoil, she sought to placate him, hold him off for as long as she could. 'I'm not ready for anything serious,' she gabbled, 'it's been a long time since I...' She flailed for words. 'You have to give me time.'

Sydney gave a grim chuckle. 'You mean just make do wi' a few kisses an' cuddles, is that it?' he sneered. 'I'm not a bloody schoolboy.'

Before she could prevent it, Grace found herself sprawled underneath him on the couch. He plastered her face with wet kisses and fondled her breasts through her nightdress, Grace choking down bile as she frantically struggled to get him off. Then, lowering his hand he yanked at the hem of her gown. 'Let's have this off,' he growled bundling her nightdress up to her chin pressing it against her throat. 'Ooh, lovely, lovely,' he gloated as with his free hand he began fiddling with the buttons on his trousers.

Panic rising inside her, Grace wanted to scream but she was finding it difficult to breathe. His trousers undone he grabbed

Grace's hand, placing it on his manhood and holding it there. In a detached manner, Grace wondered if the clammy, flaccid thing was the reason Sheila had never got pregnant. Then, pretending to be going along with him she clutched it tight.

'That's better,' he panted, 'keep going.'

'Oh! Oh! Oh!' Grace moaned loudly. Then, letting go of his penis, she let her arm fall away and her head loll to one side as she faked a fainting fit. I should have been an actress, she thought, as she lay inert, trying to still her breathing and look unconscious.

'Bloody hell!' Sydney scrabbled to his feet pulling up his trousers. 'What's wrong wi' you?'

Grace lay still for a moment longer then slowly opened her eyes. 'Where am I?' she slurred. 'What happened?'

Sydney was shaking. 'You went all funny on me,' he croaked. He looked pathetic with his shirt tails hanging out and his sparse, mousey hair standing on end. In different circumstances Grace would have laughed.

'I'm sorry, Sydney,' she mumbled. 'It must have been shock. I did tell you I wasn't ready.' She struggled to sit up, pretending to feel woozy.

Sydney stuffed in his shirt tails angrily. Grace knew that he was feeling cheated and embarrassed. She smiled inwardly as he struggled to reassert his arrogance. 'Aye, well, you'd better be ready next time,' he growled. 'I don't want any of this bloody fainting malarkey. If you want to stay here, you'd better get used to it.'

He stamped from the room and out of the front door. Adjusting her nightdress, Grace smiled grimly. *But that's just it, Sydney, I've no intentions of staying here.* He'd made her mind up for her. If the interview tomorrow went well, she'd take the job no matter how awkward and demanding Prudence Cotterill might be.

* * *

'What are you reading, Miss Cotterill?' Making it her business to find out as much as she could about her prospective employer Grace put the bowl of washing water on the bedside table and gave an enquiring smile.

Startled by the question, Prudence pushed her glasses up her nose and replied, 'Graham Greene.' She held up the copy of *The Power and the Glory*.

'I've not read that one,' Grace said, wringing out a facecloth, 'but I enjoyed his *Stamboul Train.*

Prudence looked even more surprised. 'You read Graham Greene?' she said, her shocked tone letting Grace know that she had underestimated her intelligence.

'And Hemingway and Steinbeck.' Grace handed her the facecloth.

Further brief conversations that day prompted Prudence to divulge that she liked classical music, efficiency in all things, and she didn't suffer fools gladly. During these exchanges, Grace wasn't the only one who was making an assessment. Prudence also was doing some evaluating. The young nurse clearly had a lively, intelligent mind that she hitherto hadn't equated with someone in her profession. She also liked Grace's forthright manner and the calm, assured no-fuss-and-nonsense way she responded to her own backbiting comments and snappish complaints.

At the end of her shift, Grace went to meet Prudence's nephew, Nigel Cotterill. They sat in the hospital foyer, Nigel irritable as he outlined the detail of what the job entailed. He was a scholarly looking man in his forties with an unfortunate nervous tic in his right eye. Grace could tell he wasn't enjoying the task he was faced with. She tried to put him at ease.

'You're not the first nurse we've employed to care for her,' he said uncomfortably. 'Aunt Prudence had a fall last year and broke her arm. None of the nurses we employed lasted longer than a month,' he continued, 'but it's imperative that she has someone to care for her now that she's immobile. Once she's back on her feet we would like you to stay on as a companion, thereby ensuring she doesn't have any further accidents.' He looked hopefully at Grace.

'I've only just recently met your aunt, but from what I know of her I think we might work well together,' said Grace, giving him an encouraging smile.

Nigel's eyes popped. 'Do you really?' He gazed intently into Grace's eyes wanting to believe her. 'I think it only fair to warn you she can be rude and inclined to lash out if she doesn't get her own way.'

'I'm already aware of that. Invalids often get frustrated. It's up to those who are nursing them to handle the situation carefully and ease their frustrations. There are all manner of ways of doing that.' Nigel liked the sound of that.

'However,' Grace continued, 'I have a son, and if I'm to live in I would want him to live with me.' She held her breath awaiting his response.

Nigel's face fell. 'How old is he?'

'He's two, and whilst you might see it as a drawback, I don't. A young child can have a positive effect on the wellbeing of an older person.' Grace then went on to expound her theory, bringing to bear every resource in her armoury to secure a home and an income to support her and her son.

Nigel's misgivings were easily dispelled. 'They're discharging Aunt Prudence the day after tomorrow. When can you start?'

'Immediately.' Grace's heart soared. 'I could move in tomorrow and prepare for Miss Cotterill's homecoming.' She was sitting with her hands resting in her lap looking perfectly calm and efficient but her insides were roiling with relief, and triumph. She'd swung it.

'Splendid!' Nigel stood. 'I'll call for you early tomorrow and move you and your belongings in my car.'

Grace couldn't believe her good fortune.

* * *

'Me an' Michael are leaving tomorrow, first thing. I know it's a bit sudden but something's cropped up and I have to go immediately,' she told Lily when she collected Michael.

'Eeh! I'm sorry, lass. Is it a death? Are you going back to Ireland?' Lily's face crumpled sympathetically.

Letting her believe that, and not wanting to besmirch Pam's memory by telling Lily about Sydney's unseemly behaviour, Grace said, 'I'll be sorry to go. I've loved living here and I want you to know how grateful I am for your friendship. Let everybody else know, Lily. Tell them I'll miss them. Thanks for everything.'

'You'll be missed,' Lily said tearfully, 'you're one of us, an' you've allus been on hand to tell us what do when somebody's not well.' This was true, for Grace had frequently offered advice and helped nurse neighbours suffering minor ailments.

Lily hugged and kissed Michael then Grace. Grace walked the few paces back to the house all the while wondering if she was jumping out of the frying pan into the fire.

To allay Michael's fears, Grace made a game out of packing. 'We're going on a big adventure like Mr Rabbit in your storybook so I want you to put your toys in this bag. Then you'll have them to play with in our new home,' she said putting her suitcases and bags on the bed then waiting nervously for his reaction. Michael frowned. A flutter of panic clutched her insides. How much did he understand? His face broke into a big smile. 'Mr Rabbit and my truck,' he said.

'That's right, darling, your truck and your bricks, and don't forget your ball.' Back and forth he trotted dropping his toys into the bag whilst Grace packed clothes and books and all the para-

phernalia they had acquired in their time at Pam's. Thank goodness
Nigel Cotterill had offered to help her transport it, she thought
looking at the bulging bags and suitcases.

'Percy come,' Michael said lifting the tiny dog that all this time
had been lying
        on the bed watching with his little, currant-bun eyes.

Grace gasped. She'd forgotten all about Percy. Michael was
cradling the dog in his arms, his cheek resting against Percy's knotted, white head. He'd be heartbroken if they had to leave the dog
behind. 'Yes, Percy can come too,' she said. If Prudence Cotterill
objected, she'd find the dog a new home, but for now she'd take her
chances.

'Time for you to get some sleep,' she said ruffling Michael's hair.
'We've an early start in the morning.'

She put him into his pyjamas and tucked him into bed. Percy
settled down on top of the quilt at Michael's feet. Grace fetched
Michael a cup of warm milk and biscuits for him and the dog. As he
ate his snack she told him the Mr Rabbit story. Michael handed her
his empty cup and looked at her, his sleepy blue eyes searching her
face.

'Where I going?' he asked drowsily.

Grace thought on her feet. 'To a lovely house with a big garden
for you and Percy to play in,' she replied enthusiastically. Nigel had
said 'Cawthorne's a very pretty village and the house is quite roomy
so you'll have plenty of space for you and your son.' Grace had
pictured a large house standing in its own gardens and plenty of
trees. She went back downstairs hoping she was right.

She began tidying the rooms. She wouldn't let the odious
Sydney Armitage say she had left the house in a mess. As she
dusted chalk ornaments on the mantelpiece and plumped cushions
she thought of Pam. The Tarot cards were still sitting on the table
where Pam had left them. Grace picked them up and slipped them

into her apron pocket as a reminder of her wonderful friend with a wonderful gift.

Waiting for the kettle to boil for a bedtime drink she locked the back door and wedged the chair firmly under the knob on the front door then propped the hall table up against it for good measure. If Sydney came back tonight, he'd have to break his way in. As she sipped a cup of cocoa her thoughts dwelt on the impending move. How many more would they make before they finally settled in one place they could call home, she wondered, or was this to be the pattern of their lives? A few months or a year in one place then off again in search of the impossible dream. Sad and weary, she climbed the stairs. In bed, staring up at the ceiling she whispered, 'Where are you now, Richard, when we need you?'

24

Richard Carmichael was in London, sitting in the lounge bar of a club in Lower Regent Street that was popular with ex-service men. He was on his third whisky. Since leaving the RAF he had spent many aimless hours in places like this, and although he had more or less got his desire for strong drink under control, he was still plagued by the bitter memories he struggled to obliterate.

'Same again, Carmichael?' Philip Montgomery shoved back his chair ready to go to the bar.

'Not for me, Monty.' Richard placed his hand over the top of his glass. 'I'm meeting Helen. We're going to that new Italian place in Covent Garden.'

Monty winked mischievously. 'You've been seeing quite a bit of her lately, old chap, is there something I should know?'

Richard frowned. 'Nothing like that, but you know how it is.' He shrugged.

The sardonic leer on Monty's face disappeared and was replaced with a look of compassionate understanding. 'I do,' he said. 'We were the lucky ones.'

'I suppose we were.' There was more than a hint of doubt in

Richard's voice. Monty roamed off to the bar to replenish his drink and Richard emptied his glass. It was time to go and meet Helen Rigsby, the widow of his best buddy, Bill Rigsby, or Rigs as his pals had called him. Rigs had been killed in action over the English Channel. His death, and that of Peter Hepworth – Heppy to his pals – had changed Richard's life and he couldn't find the man he had been before their deaths, a man who was worthy of the love of a woman as wonderful as Grace Murphy. She deserved better than the bitter, twisted wreck he had become and he'd let her go. But he couldn't forget her.

Helen was waiting for him in the restaurant at a table by the window. She glanced up and smiled as Richard sat down, her hazel eyes and her smooth blonde hair reflecting the light from the flickering candle in a Chianti bottle in the centre of the table. Richard liked that she bore no resemblance to Grace.

'Sorry to keep you waiting,' he said. 'How are things?'

'Oh, you know,' she said listlessly, 'I'm just muddling on from one day to the next. There are days when I feel so alone without Rigs that all I want to do is cry. What about you?'

'More or less the same.' Richard picked up the menu and glanced down it. He was beginning to wish he hadn't come. He didn't want to spend another evening salving Helen's wounds and licking his own. She had to move on, and so did he. They ordered and as they ate they made desultory conversation, the wine in one bottle and then another loosening their tongues and leading them down the same path they had trodden each time they met.

They had first got to know one another at Rigs' memorial service, each of them drawn to the other by their love and respect for Rigs. After that it only seemed natural that they should meet again to share memories of a much-loved husband, and a friend who had been like a brother.

'It seems somehow wrong to have survived when pals you loved like brothers died,' he'd said one evening as they sat drinking whisky in Helen's small flat in Bayswater. 'And then there's the terrible guilt you feel for having killed some chap who was only doing his job. Knowing that, like you, he has a mother and a girlfriend waiting for him to come home. You shoot him down and watch the clouds of black smoke as his plane spirals to the ground, and at that moment you're glad you've finished him off. You can't pity him because if it's not him, it's you.' He'd broken down in tears and Helen had held him. Then they'd made love.

Whenever they met, Helen talked about her love for Rigs and Richard told her about Grace, and how much he regretted his decision to shut her out of his life. This then became the pattern of their meetings, resurrecting memories; and as one drink followed another, they commiserated over the loves they had lost. On most evenings the only solace they could find was to fall into bed and make drunken love.

Now, as they finished the meal with glasses of brandy Richard said, 'I'm going north tomorrow to see the chap who's keeping Dad's business afloat.' He gave a wry grin. 'I'm not much use to him or anyone at the moment and John Morgan's doing a splendid job in my absence. The least I can do is show a bit of interest.' He leaned forward across the table, his face flushed with fervour. 'I'm also going to find Grace. Ask her to forgive me, take me back and make me feel whole again.'

'You're lucky you're both still alive so that you can do that,' Helen slurred. 'I wish it was that easy for me. I'll never see Rigs again.'

* * *

At the same time as Nigel Cotterill was driving Grace and Michael to their new home in Cawthorne, Richard Carmichael was driving up the A1 from London to Doncaster. The blustery March winds had driven the last of the frosty night away and a pale sun was breaking through a cloudy sky. He felt surprisingly fresh and invigorated considering the amount of drink he'd had the night before, but having made the decision to find Grace he had slept deeply for the first night in ages: he was ready to turn back time.

Grace was sitting comfortably in the passenger seat of Nigel's Rover with Michael on her lap, her arms wrapped around him. His excitement was palpable, his head turning this way and that as they drove out of Barnsley and into the open countryside. 'Moo,' he cried as they passed by a field of cows. Grace also felt a rising anticipation, and in between keeping her son entertained and pleasantly acknowledging the few comments Nigel made, she let her mind drift back to another day in the countryside: the day Richard had taken her to Sprotborough. She tilted her head, her eyes scanning the clouds, and she felt a warm hopefulness flooding through her veins as, through a break in the cumulus, she gazed at a patch of blue sky.

On the outskirts of Doncaster, Richard suddenly became aware that his hands had been clenching the steering wheel like the hands of a drowning man clinging to a spar in a storm-tossed sea. He relaxed his grip, sat back in his seat and raised his gaze to the sky. A patch of bright blue hovered over his destination. He pressed the accelerator to the floor.

* * *

Cawthorne village was just as pretty as Nigel had led Grace to believe. Mellow stone houses, an old church and shops stood at its centre and the road to Prudence Cotterill's house was lined on either side with trees and fields.

'It's much more rural than Doncaster or Barnsley,' Grace commented. 'I think we'll like living here.'

Nigel slowed the car. 'This is it,' he said, turning left into a driveway leading up to a long, low house with lots of mullioned windows and four tall chimneys.

'It's beautiful,' Grace said, pleased to see that whilst the house was long it wasn't one of those great, towering edifices with several storeys and staircases leading to dozens of rooms that no one used. Michael should feel far more at home in a house all on one level.

Nigel brought the car to a halt. 'A century ago it was a row of farm labourers' cottages and a granary. After Uncle Henry's death and the deaths of his parents the farm was sold off and Aunt Pru came to live here. In her younger days she was very creative and extremely active and...' he grinned at Grace, 'she'd stop at nothing until she got what she wanted. She converted this place practically single-handed into what you now see.'

Grace nodded thoughtfully. 'That must be why she finds her incapacity so frustrating. Being confined to a bed or a chair if you've been used to leading an active, independent life isn't easy to accept.'

'And believe me, she doesn't accept it at all gracefully.' Nigel smiled ruefully. 'Still, you seem to have the measure of her. I do hope it works out. Do say you'll stick it out for at least a month,' he joked.

'I hope it'll be a lot longer than that. I don't quit easily.'

Nigel breathed an audible sigh of relief. 'Then let me show you the house before we unload your stuff.'

'Come on, Michael,' said Grace stepping out of the car with her son in her arms. 'Look at the lovely garden for you and Percy to play in.' She set Michael on his feet and opening the rear door lifted Percy off the back seat where he had been dozing peacefully in among the baggage. Clipping on the dog's lead she handed it to Michael. 'Here, you show him the way.'

Michael gambolled off in Nigel's wake to a door at one end of the house. Inside a lobby filled with potted plants in brass urns, a hat stand, and a small table Nigel said, 'Aunt Pru lives in this end of the house. Through here is her sitting room.' He opened the door into a large, airy room tastefully furnished with couches, tables and bookcases. 'She travelled quite a bit in her younger days,' he said waving a hand at the oriental screens and rugs.

'My goodness, it's beautiful,' Grace said on her breath. She turned to Michael commanding, 'Don't touch anything, and keep a tight hold of Percy.'

'Effalump!' Michael trotted over to a small table, its base carved in the shape of an elephant complete with upturned trunk.

'Yes, darling, elephant.' Grace's anxiety showed. A room like this, full of curiosities, was a magnet to an inquisitive little boy like Michael. She wondered if the rest of the house was the same and if so would Prudence be forever ordering him not to touch anything. Beset with misgivings she heard Nigel say, 'Through here's the kitchen and her bathroom.'

Grabbing Michael, who was now inspecting a pair of bookends in the shape of two rearing lions, she dragged him and Percy to the door Nigel had gone through. An inner hallway led to a bright, well-equipped kitchen and next to it a sparkling bathroom then a bedroom with a four-poster bed covered in intricately patterned throws and cushions and more small pieces of oriental furniture. Each room was immaculate, and Grace puzzled how on earth an elderly woman who had recently suffered a broken arm managed to maintain such high standards.

She voiced her thoughts. 'Everywhere is spotlessly clean and tidy.'

'That's down to Mrs Halstead. She comes in every morning, and her husband tends to the garden,' Nigel informed her before setting off walking down the inner hallway. 'Now this end of the house is yours.' He showed her a small sitting room, two bedrooms and a bathroom. To Grace's relief the furnishings in these rooms were functional – no need to worry too much about Michael's sticky fingers – and to have all this space was beyond her wildest dreams. Even the home she had loved sharing with Pam couldn't compete with this. Recalling the shabby, little house in St Patrick's Road then Doreen Butterworth's spare bedroom and the squalor of Raby Road Grace felt as though she had died and gone to heaven.

'This will be just perfect,' she said fervently.

* * *

Richard drove into the car park at the Royal Infirmary in Doncaster. It seemed a lifetime since he'd last been here. Sitting in the car he reflected on the first time he had come here to meet Grace. Her surprise and delight when she saw him and the way she had hopped onto the back of his motorbike and held on tight. What a fool he had been to cut her out of his life, he thought, wiping his hand across his eyes. He sat for a moment longer praying that she still worked in the Royal and that she would give him the chance to make amends. Then, climbing out of the car and stretching his aching limbs, he strode into the hospital. A woman of middle years was behind the reception desk, and in front of it a queue of people awaiting her attention. Richard joined the queue.

Betty Williams, the woman behind the counter, tilted her head in annoyance as she saw the queue lengthen. No one had come to replace her and it was way past her lunch break. What's more, she needed the lavatory and her aching feet and frazzled nerves were getting the better of her. With increasing frustration, she dealt with enquiries and directed people to the wards they had come to visit. By the time it came to Richard's turn she was at her wits' end.

Richard smiled winningly at her and said, 'Could you please tell me if Grace Murphy, a midwife, still works here?'

Betty gave him a sour look as if to say she didn't have time for such trivialities. Realising this, Richard attempted to appeal to her better nature. 'Look, I've spent the last five years fighting for my country and somehow I lost touch with Nurse Murphy. She's a dear friend of mine and I would really like to see her again.' The expression on his handsome face was so desperate that Betty's heart softened.

'Yes, the war has a lot to answer for,' she said, sympathy oozing from every pore. 'Now, let me think. Grace Murphy. Oh, now I remember. A pretty girl, worked in maternity.' Richard gave an enthusiastic nod. 'She's no longer here,' Betty continued, 'she married Doctor Thompson and they...'

Richard wasn't listening. Married! Grace was married! She'd given up on him. He felt as though he was at the foot of a cliff with a landslide of rocks and mud crashing down on top of him. He turned on his heel and strode off without a thank you or a backward glance.

'Well, I never! Some people can be awfully rude,' Betty said to the woman who had been standing in the queue behind Richard. Only when Betty was hurrying to the canteen did she remember that it was a midwife called Rose Madeley who'd married Dr Thompson, not Grace Murphy.

25

'Hah! So, it is you my fool of a nephew employed,' Prudence barked as the ambulance man wheeled her out of the vehicle to where Grace stood awaiting her new employer's arrival. She had been keeping a sharp ear and eye out all morning and was now standing at the door wearing her nurse's uniform that she hadn't handed back when she left the Royal in Doncaster.

'My, aren't we smart?' Prudence scoffed, appraising Grace with gimlet eyes.

'Welcome home, Miss Cotterill.' Grace smiled then stood aside to let the ambulance man negotiate the door and then wheel his patient into her sitting room. He'd clearly been here before.

'I'll leave you to it,' he said grimacing at Grace. 'Best of luck.'

'Don't just stand there,' Prudence snapped, 'get me out of this contraption and into my chair.' She pointed to a large wing chair with a footstool close by.

Grace placed her arms under Prudence's armpits, and levering her up she deposited her in the chair then lifted her damaged leg onto the footstool. Prudence flapped her hands. 'Don't maul me, girl. I can lift my own damned leg if I choose to.'

Grace stood back. 'The less pressure you put on it for the first few days the quicker it will mend,' she said sternly.

Prudence met Grace's challenging gaze with her own. 'So, you're going to be strict with me, are you?' A glimmer of a smile curved her lips.

'If I have to,' Grace replied tersely. 'It's my job to keep you safe and make sure you make a full recovery. If you do as I say you'll be back on your feet in no time.'

Prudence chuckled. 'Quite the bossy boots, aren't you?' she said archly.

'It takes one to know one, Miss Cotterill,' Grace retorted.

Prudence burst out laughing. 'I think we're going to get on splendidly, don't you? Now, what will I call you? Murphy or Grace?'

'Grace will be fine.'

'Then you'd better call me Prudence. Now, off you go and get me a cup of proper tea. That stuff in the hospital was like dishwater.'

Grace hurried to the kitchen where Dolores Halstead, the char-cum-cook, was looking after Michael. They had both had a good laugh when they'd met the day before Dolores chirping, 'Where are ye from?' and Grace replying, 'Clare. What about you?' Now, Dolores turned from the stove and gave her an enquiring look.

'She's home then,' she said, her Cork accent as thick as the day she'd married David Halstead almost thirty years before. A coal miner, in his free time David mowed the lawns and grew magnificent vegetables.

'Aye, she's home an' glad to be so I imagine,' Grace replied.

'An' I hope ye make this your home for there's bin too many comins' an' goins' what with her bein' so hard to handle.' Dolores shook her head despairingly.

'I think we have the measure of one another,' Grace said with a grin. 'In fact, she's just told me she thinks we'll get on splendidly.'

'Saints preserve us!' gasped Dolores as she poured tea into a fine

china cup. 'Don't keep her waitin'.' Grace had gone to where
Michael was sitting by the open kitchen door playing with Percy.
The dog was tied to a long running line – David's idea – 'Gives him
a chance to run about an' keeps him from roamin' off,' he had said.
Grace smiled fondly at them, then ruffling Michael's hair and
telling him she'd be back soon she went and lifted the cup and
saucer.

* * *

The days flew by, pleasant enough even if Grace had to grit her
teeth and hold her tongue when Prudence's abrasive manner got
the better of her. She was careful to keep Michael and Percy in their
rooms, the kitchen or the garden, Dolores watching out for them
whilst Grace carried out her duties. However, one sunny afternoon,
Dolores at home and Grace bringing in the washing, Michael
decided to wander back into the house.

He hovered by the door of Prudence's room. Mammy said not to
go in, keep away, he remembered, but curiosity outweighing obedience he dropped to his knees stealthily crawling until he was under
the grand piano. Prudence was sitting in her chair reading when,
out of the corner of her eye, she saw something move. Startled, she
dropped her book into her lap.

'What are you doing under there, boy? Come where I can see
you.' She curled a beckoning finger. Michael crept from his hiding
place and approached her chair. Grace had explained that Miss
Cotterill had 'a poorly leg' and Mammy was nursing her better and
that he had to be a good boy and play on his own whilst she did her
work. Now, he gazed solemnly at Prudence for a moment or two
then very carefully he stooped over her raised leg and brushed his
lips against it.

'Poorly leg,' he said. 'Kiss it better.' He gave Prudence his most engaging smile. She was chuckling merrily when Grace burst into the room in search of him. 'I'm so sorry, Prudence...'

Prudence waved her into silence. 'He's a handsome little chap and quite a charmer,' she declared to Grace's amazement. 'What age are you, little man?'

'Two, an' I got a dog. He's Percy.'

Prudence raised amused eyes to meet Grace's reddened face. 'A dog! My goodness, Grace, what else have you got in your menagerie?'

'Just my boy and a dog, a miniature poodle to be exact,' Grace assured her. She didn't want her employer to think that Percy was a great big mongrel who'd wreak havoc on her furniture.

'Fetch him to me,' Prudence ordered. Michael skipped off willingly returning a few minutes later with Percy in his arms. He went straight up to Prudence and dumped the dog in her lap. 'Percy likes cuddles,' he said.

Grace was cringing but Prudence roared with laughter, and patting the little dog she asked Michael, 'Like this?' And running her bony fingers round Percy's ears and stroking his back she looked for Michael's approval.

'Don't let him lick your face,' Michael advised. 'Mammy says that's dirty.'

'Oh, she does, does she?' Prudence slid her eyes mischievously up at Grace. 'Well, we both must do as Mammy tells us, Michael. Isn't that right, Grace?' Her sarcasm didn't go unnoticed.

Grace, eager to divert Prudence's attention from Michael and the dog in case there were repercussions – Prudence was prone to viperish turns of mood, pointed to the photograph of a young army officer in dress uniform posing proudly in a studio portrait, his eyes focused directly into the camera and his lips curved in a superior smile under his waxed moustache. 'Is this your father?'

'Yes, Major Cotterill, King's Own Rifles. He was killed in the

Zulu Wars. I never met him, and he never knew he had a daughter. I was born some three months after.' Prudence's tone was matter of fact but Grace detected an underlying sadness in her words and in the softening of her features.

'That must have been hard to bear for your mother, and you,' said Grace musing that Michael had something in common with her irascible employer.

'It was, but it's all in the past. What you never had you never miss,' Prudence replied brusquely. 'Hankering for what might have been serves no useful purpose.' She adjusted her spectacles further up her beaky nose and looked across the room at Michael who was now crouched under the grand piano examining its stout legs. Percy dozed in Prudence's lap. 'Is that what happened to the little chap?' she asked, a hint of compassion softening her voice.

'Yes, this war deprived Michael of his father,' Grace said, leaving Prudence to believe that Richard was dead. And he might as well be, for Michael will never know him, she thought, glancing sadly at her son.

Prudence hitched her bosom with her forearm. 'Don't dwell on it,' she barked. 'Live for the present and look to the future. And now that you've finished prying into my family history pass me that box. I want to show Michael something.'

Grace went over to a side table and lifted the intricately carved box that Prudence pointed out. 'I don't want Michael – or Percy – to be nuisances to you,' she said as she handed over the box.

'Nuisances? I haven't had such fun for a long time,' Prudence hooted. 'Come here, Michael. You and I have a great deal of exploring to do.' She glanced at Grace. 'Educate him whilst he's young,' she said. 'Now, off you go, Grace, and attend to whatever it is you have to do.'

Grace walked out of the sitting room feeling slightly dazed, leaving Michael leaning over the side of Prudence's chair, his eyes intent on the contents she was taking from the box. Outside the door she stood listening as Prudence told Michael the story of the medals won in the Zulu Wars, Michael interrupting to ask, 'What this?' and Prudence patiently explaining.

* * *

Richard drove back to London in a haze of memories and regrets. Grace was married. He had lost her. Like a diminishing candle, all the hope that had burned within him on his trip to Doncaster had guttered, the flame extinguished.

Back in his flat he immediately opened a bottle of whisky and filled a tumbler. He had just refilled his glass when there was a knock at the door. At first he ignored it. Then when it came again, he impatiently set down his drink and barged to the door ready to bawl out whoever was there. Helen's anguished face stilled the words on his tongue.

'At last, you're back,' she wailed pushing past him into the room then flopping into a chair by the hearth.

Richard poured her a drink, and before Helen had a chance to speak he blurted, 'Grace's married. She didn't wait for me. I left it too late.' Without pause he told Helen about his fateful trip to the hospital.

Helen let him rant but she didn't offer any words of comfort. Then, when he ran out of steam, she leaned forward in her chair gazing intently into his face.

'It's perhaps as well you didn't find her,' she said flatly. 'I'm pregnant. I'm carrying your child.'

The whisky in Richard's glass slopped onto his trousers. He watched it seep into the fine tweed as his addled brain struggled to register Helen's words. She began to cry, softly at first then with great, heaving sobs. He sat staring at her, incapable of moving, for once he moved time would start rolling again and he knew that nothing in his life would ever be the same.

'What are we going to do?' she whispered brokenly.

'The right thing,' he muttered. 'I'll marry you.'

26

SUMMER 1948: CAWTHORNE, YORKSHIRE.

'Come along, young man, put these aside and let's go outside,' Prudence told Michael. He spun the globe of the world one last time then looked up at her, his bright blue eyes alive with expectancy. 'Hand me my stick.'

Her broken femur had healed long ago, but like most eighty-three-year-olds her steps were not the steadiest. Leaning heavily on the stick she levered herself upright and with one hand on Michael's shoulder they made their way from the sitting room to the kitchen.

'Me and Proody are going exploring,' Michael told Grace as, brushing flour from her hands, she turned to greet them. Dolores wasn't in today and Grace was making a mince and potato pie. She smiled benevolently at her son and then at Proody, as Michael had christened her. Prudence returned the smile.

'We're going to observe the ants,' she announced, 'see how they work together for the benefit of their colonies. Wonderful little creatures, and so organised.'

'Did you know that they can carry ten times their own weight?' Michael said enthusiastically. Grace said she didn't, and in reply to his 'are you coming?' she covered the pie with a clean dishtowel then washed her hands.

They trooped out into the garden, Michael gambolling ahead. Grace offered Prudence her arm and, supported by that on one side and her stick on the other, she and Grace slowly made their way across the lawn.

'Find a short, stout stick, Michael,' Prudence called, 'then poke it carefully into the soil along the bottom of the rockery. Ants like the protection of stones.'

Michael crouched and poked the stick at the base of a large stone. 'Look, Proody, look! They're coming out,' he cried excitedly. 'See this one, Proody, he's dragging a leaf.'

Prudence produced a magnifying glass from the pocket of her capacious Indian kaftan and grunted, 'Help me to my knees.' Grace lowered her gently then stood back observing the bent heads, one ensconced in a brightly coloured turban to cover her thinning hair and the other with a thatch of thick, fair hair that tore at her heart. He's so like Richard, she thought, as she watched her son and her employer explore the ant colony.

Through a haze of memories, she heard the words queen, drones and workers, then thorax, abdomen and so on, Prudence's gravelly voice echoed by Michael's as he stored the information in his acute brain. Not for the first time, Grace marvelled at how much he learned from his more than willing tutor. She blessed the day she had come to work for Prudence Cotterill.

Not that the past two years had all been plain sailing. The first time Prudence had lashed out at Grace had been the last. At the start, Grace had overlooked her impatient employer's prodding, flapping hands but not that day when she had slapped Grace so hard it made her ears ring. 'Stop that now!' Grace had bawled. 'It's demeaning to both of us. Me because I don't deserve it, and you because at your age you should know better.' Prudence had glared, shocked by Grace's unexpected anger, her own cheeks flushing with annoyance and then shame.

Gradually, the ground rules had been established, and apart from a few blips they now lived together in harmony. Much of this was due to Michael's presence. Prudence adored him and delighted in broadening the knowledge in his lively mind, Grace convinced that it gave her purpose, a reason for living. And as Prudence related stories from her travels, using the artefacts she had collected to demonstrate to Michael the different countries and cultures she had experienced, Grace acknowledged that whilst her son might not have a father to introduce the world to him, he had a wonderful role model in Proody.

In the evenings, Michael in bed and Grace with Prudence in the sitting room, Prudence with Percy in her lap, they had shared their love of reading and other interests and had talked at length getting to know each other's backgrounds. It was Prudence who had persuaded Grace to write and tell her parents about Michael. 'He's not a dirty secret or something to be kept hidden for the rest of his life,' she had snorted. Grace had taken her advice, surprised when her mother and father appeared to be unfazed by suddenly learning that they were grandparents to a four-year-old child, and thrilled when they insisted she bring him to visit them in the near future.

Grace had also found a good friend in Dolores Halstead. They helped each other with chores around the house, went shopping together, and Michael played with Dolores' grandchildren. Nigel Cotterill had long since stopped visiting, assured that Grace wasn't suddenly going to quit. All in all, life in the long, low treasure trove of a house in Cawthorne, was nigh on perfect.

* * *

'Me brother Lorchan's coming to visit us,' Dolores announced excitedly one day in the middle of August, the lashing rain keeping Michael and Percy indoors with Prudence. 'I've not seen him for near on five years,' Dolores continued, as she piled the breakfast dishes in the sink, 'but he says Sean Heffernan will mind the farm for him for a month or so an' he'll be here come September.'

'That's lovely for you. Is his farm in Cork?' Grace began wiping the dishes Dolores placed on the draining board.

''Tis so,' Dolores said proudly, 'an' Lorchan's the one that stayed at home to mind the land me family have farmed for three generations. Mammy wanted him to go for the priesthood, an' he'd o' made a gudden, but Lorchan loves his cows. He never married, you know, a nice, big fella like him. Makes you wonder, doesn't it?' She dried her hands declaring, 'There, that's me done.'

Grace was left trying to imagine Dolores' brother and coming up with nothing.

* * *

September brought the rain. Grace sat knitting in Prudence's room half-listening to her as she introduced Michael to famous landmarks in different parts of the world. The names Paris then Venice floated into her consciousness and she was overwhelmed with memories.

Richard had told her that when the war was over he would take her to Paris and Venice and that they would see all the sights before they settled down and had a family. Smiling wryly, she silently told him, *Well, wherever you are, I've yet to see the Eiffel Tower or the Bridge of Sighs but we've made a start on the family.* She thought how sad it was that he had chosen not to be a part of it. He had told her that whatever happened she had to swim with the current not against it because what will be, will be. Well, she'd done just that, she mused, she'd let it take her, storm-tossed and battered on some occasions, to where she was now. She had reached her safe haven without him, and in all that time his son had wanted for nothing. If she never achieved anything more, she'd given Michael the best start in life that she could, and she'd go on making sure that the absence of his father was in no way a deterrent to building a brilliant future.

* * *

'I don't know why they call this an Indian summer, but they can call it what they like for me as long as the weather stays like this.' After days of rain Dolores was rejoicing at the long, hot spell they were finally now having.

Grace came upright, her face flushed as much from the heat of the oven as from the warmth of the glorious September day. She put the cake on the table then stood back and asked, 'What do you think?'

'It's risen just lovely.' Dolores was admiring the perfect golden sponge as Michael, having smelled the sweetly scented aroma, rushed in from outside the kitchen door with Percy at his heels.

'Is it done?' He looked with big eyes at the cake then lifted Percy. 'Look, Percy, Proody's birthday cake,' he squealed.

'Hush, Michael, keep your voice down. You'll spoil the surprise,' his mother gently reprimanded, 'and take the dog away from the table. We don't want him scoffing it if we turn our backs.' Michael giggled and did as she asked.

Dolores made tea and they sat and sipped it as they waited for the cake to cool.

'I'll take one through for Prudence before I begin the icing,' Grace said.

'Aye, an' I'll get off. Lorchan should be up by now an' lookin' his breakfast. He was tired out after his journey, poor lamb, so I telled him to lie in. 'Tis a terrible crossing from Cork to Holyhead.' Dolores drained her cup. 'Everythin' else is ready for liftin' so I'll see ye about one,' she said, eager to be off. Grace filled a cup and took it to the sitting room. Michael and Percy followed her.

'You seem to be tied to the kitchen this morning, Grace.' With more than a hint of suspicion in her gimlet eyes Prudence accepted her cup of tea. 'I don't want any fuss, you know. I've had eighty-three birthdays. That's enough for anybody so don't go putting yourself out.'

'I'm not,' Grace said, 'I was just helping Dolores because there'll be six of us for lunch.'

'Mammy said we shouldn't leave Percy in the kitchen 'cos he might scoff...' Michael clapped his hand to his mouth remembering that the cake was a secret.

'Leave Percy with me.' Prudence held out her wrinkled arms. 'Off the two of you go and do whatever it is you're up to,' she added with a twinkle in her eye.

* * *

Dolores arrived back just before one o'clock with David and Lorchan in tow. As she arranged plates of ham salad, she commented on the beautifully iced birthday cake. Grace had coated the sponge with white icing then fashioned a large pink eight and a four on top surrounded by tiny rosebuds

'I hope you're not putting eighty-four candles on it,' David remarked. ''Cos if you are I'll ring t'fire brigade now.'

Lorchan chuckled softly. He was a tall, muscular man with a weather-beaten face and flaming red hair. Grace thought he must be in his forties, a shy, awkward man not used to company. She didn't think he was particularly handsome but he had kind brown eyes and a slow, gentle smile. She did her best to put him at ease.

At half past one they all sat down at the round table in the dining room to eat. Prudence was looking positively majestic in her kaftan and fringed shawl, its exotic colours matching that of her embroidered turban. Quite the Queen of Sheba, Grace thought.

The sky was a clear blue sheet, the sun streaming in through the open French windows winking and glinting on Prudence's best silverware as they chattered convivially.

'You did well with the tomatoes this year, David,' Prudence remarked as she pierced a tasty morsel with her fork.

'Aye, but they'll do better next time when I've pruned back that sycamore. It's a bit early to do it but it's keeping out the light, an' now Lorchan's here he'll give me a hand.' Lorchan gave a slow smile and a nod.

By now, Michael was jiggling in his chair positively bursting for the cake to be brought in. He cast big, blue, anxious eyes at his mother who grinned and gave him a nod. He slid off his chair and followed her into the kitchen, returning a minute later carefully carrying the cake, alight with eight flickering candles, and lustily singing 'Happy birthday to you.' Everyone but Prudence joined in.

'Oh, you shouldn't have,' she protested, her voice thick with emotion. 'A lot of nonsense at my age.' But Grace could tell that she was delighted.

After they'd demolished the cake, they trooped out into the garden. Michael found one of the first conkers and Prudence split its spiky case to reveal the shiny, brown nut. Leaving them to explore it Grace walked down the garden with Lorchan, talking about his farm and Grace's life in Cawthorne.

'I was sorry to hear ye'd lost your husband an' the wee feller his father,' Lorchan said, his soft lilting voice genuine with sincerity.

'We didn't lose him. It was more a case of him losing us. I wasn't married to him,' Grace found herself saying then wondering why she'd confided something so personal to a man she barely knew.

'Ach, well, the wee feller seems to be doing fine without him,' Lorchan said, and changed the subject. Grace found him easy to talk to. So easy, that the next day when Dolores asked her for a favour she readily agreed.

'He wants to see the sights but I've got to make jam and chutney whilst the fruit's good. I don't want to spoil his holiday so I thought ye an' Michael could take him,' she said hopefully. 'I'll mind Prudence while ye're gone.'

'She's having a day in bed. All the excitement yesterday tired her out. It's those party games that did it,' said Grace shaking her head. 'Charades and hide the thimble, and most of it for Michael's benefit as much as her own. Now it's taking its toll.'

* * *

Grace walked with Lorchan to the village, Michael between them holding hands and chattering nineteen to the dozen. They visited the church and the graveyard then a shop where Lorchan bought sweets for Michael. On the edge of the village, they came to a farm.

'Now, Michael, he's the bull. A big, brave feller an' the daddy to them young calves,' Lorchan said bending down to Michael's height as they peered through the fence.

'I don't have a daddy.'

Grace felt an icy hand clutch at her heart when she heard Michael's reply. She blinked back tears.

'So ye don't, Michael, but ye have your lovely mammy an' ye don't want for anything more,' Lorchan said gently. He glanced up at Grace, his eyes warm with compassion and his smile comforting. Grace gave him a wobbly smile in return thinking what a lovely, thoughtful man he was. As they walked back to the house she realised that she had really enjoyed the day.

* * *

Lorchan came the next day to help David prune the sycamore. Over a cup of tea, when he and Grace were alone in the garden, Lorchan apologised for his remark about the bull. ''Twas thoughtless of me. I never would o' said it had I thought the wee feller would take it that way.'

Grace told him it didn't matter, that it was the truth and that Michael would have to learn to live with it. Going back indoors she wondered how many other men would have been so sympathetic. Not many, she told herself.

Prudence was taking another day in bed and Grace was concerned for her usually lively employer. The doctor came and went pronouncing his verdict as 'old age'.

Sitting beside the large four-poster bed holding Prudence's hand Grace listened as Prudence drowsily reminisced about her time in India, before falling asleep. Throughout the rest of the day, Grace sat with her for much of the time often with Michael and Percy for company, Michael haltingly reading from one of Proody's favourite childhood books.

'Good boy, Michael.' Prudence lazily fondled his hair. 'You're going to be a great scholar one day. You'll make me and your mother proud.' Her usual brisk, gravelly tones were now a whisper, and whenever she spoke she appeared to be searching for the words.

That evening, after Grace had put Michael to bed, she sat with Prudence, afraid to leave her alone. Prudence drifted in and out of consciousness. At one point she squeezed Grace's hand and murmured, 'I never thought I'd have a daughter and a grandson. You gave me that gift.' Silently, Grace wept.

Dawn light crept into the bedroom. Grace woke with a start. Prudence lay swathed in her silk shawl, her sparse hair fanning the pillow and her noble features perfectly at rest. Grace kissed her forehead then sat by the bed tears streaming down her cheeks as she gazed at the woman she had grown to love and respect.

She didn't know quite how long she sat there grieving the loss of her good friend and benefactor, for that's how she had come to think of Prudence. As she sat holding the frail hand she reflected on her years in Prudence's employ. The barking voice that delivered orders like a major general gradually softening, and the childish tantrums ceasing as Grace and Michael's companionship and his thirst for knowledge gave her release to love and be loved.

'We're going to miss you dreadfully, Proody. You opened up a whole new world for me and my son, and for that you deserve your place in heaven,' Grace whispered before getting to her feet and steeling herself for what she knew she now must do.

Grace, stunned by Prudence's death, went through the motions of notifying Nigel and breaking the sad news to Dolores and David. They, of course, helped her make the necessary arrangements that would mark Prudence's passing and it wasn't until they were finalised that Grace gave some thought to her own and Michael's future. Telling him that his beloved Proody had had to go and live with the angels had been hardest of all. He'd nodded sombrely then bitten his bottom lip before saying, 'She'll see Pam, won't she? She can tell her I'm a big boy now.' In the back of her mind Grace had always been aware that there would come a time when Prudence would no longer need her, but she hadn't expected it to come so soon. Her spirit quailed at the thought of moving on.

Nigel came back to the house after the largely attended funeral.

'I think it only fair to let you know that I'll be selling up,' he said unfeelingly. 'You can stay on until the sale goes through, but I think you should start looking for somewhere else.' Grace's wounded spirits sank even lower.

When Lorchan came to make a bonfire of the sycamore

branches he had helped prune, Grace found herself confiding in him yet again. Although she couldn't quite put her finger on it there was something about him that made her feel safe and comforted whenever she was in his company.

'Back to square one,' she said trying to sound positive and hide her misery. 'Yet again I'm looking for a place for us to live.'

Lorchan heard the false bravado in her voice. He piled the branches into a steeple and stuffed twists of paper in amongst them, all the while thinking how much he admired her and wondering if he had the audacity to make the suggestion that was crowding his thoughts. She was a beautiful, young woman with a lovely nature. What would she want with a middle-aged farmer who was neither handsome nor wealthy? He struck a match, setting fire to the twists of paper.

The flames shot skyward, Michael circling the bonfire whooping and throwing on twigs. Lorchan gazed into the blaze. *Go for it, boyo, ye have nothing to lose*, he silently told himself. He rubbed his hands on the back of his trousers and cleared his throat. By God, but his mouth was dry.

'Ye an' the wee feller can always come an' live with me in Kilmallow,' he said softly. 'Ye can marry me if ye like an' live there for as long as ye so please.' He broke out in a sweat.

Grace stared at him, saw the anxiety in his eyes and heard the blood singing in her ears and felt her heartbeat quicken.

Lorchan gazed into her stunned face. 'I'm sorry if I overstepped the mark,' he muttered turning his attention back to Michael and the fire and saying, 'Keep ye well back from the blaze, son.'

Grace patted Lorchan's arm, and to his broad back she softly said, 'Let me think about it, Lorchan.'

Then she turned, running into the house to her bedroom. Lying on the bed, eyes closed, she slowed her throbbing heartbeat. She saw a young airman sauntering towards her, sunlight catching his thick, fair hair and the golden stubble on his cheeks. His firm lips broke into a wide smile and his blue eyes sparkled. Then she saw the warm, brown eyes and the tentative smile that were Lorchan Brady's. What did she have to lose? She knew the answer to that. She had lost it long ago. Lorchan was a good, kind man, a man whose company she enjoyed; he was good with Michael, and he promised them stability. You hardly know him, an inner voice warned, he might turn out to be a brute. Grace gave a little smile and shook her head. She didn't believe that.

Oh, if only Prudence was here to give her advice, thought Grace sitting up then pacing the floor. Could she give Lorchan the kind of love he might be looking for? She shivered as she recalled the night that she and Richard had made love. Could she possibly give herself to another man? But do you want to remain alone for the rest of your life? the inner voice asked. Again, she knew the answer. It was no.

Out in the garden the heart of the bonfire collapsed, sparks flying into the air. Lorchan stooped and lifted Michael up onto his broad shoulders. 'Let's go find your mammy, son.'

Grace met them in the kitchen. Lorchan set a laughing Michael down and Grace said, 'Away an' wash your hands an' face, Michael.' He scampered off. Then she looked directly into Lorchan's eyes. 'The answer's yes,' she said.

'Thank ye kindly,' he replied gruffly, choking back tears. 'I'm honoured. I'll do me best to make ye happy.' He wiped the back of his big, beefy paw over his eyes.

'Thank you for asking me,' Grace replied. 'I'll do *my* best to make *you* happy.'

27

NOVEMBER 1969: LOWER MELTON

Sara sat beside her father's bed oblivious to the hovering nurses and the medicinal smells. The tide had turned at last and the sea on which she had sailed with such hope was on its way out. 'Not long now,' the nurse had whispered.

'It's been a long day,' Richard said, his voice low and quavering. 'You must be exhausted.'

'I'm fine, Dad.' Sara gently squeezed his hand. It felt like a bundle of twigs.

'I've come to the conclusion that cancer has its merits,' Richard said wryly. Sara choked down a sob. 'What I mean is it gives you time to prepare,' he continued. 'We didn't have that with your mother she went so quick.' His blue eyes gleamed with fond memories then his lids drooped and he dozed again. The morphine was doing its trick.

Sara sat on, determined not to break down into the shuddering wreck she knew she would be once he was gone. She now knew all the answers to her questions, for in her recent visits Richard had turned back time, telling her all that he had buried in his heart. She knew about his hasty wedding to her mother, Helen, and how they had 'rubbed along nicely' delighting in her birth and gradually finding the love and respect that had been theirs to the end. She knew all about Rigs, Heppy and Grace and the horrors of a war that had changed the course of her father's life. But knowing all this didn't make it any easier to let him go. Her heart ached unbearably as she gazed into his shrunken face, the vestiges of the handsome man he had been still shining through.

Richard's eyes shot open, a startled expression in their faded blue. He glanced about him as though to ascertain where he was. 'Pass me the box,' he said.

Sara knew exactly which box he meant. Its contents had played their part in many of their conversations. She set the box on the bed so that he could reach it. He flipped the lid then removed the brooch and Grace's photograph. Smiling, he traced her image with his fingers and then rubbed his thumb over the brooch pressing the little Spitfire into his flesh.

'Find Grace, give her the brooch and tell her I'm sorry, that I've regretted what I did every day of my life and that I never forgot her,' he panted. 'Tell her to keep looking for the patch of blue sky.' The urgency of his request sapped him of what little strength he had left and the photograph and the brooch slipped from his hand. 'Promise to do that, Sara.' His head fell back on the pillow. He closed his eyes.

'I promise,' Sara said through her tears. 'I won't let you down, Dad.'

His lips curved into a slow, sweet smile. 'I love you, Sara.'

'And I love you, Dad.' Sara gazed through blurred eyes at her father's beloved face and listened to his breathing, willing it to go on forever.

28

SPRING 1970: DONCASTER, YORKSHIRE

Sara was unaware that as she parked her yellow Beetle outside Doncaster Royal Infirmary it was in the same spot her father had parked his green Triumph almost thirty years before. Or that she was treading the same ground Richard and Grace Murphy had trodden as Grace ran into his open arms.

A biting wind blew across the car park whipping at Sara's legs and making her quicken her steps. She felt guilty at having let more than three months elapse before starting her search for Grace but time spent arranging Richard's funeral and dealing with his estate then work and Christmas, and a wonderful new boyfriend, Tom, had all conspired to delay her. But now, hell-bent on keeping her promise to her father, she had driven up from London to fulfil her mission.

Inside the hospital, Sara didn't join the queue at the reception desk as her father had done on his last fateful visit. She headed straight for the maternity department: Grace had been a midwife. If anyone remembered her that would be where she might find out what had become of her.

'Could I speak to someone in charge?' Sara asked a young nurse who was just coming out of a ward lined with cribs.

'That'll be Matron,' the nurse replied. 'I'll see if she's available. Come this way.' She set off at a brisk pace leading Sara into a ward filled with women, some nursing their babies. Outside a small office partitioned off from the beds she rapped the door. When she heard the words 'Come in' she opened it and said, 'A lady to see you, Matron.'

Sara entered. A buxom middle-aged woman with a pleasant smile asked, 'How may I help you?'

'I'm making enquiries about a midwife called Grace Murphy who used to work here during the war. I'm trying to trace her whereabouts.'

'Oh, Grace. Grace Murphy, I remember her well,' said Maudie Shaw with a fond smile. 'We worked together for a couple of years back then.'

Sara's spirits soared. She was on track.

Maudie Shaw looked at her quizzically. 'Are you her daughter?'

'I could have been had things worked out differently,' Sara replied, 'but no, I'm not her daughter. Perhaps if you have time to listen, I'll explain why I'm here.'

Intrigued, Maudie told Sara to take a seat.

'No, she definitely didn't marry Dr Thompson,' Maudie intervened at one point, and later, 'Oh, yes the flyer, the chap who flew Spitfires,' Maudie said as Sara continued her story. 'She was very much in love with him.' And when Sara finished speaking Maudie smiled ruefully. 'It's sad to think they didn't end up together.'

Sara nodded. 'Have you any idea where she went after she left here?'

Maudie smiled. 'As a matter of fact, I have. I heard she'd gone to live in Wheatley with an ex-patient of ours, a Mrs Butterworth, but whether she's still in that area is anybody's guess.' Seeing

Sara's disappointment Maudie left her desk and over at a filing cabinet she withdrew a bulky file. 'We should have Mrs Butterworth's last known address,' she said confidently. 'That might help.'

Sara sat forward eagerly as Maudie flipped through the file. 'Ah, yes, here it is. I'll jot it down for you.' She handed Sara the slip of paper. 'If you do find her, give her my regards. I liked Grace. She was an excellent nurse.'

Sara thanked her and left, triumphant. Things *were* looking positive. Perusing her map, she drove to the address in Wheatley.

* * *

A tired-looking woman answered Sara's knock, and ignoring the shouts of 'Who the bloody hell is it now?' from the man wearing a string vest Sara said, 'I'm looking for Grace Murphy. Are you Mrs Butterworth?'

Doreen flushed. 'I used to be,' she said glancing nervously over her shoulder. Then pulling the door behind her she stepped outside. 'Grace,' she said with a sad smile, 'lovely Grace. Her an' me were great friends when she lived here.'

'Was she married then?'

'Married!' Doreen shook her head. 'Grace wasn't married. Her chap what flew the Spitfires let her down. She really loved him, so she did.'

That was my dad, Sara thought sadly. 'Do you know where Grace is now?' she asked without much hope.

Doreen shook her head. 'She hasn't lived here since...' Her brow creasing she mentally totted the years. 'Since nineteen forty-four.' Sounding surprised at the passage of time she added, 'She dropped me a line back then saying her and her little lad were living in Cawthorne, nursing a woman called...' Doreen pressed her fingers to her lips and said, 'Ooh, let me think... Copperhill, that wa' it. A Miss Copperhill.'

Sara was still trying to comprehend Doreen's mention of 'her and her little lad' when the door was dragged open and the man in the string vest bawled, 'Are you going to stand here yakking all bloody day?'

The woman jumped, and almost pushing Sara off the step, she cried, 'If you find her tell her I'm sorry.' She scooted inside. The door slammed. Sara stood for a moment listening to the angry shouts and feeling very confused.

Grace had a son, but no doctor husband. Silently cursing the brutish man and wishing she'd had more time to speak with the poor, bullied woman Sara got in the car and looked at the map. Cawthorne. She drove out of the town her thoughts tumbling so fast she barely concentrated on the road as she mulled over the time frame of Grace's story.

Neither her dad nor Doreen Butterworth had had contact with Grace for almost thirty years. Anything could have happened in that length of time, she thought, and yet... Her hands slipped on the steering wheel and a shiver ran down her spine. She slowed the car then pulled off the road into a farm gateway. She needed to do some serious thinking.

In nineteen forty-four Grace had given birth to a son. Her dad had last seen Grace in autumn, nineteen forty-three about the same time as he had lost his father and then his best pal, Rigs. She shivered again, her calculations jangling inside her brain. Had Grace been pregnant then? Had her dad abandoned Grace knowing that she was having his child? She didn't want to believe that of him. And why, when he'd told her everything else in such detail had he never mentioned it? Better to think that Grace had met someone else, Sara thought, but somehow, she didn't think she had. I could have a half-brother, she thought, feeling slightly sick and curiously excited as she set the car in motion. The search for Grace Murphy had suddenly taken on a whole new meaning.

* * *

'Copperhill, did you say?' The shopkeeper scratched his head. 'There's nubbdy by that name as I know of in Cawthorne.' Sara wondered if she'd been sent on a wild goose chase.

'It's actually a Grace Murphy I'm looking for,' she said. 'I was told she came here to nurse a Miss Copperhill.'

'Ah, now you're talkin'.' The shopkeeper smiled. 'It's Cotterill. Miss Prudence Cotterill as was. Grace worked for her.'

'You know Grace?' Sara's hopes rekindled.

'Oh, aye, she's a grand lass is Grace.'

'Where can I find her?' Sara's voice was high with expectation.

'Well, you'll not find her here. She left after Miss Cotterill died, but Dolores Halstead can tell you where she lives now, she's her sister-in-law.'

The sinking feeling that had been about to invade Sara's stomach suddenly bubbled with euphoria as the friendly shop-keeper gave her directions to Dolores's house. Grace had married after all.

Sara came away from the shop deep in thought. Of all the things she had learned in her search for Grace one was that everybody held her in high regard and remembered her fondly. Not once had she had to produce the photograph from her handbag to jog their memories. It seemed that Grace wasn't just beautiful on the outside but just as lovely on the inside. No wonder her dad had loved her. And twice she, Sara, had been told how much Grace had loved her father. She thought how sad it was that the war had torn them apart, that the horrors of flying too many deadly missions and losing friends had temporarily distorted her dad's self-worth to such an extent that he had given up on the woman he had so obviously loved.

She drove slowly taking her time to think, and wishing she could turn back time and bring them together as they had been in those wonderful days when they had planned a future together. But of course if she could do that she wouldn't exist, well, not as she was now. She was Richard and *Helen's* daughter. But she could so easily have been Grace's.

A matter of minutes later she brought the car to a halt outside a pretty cottage with a beautiful garden.

29

Despite having driven from London to Doncaster early that morning, Sara was itching to get back to Tom and tell him that she had succeeded in keeping her promise. So, rather than look for somewhere to stay overnight as she had intended, she drove straight back down the A1 then onto the M1, fortifying herself with cups of coffee and sticky buns on the way.

It was after eleven when she arrived at her flat in Chelsea. As soon as she was indoors she rang Tom; she knew he'd still be awake. Like her he was a night owl. Breathlessly she told him she had found Grace. 'I'm coming straight round,' he said and hung up. Sara smiled as she put the kettle on.

Tom was the love of her life. Big, bearded and handsome and blessed with a beautiful nature, Sara had liked him from the moment she met him on a photo shoot in Milan the previous autumn. They'd explored the city together, and by the time they returned to London they were in love.

Snuggled up on the couch, Sara told Tom about the helpful matron then the nervous woman with the horrible husband, and finally about meeting Dolores Halstead. 'It seems it all turned out nicely for Grace in the end,' she said dreamily. 'Just when she'd lost her good friend Miss Cotterill and had to think about finding somewhere else to live for her and Michael there was Lorchan Brady with the answer to all her problems.'

'Good old Lorchan.' Tom gave a wry grin.

'I find it hard to believe that I have a half-brother,' Sara continued with more than a hint of wonder in her voice. 'I always wanted a sibling when I was growing up.' She paused thoughtfully. 'I suppose in some way I should resent Grace for being the love of my dad's life but from what he and everybody else has told me, I just can't. I know he loved Mum as well.'

'And I love you,' said Tom dropping a kiss on her cheek. 'Now, what are you going to do with all this information you've gathered, Sherlock?'

'Write to Grace, and if she's willing I'll go to Ireland and give her the brooch in person, Dr Watson,' said Sara firmly. 'I'd like to check out this half-brother of mine. If Grace agrees, will you come with me?'

'To the ends of the earth and back,' Tom replied.

30

SUMMER, 1970: COUNTY CORK

Grace had been shopping in Cork centre and meeting up with Clodagh for lunch on the day Sara's letter arrived. A few years after marrying Lorchan Brady and going to live in Kilmallow, Grace had been in the city shopping when whom should she chance to meet but Clodagh. They had fallen into one another's arms laughing and crying at the unexpected reunion.

'Of all the people,' Grace had cried on seeing her old friend. 'I've thought of you often, Clo, and was sorry we lost touch.' She had looked at Clodagh, her eyes alight with joy but at the same time noting that Clodagh hadn't worn well. Her once red hair was pepper and salt and her face lined with the signs of a woman who had suffered.

'I'd have recognised you anywhere, you haven't changed a bit,' Clodagh had said as if she had read Grace's mind, 'though I can't say the same for meself.'

'Are you over here visiting your parents?' Grace had said as they made their way to a coffee shop.

'Nope,' Clodagh had replied with a hint of the old Clodagh. 'I've been back here near on five years. I put up with that bastard Ray

Barnes for ten then one day I decided I'd had enough and came home. But what brings you here?'

Over more than one cup of coffee they wound back the years. Grace told her about Richard and Michael, Clodagh declaring, 'The lousy glamour boy. How dare he leave you in the lurch like that.'

Grace had smiled at the old expression 'glamour boy' then excused Richard's behaviour by saying, 'I think the war got the better of him. He doesn't know about Michael.' Then she told her about Lorchan, and Clodagh had gone on to tell her that life in Scotland on a remote RAF base had been horrendous and that Ray's infidelity had almost crippled her.

'I was already pregnant with Ryan, my eldest, when I married him, an' a year later I had Roisin. When the war ended, we went to live near his family in Chesterfield.' Clodagh had given a long groan. 'It was bloody awful. I don't know how I stuck it so long but I kept thinking things would come right.' She shrugged. 'But they never did.'

Grace had sympathised. She didn't say she had predicted it, and was pleased to learn that Clodagh had married again, this time to a fisherman in Kinsale. Since then the old friends met on a regular basis. They'd even been to visit Patsy, still single and living in Tralee with two budgerigars, and working as a matron in the hospital there. Now, having lunched and swapped the latest news, they went their separate ways, Clodagh to Kinsale and Grace to Kilmallow.

No matter how many times Grace returned to the pretty, white farmhouse she always felt that same warm glow she had experienced when Lorchan had brought her and Michael to live with him. It made her feel safe and loved.

Lorchan greeted her with a big smile. 'I see ye kept the shops busy.' His eyes twinkled when he saw her bags and his chest visibly swelled as he added, 'Hannah rang. She's coming down next weekend.'

Hannah, the daughter Grace had given him three years after their marriage, was the pride and joy of Lorchan's life: he had never expected to be a father in his own right. Although he had readily taken Richard's son as his own, and Michael just as readily accepted Lorchan as his father, Hannah was the icing on the cake. She was now working as a librarian in the university in Galway.

Grace dropped her bags, smiling at the news. She had been thrilled when she discovered she was pregnant and considered Hannah the perfect gift to repay Lorchan for his love and kindness. 'That's grand,' she said. 'We'll do something special.' She missed her much-loved daughter now that she was away from home, and was glad that Michael had decided to work in the local vets' practice.

Michael was engaged to the lovely Noreen, also a vet, and Grace was looking forward to the wedding later in the year.

'Oh, by the way, there's a letter for ye from England.' Lorchan nodded at the mantelpiece.

Grace didn't recognise the writing so it wasn't from Dolores. Intrigued, she opened the envelope and withdrew two crisp sheets of paper. Feeling as though her legs didn't belong to her, she sat down with a thump. 'Oh, my goodness!'

'What is it?' Lorchan cried.

Grace was still reading, a gamut of emotions flitting across her face from astonishment to curiosity then deep sorrow. Lorchan bounced on his heels, his concern for her growing. 'Who is it from? Is it bad news?'

'It's from Richard's daughter.' Grace raised her tear-stained face. She sounded utterly bemused. 'Richard Carmichael. He died last November. He asked her to find me,' she continued in a wobbly voice. 'He gave her a gift for me.' She let the letter fall into her lap and sat biting her lip and silently crying.

Lorchan lifted the letter and read it. He knew all about Richard and had no fear of him coming between himself and Grace. He was wise enough to know that she would never forget her first love. How could she when Michael was a constant reminder? But he also knew that her love for him was as strong as his love for her. He lifted her up from the chair and held her close. Grace leaned into his broad chest finding comfort there.

'She wants to come and visit,' Lorchan said. 'What are ye going to do?' He paused, and in his gruff, kindly way he added, 'Whatever ye decide, it's fine by me.' Grace gazed up at him and smiled gratefully.

'I know,' Grace replied softly. How lucky she was to have found such a kind, understanding man. 'Let me think about it.'

* * *

In the small garden she'd created by the back door Grace knelt to weed the border barely aware of bits of chickweed and sprouting dandelions as she mulled over Sara's letter. To know that Richard had never forgotten her, that on his deathbed he had tried to make amends for abandoning her had opened so many old wounds that she didn't know what to think. Forking up a clump of chickweed, she acknowledged that she had never forgotten him, but her memories felt more like something she had dreamed rather than reality. Only every now and then when Michael would say or do a certain thing was she able to picture clearly the man she had loved and lost. They were for the most part happy memories that no longer tore at her heart.

Then, as she got to her feet, it suddenly dawned on Grace that Sara was a half- sister to Michael. Whatever would he make of that? Sara had written that Richard had married his pal Rigs's widow and that she was their only child. Poor Rigs, his and Garvey Carmichael's death had been the catalyst that had tipped Richard over the edge. The bloody war had a lot to answer for, she thought bitterly, reliving for a moment how heartbroken she had been when Richard had gone out of her life. *But if he hadn't, I wouldn't have had the happiness I've known with Lorchan, and I am happy. I can't deny that.*

Grace wondered if Michael would take kindly to meeting Sara. He never thought of anyone other than Lorchan as being his father, and why would he? He'd never known Richard Carmichael and Richard Carmichael had never known he had a son. Putting away her fork and trowel and going inside to wash her hands, she decided she would talk to Michael before replying to Sara's letter.

* * *

'She wants to meet you and give you something he wants you to have,' Michael said caustically. 'A bit late for that, isn't it?'

'She made a promise,' Grace said rationally. 'She's just keeping it.'

'And he was salving his conscience before he went to meet his Maker,' Michael replied dryly. 'And don't go thinking that I'm saying this because I feel bitter about him. I don't. I don't think anything about him. Lorchan Brady's my father.' Michael looked at his mother, his eyes filled with love. 'All I'm saying is, I don't want it to stir up old memories that might hurt you. If you want to meet the girl then it's all right by me, but be aware of the consequences.'

'She's your half-sister. Maybe it's only right you should meet her.'

Michael looked surprised. 'I hadn't thought of that,' he said pulling a face so like his father's that Grace's heart flipped.

* * *

Sara and Tom travelled to Ireland on the night boat, and with Tom at the wheel of Sara's little yellow Beetle they drove through the early morning mists to their destination, County Cork. Getting out of Dublin was a nightmare, the city heaving with traffic, but soon they were in the hinterlands the sun rising higher in the sky and promising a glorious day. They drove along roads bordered by high hedges bright with golden gorse and yellow rattle, and in the distance blue-grey mountains as ethereal as a fairy story. They passed by imposing entrances to grand mansions, some of them in ruins, Sara twisting and turning in her seat and commenting, 'My dad would grieve to see the demise of such magnificent architecture,' and Tom replying in his practical, no-nonsense way, 'Nobody can afford the upkeep on places like that any more.' As the little car ate up the miles, they drove through small towns with castles standing guard over them, and one with thatched cottages on either side of the road. 'Look, Tom, look! It's absolutely magical,' Sara cried.

'Ireland's clearly cast its spell on you,' said Tom keeping his eye on the roads and the signposts and chuckling. Sara's exuberance for life was just one of the reasons he loved her. Sara let out a whoop as they crossed the border between Waterford and Cork. Tom jumped.

'Calm down,' he exhorted, 'you're distracting me. What's more, the Irish have suffered enough at the hands of the English without them thinking I've brought a banshee to visit them. They're a pretty superstitious lot you know. They'll set the priests on you.'

Sara fell about laughing. She loved Tom's irreverent humour. In some ways he reminded her of her dad. Musing on if, like her father, she had found a love that would last a lifetime she watched the landscape unfolding before them, green, wild and mysterious.

'Now, Alice in Wonderland, keep an eye out and look for signs for Kilmallow. We must be near by now,' said Tom.

'Here, turn right,' Sara cried.

Tom swung the car round a corner and soon they were tootling down Kilmallow's main street past several pubs, a filling station with one pump – they laughed at that – and houses and a church. 'Now all we need to do is ask for directions to the Bradys' farm.' Her enthusiasm suddenly evaporated, nerves kicking in at what she was about to do. Keeping her dad's promise might not be that easy after all.

* * *

Grace was nervous. She'd been jittery ever since Sara's visit had been confirmed. It was Lorchan who had persuaded her to invite Sara. 'Sure, if the wee girl promised her dying father to look ye up, the least ye can do is be civil an' let her keep it,' he had said sagely. 'What harm can it do?'

What harm indeed, thought Grace. It might stir too many unhappy memories. And shrouded in doubt she flipped the bacon in the pan and left it to cook slowly on the Aga. Sara and Tom were bound to be hungry after their journey and what better than a tasty Irish breakfast to welcome them. They were due anytime soon. She was alone in the farmhouse, Lorchan and Michael having gone to look at a cow suffering from mastitis, and Hannah away to the village to buy fresh bread. Grace found the waiting difficult. It brought back memories of waiting in the telephone box in Plunket Road for Richard's call, and the long, lonely weeks she'd spent waiting to see him again. Keep busy, she told herself lifting fried potato bread from a pan to a plate then into the oven to keep warm.

* * *

In Kilmallow's main street, Hannah Brady was putting freshly baked loaves into the basket on her bike when a yellow car slowed to halt beside her. A girl with long, straight blonde hair leaned out of the car's passenger window. 'Excuse me, we're looking for directions to Lorchan Brady's farm,' she said eagerly.

Hannah grinned. 'You must be Sara Carmichael,' she said, making Tom chuckle and causing Sara's jaw to drop. The girl looked familiar, her tangle of black, curly hair and luminous grey eyes reminding Sara of someone she couldn't place.

'However do you know that?' Sara's eyes boggled.

'I'm Hannah Brady, Lorchan and Grace's daughter. We're expecting you. I've just been to get bread.' She threw her leg over the bar of her bike. 'Follow me and I'll show you the way.'

'What about that? It's like an omen,' Sara said, amazed, as Tom started to drive slowly behind Hannah's bike down the main street then into a narrow winding road. She wouldn't admit it to Tom, but now her stomach was churning. What if the meeting went horribly wrong? Would Grace be full of recrimination? She had every reason to be bitter. After all, she had been abandoned with a baby to care for all on her own.

Hannah led them to a pretty, white farmhouse with a bright, red door. Tom parked the car then climbed out, stretching his long arms and legs, but Sara stayed where she was, filled with apprehension. She drew a deep breath, steeling herself to meet Grace and hear whatever it was she might say.

Grace heard the hum of the car's engine and Hannah appeared in the kitchen door. 'They're here. I met them in the village.' Grace wiped her hands on the tea towel and patted her hair. Then, holding her breath, she went to the door and stepped out to meet them.

For some strange reason Grace was pleased to see that Richard's daughter bore no resemblance to him. She hurried forward, her hand outstretched. 'You found us then,' she said forcing a wide smile. 'Welcome to Kilmallow.'

Sara was shocked by how beautiful and young Grace looked. There was little sign of grey in her black, curly hair and her face was without wrinkles, but it was her opalescent grey eyes so gentle and kind that captivated Sara. Quite out of character, Sara was lost for words. Tom came to her rescue.

'Thank you,' he said. 'It's a beautiful part of the world you have here, and we were lucky enough to bump into Hannah to show us the way.'

Grace instantly liked the big, bearded man at ease in his own skin. He reminded her of Lorchan. She wasn't sure what to make of the tall, slim blonde girl who was looking as nervous as Grace felt.

'Come in,' she said leading them into the large, cosy kitchen. 'Make yourselves at home.' She indicated chairs at the table already set for a meal.

'Something smells good.' Tom wrinkled his nose appreciatively as he sat down. 'By the way,' he continued pleasantly, 'I'm Tom Whittaker, seeing as nobody bothered to introduce me.' He glanced at Sara, bemused by her uncustomary silence. 'Are you okay?' he muttered anxiously as she sat down beside him. Sara nodded and managed a weak, tight-lipped smile.

'I thought you'd be hungry,' Grace said glad of the diversion as she removed plates and dishes from the Aga, 'so I've cooked up a good Irish breakfast for you – and for these two,' she added as Lorchan and Michael walked in.

Sara turned her head and drew a sharp breath when she saw the younger of the two men. It was just like looking at photographs of her dad as a young man. Introductions were made, the giant that was Lorchan making them welcome. Michael had gone straight to the sink and was washing his hands. He merely nodded when Grace introduced him. Sara thought he didn't look pleased. Grace served breakfast with Hannah's assistance and they all tucked in,

Lorchan enquiring about Sara and Tom's journey and Tom doing the answering.

'What do you do for a living, Sara?' Hannah asked brightly as the conversation about the journey petered out.

'I'm a photographer. We both are,' she said nodding at Tom. 'We work on promotional shoots, landscapes, fashion, wildlife, whatever comes up,' she continued, the interest in her work helping her to find her tongue. 'What about you?'

'Stuffy old librarian, I'm afraid. It sounds pretty boring compared with what you do.' Hannah didn't look as though she meant it.

'Less o' the old,' Lorchan said. Then addressing Sara and Tom he proudly added, 'She's at the university in Galway doing research into Celtic folklore.'

Sara noted the adoration in his eyes as he smiled at his daughter. 'An' the big feller here,' he waved his fork at Michael, 'is the local vet.' Again, Sara heard the pride in Lorchan's voice.

They talked on, the conversation revolving around folklore, photography and veterinary work, everyone contributing and all of them avoiding the reason for Sara and Tom's visit. Sara's eyes were drawn time and time again to Michael. It wasn't just his looks but his mannerisms that reminded her of her father, and she wondered how was it that Michael was so like him when they had never met? Blood's definitely thicker than water, she thought.

The meal over, Hannah suggested that they go and sit outside and take advantage of the brilliant sunshine. They all trooped after her to the garden at the front of the house to lounge on the summer seats. Michael sat down beside Sara, and as Tom enquired about the distant mountains and Lorchan and Hannah gave him a mental geographic tour of the scenery Michael turned to Sara. 'Well, go on then, tell me what he was like,' he said his tone verging on a sneer.

'If you really want to know, stand in front of a mirror to see

exactly what he looked like and then think about your own character to know exactly what sort of man he was,' Sara replied, her
words spilling out sharper than she intended.

Michael flushed. 'Sorry.' He smiled contritely. 'I thought I didn't
care but now I find that I do. I've always looked on Lorchan as my
father, and in many ways he is. When your letter arrived, I was
worried that you'd upset Mam. I can see by the look in her eyes and
the smile on her face that you've done the opposite.' He gave Sara a
friendly nudge. 'Now I've got two little sisters to pester me, and I'm
not complaining.' Sara giggled. Michael was her dad all over.

Lorchan pushed back his chair, and giving Grace a meaningful
look he said, 'Come on, Tom. I'll show ye round my empire.' With a
glance at Sara, Tom followed Lorchan around the side of the house.

'I've some notes I need to catch up on,' Hannah said. 'I'll see you
all later.'

'I'm away to check on that cow,' Michael said gruffly.

And just like that, Grace and Sara found themselves alone.

Grace broke the silence. 'How ever did you find me?'

Sara told her about Matron Maudie Shaw and Grace smiled
fondly. 'Maudie was lovely. We worked well together.' Then Sara
rather dramatically described her visit to Doreen Butterworth.
'Poor Doreen,' Grace said. 'Ronnie was an awful chap. I knew he'd
make her life a misery.' And when Sara went on to tell her about
Dolores, Grace laughed. 'The sly old puss. Her last letter never let
on that she'd met you.'

'Perhaps she didn't want you to have too much time to think it
over and then refuse to see me,' Sara said. 'I was terrified that might
happen.'

'I did think about refusing.' Grace smiled at Sara. 'I'm so glad I
didn't.'

'So am I,' Sara said, her voice high with relief. 'I would have
hated not being able to keep my promise to Dad.'

Grace's sympathy was aroused to think that this young girl was bearing the burden of Richard's request all on her own. 'Do you have brothers or sisters, Sara?'

'No, I'm an only child.' The corners of Sara's mouth twitched. 'Or at least I thought I was until I learned about Michael. He's incredibly like my father, isn't he?'

Grace gazed towards the distant mountains. 'You don't look a bit like your dad,' she said standing quickly and clattering pots of geraniums into a different formation to hide her emotions.

'No, I take after Mum, but I'd like to think I have something of Dad's sweet nature. He was a lovely man.'

A gulping sob suddenly erupted from Grace's throat as she struggled to get a grip on the rising tide of agitation that was threatening. She wasn't ready to talk about Richard. Instead, she remarked, 'As was his father, Garvey. But of course, you never met him.'

Sara pulled a face. 'I still have my grandmother, Cecily.'

'Ah, yes, Cecily. She didn't approve of me,' said Grace, her smile grim as she continued moving pots from one place to another.

'There's not much she does approve of,' Sara said heatedly. 'She was horrible when Dad was dying.'

Grace's hands stilled and her head drooped, the will to prevaricate draining from her. She leaned heavily against the back of a chair, her knuckles whitening. 'How did he die? Had he been ill?' Her voice was barely above a whisper.

After all this time she still cares deeply about him, Sara thought sadly as, gazing at Grace's dejected figure, she told her about Richard's cancer and how bravely he'd fought against it. 'He didn't deserve that, nobody does,' Grace murmured coming to sit next to Sara. 'Tell me about him,' she said brokenly, 'about his life with you and your mother.' Her plea tugged at Sara's heartstrings.

Sara began talking quite simply about her happy childhood,

about Helen being a schoolteacher and how Richard had returned to work as an architect. 'He knew a lot about architecture,' Grace intervened. 'We'd go to grand houses and he'd educate me as we toured the properties.'

Sara was struck that they had clearly shared a lot of moments she knew nothing about. They hadn't just been a couple of young people in the heat of a raging war who had had a fling because they had thought they might not live to see tomorrow. Theirs had been a deep and meaningful love that they had thought would last a lifetime. She had to do her utmost to let this lovely woman know how much she had meant to her father. Sara took a deep breath.

'At first, when he told me about you, I felt resentful. I'd always thought Mum was the great love of his life and when he said they "rubbed along nicely" I was hurt for her. But the more we talked the better I understood.' She gave a little smile. 'I've done a lot of growing up since Dad died. I've accepted that they only got married because I was on the way. That they had both lost the person they wanted to spend their lives with.' She paused thoughtfully. 'When I was a teenager, I can remember thinking it odd that Mum still wore Bill Rigsby's wedding ring along with the one Dad gave her and kept his photograph by her bed. Then, when I learned about you, I realised that although Mum and Dad had grown to love and respect one another and were very happy, Mum's heart still truly belonged to Bill and my dad's to you, Grace.'

'Thank you for telling me that.' Grace's eyes filled with tears.

'He made me promise,' Sara went on hastily in case she lost her nerve, 'to tell you that he only gave up on you because he had given up on himself. He hated the man he had become – a killer who could be killed at any moment was how he described himself – and he didn't want you to suffer being tied to that man. He thought you deserved better. He sorely regretted that decision and wanted to make his peace with you before he died. He asked me to tell you he was sorry and that he never forgot you.' Sara delved in her handbag. 'He wanted to give you this.' She withdrew the brooch. 'He had it made especially for you. Then when he lost his father and Rigs he seemed to have lost his way, but he wanted you to have it now to remember the love you shared.' Sara handed the brooch to Grace.

'As if I ever could forget,' Grace murmured. She held the brooch reverently in her palm gazing at it through eyes misted with tears. 'A patch of blue sky,' she whispered more to herself than to Sara.

Sara's heart crumbled. 'Dad said to tell you to keep looking for the patch of blue sky,' she said choking with emotion.

Grace closed her fingers tightly round the brooch feeling the weight of it in her palm. She felt as though she was holding Richard's heart in her hand. She set the brooch on the table. Then she raised her gaze to look directly at Sara.

'Thank you,' she said, 'thank you for keeping your promise. You'll never fully understand what it means to me, but just let me say that you coming here lays so many ghosts to rest that it makes me appreciate what Richard and I have had in our lives. We were fortunate to have had our love for one another, and then to find love again, your dad with Helen and me with Lorchan.' She smiled wistfully as she took Sara's hands. 'Not everyone is as lucky as that, Sara.'

Grace gazed at the brooch for a moment longer then pinned it to her dress just above her heart sure in the knowledge that Lorchan would not object to her wearing it. He had nothing to fear from a dead man, he knew her love for him was as strong as his for her, and jealousy was not in his nature.

Sara gazed at the brooch, the white enamelled clouds standing proud against the grey linen of Grace's dress and the little Spitfire looking as though it was flying from her heart. She breathed a huge sigh of relief. She had kept her promise and in doing so she had laid to rest the ghosts that had haunted her father and Grace, and more recently had troubled her own thoughts and dreams.

'That's where it belongs,' she said nodding at the brooch then smiling at Grace, 'and it looks just perfect.' Her eyes filled with tears to think of the wasted years. She'd make sure she didn't make the same mistake her father had made, she told herself, thinking of Tom. She wasn't going to let him slip through her fingers no matter what problems life threw at her.

'I take it that you and Tom are in love,' Grace said as though she had read Sara's mind. Sara nodded. 'Then make the most of it,' Grace said fervently, 'don't let circumstances tear you apart. Swim with the current, your dad would say, not against it. Otherwise, you might not be as fortunate as he and I were. It took a lot of courage for you to find me and put my mind at rest. Richard must be very proud of you.'

By now they were both in tears but they were tears of joy as the two women, separated by a generation, were connected by their love for the man who had shaped their lives.

Grace placed her hand over the brooch, and her eyes alight with love and wonder she said, 'To love and be loved is a very precious thing, Sara, even when the person you shared that love with is no longer part of your life. It isn't something you can forget. It's there deep inside you even when you're not aware of it. You carry it with you through life and it gives you the strength to keep on looking for the patch of blue sky.'

ACKNOWLEDGMENTS

For every book that eventually reaches the shelves there is an entire army working to make it right; a book doesn't just happen because it has been written. The inspiration for the plot might belong to the author but behind the scenes there is an army of dedicated agents, publishers, editors and marketers who make the book as good as it can be. Therefore, I'd like to give a massive thank you to my agent, Judith Murdoch for her constant support and wise advice. I wouldn't be where I am without her. I am also deeply grateful to the wonderful team at Boldwood for their unstinting support and attention to detail. They are blessed with great minds and sharp eyes.

In particular, I must show my appreciation for Sarah Ritherdon, Boldwood's Publishing Director for her friendly, good-humoured and brilliant advice; she's a pleasure to work with. Grateful thanks are also due to the wonderful marketing team, Claire Fenby, Nia Benyon and Marcela Torres: isn't the book cover terrific? Thanks also to Clare Black and Sandra Ferguson for editing and proof-reading. And a huge thanks to Amanda Ridout for heading up this wonderful team. You all make my ideas a reality.

The inspiration for *The Midwives' War* came from something that happened in my childhood. Kitty, a young Irish girl came to live near us. She had a boyfriend, Robbie, who was a pilot. When she learned that she was pregnant with Robbie's baby and without any family to support her, my mother befriended her. When the war ended, Robbie came back a changed man. He told Kitty that what he had experienced in the war had made him unfit to be a married man or support a child, and went out of their lives.

A novel written about a particular time in history always requires research and I found the following especially helpful so thanks to them: *Air Force Blue* by Patrick Bishop, *A Higher Call* by Adam Makos, and the RAF Archives. Special thanks to Elma Cassidy of Downpatrick, Co. Down. Whenever I have needed advice about nursing and midwifery Elma, a now retired highly respected health care worker, has given me invaluable information.

Thanks also to the book bloggers, reviewers and most of all my readers. It is most gratifying to read their opinions and to know that they enjoyed what they read.

I've dedicated this book to my late father, Eddie Manion, who always claimed that the best years of his life were spent in the RAF. I only wish I had listened more carefully to his stories.

Finally, thanks to my family without whom none of this would be possible. Their love and support keep me going.

ABOUT THE AUTHOR

Chrissie Walsh was born and raised in West Yorkshire and is a retired schoolteacher with a passion for history. She has written several successful sagas documenting feisty women in challenging times.

Sign up to Chrissie Walsh's mailing list here for news, competitions and updates on future books.

Follow Chrissie on social media:

twitter.com/walshchrissie

facebook.com/100063501278251

ALSO BY CHRISSIE WALSH

The Weaver Street Series

Welcome to Weaver Street

Hard Times on Weaver Street

Standalones

The Midwives' War

Sixpence Stories

Introducing Sixpence Stories!

Discover page-turning historical novels from your favourite authors, meet new friends and be transported back in time.

Join our book club
Facebook group

https://bit.ly/SixpenceGroup

Sign up to our
newsletter

https://bit.ly/SixpenceNews

Boldwood

Boldwood Books is an award-winning fiction publishing company seeking out the best stories from around the world.

Find out more at
www.boldwoodbooks.com

Join our reader community for brilliant books, competitions and offers!

Follow us

#BoldBookClub

Sign up to our weekly deals newsletter

https://bit.ly/BoldwoodBNewsletter

Printed in Great Britain
by Amazon